新概念英语

（第一册）

一课一练

1

新概念英语学习中心 编

中国石化出版社
HTTP://WWW.SINOPEC-PRESS.COM
教·育·出·版·中·心

图书在版编目（CIP）数据

新概念英语一课一练. 第1册／新概念英语学习中心编.
北京：中国石化出版社，2009
ISBN 978-7-80229-970-2

Ⅰ. 新… Ⅱ. 新… Ⅲ. 英语-习题 Ⅳ. H319.6

中国版本图书馆 CIP 数据核字（2009）第 090864 号

中国石化出版社出版发行
地址:北京市东城区安定门外大街58号
邮编:100011　电话:(010)84271850
读者服务部电话:(010)84289974
http://www.sinopec-press.com
E-mail:press@sinopec.com.cn
河北天普润印刷厂印刷
全国各地新华书店经销
＊
787×1092 毫米 16 开本 13.25 印张 391 千字
2009 年 6 月第 1 版　2009 年 6 月第 1 次印刷
定价:22.00 元
（购买时请认明封面防伪标识）

前　　言

　　说起《新概念英语》，只要学习英语的中国人几乎都知道。这套教材在中国已经流行了近 30 年，仍经久不衰。《新概念英语一课一练》系列丛书既紧贴《新概念英语》的课文内容，又增添了很多相关练习。它的最大特点是从语法、词汇、阅读、翻译和写作等方面对学习者进行同步辅导。

　　结合中考、高考、大学英语四六级、考研等考试的要求，编者从应试和应用的角度出发，把教材的精华和学习的重点、难点全部融入习题中，从而有效帮助学习者巩固课文知识、加深记忆、训练技能，最终全面提高英语听、说、读、写能力。

　　本套丛书既可供自学《新概念英语》的读者使用，也可供相应水平的自学者查漏补缺，进一步提高自己的英语水平。

　　由于编者水平有限，编写时间仓促，书中不妥和错误之处在所难免，恳请广大读者提出宝贵意见，以待再版修订。

编　者

目　　录

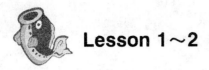

Lesson 1~2

一、单词拼写：根据所给中文意思补全下列单词

1. p____don（原谅,再说一遍 *n.* / *vt.*）   2. sk____t（裙子 *n.*）   3. dr__ss（裙子 *n.*）

4. y____（是的 *adv.*）   5. c____（小汽车 *n.*）

二、语法和词汇：从 A、B、C、D 中选出正确答案

1. —What _____ the number of the girls in your class?

—About twenty.   （哈尔滨,中考）

A. is   B. am   C. are   D. be

2. —Do you know the woman in the red dress?

—Certainly. She's Mrs. Xu. She teaches _____ English.   （吉林,中考）

A. our   B. us   C. my   D. ours

3. My parents gave _____ a nice toy dog for my birthday.   （北京,中考）

A. I   B. me   C. my   D. mine

4. I met Kate on _____ way home yesterday.   （北京,中考）

A. my   B. me   C. his   D. him

5. When Yang Liwei came back from space, many reporters interviewed _____ and got some first-hand information.   （上海,中考）

A. he   B. him   C. his   D. himself

6. —Thank you very much.

—_____.

A. Please   B. Yes   C. Thank you   D. Not at all

7. —Look! That man looks like Mr. Brown.

—It _____ be him, for he _____ America.

A. can't; has gone to   B. may not; has gone

C. mustn't; has been to   D. can't; has been to

8. You _____ go and ask Meimei. She _____ know the answer.

A. must; can   B. must; may

C. need; can   D. can; may

9. John has never been to China, _____?

A. has she   B. hasn't she

C. hasn't he   D. has he

10. There is little milk in the bottle, _____?

A. is there   B. isn't there   C. is it   D. isn't it

11. Mr. Wang asked me _____ him.   （北京,中考）

A. help   B. helps   C. to help   D. helping

12. —You're very _____, aren't you?

—Yes. Our team has won the game.   （北京,中考）

A. happy   B. worried   C. sad   D. afraid

13. —Is this pen yours?

—No, it's not _____. It's Elsa's.　　　　　　　　　　　（北京，中考）

　　A. I　　　　　　B. me　　　　　　C. my　　　　　　D. mine

14. _____ book is this?　　　　　　　　　　　　　　　　（北京，中考）

—It's Kate's.

　　A. When　　　　B. Why　　　　　C. Where　　　　　D. Whose

15. Don't _____ Chinese in your English class.　　　　　　（北京，中考）

　　A. say　　　　　B. tell　　　　　C. speak　　　　　D. talk

三、翻译句子

　　甲：这是你的手表吗？　　　　　_____

　　乙：对不起，请再说一遍。　　_____

　　甲：这是你的手表吗？　　　　　_____

　　乙：是的，是我的。　　　　　　_____

　　甲：非常感谢你。　　　　　　　_____

四、用所给的词完成句子

┌────────────────────────────────────┐
│　　excuse me, pardon, thank you　　　│
└────────────────────────────────────┘

　1. A：_____, is this your book?

　　　B：_____?

　　　A：Is this your book?

　　　B：Yes, it is. _____.

　2. A：_____, could you tell me the time?

　　　B：_____?

　　　A：Could you tell me the time?

　　　B：Oh, it is 5∶30.

　　　A：_____ very much.

五、按照字母排列，写出所缺的字母

　1. A B _ D E _ G H _ J K _ M _ O P _ R S _ U V _ X Y _

　2. _ b c _ e f _ h i _ k l _ n o _ q r _ t u _ w x _ z

六、完成句子

　1. Everybody is in the classroom.

　　　_____ _____ in the classroom?

　2. She's never helped others.

　　　_____ _____ never helped others?

　3. The boy does some housework at home.

　　　_____ the boy _____ _____ housework at home?

　4. The children had a good time in the park.

　　　_____ the children _____ a good time in the park?

　5. Jim has some story-books.

　　　_____ Jim _____ story-books? _____ Jim _____ story-books?

　6. Jo read today's newspaper.

　　　_____ Jo _____ today's newspaper?

　7. Mr. Hunt told us something important at the meeting.

　　　_____ Mr. Hunt tell you _____ important at the meeting?

2

8. The plane has already landed.

_____ the plane landed _____?

9. The old man often does morning exercises.

_____ the old man often _____ morning exercises?

10. They'll meet you at the station.

_____ they _____ you at the station?

11. We're from the United States.

_____ _____ from the United States?

12. They have an expensive DVD.

_____ _____ an expensive DVD? _____ _____ _____ an expensive DVD?

13. The building was built many years ago.

_____ the building _____ many years ago?

14. He has already gone to England.

_____ he _____ to England _____?

15. I must finish my homework before eight o'clock.

_____ you _____ your homework before eight o'clock?

16. He often goes to the library.

_____ he often _____ to the library?

17. They have a class meeting every other week.

_____ they _____ a class meeting every other week?

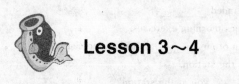

Lesson 3~4

一、单词拼写：根据所给中文意思补全下列单词

1. n__mb___ （号码 *n.*） 2. cl___kr___m（衣帽存放处 *n.*） 3. d___ght___ （女儿 *n.*）
4. tea _____ （老师 *n.*） 5. h _____ （这里 *adv.*）

二、语法和词汇：从 A、B、C、D 中选出正确答案

1. —It isn't my pen. Whose is it?
   —It's _____. （PETS 一级）
   A. he   B. him   C. his   D. he's

2. —How's your mother?
   —She's _____. （湖北，中考）
   A. very well   B. over there   C. a doctor   D. fifty

3. Some of the stamps belong to me while the rest are _____.
   A. him and her   B. his and hers   C. yours   D. him and hers

4. Which one is _____ most favourite?
   A. you   B. your   C. yours   D. yous

5. This woman has teaching _____ for five years.
   A. they   B. them   C. their   D. theirs

6. —Is this your coat?
   —_____.
   —Sorry, Sir.
   A. Yes, it is   B. No, it is   C. No, it isn't   D. No, it's

7. —_____?
   —Yes, she is my daughter.
   A. Is it your daughter   B. Is this your daughter
   C. Is your daughter   D. Is it this your daughter

8. —What's your name?
   —_____.
   A. No, it is   B. My name is David
   C. Yes, it is his   D. Sure, it's hers

9. —Is that blouse Mary's?
   —_____.
   A. No, it is   B. Yes, it's her   C. Yes, it is his   D. Sure, it's hers

10. —_____ is that red car?
    —It is Mr. Wang's.
    A. Whose   B. What   C. Who   D. This

11. If you don't know a word, you must _____ in a dictionary.
    A. look it up   B. look it down   C. look over it   D. look up it

12. —Can you go swimming with us this afternoon?
    —Sorry, I can't. I _____ take care of my little sister at home because my mother is ill.
    A. can   B. may   C. must   D. have to

13. —Can you _____ me your car?

—Sorry, I can't. Because I must go out this afternoon. You can _____ one from Mike.

　　A. lend，borrow　　B. borrow，lend　　　C. borrow，borrow　　D. lend，lend

14. We couldn't find out _____ ，so we asked a policeman.

　　A. whose bike it was　　　　　　　B. whose bike was it

　　C. whose it was bike　　　　　　　D. whose was it bike

15. I don't know _____ for me.

　　A. if is he waiting　　　　　　　　B. he is waiting

　　C. if he is waiting　　　　　　　　D. if he was waiting

16. —This is John speaking. Who's that?

　　—_____.

　　A. I'm Kate　　　　　　　　　　B. This is Kate

　　C. I'm your friend　　　　　　　　D. This is Kate's speaking

17. Mum，I'm thirsty. Will you please give me some _____?　　　　（北京，中考）

　　A. pencils　　　　　B. cake　　　　　C. water　　　　　D. books

18. Our English teacher comes _____ England.　　　　　　　　　（北京，中考）

　　A. at　　　　　B. on　　　　　C. of　　　　　D. from

三、翻译句子

甲：请把我的伞给我，这是我的票。　　_____

乙：谢谢，先生，五号。　　　　　　　_____

乙：这是你的伞。　　　　　　　　　　_____

甲：这不是我的伞。　　　　　　　　　_____

乙：对不起。　　　　　　　　　　　　_____

四、完成对话

1. A：Excuse me!　　　　　　　　　B：_____

2. A：Here is your coat.　　　　　　　B：_____

3. A：This is not my umbrella.　　　　B：_____

4. A：_____　　　　　　B：No，it isn't my coat.

5. A：Is this?　　　　　　　　　　　B：Yes，it is. _____.

五、将下列句子改成否定句和一般疑问句

1. This is my bicycle.

2. This is my shoe.

3. This is my shirt.

4. This is my bag.

5. This is my book.

六、完成句子：仿照例句写出相应的疑问句，并回答

Is this your coat?

No. It isn't my coat. It's your coat.

1. Is this your skirt?　　　　　　　6. Is this your pen?

2. Is this your house?　　　　　　　7. Is this your book?

3. Is this your dress?　　　　　　　8. Is this your shirt?

4. Is this your watch?　　　　　　　9. Is this your car?

5. Is this your umbrella?　　　　　　10. Is this your pencil?

5

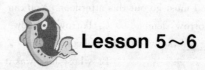
Lesson 5~6

一、单词拼写：根据所给中文意思补全下列单词

1. Jap__n_____（日本人 *n.*）　　2. Sw__d_____（瑞典人 *n.*）

3. It_____n（意大利人 *n.*）　　4. m__k__（牌号 *n.*）

5. m___n___g（早上 *n.*）

二、语法和词汇：从 A、B、C、D 中选出正确答案

1. You are reading English; I am _____ reading English.　　（北京，中考）

　　A. also　　　　　B. too　　　　　C. either　　　　　D. to

2. Jim doesn't know Japanese, and his brother doesn't know Japanese, _____.　　（重庆，中考）

　　A. also　　　　　B. too　　　　　C. either　　　　　D. to

3. Last Sunday, my parents took me to the zoo. In the zoo we saw _____ elephant. _____ elephant was from Africa.　　（新疆，中考）

　　A. a/The　　　　B. the/An　　　　C. an/The　　　　D. the/A

4. Kate is nice. I like to work with _____ very much.　　（河南，中考）

　　A. she　　　　　B. her　　　　　C. hers　　　　　D. she's

5. —Happy birthday to you, Ann!

　　—_____.　　（山东，中考）

　　A. Thank you　　B. The same to you　C. Me, too　　　D. OK

6. We'll go for a picnic if it _____ this Friday.

　　A. won't rain　　B. isn't raining　　C. doesn't rain　　D. don't rain

7. It was already eight o'clock _____ we got there.

　　A. when　　　　B. while　　　　C. if　　　　　D. because

8. Mary said that she _____ me for a long time.

　　A. hadn't seen　　B. hasn't seen　　C. didn't see　　D. couldn't see

9. I would like to go swimming _____ the weather is good.

　　A. for　　　　　B. since　　　　C. if　　　　　D. whether

10. _____ he had finished his work, he left his office.

　　A. Until　　　　B. After　　　　C. If　　　　　D. Before

11. The result of the experiment was very good, _____ we hadn't expected.　　（北京，中考）

　　A. when　　　　B. that　　　　C. which　　　　D. what

12. Miss Green didn't tell us _____ in 2002.　　（北京，中考）

　　A. where does she live　　　　　B. where she lives

　　C. where did she live　　　　　D. where she lived

13. I've worked with children before, so I know what _____ in my new job.　　（北京，中考）

　　A. expected　　B. to expect　　C. to be expecting　　D. expects

14. She is a good student, _____ she?　　（北京，中考）

　　A. is　　　　　B. isn't　　　　C. does　　　　D. doesn't

15. Which language is _____, English, French or Chinese?　　（北京，中考）

　　A. difficult　　B. the difficult　　C. more difficult　　D. the most difficult

16. —What a nice bike! How long _____ you _____ it?

    —Just two weeks.　　　　　　　　　　　　　　　　　　　　　（北京，中考）

    A. will；buy　　　　B. did；buy　　　　C. are；having　　　　D. have；had

17. We'll have a sports meeting if it _____ rain tomorrow.　　（北京，中考）

    A. won't　　　　　B. isn't　　　　C. don't　　　　D. doesn't

18. —Can you speak Japanese?

    —No，I _____ .　　　　　　　　　　　　　　　　　　　（北京，中考）

    A. mustn't　　　　B. can't　　　　C. needn't　　　　D. may not

19. Chinese _____ by more and more people in the world now.　（北京，中考）

    A. is spoken　　　　　　　　　　B. is speaking

    C. speaks　　　　　　　　　　　D. spoke

20. Aunt Li often asks her son _____ too much meat. It's bad for his health.　（北京，中考）

    A. don't eat　　　　　　　　　　B. not to eat

    C. not eat　　　　　　　　　　　D. to not eat

21. —_____ do you have an English party?

    —Once a month.　　　　　　　　　　　　　　　　　　　　（北京，中考）

    A. How old　　　　B. How far　　　　C. How often　　　　D. How long

三、翻译句子

甲：早上好，布莱克先生。　　　　　　　　　_____

乙：早上好。　　　　　　　　　　　　　　_____

甲：这位是索菲小姐。她是美国人，是个新学生。　_____

乙：这位是索菲娅小姐。她是日本人，是个新学生。　_____

甲：很高兴认识你。　　　　　　　　　　　_____

7

四、答句配对

1. Good morning.　　　　　　　　A. Thank you.

2. Excuse me.　　　　　　　　　　B. Glad to see you，too.

3. Nice to meet you.　　　　　　　C. Yes?

4. Glad to see you.　　　　　　　　D. Good morning.

5. Here is your dress.　　　　　　　E. Nice to meet you，too.

五、用适当的人称代词填空

1. Miss Jane is Italian. _____ isn't Spanish. _____ is an Italian actress（女演员）. That is _____ car. _____ is a Citroen.

2. Hans is forty-one. Mary is _____ daughter. _____ is five.

3. George is English. _____ is an English teacher. This is _____ car. _____ is a Ford.

4. Jim is five years old. _____ is in a nursery（托儿所）. Miss Laura is _____ teacher.

5. That woman is a new teacher. _____ name is Susan. _____ is from Italia，but _____ husband（丈夫）is not from Italia. _____ is from Japan.

六、完成句子：就划线部分提问

1. Miss Chen teaches Chinese in a middle school.

2. Li Lei is a student.

3. The book cost me 23 yuan.

4. He writes to his friend three times a month.

5. We write words with our hands.

6. He has three pens.

7. His father is 78 years old.

8. He can't ride a bike <u>because he's too young</u>.

9. I like <u>the black</u> cat best of all.

10. It's <u>about 5 kilometres away</u> from here to the People's Hospital.

11. Lucy and Lily are in <u>Grade Two</u>.

12. <u>The old man</u> often tells <u>the boys</u> about <u>his stories</u>.
         ①   ②   ③

13. <u>Han Meimei's</u> coat is <u>black</u>.
        ①   ②

Lesson 7～8

一、单词拼写：根据所给中文意思补全下列单词

1. h ＿＿rdresser（理发师 *n.*） 2. op ＿＿at ＿＿（操作人员 *n.*）3. na ＿＿＿＿ality（国籍 *n.*）

4. m ＿＿kman（送牛奶的人 *n.*）5. p ＿l ＿ceman（警察 *n.*）

二、语法和词汇：从 A、B、C、D 中选出正确答案

1. —Have you got a letter from your daughter?

　 —Yes, I've got a letter from ＿＿＿＿＿. 　　　　　　　　　　　（陕西, 中考）

　 A. her 　　　　　B. hers 　　　　　C. she 　　　　　D. herself

2. —＿＿＿＿＿ are you?

　 —I am a teacher.

　 A. What 　　　　B. Who 　　　　　C. Who's 　　　　D. How

3. ＿＿＿＿＿ your teacher?

　 A. How are 　　　B. How old 　　　C. How old are 　　D. How is

4. Mr. Hyde's possible full name is ＿＿＿＿＿.

　 A. Emma hyde 　　　　　　　　　B. Hyde K. John

　 C. Peter A. Hyde 　　　　　　　　D. Hyde Wiliam John

5. —＿＿＿＿＿ ?

　 —I am a boss.

　 A. What are you doing 　　　　　B. What do you do

　 C. How are you 　　　　　　　　D. What's your name

6. It's too hot today. Why not ＿＿＿＿＿ your coat?

　 A. take off 　　　B. take up 　　　C. take away 　　　D. take out

7. —＿＿＿＿＿?

　 —I am a French.

　 A. What are you from 　　　　　B. What nationality are you

　 C. Where are you from 　　　　　D. What nationality have

8. —What's his job?

　 —＿＿＿＿＿.

　 A. She is worker 　　　　　　　B. I am a worker

　 C. He is a worker 　　　　　　　D. His job is a worker

9. —Are you Spanish?

　 —＿＿＿＿＿.

　 A. Yes, you are 　　B. No, I are not 　C. Yes, I am 　　D. No, I isn't

10. —＿＿＿＿＿?

　 —I am Bob.

　 A. What's your job 　　　　　　B. Where are you from

　 C. What's your name 　　　　　　D. What's you name

11. —What's your name?

　 —＿＿＿＿＿.

　 A. My name's Relly 　　　　　　B. Relly is me

9

C. My name are Relly   D. Relly is I

12. —Hi, Peter. Why are you in such a hurry?

—_____ the 7 : 30 train.

A. Catch   B. To catch   C. Catching   D. Caught

13. —What is in the box on the table?

—There _____ a knife, two books, and three pencils in it.

A. will be   B. are   C. is   D. am

14. —When _____ you _____ the floor?

—I swept the floor last week.

A. did, swept   B. were, sweep   C. did, sweep   D. were, swept

15. I'm going to visit the Great Wall _____.

A. the day before yesterday   B. the day after tomorrow

C. last Friday   D. yesterday afternoon

16. —Where were they _____ September 2nd?

—They were _____ Dalian.

A. on, at   B. on, in   C. in, in   D. in, at

17. I like fish, _____ my brother doesn't like it.   (北京, 中考)

A. so   B. or   C. for   D. but

18. —What are the girls doing?   (北京, 中考)

—They're _____ the music.

A. listening to   B. talking with   C. coming from   D. looking for

19. _____ name is Lin Tao.   (北京, 中考)

A. He   B. Himself   C. Him   D. His

20. "What's wrong _____ you?" the doctor asked.   (北京, 中考)

A. from   B. with   C. for   D. at

21. Nick is looking for another job because he feels that nothing he does _____ his boss.

(北京, 中考)

A. serves   B. satisfies   C. promises   D. supports

三、翻译句子

1. 我是一个新学生,我叫罗伯特。   _____

2. 你是哪国人? 我是意大利人。   _____

3. Are you a postman?   _____

4. No, I am not. I am an engineer.   _____

5. Nice to meet you.   _____

四、在需要的地方填 a 或 an

1. Alice is _____ air-hostess.   His father is _____ engineer.

2. He has _____ mother.   His mother is _____ housewife.

3. Christine is _____ new student.   His sister is _____ air-hostess.

4. Mary is not _____ nurse.   She is _____ policewoman.

五、用 too 和 either 填空

1. I don't study English. My friend doesn't study English, _____.

2. This is not my book. That is not my book, _____.

3. We go to school by bicycle. They go to school by bicycle, _____.

4. She is not from Japan. His husband is not from Japan, _____.

5. I am a student. Are you a student, _____?

6. They don't work on Saturday. We don't work on Saturday, _____.

7. She has a new coat. I have a new coat, _____.

六、完成句子：仿照例句写出相应的疑问句，并回答

选用 his，her，he，she，a 或 an 等词。

Examples：

keyboard operator

What's her job? Is she a keyboard，operator? Yes，she is.

engineer

What's his job? Is he an engineer? Yes，he is.

1. policeman   6. nurse

2. policewoman   7. mechanic

3. taxi driver   8. hairdresser

4. air hostess   9. housewife

5. postman   10. milkman

Lesson 9～10

一、单词拼写:根据所给中文意思补全下列单词

1. th _____ s（谢谢 *n.*） 2. s ___（看见 *v.*） 3. t _ d ___（今天 *n.*）

4. w _ m _ n（女人 *n.*） 5. d ___ t __（脏的 *adj.*）

二、语法和词汇:从 A、B、C、D 中选出正确答案

1. How are you today? Fine, _____.

   A. please   B. pardon   C. sorry   D. thanks

2. The housewife isn't busy. She is _____.

   A. hot   B. dirty   C. free   D. thin

3. —Would you like some more milk?

   —_____. I have had enough.

   A. Yes, please   B. All right   C. I would   D. No, thanks

4. —Would you help me to repair my bike?

   —_____.

   A. Yes, please   B. No, thanks

   C. Certainly, I'll be glad to   D. Of course, I would like

5. —Have a good winter holiday!

   —_____.

   A. I'm afraid I won't   B. OK. Let's have a good time

   C. All right, I will   D. Thanks and you too

6. —_____ you ever _____ to Beijing?

   —Yes, I have.

   A. Have; gone   B. Did; go   C. Do; go   D. Have; been

7. —_____ will your parents come back from abroad?

   —In two months.

   A. How long   B. How soon   C. How often   D. How many

8. —_____ desk is yours?

   —The one on the left.

   A. What   B. How   C. Which   D. Where

9. —How are you today?   (北京,中考)

   —Oh, I _____ as ill as I do now for a very long time.

   A. didn't fell   B. wasn't feeling C. don't fell   D. haven't felt

10. —Is Tom at school today?

    —No. He's at home _____ he has a bad cold.   (北京,中考)

    A. because   B. if   C. until   D. before

11. —Hi, Kate. You look tired. What's the matter?

    —I _____ well last night.   (北京,中考)

    A. didn't sleep B. don't sleep   C. haven't slept D. won't sleep

12. The managers discussed the plan that they would like to see _____ the next year.

                                                          (北京,中考)

A. carry out   B. carrying out

C. carried out   D. to carry out

13. There is _____ old woman in the car.   （北京，中考）

　　A. 不填   B. the   C. a   D. an

14. When he _____ home，he saw his mother cleaning the room.   （北京，中考）

　　A. got up   B. got back   C. got off   D. got on

15. —How old are you?

　　—I'm fifteen. I was born _____ 1990.   （北京，中考）

　　A. in   B. at   C. on   D. for

16. My cousin is very busy with his work. He has _____ time to read newspapers.

　　　　　　　　　　　　　　　　　　　　　　　　　　　　　（北京，中考）

　　A. little   B. few   C. a little   D. a few

三、翻译句子

1. Hello，Hellen.   _____

   Hello，Steven.   _____

2. How are you today?   _____

3. I'm fine，thank you.   _____

4. Nice to see you.   _____

5. Nice to see you，too.   _____

四、用 am，is，are 填空

1. Mary _____ a teacher.   4. _____ you French?

2. Sue _____ my daughter.   5. Yes，I _____.

3. What nationality _____ you?   6. My name _____ Alice.

五、根据课文内容完成下列会话

Mr. Steven：Good afternoon，Mrs. Helen.

Mrs. Helen：_____.

Mr. Steven：How are you today?

Mrs. Helen：_____. And you?

Mr. Steven：I'm fine，_____.

Mr. Steven：_____ Mr. Helen?

Mrs. Helen：He's fine，thanks.

Mrs. Helen：_____ Mrs. Steven?

Mr. Steven：She's very well，too，Mrs. Helen.

Mr. Steven：Goodbye，Mrs. Helen. Nice to see you.

Mrs. Helen：_____，too，Mr. Steven. Goodbye.

六、完成句子：将下列句子译成英语

1.布朗先生，你身体好吗？

2.布朗夫人身体好吗？

3.我很好，谢谢。你身体怎样？

13

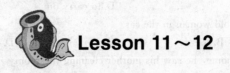

Lesson 11～12

一、单词拼写：根据所给中文意思补全下列单词

1. c _ t ___（抓住 v.）   2. b ___th ___（兄弟 n.）   3. h ___（她的 pron.）

4. bl ___（蓝色的 adj.）   5. who ___（谁的 pron.）

二、语法和词汇：从 A、B、C、D 中选出正确答案

1. —_____ are they?
   —They are my friends.   （北京,中考）
   A. Who   B. Whose   C. Which   D. What

2. —_____ are you in?
   —Class Five.   （天津,中考）
   A. What class   B. What grade   C. What colour   D. What number

3. —Paul,do you know the man standing at the door?
   —Yes,he is one of _____ friends.   （吉林,中考）
   A. I   B. me   C. my   D. mine

4. —Tina,could you please play _____ piano for me while I am singing.
   —With pleasure.   （吉林,中考）
   A. a   B. an   C. the   D. 不填

5. Betty and her sister went to the museum with a realtive of _____.   （无锡,中考）
   A. her   B. hers   C. their   D. theirs

6. —What is his job?
   —_____ an engineer?
   A. Is she   B. She is   C. Is he   D. He is

7. —_____ is your pencil?
   —The red one.
   A. What colour   B. Whose   C. Which   D. Where

8. Summer is coming, and the _____ is going much higher.
   A. warm   B. hotness   C. temperature   D. temperatures

9. It's cold outside. You had better _____ your room much warmer.
   A. keep   B. does   C. find   D. made

10. Before you walk into the room, you have to _____ your shoes.
    A. take down   B. take with   C. take off   D. take on

11. That was all _____ we had done.
    A. which   B. who   C. that   D. whom

12. The bag _____ on the desk is now missing.
    A. I have put it B. that I have put C. as I put it   D. which I had put

13. He _____ see a doctor before it is too late.
    A. must   B. could   C. have to   D. can

14. Jim is the boy _____ from England.
    A. who are   B. who is   C. that come   D. which comes

14

15. Jim is one of the boys _____ from England.

    A. who are   B. who is   C. that comes   D. which come

16. This is the longest train _____ I have ever seen.

    A. which   B. that   C. what   D. whom

17. _____ some of this juice — perhaps you'll like it.   （北京，中考）

    A. Trying   B. Try   C. To try   D. Have tried

18. The white shirt is as _____ as the yellow one.   （北京，中考）

    A. cheap   B. cheaper   C. cheapest   D. the cheapest

19. If he _____ harder，he will catch up with us soon.   （北京，中考）

    A. study   B. studies   C. will study   D. studied

20. Father is sleeping. You'd better _____ quiet.   （北京，中考）

    A. to keep   B. keep   C. keeping   D. kept

21. —_____ does your mother work?   （北京，中考）

    —In a factory.

    A. Where   B. When   C. Which   D. Who

22. —_____ is your sister?   （北京，中考）

    —She's eleven years old.

    A. How old   B. How many   C. How much   D. How long

23. He is so careful that he always looks over his exercises to _____ there are no mistakes.

                                             （北京，中考）

    A. make sure   B. find out   C. think about   D. try out

三、翻译句子

1. 蒂姆，这是你的衬衫吗？   _____

2. 不，先生，这不是我的，我的是蓝色的。   _____

3. 那么这是谁的？   _____

4. 也许是戴姆的。   _____

5. 给你，接着。谢谢，先生。   _____

四、根据课文内容填空

A：Whose is that shirt?

B：Which ① ?

A：The white ② .

B：It is not ③ . Perhaps it is ④ shirt，Sir.

A：Here you are. ⑤ !

C： ⑥ .

五、将下列短语译成英语

    1. 张先生的办公室_____   2. 我妈妈的书_____   3. 苏珊的汽车_____

    4. 我姐的裙子_____   5. 吉姆的衬衣_____

六、完成句子：仿照例句写出相应的疑问句，并回答

car/Paul

Whose is this car? It's Paul's. It's his car.

Now you do the same. Use It's，his，and her.

1. tie/my brother   6. coat/Miss Dupont

2. shirt/Tim   7. suit/my father

3. dress/my daughter   8. umbrella/Mr. Ford

4. skirt/my mother   9. blouse/my sister

5. pen/my son   10. handbag/Stella

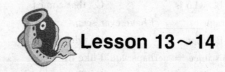

Lesson 13~14

一、单词拼写:根据所给中文意思补全下列单词

1. sm___t(聪明的、漂亮的 *adj.*) 2. s__m__(相同的 *adj.*) 3. h__t(帽子 *n.*)

4. d__g(狗 *n.*) 5. ___pst_____s(楼上 *adv.*)

二、语法和词汇:从 **A、B、C、D** 中选出正确答案

1. _____ turn is now? （太原,中考）

A. Who's   B. Whose   C. Who   D. Whom

2. The man _____ the bike is our teacher. （焦作,中考）

A. at   B. in   C. on   D. by

3. I am _____. （吉林,中考）

A. an Chinese   B. Chinese   C. the Chinese   D. one Chinese

4. Please look _____ the picture on the wall. （重庆,中考）

A. in   B. at   C. to   D. on

5. —Hello,Here is your pencil-box.

— _____ very much.

— _____. （重庆,中考）

A. Thank/That's right.

B. Thank you/That's all

C. Thank you/You're welcome

D. Thank you/No,no

6. That is a _____ hat!

A. love   B. lovly   C. lovely   D. lovlly

7. —Does she like steak or lamb?

— _____.

A. Lamb   B. Yes, she does   C. Yes, she likes   D. She likes

8. —Where is Mrs. Clinton?

—She is _____.

A. at the butcher   B. in the butcher   C. at the butcher's   D. at butcher's

9. This apple is small. Give _____ a big _____.

A. he, apple   B. him, apples   C. him, one   D. he, /

10. —Are you _____?

—No, we're _____.

A. Germany, America

B. America, German

C. Germany, American

D. German, American

11. —These girls are from _____.

—They're _____.

A. England, English

B. English, English

C. England, England

D. English, England

12. —Which is your skirt?

— _____.

A. The one brown   B. A green one

C. The brown one   D. It's green

13. —Can you spell "number", please?

    —_____.

    A. Yes, I can   B. Yes, N—U—M—B—E—R, number

    C. I can   D. Excuse me

14. —What is this?

    —_____.

    A. This a book   B. This's an book

    C. It's book   D. It's a book

15. —Where _____ Peter?

    —He _____ at school.

    A. is, is   B. is, am   C. am, is   D. is, are

16. John may phone tonight. I don't want to go out _____ he phones.   （北京，中考）

    A. as long as   B. in order that   C. in case   D. so that

三、翻译句子

1. 你的新套装是什么颜色的？   _____

2. 是绿色的。   _____

3. 到楼上来欣赏吧。   _____

4. 谢谢。   _____

5. What a lovely hat!   _____

四、改错

1. the boy is my brother.

2. He are 15. How old are she?

3. They are in same class.

4. My hats green.

5. Come or see my car.

五、将下列短语译成英语

1. 黄色的书包_____   2. 红色的汽车_____   3. 灰色的衬衣_____

4. 黑色的手提箱_____   5. 绿色的帽子_____   6. 白色的裙子_____

7. 蓝色的天空_____   8. 褐色的眼睛_____   9. 黑灰色的外套_____

10. 棕白色的猫_____

六、完成句子:补全下列对话并进行练习

A: 你的车是什么颜色?

    Is it black?

B: 它不是黑色的,是白色的,但是我父亲的车是黑色的。

    Come and see my car.

A: 好的。

B: My father says it is a lovely car.

A: 这辆车的确漂亮。

17

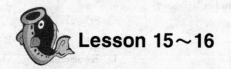

Lesson 15～16

一、单词拼写:根据所给中文意思补全下列单词

1. N＿＿w＿＿g＿＿n(挪威人 *n.*)　2. t＿＿r＿st(旅游者 *n.*)　3. g＿＿l(女孩 *n.*)

4. bl＿ck(黑色的 *adj.*)　　5. th＿＿＿＿(这些 *pron.*)

二、语法和词汇:从 A、B、C、D 中选出正确答案

1. Do you have five ＿＿＿＿ or ＿＿＿＿?　　　　　　　　　　(太原,中考)

　A. watchs/knives　　　　　　　　B. watches/knives

　C. watches/knifes　　　　　　　　D. watchs/knife

2. Both my sister and my brother are ＿＿＿＿.　　　　　　　(桂林,中考)

　A. a police　　　　　　　　　　　B. policemen

　C. policewomen　　　　　　　　　D. polices

3. Look at this picture—there are 5 ＿＿＿＿ in it.　　　　　(哈尔滨,中考)

　A. countries　　　　　　　　　　B. country's

　C. countries's　　　　　　　　　　D. countrys

4. There are 15 ＿＿＿＿ and ＿＿＿＿ in the basket.　　　　(武汉,中考)

　A. tomatoes/potatos　　　　　　　B. tomatos/potatos

　C. tomatoes/potatoes　　　　　　　D. tomatos/potatoes

5. —＿＿＿＿ is your grandpa, Emma?

　—He's watering the flowers in the garden.　　　　　　　(北京,中考)

　A. When　　　B. What　　　C. Where　　　C. How

6. —Is your daughter French?

　—＿＿＿＿.

　A. No, she isn't　　B. Yes, he is　　C. No, they aren't　　D. Yes, I am

7. —＿＿＿＿?

　—They are blue.

　A. Whose colour are your shoes　　B. What colour is your shoes

　C. How colour are your shoes　　　D. What colour are your shoes

8. You'd better ＿＿＿＿ your coat. It's cold outside.

　A. put on　　　B. to put on　　　C. putting on　　　D. puts on

9. Your coat is in the box. ＿＿＿＿ if you go out, for it is cold outside.

　A. Take away it　　B. Take it off　　C. Put on it　　D. Put it on

10. Look! The cat is running ＿＿＿＿ to catch the mouse.

　　A. slow enough　　B. fast enough　　C. enough fast　　D. as quickly as

11. —Where is Professor Lee?

　　—He ＿＿＿＿ to the library. He'll come back soon.

　　A. went　　　B. goes　　　C. has gone　　　D. has been to

12. —Do you know our town at all?

　　—No, this is the first time I ＿＿＿＿ here.

　　A. was　　　B. have been　　　C. came　　　D. am coming

18

13. —What nationality is she?

—She is _____.

A. Germany B. France C. Sweden D. Korean

14. —Is it an English car?

—_____.

A. It's not B. No, it isn't C. Yes, it's D. No, it is

15. —Dad, this is my teacher Mr. Smith.

—_____

A. How are you?   B. Thank you!

C. How do you do?   D. See you later!

16. —How are you?

—_____

A. How are you? B. Fine, thanks! C. Thank you! D. Sorry.

17. Mrs. Brown came to China _____ 1996. （北京，中考）

A. From B. of C. to D. in

18. It was an exciting moment for these football fans this year, _____ for the first time in years

their team won the World Cup. （北京，中考）

A. that B. while C. which D. when

19. Cars, buses and bikes _____ stop when the traffic light is red. （北京，中考）

A. can B. must C. may D. need

20. One of the sides of the board should be painted yellow, and _____. （北京，中考）

A. the other is white   B. another white

C. the other white   D. another is white

21. —When will Mr. Black come to Beijing? （北京，中考）

—_____ September 5.

A. On B. To C. At D. In

19

三、翻译句子

1. Are you Spanish? _____

2. No, we aren't. We are Danish. _____

3. 你们的朋友也是丹麦人吗？ _____

4. 不，他们是挪威人。 _____

5. 这些是我们的护照。 _____

四、用人称代词填空

1. My father is 55 years old. _____ is a teacher.

2. Whose books are those? _____ are my books.

3. I love my parents. _____ are teachers.

4. My daughter is a lovely girl. I love _____ very much.

5. Get up. _____ is 8 o'clock.

五、将下列名词复数按发音归类

books, suits, handbags, teachers, ties, beds, dresses, blouses, coats, friends, tourists, boxes, carpets, nurses, mechanics, students, shoes, umbrellas, makes, Spaniards, maps, Swedes

/s/ _____

/z/ _____

/ts/ _____

/dz/ _____

/iz/ _____

六、完成句子

1. _____ he your brother? Yes, he _____. His name _____ Alan.

2. Excuse me, _____ your name Smith? No, it _____ not. I _____ John White.

3. We _____ students. Mr. Blake _____ our teacher.

4. John and Tom _____ good friends. They _____ both Spanish.

5. Miss Dupont _____ a nurse. She _____ Mr. and Mrs. Dupont's daughter. They _____ French.

6. What colour _____ your umbrellas? My umbrella _____ red and my sons' umbrellas ____ black.

7. What _____ your jobs? We _____ air-hostesses.

8. Which _____ your pencils? _____ these your pencils?

9. Whose _____ these cases? _____ they Mr. Blake's?

10. _____ these your ties? No, they _____ not. My ties _____ orange.

Lesson 17~18

一、单词拼写：根据所给中文意思补全下列单词

1. off _____（办公室 *n.*）   2. s __ l __ s（推销的 *adj.*）

3. __ mpl __ ee（雇员 *n.*）   4. l __ z __（懒的 *adj.*）

5. v __ r __（非常 *adv.*）

二、语法和词汇：从 A、B、C、D 中选出正确答案

1. —The books on the chair _____ Millie's, right?

   —Yes，they are.   （柳州，中考）

   A. is   B. they're   C. it's   D. are

2. Are they from _____ ?   （北京，中考）

   A. Australian   B. English   C. American   D. Canada

3. —_____ is this boy in the art room?

   —He's my new friend.   （湖南，中考）

   A. Who's   B. What   C. How   D. Who

4. —How many policemen are there in this police station?

   —There are 54 _____ and 18 _____ .

   A. policeman/policewoman   B. policeman/policewomen

   C. policemen/policewoman   D. policemen/policeman

5. Mr. White，with his friends，_____ on a trip.   （黄冈，中考）

   A. have   B. has   C. is   D. are

6. —What are their jobs?

   —They are _____ .

   A. engineeres   B. engineers   C. engineer   D. engineermen

7. How have you been _____ ?

   A. recent   B. to   C. lately   D. late

8. She was heard _____ an English song in her room last night.

   A. sings   B. sang   C. to sing   D. singing

9. There _____ a box on the desk.

   A. am   B. is   C. are   D. have

10. This is _____ classroom. That is _____ classroom.

    A. we, their   B. our, their   C. my, they   D. we, their

11. These _____ my friends Cathy and _____ brother Jim.

    A. are, her   B. is,her   C. are,she   D. is,she

12. John is _____ boy.

    A. a American   B. a America   C. an American   D. an America

13. Is that a television _____ a computer?

    A. or   B. and   C. but   D. about

三、翻译句子

1. 来见见我们的雇员,李先生。
2. 谢谢,杰克先生。
3. 那些姑娘很勤劳,她们是做什么工作的?
4. 她们是电脑录入人员。
5. 她们很勤劳。
6. Who is this young man?
7. This is Jim.
8. He is our office assistant.
9. How do you do?
10. He is very hard-working.

四、将下列各词变为复数

1. policewoman _____
2. milkman _____
3. book _____
4. carpet _____
5. tie _____
6. student _____
7. operator _____
8. housewife _____
9. box _____
10. nationality _____
11. policeman _____
12. air hostess _____
13. house _____
14. knife _____
15. man _____
16. postman _____

五、用 a 或 an 填空

1. That's _____ lovely hat. It's green.
2. Is this _____ umbrella?
3. What's Jim's job? He's _____ office assistant.
4. Michael Baker isn't _____ assistant. He's _____ Sales Rep.
5. My sister is _____ air hostess.
6. Claire Taylor is _____ employee.
7. He isn't _____ postman. He's _____ milkman.
8. What's Tom's job? He's _____ taxi driver.
9. Is she _____ nurse or _____ housewife? She isn't _____ housewife. She's _____ nurse.
10. Is it _____ French car? Yes, it is. It's _____ Peugeot.

六、书面表达

假设你在国外某城市参观访问,准备启程回国。舞会上要向外国朋友讲几句话。请事先拟一篇80—100词的发言稿。要求包括如下内容:

1. 美丽的城市,美丽的风光使你度过难忘的时光。
2. 感谢朋友们的盛情,祝他们一切顺利。
3. 欢迎朋友来中国参观,愿友谊地久天长。

七、完成句子

1. _____ is he? He's Jim.
   A. What   B. Who   C. Whose   D. Whom
2. Who's that at the door? _____ is Lucy.
   A. It   B. He   C. She   D. This
3. Who's this meal for? For _____.
   A. her   B. she   C. her's   D. he

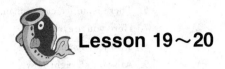 # Lesson 19～20

一、单词拼写:根据所给中文意思补全下列单词

1. M＿m（妈 *n.*）   2. t＿＿＿＿d（累的 *adj.*）   3. r＿gh＿（对的 *adj.*）

4. b＿g（大的 *adj.*）   5. l＿n＿（长的 *adj.*）

二、语法和词汇:从 A、B、C、D 中选出正确答案

1. There is ＿＿＿＿ ice cream.

    A. a   B. the   C. /   D. an

2. Look at ＿＿＿＿.

    A. they   B. he   C. she   D. them

3. —Are his shoes dirty or clean?

    —＿＿＿＿.

    A. Dirty   B. Yes   C. No   D. old

4. —Are they open or shut?

    —＿＿＿＿.

    A. Yes   B. No   C. Shut   D. Good

5. —Are they hot or cold?

    —＿＿＿＿.

    A. Yes   B. No   C. Long   D. Cold

6. —Are you all right now?

    —＿＿＿＿.

    A. Yes,we are   B. No,I am   C. No,we are   D. Yes,we aren't

7. —What's the matter?

    —I ＿＿＿＿ tired.

    A. are   B. is   C. am   D. /

8. How many boys ＿＿＿＿ there in Class One?　　　　　　　　　　（北京,中考）

    A. be   B. is   C. are   D. am

9. —Is that Jack speaking?

    —Sorry, he isn't in right now. He ＿＿＿＿ the cinema with his aunt.　　（北京,中考）

    A. has been to   B. has gone to

    C. have been to   D. have gone to

10. There ＿＿＿＿ a big tree near the house.　　　　　　　　　　（北京,中考）

    A. Are   B. is   C. have   D. has

11. —You've left the light on.　　　　　　　　　　　　　　　（北京,中考）

    —Oh , so I have . ＿＿＿＿ and turn it off.

    A. I'll go   B. I've gone   C. I go   D. I'm going

12. The changes in the city will cost quite a lot, ＿＿＿＿ they will save us money in the long run.

    　　　　　　　　　　　　　　　　　　　　　　　　　　（北京,中考）

    A. or   B. since   C. for   D. but

23

三、翻译句子

1. 怎么啦,孩子?
2. 我们又累又渴。
3. 坐在这儿吧。
4. 现在好些吗?
5. 不,还没有。

6. There is an ice cream man.
7. Here you are, children.
8. Two ice creams, please.
9. Are you all right now?
10. Thank you.

四、反义词连线

1. cold
2. clean
3. fat
4. young
5. open

A. shut
B. thin
C. hot
D. dirty
E. old

五、改变下列句型,将形容词改成定语或表语

1. Their house is small.
2. The untidy room is mine.
3. The lovely cat is my aunt's.
4. Our coats are clean.
5. Your sister's dress is beautiful.
6. The old book is Jim's.
7. My father is thin.

六、书面表达

24

英国中学生代表团来你校访问,校长给你一张时间表,请你用英语向外国朋友介绍在北京逗留三天的活动安排。

时间表:1. 周一上午,校长会见之后介绍学校情况,下午参观实验楼、图书馆。

2. 周二,两国学生共同游览长城,张老师讲长城趣闻。晚上在402室举行联欢会。

3. 周三,两校学生座谈,下午自由活动。

4. 周四,上午9:45乘火车去西安。

要　求:以讲话稿的形式把上述内容表达清楚,并有恰当的开头与结尾。

字　数:100　120词。

七、完成句子:补全下列对话并进行练习

A:我很热,又很渴。

B:Me, too.

A:Look,那儿有一家食品杂货店(grocery)。

B:Let's 去买两瓶可口可乐。

A:Oh.

B:怎么啦?

A:店关门了。What a pity!

A:看! 那儿有个卖冰淇淋的人。

B:请拿两个冰淇淋。

B:How much are they?

C:两元四角。

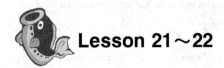 **Lesson 21～22**

一、单词拼写：根据所给中文意思补全下列单词

1. f＿ll（满的 *adj.*）　　2. sh＿＿p（尖的 *adj.*）　　3. f＿＿k（叉子 *n.*）

4. bl＿＿t（钝的 *adj.*）　　5. kn＿f＿（刀子 *n.*）

二、语法和词汇：从 A、B、C、D 中选出正确答案

1. It's not good to be late ＿＿＿＿＿＿＿ school.　　　　　　　　　　（长沙，中考）

　　A. for　　　　　B. she　　　　　C. about　　　　　D. to

2. —Whose book is this? Is this yours?

　　—No, it's ＿＿＿＿＿＿＿.　　　　　　　　　　　　　　　　　　（永州，中考）

　　A. her　　　　　B. she　　　　　C. my　　　　　D. hers

3. —Would you like some tea?

　　—Yes, ＿＿＿＿＿＿＿.　　　　　　　　　　　　　　　　　　　（哈尔滨，中考）

　　A. thank you　　B. here you are　　C. give me　　D. show me

4. I am a student. ＿＿＿＿＿＿＿ name is Tom.　　　　　　　　　　（朝阳，中考）

　　A. My　　　　　B. Your　　　　　C. His　　　　　D. Her

5. —Which football match do you like better?

　　—＿＿＿＿＿＿＿ between South Korea and Japan.　　　　　　　　（杭州，中考）

　　A. The one　　　B. One　　　　　C. The ones　　　D. Ones

6. Give ＿＿＿＿＿＿＿ a spoon.

　　A. we　　　　　B. they　　　　　C. I　　　　　　D. us

7. "Give me a bottle.""Which one, the old one or the new one?""The ＿＿＿＿＿＿＿ one."

　　A. sharp　　　　B. blunt　　　　C. old　　　　　D. full

8. "This green one?""No, not that one. The ＿＿＿＿＿＿＿ one."

　　A. big　　　　　B. small　　　　C. old　　　　　D. red

9. "Give me a book please.""Which ＿＿＿＿＿＿＿?"

　　A. this　　　　　B. that　　　　　C. bottle　　　　D. one

10. "Which books?""＿＿＿＿＿＿＿?"

　　A. This one　　　B. These ones　　C. This ones　　D. These one

11. "Is this your coat?""No. ＿＿＿＿＿＿＿ coat is white."

　　A. His　　　　　B. Your　　　　　C. My　　　　　D. His

12. "Is this your father's hat?""No. ＿＿＿＿＿＿＿ is orange."

　　A. My　　　　　B. Your　　　　　C. Her　　　　　D. His

13. "Are those your pens?""No. ＿＿＿＿＿＿＿ pens are red."

　　A. Our　　　　　B. Their　　　　C. Your　　　　　D. His

14. "Is this Miss Alice's hat?""No. ＿＿＿＿＿＿＿ hat is new."

　　A. His　　　　　B. Her　　　　　C. Your　　　　　D. My

15. I want something to eat. Please give me a ＿＿＿＿＿＿＿.　　　　（北京，中考）

　　A. book　　　　B. watch　　　　C. shirt　　　　D. cake

16. The WTO cannot live up to its name ＿＿＿＿＿＿＿ it does not include a country that is home to one fifth of mankind.　　　　　　　　　　　　　　　　　　　　　（北京，中考）

25

A. as long as   B. while   C. if   D. even though

17. —Which is _____, the sun, the moon or the earth?

    —Of course, the moon is.   (北京,中考)

    A. small   B. smaller   C. smallest   D. the smallest

18. The box is light. Wang Ping can _____ it by herself.   (北京,中考)

    A. find   B. watch   C. carry   D. learn

三、翻译句子

1. 请拿本书给我。   6. Give me a tie please.

2. 哪一本,这一本吗?   7. Which one? The old one?

3. 不,红色的那本。   8. No. The new one.

4. 这本?   9. Here you are.

5. 是的,谢谢。   10. Thank you.

四、用代词的主格、宾格或所有格填空

1. A: Can you lend me your book?

    B: Yes, Here _____ are. But please return _____ to _____ tomorrow.

2. I love _____ parents. _____ are teachers and _____ are very kind to _____ students.

3. Are those your pens? No. _____ are not. _____ pens are blue.

4. This is my danghter's dog. _____ likes it very much. _____ hair is white and black.

五、用 large, big, small 或 little 填空

1. The girl is _____ (矮小) for her age.

2. Don't cry. You're a _____ (大) boy now.

3. When I was a _____ (小) boy, I lived in countryside.

4. I want a _____ (小) box. This is too _____ (大).

5. A _____ (大) piano stood against the wall.

6. I think you've made a _____ (大) mistake.

六、书面表达

    假定你在下午放学骑车出校门时,由于车速太快,与从左面驶来的一辆卡车相撞,多亏司机停车及时,尽管如此,你还是被撞倒在地,车子坏了,腿也破了,眼镜也碎了。你下决心以后骑车一定要小心。

要求:一篇 100—120 词的日记。时间:2002 年 10 月 28 日

注意:该文要求写一篇日记,并且是一件亲身经历的事。在写之前,要先构思。首先应是日记的格
      式,其次是叙述事故发生的整个过程及其感受,用学过的语言安排一下顺序。在写时注意如
      下几个语言点线索:

      1. a terrible day   2. after school

七、完成句子:把括号内的词语译成英语

1. A: Give(我) a cup please.

    B: Which one? (是这只脏的吗?)

    A: No, not this dirty one. (是那只干净的。)

    B:(给你。)

    A: Thank you.

2. A: Give(他) a bottle please.

    B: Which one? (是这只空的吗?)

    A: No, not this empty one. (是那只满的。)

3. A: Give(他们) a knife please.

    B:(哪一把?)This sharp one?

    A: No, (不是这一把。)The blunt one.

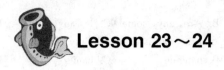

Lesson 23~24

一、单词拼写：根据所给中文意思补全下列单词

1. st __ r ___（立体声音响 *n.*）　　2. t __ b ___（桌子 *n.*）

3. c __ pb ___ rd（食橱 *n.*）　　4. pl __ t __（盘子 *n.*）

5. n __ w __ p __ p ___（报纸 *n.*）

二、语法和词汇：从 A、B、C、D 中选出正确答案

1. Some journalists went to Germany to work for the World Cup _____ June 2nd.　　（天津，中考）

  A. on　　　　　B. in　　　　　C. at　　　　　D. with

2. Oh，boys and girls，come in please. And make _____ at home.　　（石家庄，中考）

  A. yourself　　　B. us　　　　　C. you　　　　D. yourselves

3. There _____ some old people taking a walk in the park.　　（重庆，中考）

  A. is　　　　　B. are　　　　　C. has　　　　D. have

4. They usually have a football match with their foreign friends _____ fine afternoons.

                                         （桂林，中考）

  A. in　　　　　B. on　　　　　C. at　　　　　D. to

5. Gina was born _____ 1999. She is old enough to go to school.　　（北京，中考）

  A. to　　　　　B. on　　　　　C. at　　　　　D. in

6. There's enough bird food _____ for a month.

  A. to last　　　B. last　　　　C. lasts　　　D. lasted

7. How have you been _____?

  A. recent　　　B. to　　　　　C. lately　　　D. late

8. —Give me some glasses.

  —Which _____?

  A. glass　　　　B. one　　　　C. it　　　　　D. glasses

9. Give me some _____.

  A. pen　　　　B. pencil　　　C. desk　　　D. desks

10. Give me some _____.

  A. box　　　　B. boxs　　　　C. boxes　　　D. box-es

11. Give me some _____.

  A. fork　　　　B. forks　　　　C. forkes　　　D. fork-es

12. Give me some _____.

  A. bottle　　　B. bottles　　　C. bottlees　　D. bottle-es

13. Give me some _____.

  A. magazine　　B. magazines　　C. magazinees　　D. magazine-es

14. —Which ones?

  —The ones _____ the floor.

  A. and　　　　B. or　　　　　C. in　　　　　D. on

15. —Which ones?

  —The ones _____ the bed.

  A. in　　　　　B. or　　　　　C. and　　　　D. on

27

16. — _____ there _____ fish in the river?
   —Yes, there is _____ fish.
   A. Is, some, some　　B. Are, any, some　　C. Is, any, some　　D. Are, any, any

17. The picture _____ on the wall is painted by my nephew.　　　　（北京，中考）
   A. having hung　　　B. hanging　　　　C. hangs　　　　D. being hung

18. My book _____ on the desk.　　　　（北京，中考）
   A. is　　　　　B. am　　　　C. are　　　　D. be

三、翻译句子

1. 盘子里的匙很脏。
2. 餐柜里的杯子是空的。
3. 地板上的箱子很重。
4. 书架上的书是旧的。
5. 桌上的那些杂志是新的。

6. The ties on the chair are short.
7. The newspapers on the floor are dirty.
8. Which ones?
9. Here you are.
10. Thank you.

四、改错

1. What's it? It's a apple.
2. Who are those young woman?
3. The policemen works very hard.
4. Those American are visitors.
5. My parent is workers.

五、翻译下列句子(注意介词短语的用法)

1. The book on your desk is very famous.
2. The spoons on the plate are dirty.
3. The girl in red is my classmate.
4. I want to buy the book on this shelf.
5. The case on the floor is very heavy.
6. The book in your hand is mine.
7. I'm sorry. The cup on the sideboard is empty.
8. The pictures on the wall are valuable (有价值的).

六、书面表达

　　假设你是校报英文刊物的记者,请就你校最近举办的一次英语晚会情况写一篇英文报导,要求包括以下内容:
　　1. 时间:十二月三十日(星期三)晚七点。
　　2. 地点:学校第二会议室。
　　3. 内容:歌舞,短剧,用英语表演。
　　4. 晚会还有来自澳大利亚的布朗先生,演唱了吉它伴奏歌曲。
　　5. 大家玩得很痛快。
　　(限词100左右)
注意:要求把这篇报导用自己所学知识,力求表达清楚,文理要通顺,形式要正确。在避免逐字逐句翻译的基础上,做到内容要点不要遗漏,文题相符。

七、完成句子:将下列短语译成英语

1. 架子上的杂志
2. 电视机上的报纸
3. 梳妆台上的领带

4. 地板上的箱子
5. 餐桌上的盘子
6. 碗柜上的瓶子

Lesson 25～26

一、单词拼写:根据所给中文意思补全下列单词

1. m＿dd＿＿＿ (中间 *n.*)   2. ele＿＿＿r＿＿＿ (带电的 *adj.*)   3. wh＿＿＿＿＿ (哪里 *adv.*)

4. ＿f(……的 *prep.*)   5. M＿＿＿ (夫人 *n.*)

二、语法和词汇:从 A、B、C、D 中选出正确答案

1. —Have you had ＿＿＿＿＿＿＿ breakfast yet?

   —No,not yet.

   A. 不填   B. a   C. the   D. an

2. Look! Lily with her sister ＿＿＿＿＿＿＿ flying a kite on the playground.

   A. is   B. are   C. this   D. that

3. We are doing much better ＿＿＿＿＿＿＿ English ＿＿＿＿＿＿＿ our teacher's help.

   A. in/at   B. at/in   C. in/with   D. with/with

4. There ＿＿＿＿＿＿＿ two spoons and a knife on the table.

   A. are   B. is   C. am   D. be

5. There ＿＿＿＿＿＿＿ a knife and two spoons on the table.

   A. are   B. is   C. am   D. be

6. There is ＿＿＿＿＿＿＿ glass on the table.

   A. a   B. an   C. /   D. the

7. There is a fox ＿＿＿＿＿＿＿ the tin.

   A. into   B. on   C. of   D. /

8. There is a spoon ＿＿＿＿＿＿＿ the cup.

   A. on   B. in   C. of   D. /

9. There is a box ＿＿＿＿＿＿＿ the floor.

   A. in   B. on   C. of   D. /

10. "＿＿＿＿＿＿＿ is it?""In the room. "

    A. What   B. Who   C. Which   D. Where

11. Give ＿＿＿＿＿＿＿ please,Jack.

    A. some glasses me   B. I some glasses   C. some glasses me   D. me some glasses

12. Tom didn't the coat, ＿＿＿＿＿＿＿?

    A. didn't he   B. doesn't he   C. did he   D. does he

13. I have made a ＿＿＿＿＿＿＿ to work hard at English.

    A. decision   B. decide   C. idea   D. belief

14. I ＿＿＿＿＿＿＿ here for 5 years.

    A. have been   B. have come   C. came   D. will be

15. Someone called me up in the middle of the night , but they hung up ＿＿＿＿＿＿＿ I could answer the

    phone.   (北京,中考)

    A. as   B. since   C. until   D. before

16. Dorothy was always speaking highly of her role in the play, ＿＿＿＿＿＿＿,of course , made the oth-

    ers unhappy.   (北京,中考)

29

A. who   B. which   C. this   D. what

17. If you want to change for a double room you'll have to pay _____ $ 15.   (北京,中考)

    A. another   B. other   C. more   D. Each

18. —Where are you going?

    —I'm going to the _____ to fly a kite.   (北京,中考)

    A. shop   B. library   C. park   D. post office

19. —Can you write a letter in English?   (北京,中考)

    —No, I _____.

    A. may not   B. mustn't   C. can't   D. needn't

三、翻译句子

1. 冰箱里有个瓶子。   6. Give me a book.
2. 是空的吗?   7. Which book?
3. 不满的。   8. The book on the shelf.
4. 瓶子里有什么?   9. There are some books on the shelf.
5. 有牛奶。

四、介词填空

1. _____ the kitchen   2. _____ the left   3. _____ the middle of
4. _____ the shelf   5. _____ the floor

五、用 there's 或 there're 填空

1. _____ a new manager. His name is Michael.
2. _____ some typists in the office.
3. _____ a pen and two books on the desk.
4. _____ a lot of students in the hall.
5. _____ twelve months in a year.
6. _____ twenty-nine days in February this year.

六、书面表达

请用英语为《中学英语指导》写一篇习作,题为"Our School",内容要点如下:

1. 学校概况:学校位于城西,虽然不大,但历史悠久,老师约150人,学生1500人。
2. 学校设施:三幢教学楼,一个图书馆,校园东边是大操场。
3. 校园景色:到处是树木、花草,美极了。
4. 教学情况:学校有市里最好的老师,他们乐于助人;学生学习努力,积极参加各种活动。学校生
   活充满欢乐,大家都热爱学校生活。
5. 字   数:80—120 词。

七、完成句子:根据课文内容完成下列会话

B:There is a blue electric cooker in Mrs. Smith's kitchen.

A:Where is the _____?

B:_____.

A:Is there a table or a desk in the kitchen?

B:There isn't _____ in the kitchen.

    There is _____.

A:Where _____?

B:It is in the middle of the room.

A:Is there an _____ bottle and a _____ cup on the table?

B:Yes, there is.

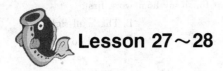

Lesson 27～28

一、单词拼写:根据所给中文意思补全下列单词

1. d _____（门 *n.*）   2. pi ___ure（图 *n.*）   3. liv __ng（活着的 *adj.*）

4. armch _____（扶手椅 *n.*）   5. s __m __（一些 *adj.*）

二、语法和词汇:从 A、B、C、D 中选出正确答案

1. There are two _____ in my pencil-box.   （永州,中考）

    A. knife   B. knifes   C. knives   D. a knife

2. They have _____ on the hill.   （昆明,中考）

    A. apple tree   B. apple trees   C. apples tree   D. apples trees.

3. There _____ a great number of students over there. The number of the students _____ five thousand.   （黄冈,中考）

    A. are/is   B. are/are   C. is/are   D. is/is

4. There is not _____ in the purse.   （北京,中考）

    A. some money   B. some money's

    C. any money   D. any moneys

5. There is no orange in the bottle. Would you like _____ to drink?   （杭州,中考）

    A. something else   B. else something   C. else   D. something

6. There are some newspapers _____ the table.

    A. in   B. on   C. at   D. near

7. There are _____ books on the desk.

    A. a   B. an   C. some   D. /

8. _____ there a book on the shelf?

    A. Am   B. Are   C. Is   D. /

9. Are there _____ dresses in the room?

    A. a   B. an   C. some   D. any

10. There are some trousers _____ the bed.

     A. in   B. on   C. near   D. at

11. There are some glasses _____ the television.

     A. in   B. on   C. near   D. at

12. There are some bottles _____ the refrigerator.

     A. in   B. on   C. near   D. at

13. I _____ buy a car next month.

     A. would   B. should   C. am going to   D. am about to

14. She _____ that the book was not Mrs. Wang's, but Mr. Li's.

     A. listened   B. spoke   C. thought   D. thinks

15. The plane _____ at 10 o'clock. Are you ready?

     A. will fly   B. flies   C. has flown   D. to fly

16. Mary, please show _____ your picture.   （北京,中考）

     A. my   B. mine   C. I   D. me

17. —Would you like to go out for a walk with us?

—_____ , but I must finish my homework first.　　　　　　　(北京，中考)

A. Of course not　　　　　　　B. That's all right

C. I'd love to　　　　　　　　D. Yes，I do

三、翻译句子

1. 梳妆台上有车票吗？

2. 有的。

3. 它们在哪？

4. 它们靠近那只盒子。

5. 谢谢。

6. Are there any forks on the table?

7. There aren't any on the table.

8. There are some on the cupboard.

9. Whose are these forks?

10. They are Mrs. Smith's.

四、将下列句子改成疑问句

1. There is a desk near the window.

2. There are some books on the book-shelf.

3. There is a picture on the wall.

4. There are some girls in the shop.

五、用 some，any 填空

1. Put _____ bread on the table；we shall need _____ more.

2. Do you see _____ people?

3. We need _____ vegetables every day.

4. There are _____ new words in the text.

5. Do you have _____ friends in the city?

6. There isn't _____ water left. Please go and get _____ .

7. There aren't _____ desks in the room. There are only _____ chairs in it.

8. I have _____ questions about the text.

六、书面表达

说明：根据提示用英语写一封信。

提示：你的朋友 Mr. Carl Hill 写信告诉你他下月从美国来京，你邀请他来你家住，你还愿为他提供一间卧室，一日三餐，并带他逛北京。你准备去机场接他，请他抵京时通知你。

七、完成句子：将下列句子改成否定句和疑问句

1. There is a desk near the window.

2. There are some English books on the book-shelf.

3. There is a blackboard in the classroom.

4. There is a map on the wall.

5. There are some cars in the street.

6. There are many people in the shop.

7. There is some water in the glass.

Lesson 29～30

一、单词拼写：根据所给中文意思补全下列单词

1. cl__th___（衣服 *n.*）　2. d__st（扫去灰尘 *v.*）　3. _____（换空气 *v.*）

4. sh__t（关 *v.*）　5. sw___p（扫 *v.*）

二、语法和词汇：从 A、B、C、D 中选出正确答案

1. —Mum，may I watch TV now?

　—No，you _____ finish your homework first.　　　　　　　（天津，中考）

　A. mustn't　　　　B. must　　　　C. need　　　　D. can't

2. —Must they clean the classroom now?

　—No，they _____.　　　　　　　　　　　　　　　　（永州，中考）

　A. can't　　　　B. needn't　　　　C. don't　　　　D. mustn't

3. —Must I clean the room now?

　—No，you _____.　　　　　　　　　　　　　　　　（焦作，中考）

　A. can't　　　　B. may not　　　　C. mustn't　　　　D. needn't

4. Henry _____ be at home because he phoned from the farm just now.　（桂林，中考）

　A. mustn't　　　　　　　　　B. isn't able to

　C. may not　　　　　　　　　D. can't

5. —Excuse me. Look at the sign _____ !

　—Sorry，I didn't see it.　　　　　　　　　　　　　　（南宁，中考）

　A. NOT SMOKING　　　　　　　B. NO SMOKING

　C. DONT SMOKE　　　　　　　　D. DO NOT SMOKE

6. _____ the clothes.

　A. Make　　　　B. Wash　　　　C. Open　　　　D. Put

7. _____ the pencil.

　A. Open　　　　B. Shut　　　　C. Make　　　　D. Sharpen

8. _____ the bottle.

　A. Wake　　　　B. Sweep　　　　C. Shut　　　　D. Open

9. _____ off the television.

　A. Put　　　　B. Open　　　　C. Turn　　　　D. Shut

10. Take _____ your trousers.

　A. on　　　　B. off　　　　C. in　　　　D. of

11. This bedroom's _____. What must I do?

　A. clean　　　　B. nice　　　　C. tidy　　　　D. untidy

12. He said he _____ up at six every morning as a rule.

　A. get　　　　B. gets　　　　C. would　　　　D. got

13. She said that she would go there _____.

　A. that day　　　　B. then　　　　C. the next day　　　　D. tomorrow

14. Is your brother an engineer _____ a teacher?

　A. of　　　　B. but　　　　C. or　　　　D. and

33

15. _____ live at 34 Queen Street.

    A. The Smiths   B. The Smith   C. Smiths   D. Smith

16. The air in Beijing is getting much _____ now than a few years ago.   (北京,中考)

    A. clean   B. cleaner   C. cleanest   D. the cleanest

17. —May I put my bike here?

    —No, you _____. You should put it over there.   (北京,中考)

    A. couldn't   B. needn't   C. mustn't   D. won't

三、翻译句子

1. 进来。

2. 请把灯关上。

3. 这卧室不整洁。

4. 我应该做什么?

5. 扫扫地,通通风。

6. Put these clothes in the wardrobe.

7. Open the window and air the room.

8. Make the bed.

9. Dust the dressing table.

10. Empty the bottle.

四、词语搭配

1. shut the

2. open the

3. put on your

4. take off your

5. turn on the

6. turn off the

7. clean the

8. dust the

9. sweep the

10. sharpen the

A. clothes

B. radio

C. door

D. window

E. blackboard

F. floor

G. dressing table

H. pencil

五、用介词填空 (of, in, under, on, at, near)

1. There is a desk _____ the window.

2. There are two pairs of shoes _____ the bed.

3. Are there any pictures _____ the wall?

4. There are some cars _____ the street.

5. There is a table in the middle _____ the kitchen.

6. There is a man _____ the door.

7. I put the pen _____ the table.

8. The boys are swimming _____ the river.

六、书面表达

    假如你是个过路人,看到圣保罗 Capital Building 的大火,以及救火人员奋力灭火和抢救被困人员的情景。描写一下当时的情况,可以使用下列短语:

do some shopping in the market

go over to see it

many people escape into the street

some helicopters

land on the roof

see a big fire in the distance

fire breaks out on the 11th floor

many others be trapped

very thick smoke

save about 70 people

七、完成句子

1. You _____ tell somebody else about it;this is secret between us.

    A. don't   B. needn't   C. mustn't   D. won't

2. You _____ be tired;you have been working for so long a time,but he _____ be tired;he

34

has just begun to work.

  A. must, can't   B. must, may no

  C. can't, must   D. may, not, must

3. The general himself _____ attend the meeting, but I'm not very certain.

  A. must   B. should   C. caught to   D. may

4. —Shall I tell John about it?

  —No, you _____. I have told him already.

  A. needn't   B. mustn't   C. shouldn't   D. wouldn't

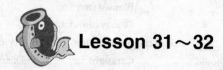

Lesson 31～32

一、单词拼写:根据所给中文意思补全下列单词

1. t____th(牙 n.)　　2. b__sk___（篮子 n.）　　3. t__p__（打字 v.）

4. cl__m__（爬 v.）　　5. ___d___（在……下 prep.）

二、语法和词汇:从 A、B、C、D 中选出正确答案

1. —Excuse me. Who _____ eating the bones?
   —The dogs.　　　　　　　　　　　　　　　　　（大同,中考）
   A. are　　　　　B. is　　　　　C. must　　　　　D. will

2. Is your brother _____ all at home this evening?　（襄樊,中考）
   A. reading/looking　　　　　　B. reading/watching
   C. watching/looking　　　　　　D. looking/watching

3. My family _____ all at home this evening.　（郑州,中考）
   A. are　　　　　B. is　　　　　C. am　　　　　D. be

4. Look! There are some _____ on the table.　（云南,中考）
   A. photoes　　　B. photos　　　C. meat　　　　D. photo

5. Look! There are some children _____ in the park.　（北京,中考）
   A. play　　　　　B. playing　　　C. plays　　　D. played

6. What's she _____?
   A. do　　　　　B. doing　　　C. dos　　　　D. does

7. What _____ it doing?
   A. is　　　　　B. am　　　　　C. are　　　　D. do

8. He has _____ friends than you have.
   A. fewer　　　　B. fewest　　　C. little　　　D. less

9. Tom didn't go to the cinema yesterday，I didn't go _____.
   A. instead　　　B. as well　　　C. too　　　　D. either

10. He is _____ intelligent person I have ever met.
    A. least　　　　B. the least　　C. more　　　　D. very

11. Jack is _____ a magazine.
    A. readding　　B. reading　　　C. reads　　　D. read

12. The boy is _____ on his shirt.
    A. puting　　　B. putting　　　C. puts　　　　D. put

13. Army is _____ the floor.
    A. sweeping　　B. sweeping　　C. sweep　　　D. sweeps

14. The cat is _____ its milk.
    A. drink　　　　B. drinks　　　C. drinking　　D. drinkking

15. I am _____ the dressing table.
    A. dresing　　　B. dressing　　C. dress　　　D. dresses

16. We _____ got any money at all.
    A. haven't　　　B. didn't　　　C. have　　　　D. did

36

17. —_____ is your grandpa, Emma?
　　—He's watering the flowers in the garden.　　　　　　　　　　　（北京，中考）
　　A. When　　　　B. What　　　　C. Where　　　　D. How

18. —It's a good idea. But who's going to _____ the plan?
　　—I think Tom and Greg will.　　　　　　　　　　　　　　　　　（北京，中考）
　　A. set aside　　　B. carry out　　　C. take in　　　　D. get through

19. —Waiter!　　　　　　　　　　　　　　　　　　　　　　　　　（北京，中考）
　　— _____
　　—I can't eat this, It's too salty.
　　A. Yes, sir?　　　B. What?　　　C. All right?　　　D. Pardon?

20. —What about having a drink?　　　　　　　　　　　　　　　　（北京，中考）
　　— _____
　　A. Good idea.　　B. Help yourself.　　C. Go ahead, please.　　D. Me, too.

三、翻译句子

1. 公园里有个女孩。
2. 她在干什么？
3. 她正在看一本杂志。
4. 那只狗在干什么？
5. 它正在啃骨头。
6. The cat is drinking milk.
7. You are turning on the radio.
8. He is opening the window.
9. She is shutting the door.
10. What are you doing?

四、用动词适当形式填空

1. What is he _____ (do)? He is _____ (talk) to his friend.
2. What are you _____ (do)? I am _____ (sweep) the floor.
3. What are they _____ (do)? Are they _____ (play) in the garden?
4. No, they are _____ (have) lunch now.

五、将下列句子改成一般疑问句和否定句

1. The children are playing on the playground.
2. The students are planting trees.
3. Jenny is reading a picture book.
4. He is drawing on the wall.
5. They are having a good time.
6. They are drinking coffee.
7. His son is studying hard.
8. They are watching TV at the moment.

六、书面表达

　　在一次有关防火知识宣传的中外学生联欢会上，你代表某中学向与会者用英语讲一个幽默而又不失教育意义的小故事。大意如下：
　　某消防队接到火警电话，由于双方都缺乏防火知识造成误会。报警者说，我家着火，请快来救火，值班者问：在哪儿？回答：在厨房。值班者问：怎么去？回答：难道你们不是乘消防车来吗？
　　要求：写成讲说稿，开始部分已给出。
　　Hello, friends. Next I will tell you an interesting story about a fire. I think every one of us should learn something useful and instructive from my story...

七、完成句子：用动词的适当形式填空

1. Look, your dog _____ (run) after a cat.
2. What are you doing? I _____ (read) a book.
3. Where is Tom? He _____ (go) over his lessons in his room.
4. She says that she _____ (write) a novel.
5. My father _____ (sharpen) the pencil for me at this moment.

37

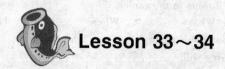

Lesson 33~34

一、单词拼写：根据所给中文意思补全下列单词

1. sh __ v __ （刮脸 v.）　　2. w _____ （洗 v.）　　3. j ___ p（跳 v.）

4. sh _ n _ （照 v.）　　5. b ___ t（船 n.）

二、语法和词汇：从 A、B、C、D 中选出正确答案

1. _____ my parent's help, I begin to catch up _____ my classmates.

   A. With/to　　　B. Under/with　　　C. With/with　　　D. To/to

2. —Do you know the differences _____ the three words?

   —Sorry，I don't know.

   A. among　　　B. between　　　C. with　　　D. about

3. Jenny and her parents _____ going to visit the Palace Museum tomorrow.

   A. is　　　B. am　　　C. are　　　D. be

4. My family _____ the best one in the world.

   A. are　　　B. is　　　C. am　　　D. be

5. —Class is _____. See you tomorrow.

   —See you!

   A. on　　　B. in　　　C. over　　　D. with

6. Mr. Jones is _____ his family.

   A. in　　　B. on　　　C. at　　　D. with

7. There are some boats _____ the river.

   A. in　　　B. on　　　C. at　　　D. over

8. The aeroplane is flying _____ the river.

   A. over　　　B. under　　　C. at　　　D. on

9. Tim is looking _____ them.

   A. over　　　B. under　　　C. on　　　D. at

10. —What are they doing?

   —They are _____.

   A. wash　　　B. washs　　　C. washes　　　D. washing

11. —What are they doing?

   — They are _____.

   A. walking　　　B. walks　　　C. walk　　　D. walkking

12. —What are the birds doing?

   —They are _____.

   A. flies　　　B. fling　　　C. flying　　　D. fly

13. Tom can run _____ fast as Jason.

   A. as　　　B. so　　　C. such　　　D. very

14. I don't like Chinese，I like English _____.

   A. instead of　　　B. as well as　　　C. too　　　D. instead

15. She is good at running，and she is good at jumping _____.

    A. instead of   B. as well   C. neither   D. instead

16. He has _____ money.

    A. many   B. much   C. a lots of   D. lot of

17. I want to know _____ the day after tomorrow.   (北京,中考)

    A. what he will do   B. what will he do

    C. what he did   D. what did he do

18. —Would you like to go to the concert with me?

    —I'd love to, _____ I can't. I have a lot of homework to do.   (北京,中考)

    A. or   B. but   C. so   D. and

19. The doctor looked over Peter carefully after he _____ to the hospital.   (北京,中考)

    A. takes   B. is taken   C. took   D. was taken

20. Sorry I'm late. I _____ have turned off the alarm clock and gone back to sleep again.

    (北京,中考)

    A. might   B. should   C. can   D. will

三、翻译句子

1. Sholly 正坐在树下。

2. 椅子下面有只猫。

3. 桌子上方有一盏灯。

4. 我和父母在一起。

5. 请给我几只玻璃杯。

6. It is raining.

7. There are some clouds in the sky.

8. They are walking over the bridge.

9. There are some boats on the river.

10. She is looking at the ship.

四、介词填空 (on, in, at, near, over, under)

1. There is a picture _____ the wall _____ the door.

2. There is a bridge _____ the river. A ship is going _____ the river.

3. Mr. Black lives _____ his family _____ the fifth floor _____ that building.

4. A bird is flying _____ the house. Tom is looking _____ it.

五、将下列句子改为现在进行时的句子(把时间状语部分改为 now)

1. He eats her breakfast every day.

2. She types letters every morning.

3. I do my homework every evening.

4. My father shaves every day.

5. My grandfather cooks for us every day.

6. Bessie dusts the dressing table every morning.

7. I make the bed every morning.

8. My brother sharpens his pencils every day.

六、书面表达

    给你的笔友 Fred 写信,告诉他你很高兴收到他七月二日的信,同时将你现在英语学习中遇到的一些困难,例如:易忘所学过的单词和词组,对一些习惯用语和语法规则未能弄懂,在习作中常犯错误等,请他帮助你提出如何学好英语的意见。你叫李英,在广州市第一中学高一·三班学习,发信日期为 2002 年 7 月 5 日。全文约 100—120 词。

七、完成句子:仿照例句写出相应的特殊疑问句,并回答。

the man and the woman/waiting for a bus

What are the man and the woman doing?

They're waiting for a bus.

1. the men/shaving

2. the children/crying
3. the men/cooking a meal
4. the dogs/eating bones
5. the women/washing dishes
6. the women/typing letters
7. they/walking over the bridge
8. the birds/flying over the river
9. the children/doing their homework
10. the children/looking at the boats on the river

Lesson 35～36

一、单词拼写：根据所给中文意思补全下列单词

1. o____（离开 *adv.*）　　2. p____k（公园 *n.*）　　3. ph__t__gr_____（照片 *n.*）

4. __l__ng（沿着 *prep.*）　　5. __nt__（进入 *prep.*）

二、语法和词汇：从 A、B、C、D 中选出正确答案

1. Don't tell anybody about it. Keep it _____ you and me.　　（哈尔滨，中考）

　　A. among　　　　　B. between　　　　C. in　　　　　　D. with

2. —Somebody is waiting outside. He wants to see you.　　（苏州，中考）

　—_____ no one knows I'm here.

　　A. For　　　　　　B. And　　　　　　C. But　　　　　　D. So

3. The doctor is _____ the crying baby, but he can't find out what is wrong with it.

　　　　　　　　　　　　　　　　　　　　　　　　　　　　（安徽，中考）

　　A. looking over　　B. looking after　　C. looking for　　D. looking out

4. Don't forget to _____ your school things when you have finished your homework.

　　　　　　　　　　　　　　　　　　　　　　　　　　　　（常州，中考）

　　A. put off　　　　　B. put up　　　　　C. put down　　　D. put away

5. Sorry, there is no direct airline _____ Taiwan and the mainland.　　（莱芜，中考）

　　A. along　　　　　B. in　　　　　　　C. between　　　　D. at

6. The Chinese history deeply _____ him.

　　A. interesting　　　B. interest　　　　C. interests　　　D. interested

7. It is _____ a park.

　　A. on　　　　　　B. of　　　　　　　C. between　　　　D. beside

8. Some of them are coming _____ the park.

　　A. out　　　　　　B. of　　　　　　　C. out of　　　　　D. of out

9. —Where is he?

　—He is _____ the park.

　　A. sitting near　　　B. sitting on　　　C. sitting in　　　D. sitting of

10. The car is coming _____ the road.

　　A. of　　　　　　B. in　　　　　　　C. on　　　　　　D. along

11. The plane is flying _____ the bridge.

　　A. on　　　　　　B. in　　　　　　　C. under　　　　　D. of

12. The man is walking _____ two policemen.

　　A. on　　　　　　B. in　　　　　　　C. between　　　　D. of

13. She is going _____ the shop.

　　A. out　　　　　　B. out of　　　　　C. of　　　　　　D. on

14. They are jumping _____.

　　A. of　　　　　　B. off　　　　　　　C. in　　　　　　D. on

15. A town is _____ than a city.

　　A. smaller　　　　　B. smallest　　　　C. bigger　　　　D. biggest

41

16. —Would you like something to eat?

　—_____.

　　A. I'd like to　　　B. No, thanks　　　C. Yes, I like　　D. No, I don't

17. _____ production up by 60％, the company has had another excellent year. （北京，中考）

　　A. As　　　　　B. For　　　　C. With　　　　D. Through

18. We often go to the park _____ Sundays. （北京，中考）

　　A. on　　　　　B. in　　　　C. at　　　　D. from

三、翻译句子

1. 我和汤姆正在打扫房间。

2. 玛丽在教我和李平英语。

3. 我和他们正坐在树下。

4. 女儿走在我和妻子之间。

5. 我正在横穿马路。

6. She is going into shop.

7. Jack is sitting under the tree.

8. The plane is flying over my head.

9. The boat is going under the bridge.

10. We are walking along the street.

四、介词填空(with, on, in, along, across, between)

1. There are many trees _____ the streets.

2. Mr. Tone lives _____ the first floor.

3. We often swim _____ the river.

4. Our village is _____ two hills.

5. Mr. David goes to work _____ his wife.

五、用现在进行时改写下列句子

1. Mother mops the kitchen floor.

2. I sit on the grass.

3. They plan to visit London this summer.

4. How do you get along with your classmates?

5. He digs a hole in the garden to plant the tree.

六、书面表达

请以 Information and life 为题写一篇短文。

提示：

1. 信息的重要性

2. 获知消息的途径

3. 如何运用知识

七、完成句子:用下列介词填空

with, on, in, along, across, between

1. There are many trees _____ the streets.

2. Mr. Jones lives _____ the first floor.

3. My father often walks _____ the river after supper.

4. We often swim _____ the river.

5. Be careful(当心)when you are walking _____ the street.

6. The children are looking at a ship _____ the river.

7. Our village is _____ two hills.

8. Mr. David often goes to work(上班) _____ his wife.

Lesson 37～38

一、单词拼写:根据所给中文意思补全下列单词

1. h＿mm＿＿＿（锤子 *n.*）　　2. p＿nk（粉色 *n.*）　　3. m＿k＿（做 *v.*）

4. h＿＿＿d（努力地 *adv.*）　　5. h＿m＿w＿＿k（作业 *n.*）

二、语法和词汇:从 A、B、C、D 中选出正确答案

1. The child _____ his mother carefully but he can't _____ anything. 　　（江西,中考）
   A. listens/hear　　B. is listening to/hear　　C. hears/listen　　D. hears/listen to

2. Don't make me _____ this or that. I'm too busy! 　　（徐州,中考）
   A. to do　　B. do　　C. doing　　D. done

3. I _____ my homework while my parents _____ bed for me. 　　（浙江,中考）
   A. am making/are doing　　　　B. am doing/are making
   C. am making/are making　　　　D. am doing/are doing

4. There _____ a Model Contest in our city this afternoon. 　　（浙江,中考）
   A. are going to have　　　　B. is going to have
   C. are going to be　　　　D. is going to be

5. _____ is really hard _____ them to climb Mount Qomolangma. 　　（黄冈,中考）
   A. This/to　　B. It/for　　C. This/for　　D. It/to

6. This is my book. Please give _____.
   A. I it　　B. it I　　C. me it　　D. it me

7. It is _____ my daughter.
   A. at　　B. in　　C. on　　D. for

8. I am going to paint it _____.
   A. good　　B. pink　　C. nice　　D. hardly

9. —What are you going to do?
   —We are _____.
   A. painting　　B. going to paint　　C. going to painting　　D. paint

10. What _____ you doing?
    A. is　　B. am　　C. are　　D. be

11. What _____ they doing?
    A. is　　B. am　　C. are　　D. be

12. What _____ he going to do?
    A. is　　B. are　　C. am　　D. be

13. We are _____ to the tap.
    A. listen　　B. listening　　C. to listen　　D. listens

14. We are _____ our homework.
    A. do　　B. doing　　C. to do　　D. does

15. We are going to _____ the bus.
    A. wait for　　B. waiting for　　C. to wait for　　D. waits for

16. Lucy is one of _____ students in our class.

43

A. good   B. better   C. best   D. the best

17. Mr. Gao is a teacher. He work in a new _____.   (北京,中考)

A. shop   B. school   C. factory   D. hospital

三、翻译句子

1. 你在干什么?
2. 我正在等车。
3. 你在等哪辆车?
4. 401 车。
5. 我不准备等车。

6. Are you doing your homework?
7. No, I am not.
8. What are you doing?
9. I'm watching TV.
10. I am going to do homework after it.

四、用所给动词适当形式填空

1. George _____ (make) a bookcase now. He _____ (work) very hard.

The book case _____ (be not) for himself. It _____ (be) for his daughter.

2. I _____ (do) my homework now. I _____ (go) to see a film today.

So I must _____ (finish) it.

3. Suen _____ (go) to paint the shelf. Because pink _____ (be) his favourite colour.

五、书面表达

高一(1)班学生写信邀请迈克先生参加周末音乐会,迈克阅后,回信如下:"感谢大家的邀请。遗憾的是我周末晚上另有安排,届时不能参加。祝大家晚会快乐。"2002 年 4 月 14 日

请将迈克的回答信用英文表达出来(字数 40—60)。

六、完成句子:以 be going to 形式将括号内的动词填入空内

44

1. My son says he _____ (be) a doctor when he grows up.

2. My brother _____ (sell) his old car and buy a new bicycle.

3. You _____ (miss) your train.

4. When _____ your husband _____ (cut) the grass?

5. What _____ you _____ (do) with this room?

   I _____ (paint) the walls in black and white stripes(条).

6. It _____ (rain). Look at those clouds(云).

7. The cat _____ (have 生)kittens(猫仔).

8. That rider(骑手) _____ (fall) off.

9. Mr. Smith is standing up. He _____ (make) a speech.

10. I _____ (not sleep) in this room. It is haunted(闹鬼的).

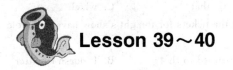

一、单词拼写：根据所给中文意思补全下列单词

1. c_____ful（小心的 *adj.*） 2. fl_____（花 *n.*） 3. ___ow（给…看 *v.*）

4. s__nd（送给 *v.*） 5. g__（去 *v.*）

二、语法和词汇：从 A、B、C、D 中选出正确答案

1. —Don't be late again，Mike.

  —_____. （上海，中考）

  A. No，I don't B. Don't worry C. Sorry，I won't D. No，I will

2. A strong wind will arrive in Harbin. It will _____ much rain.

  （哈尔滨，中考）

  A. bring B. take C. carry D. get

3. Jim asks Lin Feng _____ forget to change water. （武汉，中考）

  A. to not B. don't C. not D. not to

4. Tomorrow's meeting is very important. Please ask them _____ there on time. （黄岩，中考）

  A. go B. going C. to go D. went

5. He is kind and always _____ his help to others. （上海，中考）

  A. receives B. brings C. takes D. gives

6. I am going to put _____ the table.

  A. on it B. it on C. it to on D. on to it

7. Don't _____ it there.

  A. put B. to put C. putting D. puts

8. It's a _____ vase.

  A. love B. lovly C. lovely D. loveful

9. I am going to _____ it off.

  A. taking B. takeing C. to take D. take

10. I am going to show _____ my wife.

  A. to it B. to C. it D. it to

11. I am going to give _____ my children.

  A. them to B. to them C. them D. to

12. I didn't go _____ for this summer vacation.

  A. somewhere B. everywhere C. nowhere D. anywhere

13. It _____ heavily when I was driving to Beijing.

  A. wills B. raining C. rains D. rained

14. Tom _____ his homework at this time yesterday.

  A. was doing B. did C. would do D. has done

15. In the last few years Beijing _____ greatly.

  A. has changed B. has been changed C. changed D. was changed

16. _____ your homework _____ in half an hour?

  A. Will；finish B. Is；finished C. Will；be finished D. Does；be finish

17. These wild flowers are so special that I would do _____ I can to save them. (北京,中考)

A. whatever   B. that   C. which   D. whichever

18. —I just heard that the tickets for tonight's show have been sold out.

—Oh no! _____.   (北京,中考)

A. I was looking forward to that   B. It doesn't matter

C. I knew it already   D. It's not at all interesting

19. _____ the general state of his health, it may take him a while to recover from the operation.   (北京,中考)

A. Given   B. To give   C. Giving   D. Having given

三、翻译句子

1. 你打算如何处理那花瓶?   6. Don't drop it.

2. 我打算把它放在这张桌上。   7. Put it here on the shelf.

3. 不要放在那儿。   8. There we are.

4. 把它给我。   9. It's a lovely vase.

5. 小心点。   10. Give it to me.

四、用动词适当形式填空

1. _____ (not make) too much noise. They _____ (have) lessons.

2. We are not going to _____ (take) her any flowers.

3. _____ (Be careful). The bus _____ (come) to us.

4. _____ he _____ (listen) to the radio now?

5. Please _____ (wait) for a minute.

五、介词填空

1. Put the box _____ the shelf.

2. A: What are you going to do _____ the worn shoes?

B: I'm going to put them _____ the wardrobe.

3. Take _____ your books and read _____ me.

4. A: What's that?

B: It's coffee _____ cream and sugar.

5. She's looking _____ the new dress _____ the shop window.

6. Lucy is sitting _____ her father and mother.

7. Who's the boy _____ Jim?

8. A: Where are you going?

B: I'm going _____ the park _____ Jim.

六、书面表达

请给同学写一封信,谈谈自己的理想(字数 120—150)。

七、完成句子:仿照例句将下列句子改为祈使句

e. g. My wife told me to be patient with the children.

＝Be patient with the children.

My wife told me not to be angry with the children.

＝Don't be angry with the children.

1. Father told me not to read in bad light.

2. He told me not to worry.

3. She asked me to be patient.

4. She asked him to be kind to the child.

5. The boss ordered me not to leave the office.

6. He told me not to miss my train.

7. I warned her not to go alone.

8. Mr. Smith advised me not to believe him.

9. Mother told the boy not to put the wine near the fire.

10. Father advised me to be careful with that knife.

11. He told John not to be foolish.

12. The teacher ordered the boy not to argue(争论) with her.

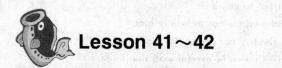

Lesson 41～42

一、单词拼写:根据所给中文意思补全下列单词

1. b___d(小鸟 n.)   2. ch___s_(干酪 n.)   3. ch_c_l_t_(巧克力 n.)

4. c__ff___(咖啡 n.)   5. br___d(面包 n.)

二、语法和词汇:从 A、B、C、D 中选出正确答案

1. —Can I help you?

—I'd like _____ for my twin daughters. (滨州,中考)

A. two pair of shoes   B. two pairs of shoes

C. two pair of shoes   D. two pairs of shoes

2. We have bought two _____ for the coming party. (烟台,中考)

A. box of apple   B. boxes of apples

C. box of apples   D. boxed of apple

3. —How much _____ the shoes?

—Five dollars _____ enough. (郑州,中考)

A. is/is   B. are/is   C. are/are   D. is/are

4. I'd like some water，but he wants _____. (北京,中考)

A. two bottle orange   B. two bottles of orange

C. two bottle oranges   D. two bottles of oranges

5. Mr. Smith always has _____ to tell us. (邢台,中考)

A. some good pieces of news   B. some pieces of good news

C. some good piece of news   D. some piece of good news

6. Is there _____ in the room?

A. tin of tobacco   B. a tobacco   C. a tin of tobacco   D. some tobaccos

7. My teacher wants me to _____ my homework this afternoon.

A. be doing   B. doing   C. not do   D. did

8. We _____ go there by bus.

A. have to not   B. wil has to   C. have not to   D. don't have to

9. I think she is _____ an engineer.

A. not possible   B. must   C. be   D. probably

10. Is there a _____ in the room?

A. photograph   B. milk   C. tea   D. coffee

11. There is _____ coffee here.

A. a   B. an   C. some   D. any

12. There is _____ car on the bridge.

A. a   B. an   C. some   D. any

13. —Is there a passport here?

—Yes，there is _____ here.

A. a   B. an   C. one   D. some

48

14. —Are there any newspapers here?

   —Yes, there are _____ here.

   A. a   B. an   C. any   D. some

15. —Is there any milk here?

   —No, there isn't _____ here.

   A. a   B. an   C. any   D. one

16. There is _____ with my eyes. So I always see the _____. My classmates often laugh at me.

   A. something wrong; things wrong   B. something wrong; wrong things

   C. wrong something; things wrong   D. wrong something; wrong things

17. —Do you want tea or coffee?   (北京，中考)

   —_____. I really don't mind.

   A. Both   B. None   C. Either   D. Neither

18. Some birds _____ to the south before winter.   (北京，中考)

   A. run   B. swim   C. walk   D. fly

19. "Help _____ to some meat, Mary," my aunt said to me.   (北京，中考)

   A. themselves   B. ourselves   C. yourself   D. himself

三、翻译句子

1. 桌上有茶叶吗？

2. 没有。

3. 桌上有咖啡吗？

4. 有，给你。

5. 谢谢。

6. Is there any beer in the refrigerator?

7. Yes, there are two bottles of beer.

8. Give me a bottle, please.

9. Here you are.

10. Thank you.

49

四、词组配对

1. a loaf of

2. a tin of

3. a bottle of

4. a bar of

5. a piece of

bread

cheese

soap

milk

tobacco

五、将下列句子改成否定句与疑问句

1. There's some tea in the tin.

2. There's some cheese on the plate.

3. There's some bread on the table.

4. There's some milk in the bottle.

5. There's some coffee in the cup.

6. There's some soap on the dressing table.

7. There's some fruit in the fruit bowl.

8. There's some meat in the fridge.

六、书面表达

假如你是李华，正在上海出差，当得知 Robin 来京，但又无法到火车站接 Robin 时，就给 Robin 写信，告知他到你家的路线，父亲在家中接待他，你很快就会回家带他一块儿参观北京。

七、完成句子：仿照例句写出相应的疑问句，并回答

spoon/on the plate

Is there a spoon here?

Yes, there is. There's one on the plate.

milk/on the table

Is there any milk here?

Yes, there is. There's some on the table.

1. passport/on the table
2. tobacco/in the tin
3. bread/on the table
4. vase/on the radio
5. tea/on the table
6. hammer/on the book-case
7. suit/in the wardrobe
8. tie/on the chair
9. chocolate/on the desk
10. cheese/on the plate

Lesson 43～44

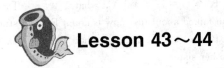

一、单词拼写:根据所给中文意思补全下列单词

1. n ＿＿＿（现在 *adv.*）　　2. b ＿＿l（沸腾 *v.*）　　3. k ＿ttl ＿（水壶 *n.*）

4. ＿f（的 *prep.*）　　5. m ＿k ＿（做 *v.*）

二、语法和词汇:从 A、B、C、D 中选出正确答案

1. The World Wide Web is sometimes jokingly（开玩笑地）called the World Wide Wait because it
   is always ＿＿＿＿ slow.　　　　　　　　　　　　　　　　　　（苏州,中考）

   A. much　　　　　B. too　　　　　C. go　　　　　D. a little

2. —May I talk in class?

   —No,you ＿＿＿＿.　　　　　　　　　　　　　　　　　　　（上海,中考）

   A. don't　　　　　B. needn't　　　　C. mustn't　　　D. may

3. Henry ＿＿＿＿ be at home；his mother is looking for him.　　　（无锡,中考）

   A. mustn't　　　　B. isn't able to　　C. may　　　　D. can't

4. —Mum, ＿＿＿＿ I play computer games?

   —Yes,you can. But you have to finish your homework first.　　（广州,中考）

   A. must　　　　　B. may　　　　　C. should　　　　D. can't

5. —Must I go and do it now?

   —No,you ＿＿＿＿. We still have two more days.　　　　　　（广州,中考）

   A. shouldn't　　　B. can't　　　　C. needn't　　　D. won't

6. The kettle's ＿＿＿＿.

   A. boiling　　　　B. boilling　　　C. boil　　　　　D. boils

7. ＿＿＿＿. It's in front of you.

   A. There they are　B. There are they　C. There it is　　D. There is it

8. ＿＿＿＿ there any bread here?

   A. Is　　　　　　B. Are　　　　　C. Am　　　　　D. Be

9. ＿＿＿＿ there any cups on the table?

   A. Is　　　　　　B. Am　　　　　C. Are　　　　　D. Be

10. ＿＿＿＿ there any soap on the cupboard?

    A. Be　　　　　B. Am　　　　　C. Are　　　　　D. Is

11. ＿＿＿＿ there any water in the glasses?

    A. Be　　　　　B. Am　　　　　C. Are　　　　　D. Is

12. ＿＿＿＿ there any chocolate here?

    A. Be　　　　　B. Am　　　　　C. Are　　　　　D. Is

13. ＿＿＿＿ there any hammers on the table?

    A. Be　　　　　B. Am　　　　　C. Are　　　　　D. Is

14. Are there any buses ＿＿＿＿ that building?

    A. over　　　　　B. on　　　　　C. under　　　　D. in front of

15. Is there any milk ＿＿＿＿ the door?

    A. in　　　　　　B. on　　　　　C. behind　　　　D. under

16. Is his book _____ you talked about just now?

    A. the one   B. ×   C. what   D. who

17. The one _____ you talked about just now is about English study.

    A. the one   B. ×   C. what   D. where

18. Jane is _____ than her sister.

    A. much stronger   B. more strong   C. very strong   D. more strongly

19. There is _____ in today's newspaper.

    A. new anything   B. new something   C. anything new   D. something new

20. While she _____ TV in the living room, the telephone _____.

    A. watches, rings   B. is watching, rang

    C. was watching, rang   D. watched, was ringing

三、翻译句子

1. 你会沏茶吗？

2. 这水壶里有水吗？

3. 茶叶在茶壶后面。

4. 我现在看见了。

5. 我找到了。

6. Hurry up.

7. Here they are.

8. There it is.

9. It's in front of you.

10. Of course I can.

四、变换单复数

    boy   fox   glass   tomato   bird   child   dish

五、填入适当的量词

1. a _____ of sugar

2. two _____ of tea

3. three _____ of coffee

4. four _____ of milk

5. five _____ of bread

6. two _____ of chocolate

7. a _____ of cheese

8. a quarter of a _____ of tobacco

六、书面表达

    围绕吸烟有害健康这一题材，以 Give up Smoking 为题写一篇短文。注意要把劝告人们戒烟的理由陈述出来，字数在 120 字左右。

七、完成句子:完成下列对话

A：Can you see two cars in front of that building?

B：No, _____

A：Stand on this chair and have a look.

B：_____ right.

A：Can you _____ now?

B：Yes, but I can see only one car.

A：Get down please. Let me have a look.

B：What _____?

A：I can see only _____, but I can't see the _____, either.

Lesson 45～46

一、单词拼写：根据所给中文意思补全下列单词

1. c__k__（蛋糕 *n.*）　　2. t__rr__b___（可怕的 *adj.*）　　3 __sk（要求 *v.*）

4. c__n（能 *v.*）　　　5. b__h__n__（后面 *prep.*）

二、语法和词汇：从 A、B、C、D 中选出正确答案

1. _____ I fill in check-in form right now，sir?

　—No，you needn't. You can complete it this afternoon.　　　　　　　（广东，中考）

　A. May　　　　　B. Can　　　　　C. Would　　　　　D. Must

2. —May I go to the cinema，mum?

　—Certainly. But you _____ be back by 11 o'clock.　　　　　　　（安徽，中考）

　A. can　　　　　B. may　　　　　C. must　　　　　D. need

3. Mrs. Green is out. I have to _____ her baby.　　　　　　　　　（南宁，中考）

　A. look around　　B. look up　　　C. look for　　　D. look after

4. —Boss，must I finish typing this letter today?

　—No，you _____. You may finish it tomorrow.　　　　　　　　　（兰州，中考）

　A. needn't　　　　B. mustn't　　　C. don't　　　　　D. won't

5. —Can you understand me?

　—Sorry，I can _____ understand you.

　A. hardly　　　　B. almost　　　　C. nearly　　　　　D. ever

6. Can you _____ the bird?

　A. to see　　　　B. seeing　　　　C. sees　　　　　　D. see

7. Can you _____ the book?

　A. to read　　　　B. reading　　　C. reads　　　　　　D. read

8. Can you _____ the aeroplane?

　A. to see　　　　B. seeing　　　　C. see　　　　　　D. sees

9. Can you _____ cakes?

　A. to make　　　　B. make　　　　C. making　　　　　D. makes

10. Can _____ listen to the radio?

　A. Sam and you　　B. you and Sam　C. I，you and Sam　D. you，I and Sam

11. When I was young，I _____ go swiming myself.

　A. often　　　　　B. was going to　C. shall　　　　　　D. used to

12. He used to help you do some housework，_____?

　A. wouldn't he　　B. didn't he　　C. was he　　　　　D. did he

13. I saw Jane just now. She _____ have gone to school.

　A. needn't　　　　B. must　　　　C. couldn't　　　　　D. could

14. —Can you ride a bike?　　　　　　　　　　　　　　　　　　　　（北京，中考）

　—No，I _____.

　A. may not　　　　B. can't　　　　C. needn't　　　　　D. mustn't

53

三、翻译句子

1. 你能为我打一下这封信吗？
2. 请你呆一会儿好吗？
3. 我打不了这封信。
4. 我看不懂这封信。
5. 老板的书写太糟糕了。

6. What's the matter?
7. Here you are.
8. Can the cat drink its milk?
9. Can George take these flowers to him?
10. I can't put it on the shelf.

四、用所给动词适当形式填空

1. Can you _____ (see) the plane in the sky?
2. There _____ (be) some cheese on the plate.
3. Must I _____ (open) the door now?
4. _____ (be) there any chairs in the room?
5. _____ (sweep) the floor and _____ (dust) the sideboard.

五、将下列句子改为一般疑问句和否定句

1. I can tell him the truth.
2. Mr. Zhang can speak Japaness.
3. I can see the words on the blackboard clearly.
4. I can help you.
5. We can go to Hong Kong for a holiday.
6. Tom can stay up till tomorrow.
7. We can do our best for our construction.
8. He can move the stone.

六、书面表达

根据提示的情景用英语写出一段通顺恰当的短文，约 80～100 词。不必根据中文逐字逐句翻译。

李磊对英语很感兴趣。上星期他看了英语影片《音乐之声》(The Sound of Music)，非常喜欢影片中的英语歌曲，但听不懂其中的对话。他决心今后更努力地学好英语。

七、完成句子：将 can 和括号中的动词填入空内

1. I _____ (not remember) his address.
2. When the fog(雾) lifts, we _____ (see) where we are.
3. I _____ (not do) anything about it.
4. _____ you _____ (type) this letter?
5. I _____ (not understand) what he is saying.
6. He says that he _____ (not come); he is having a bath now.
7. _____ Tom _____ (swim) across this river?
8. She _____ (not speak) English but she _____ (understand) French.
9. He _____ (climb) over the gate and get a ladder(梯子).
10. I _____ (not eat) any more.

Lesson 47~48

一、单词拼写:根据所给中文意思补全下列单词

1. w__n__（想 *v.*）　　　2. __r__ng__（桔 *n.*）　　　3. __pp___（苹果 *n.*）

4. fr_____（新鲜的 *adj.*） 5. b_____（啤酒 *n.*）

二、语法和词汇:从 A、B、C、D 中选出正确答案

1. —Do you have a baseball?
　—_____.　　　　　　　　　　　　　　　　　　　　　（上海,中考）
　A. No,I do　　　B. Yes,I don't　　　C. Yes,he does　　　D. Sorry,I don't

2. _____ do you spell it?　　　　　　　　　　　　　　　　（贵州,中考）
　A. What　　　B. How　　　C. How's　　　D. Which

3. —Do you mind if I smoke here?
　—_____. No smoking here.　　　　　　　　　　　　　　　（上海,中考）
　A. No,I don't　　　B. Yes,I don't　　　C. Yes,I do　　　D. No,I do

4. Where _____ your hometown?　　　　　　　　　　　　　　（焦作,中考）
　A. is　　　B. was　　　C. are　　　D. were

5. Many people think that beer _____ better than alcohol(酒,白酒).　（兰州,中考）
　A. is　　　B. was　　　C. are　　　D. were

6. "Do you like tea?" "No,_____."
　A. I do　　　B. I don't　　　C. you do　　　D. you don't

7. "Do you like butter?" "Yes,I do,but I don't want _____."
　A. one　　　B. a　　　C. an　　　D. any

8. "Do you like apples?" "Yes,I do,but I don't want _____."
　A. one　　　B. a　　　C. an　　　D. some

9. "Do you like biscuits?" "Yes,I do,but I don't want _____."
　A. one　　　B. any　　　C. some　　　D. a

10. "Do you like honey?" "Yes,I do,but I don't want _____."
　A. one　　　B. a　　　C. some　　　D. any

11. "Do you like bananas?" "Yes,I do,but I don't want _____."
　A. one　　　B. a　　　C. an　　　D. some

12. "Do you like oranges?" "Yes,I do,but I don't want _____."
　A. one　　　B. a　　　C. an　　　D. some

13. The ship is going _____ the bridge.
　A. over　　　B. on　　　C. under　　　D. off

14. Two cats are running _____ the wall.
　A. off　　　B. along　　　C. over　　　D. across

15. The girl is sitting _____ her mother and father.
　A. off　　　B. across　　　C. between　　　D. along

16. The boy feels _____ when he shook the toy.
　A. to be amused　　　B. amusing　　　C. amused　　　D. amuses

55

17. She is _____ about the compass.

    A. exciting   B. amusing   C. curiously   D. curious

18. What you said makes me feel _____ .

    A. embarrassed   B. embarrassing

    C. to be embarrassed   D. has felt embarrassed

19. Will Tom _____ attend the meeting?

    A. ask   B. be asked to   C. be asking   D. be asked

20. The meeting _____ tomorrow is important to us.

    A. will hold   B. to have been hold   C. to be held   D. to hold

21. The boy was _____ work hard by his father to learn English well.

    A. made with   B. making to   C. made   D. made to

三、翻译句子

1. 冬天,这里经常下雪。   6. Do you want a cup of coffee?

2. 他有一个大家庭,家里有 10 个人。   7. No, thanks.

3. 你喜欢咖啡吗?   8. Do you like any sugar?

4. 要在咖啡中放牛奶吗?   9. I don't like milk in my coffee.

5. 好的,请来一块。   10. I like butter, but I don't want any.

四、用所给动词适当形式填空

1. The shop _____ (open) at 8 every morning.

2. My sister _____ (do) her homework every day.

3. Tom _____ (study) Chinese in our school.

4. The little girl _____ (dress) herself.

五、用 one 或 ones 填空

1. There are only hard chocolates left. We've eaten all the soft _____ .

2. Give me some apples. I want big _____ .

3. This story is a true _____ .

4. Which _____ is his, this _____ , that _____ , or the _____ on the table?

5. He has several pens and lends me _____ .

6. Here are some postcards. I prefer used _____ to those mint _____ .

7. I've got many nice books. Do you want _____ ?

8. A: Do you want an egg?

    B: I don't want _____ .

六、完成句子:仿照例句改写下列句子

Do you like apples?

Yes, I do. I like apples, but I don't want one.

Do you like ice-cream?

Yes, I do. I like ice-cream, but I don't want any.

1. Do you like beer?   6. Do you like oranges?

2. Do you like whisky?   7. Do you like eggs?

3. Do you like jam?   8. Do you like wine?

4. Do you like biscuits?   9. Do you like honey?

5. Do you like butter?   10. Do you like bananas?

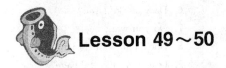

Lesson 49~50

一、单词拼写:根据所给中文意思补全下列单词

1. m__nc__ (肉馅 n.)　　2. tr_____ (真实 n.)　　3. st___k (牛排 n.)

4. h___b___d (丈夫 n.)　5. b___n (豆角 n.)

二、语法和词汇:从 A、B、C、D 中选出正确答案

1. Jim is American, _____ he can speak Chinese very good. 　　(江西,中考)

　A. if　　　　　B. so　　　　　C. but　　　　　D. because

2. —Who cleans the room every morning?

　—Jimmy _____. 　　(武汉,中考)

　A. cleans　　　B. does　　　　C. is cleaning　　D. is doing

3. —We never know _____ he wants.

　—They say he wants a baby boy. 　　(北京,中考)

　A. whom　　　B. what　　　　C. which　　　　D. where

4. He is thirsty. Please give him some _____ to drink. 　　(北京,中考)

　A. rice　　　　B. meat　　　　C. water　　　　D. oranges

5. Don't forget to _____ "thank you" when someone has helped you. 　(重庆,中考)

　A. speak　　　B. tell　　　　　C. say　　　　　D. talk

6. What time _____ he would be here?

　A. did Tom say　B. Tom said　　C. said Tom　　D. would Tom say

7. Jane does not know when she _____ her homework.

　A. had finished　B. will finish　　C. finishes　　D. finished

8. My brother is busy _____ my mother do the cooking.

　A. help　　　　B. to help　　　C. helping　　　D. helped

9. This is _____.

　A. a nice piece　B. nice piece　　C. a nice pieces　D. nice pieces

10. I _____ potatoes, but I _____ want any.

　A. like...doesn't　　　　　　B. like...doesn't

　C. likes...don't　　　　　　D. like...don't

11. He is reading a magazine, but I _____.

　A. am not　　　B. isn't　　　　C. aren't　　　　D. don't

12. She can type very well, but he _____.

　A. is not　　　B. are not　　　C. doesn't　　　D. can't

13. She likes tea, but he _____.

　A. isn't　　　　B. aren't　　　C. don't　　　　D. doesn't

14. _____ you like bananas?

　A. Do　　　　B. Does　　　　C. Is　　　　　D. Are

15. _____ Carol like peaches?

　A. Do　　　　B. Does　　　　C. Is　　　　　D. Are

三、翻译句子

1. 你想吃点牛肉吗？
2. 我儿子喜欢吃面包。
3. 我正在吃羊肉。
4. 要土豆还是西红柿。
5. 实话说，我不喜欢土豆。

6. Do you like lamb?
7. Do you want beef?
8. Does Tim want peaches?
9. Does Sam like cabbage?
10. She likes tomatoes, but she doesn't want any.

四、用动词适当形式填空

1. _____ you _____ (clean) your classroom now?
   Yes, we _____ (be). We _____ (clean) it every day.
2. _____ he often _____ (watch) TV?
   Yes, he _____ (do). Look! He _____ (watch) TV.
3. _____ they _____ (have) lunch now?
4. Can you _____ (answer) the question in English?

五、用 too 或 either 填空

1. I shalln't be in and Jane won't be, _____.
2. Does the butcher like chicken? No, he doesn't, _____.
3. Jane went to the cinema and her brother went, _____.
4. There was rain last night and in May, _____.
5. I don't know how to repair a radio. My brother doesn't, _____.
6. A: I'm hungry.
   B: Me, _____.
7. I don't like this coat and I don't like that one, _____.
8. We, _____, are going away.

六、书面表达

假定你叫 Tom，你的朋友 Jack 是一名中学生，下面是他给你的来信：

Dear Tom,

Thank you for your letter. You asked me if I was well these days. In fact, I have had so much work to do that I don't have enough time to have sports. Could you tell me what I should do to keep healthy?

Best wishes.

Yours,
Jack

请你用英文给他回一封信，字数不少于 50 个。

七、完成句子:用所给动词的适当形式填空

1. _____ you _____ (clean) your classroom now?
   Yes, we _____ (be). We _____ (clean) it every day.
2. _____ he often _____ (watch) TV?
   Yes, he does. Look! He _____ (watch) TV there.
3. _____ they _____ (have) an examination now?
4. Can you _____ (answer) the question in English?
5. Julie _____ (not live) on the campus(校园).

Lesson 51～52

一、单词拼写:根据所给中文意思补全下列单词

1. R __ ss ___ （俄罗斯 *n.*）　　2. Sw __ d ___ （瑞典 *n.*）　　3. Gr ___ c __ （希腊 *n.*）

4. D __ c __ m ____ （十二月 *n.*）5. S __ p ___ mb ___ （九月 *n.*）

二、语法和词汇:从 A、B、C、D 中选出正确答案

1. I am _____. I come from _____ People's Republic of China.　　　　（西宁,中考）

A. Chinese/不填　　B. Chinese/the　　C. Chinese/a　　D. Chinese/an

2. When do you usually have _____ dinner in _____ summer?　　（广东,中考）

A. 不填/不填　　B. 不填/the　　C. the/不填　　D. the/the

3. My mother has gone to Hong Kong. She is going to stay there for _____.　　（武汉,中考）

A. sometime　　B. some time　　C. sometimes　　D. some times

4. _____ basketball is my favourite sport.　　　　（郑州,中考）

A. The　　B. 不填　　C. This　　D. That

5. A lot of _____ people in the USA have come back to _____ for a visit these years.

（广西,中考）

A. China's/China　　B. Chinese/China　　C. Chinese's/China　　D. China/Chinese

6. Is it cold _____ warm in autumn?

A. and　　B. but　　C. or　　D. /

7. It is too cold. We must keep the room _____.

A. warmly　　B. warm　　C. warmth　　D. warmer

8. It is warm in spring. The sun shines in _____.

A. September　　B. July　　C. December　　D. April

9. It is windy in autumn. It rains in _____.

A. September　　B. July　　C. December　　D. April

10. The weather is very _____.

A. rain　　B. pleasant　　C. snow　　D. wind

11. We _____ from France.

A. come　　B. comes　　C. to come　　D. coming

12. They _____ from Norway.

A. come　　B. comes　　C. to come　　D. coming

13. You _____ from Germany.

A. coming　　B. to come　　C. comes　　D. come

14. You and Dimitri _____ from Brazil.

A. comes　　B. come　　C. to come　　D. coming

15. She and I _____ from America.

A. comes　　B. coming　　C. come　　D. to come

16. —Is this _____ English car?

—No, it's _____ Chinese car.

A. an,an　　B. a,an　　C. an,a　　D. a,a

17. —Are those pictures yours?

　　—Yes,_____.

　　A. they're　　　　　B. they are　　　　　C. those are　　　　　D. it is

18. —Is George at school?

　　—_____,I don't know.

　　A. Sorry　　　　　B. Hello　　　　　C. Excuse me　　　　　D. Oh

19. —Is your friend Chinese or English?

　　—_____.

　　A. Yes，he is.　　　　　　　　　　B. No，he is English.

　　C. He is English.　　　　　　　　　D. He's Chinese or English.

20. It's always difficult being in a foreign country, _____ if you don't speak the language.

（北京，中考）

　　A. extremely　　　B. naturally　　　C. basically　　　D. especially

21. —It's 9 o'clock now. I must go.

　　—It's raining outside. Don't leave _____ it stops. （北京，中考）

　　A. when　　　　　B. since　　　　　C. while　　　　　D. until

22. Summers in _____ south of France are for _____ most part dry and sunny.

（北京，中考）

　　A. 不填；a　　　B. the；不填　　　C. 不填；不填　　　D. the；the

三、翻译句子

1. 你们国家气候怎么样？

2. 春天天气怎么样？

3. 夏天很热，每天阳光灿烂。

4. 冬天很冷，有时要下雪。

5. 秋天风多，但很暖和。

6. It's always hot in July and April.

7. It's always warm in autumn.

8. It's cold in winter.

9. It rains in December.

10. It's very pleasant.

四、词义转换

America→美国人　　　England→英国人　　　Norway→挪威人　　　Germany→德国人

Brazil→巴西人　　　Sweden→瑞典人　　　France→法国人　　　Russia→俄国人

五、介词填空

1. There are many flowers _____ May _____ Beijing.

2. We'll have our Beijing TV Festival _____ Autumn _____ 1998.

3. My father always arrive home _____ 6：30.

4. He doesn't live here. He lives _____ Hong Kong now.

5. He is English. He comes _____ England.

6. We like to walk _____ the banks of the river.

7. The cake is _____ the refrigerator.

8. There are some clouds _____ the sky.

六、书面表达

　　假如你叫李华,4月8日去长城宾馆通知 Smith 先生去听演讲。不巧,Smith 先生不在。请你给他留个便条,按活动日程表简述活动内容,按应走路线写明步行去科学宫的路线。

时间:明天上午 9：00
地点:科学宫(旅馆附近)
内容:北京大学刘教授关于环境污染的讲座。

60

七、完成句子:将下列句子译成英语

1. 你们国家的气候怎样?

2. 春天天气怎样?

3. 夏天很热,每天阳光灿烂。

4. 冬天很冷,有时要下雪。

5. 春天和秋天多风,但很暖和。有时要下雨。

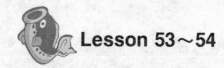

一、单词拼写:根据所给中文意思补全下列单词

1. int _____ st _ng(有趣的 *adj.*)　　　　2. K _____ (韩国 *n.*)

3. N _ g _____(尼日利亚 *n.*)　　　　4. C _ n _ d _ (加拿大 *n.*)

5. ___ str ___ (奥地利 *n.*)

二、语法和词汇:从 A、B、C、D 中选出正确答案

1. Soccer is different _____ American football. It's played all over the world.　(西安,中考)

 A. from   B. for   C. in   D. on

2. I enjoyed the scenery of the Huangpu River _____ the night of May 1st.　(上海,中考)

 A. at   B. in   C. on   D. over

3. Mother usually goes to bed late _____ night.　(太原,中考)

 A. in   B. on   C. at   D. to

4. —Would you like to come to dinner tonight?

 —I'd like to, _____ I'm too busy.　(无锡,中考)

 A. and   B. if   C. so   D. but

5. —Do you have today's newspaper,please?

 —Only several left. Would you like to have _____ ,sir?　(西安,中考)

 A. it   B. one   C. this   D. that

6. The sun rises _____ and sets _____

 A. late... early B. lately... early C. late... earily D. lately... earily

7. It's _____ .

 A. certain interesting   B. interesting certain

 C. certainly interesting   D. certainly interesting

8. It's our _____ .

 A. favourite conversation of subject B. conversation of favourite subject

 C. favourite subject of conversation D. subject of favourite conversation

9. _____ the sun set late?

 A. Do   B. Is   C. Does   D. Are

10. I am _____ . I come from _____ .

 A. Australia... Australia   B. Australian... Australian

 C. Australia... Australian   D. Australian... Australia

11. She is _____ . She comes from _____ .

 A. Austria... Austria   B. Austrian... Austria

 C. Austrian... Austrian   D. Austria... Austrian

12. They are _____ . They come from _____ .

 A. Chinese... Chinese   B. China... China

 C. Cnina... Chinese   D. Chinese... China

13. He is _____ . He comes from _____ .

 A. Finland... Finnish   B. Finnish... Finland

C. Finnish...Finnish   D. Finland...Finland

14. He is _____. He comes from _____.

    A. Turkey...Turkish   B. Turkish...Turkey

    C. Turkey...Turkey   D. Turkish...Turkish

15. The reporter said that the UFO _____ east to west when he saw it.   （北京，中考）

    A. was travelling   B. travelled

    C. had been traveling   D. was to travel.

16. I _____ my homework when Mike came last night.   （北京，中考）

    A. do   B. was doing   C. am doing   D. have done

17. —What's on TV tonight? Is there _____ interesting?

    —I'm afraid not.   （北京，中考）

    A. something   B. anything   C. nothing   D. everything

三、翻译句子

1. 我最喜欢春天和夏天。   6. Which season do you like best?

2. 我丈夫不喜欢春天和夏天。   7. I like winter best.

3. 夏天白天很长，夜晚很短。   8. Is it very cold in winter?

4. 天气是我们最喜欢谈的话题。   9. The days are long and the nights are short.

5. 你家乡气候怎么样？   10. The sun rises early and sets late.

四、用 What，Which，Where，Who，Whose 完成下列句子

1. _____ do you want，coffee or tea?

2. _____ does he study in this school?

3. _____ dress do you buy? The blue one.

4. _____ season do you like best?

5. _____ colour must I paint the bed?

6. _____ shirt is this?

五、将下列句子改成一般疑问句

1. Tom comes from Nigeria. _____

2. Mary comes from Austria. _____

3. The climate is mild in England. _____

4. The sun sets late in winter. _____

5. The sun rises early in the morning. _____

6. He likes to go to the south in summer. _____

7. They both come from Finland. _____

8. Jim comes from Poland. _____

六、书面表达

请你以 Saving Our City 为题，写一篇 100 字左右的短文。文章的第一句已给出。

提示：

1. 城市垃圾的危害。

    1)污染环境(水源、空气)；

    2)有害健康。

2. 你所在的城市是如何处理垃圾的。

    1)垃圾分类；

    2)报纸、玻璃的再利用；

    3)有害垃圾的填埋；

    4)废水、废气处理；

63

5) 制订了法律。

3. 尽我所能,保护环境。

　It's very important to deal with the rubbish in cities. ...

七、完成句子:指出下列句子中的 like 是动词还是介词

1. What's your father like? (　　　)

2. I like spring and summer. (　　　)

3. What's the weather like in Paris? (　　　)

4. I like fish very much. (　　　)

5. My teacher never speaks English like that. (　　　)

Lesson 55～56

一、单词拼写:根据所给中文意思补全下列单词

1. t_g_th___ (一起 *adv.*)　　2. __rr__v__ (到达 *v.*)　　3. __ft___n___n (下午 *n.*)

4. l___ch (午饭 *n.*)　　　　5. h___sew___k (家务 *n.*)

二、语法和词汇:从 A、B、C、D 中选出正确答案

1. I live _____ my grandparents. Now we are having dinner _____ at home. (宁夏,中考)

  A. together/with　　B. with/together　　C. at/with　　D. at/不填

2. _____ you _____ your homework now? (上海,中考)

  A. Do/doing　　B. Are/doing　　C. Were/doing　　D. Does/do

3. Lucy is very free. Look, she _____ a model ship. (北京,中考)

  A. makes　　B. made　　C. has made　　D. is making

4. The fifth month of the year is _____. (广东,中考)

  A. February　　B. May　　C. April　　D. August

5. She _____ her lunch at noon.

  A. eats always　　B. always eat　　C. always eats　　D. eat always

6. They _____ tea together.

  A. often drinks　　B. often drink　　C. drink often　　D. drinks often

7. They arrive _____ late.

  A. to home　　B. in home　　C. on home　　D. home

8. They go _____ bed.

  A. the　　B. to the　　C. to　　D. /

9. They watch _____ television.

  A. the　　B. a　　C. to　　D. /

10. What _____ Tom usually _____?

  A. do...do　　B. does...do　　C. do...do　　D. does...does

11. What _____ you usually _____?

  A. do...do　　B. does...does　　C. does...do　　D. do...does

12. He usually _____.

  A. shoves　　B. shovs　　C. shovees　　D. shove

13. She usually _____ to school.

  A. go　　B. gos　　C. goes　　D. to go

14. He usually _____ bed.

  A. make　　B. makes　　C. maks　　D. to make

15. _____ book _____ you want?

  A. Which, does　　B. Which, do　　C. Which the, do　　D. There, are

16. Can you tell me _____ an e-mail?

  A. write　　B. how to write　　C. what to write　　D. to write

17. Which _____ are Mr. Wang's?

  A. book　　B. a book　　C. books　　D. one

18. My knife is not sharp. It is _____.

  A. smart　　B. nice　　C. blunt　　D. great

19. We'll stay at home if it _____ tomorrow.　　　　　　　　　　(北京,中考)
   　A. rain　　　　　　B. rains　　　　　　C. is raining　　　D. will rain
20. Liu Ying told me _____ for her at home.　　　　　　　　　　(北京,中考)
   　A. waits　　　　　　B. wait　　　　　　C. to wait　　　　　D. waiting
21. They usually _____ TV in the evening.　　　　　　　　　　(北京,中考)
   　A. watch　　　　　　B. will watch　　　　C. are watching　　D. watches

三、翻译句子

1. Their father takes them to school every day.　　　6. 他通常喝牛奶。
2. Mr. White usually reads newspapers every evening.　7. 他每天去上学。
3. She usually eats her lunch at noon.　　　　　　　8. 他每天晚上上床睡觉。
4. They often listen to the radio at night.　　　　　9. 他到家很早。
5. What do they usually do?　　　　　　　　　　10. 我们每天做作业。

四、用动词适当形式填空

1. Mr. Smith _____ (live) with his family.
2. My father often _____ (listen) to the radio everyday.
3. The child _____ (do) his homework in the evening.
4. She often _____ (wash) her clothes.
5. What _____ you usually _____ (do) in the evening?
6. Mrs. Smith always _____ (stay) at home.

五、介词填空

1. School begins _____ 8:30 a. m.
2. Is Lily _____ home? No. She's _____ the hairdresser's now.
3. I'll phone you when I arrive _____ London.
4. What do you usually do _____ the evening?
5. Mrs. Green usually eats her lunch _____ noon.
6. It's time _____ class.
7. Mr. Jackson arrived _____ the airport _____ time.
8. I visited Professor Wang _____ Sunday afternoon.

六、书面表达

　　星期日,你们班的同学参加了植树活动,请写一篇日记,并说出自己对这次活动的看法。

七、完成句子:用所给动词的适当形式填空

1. Mr. Smith _____ (live) with his family at 125 King Street.
2. My father often _____ (listen) to the radio in the evening.
3. The children _____ (do) their homework now. They usually _____ (go) to bed at nine o'clock.
4. It is ten o'clock now. I _____ (go) to bed. I usually _____ (go) to bed at nine o'clock.
5. She often _____ (wash) the dishes after supper,but now she _____ (watch) television.
6. Mr. Smith _____ (shave) at seven every day.
7. Mrs. Sawyer always _____ (stay) at home in the morning. Now she _____ (do) the house-work. She _____ (go) to see her friends in the afternoon.
8. What _____ you usually _____ (do) in the evening?
9. When _____ he _____ (eat) his lunch every day?
10. What _____ she _____ (do) now? _____ she _____ (read) a magazine in the living-room?

66

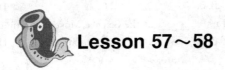

Lesson 57～58

一、单词拼写:根据所给中文意思补全下列单词

1. sh___p (商店 *n.*)　　2. ___s___lly (通常 *adv.*)　　3. t__n (十 *n.*)

4. s___ (六 *n.*)　　5. th_____ (三 *n.*)

二、语法和词汇:从 A、B、C、D 中选出正确答案

1. English people _____ use Mr. before a man's first name.　　(北京,中考)

  A. never　　　　B. usually　　　　C. often　　　　D. sometimes

2. _____ he _____ on well with his friends this term?　　(北京,中考)

  A. Does/gets　　B. Do/get　　　C. Is/getting　　D. Is/get

3. Listen! Class Two _____ an English song in the next room.　　(乐山,中考)

  A. are singing　　B. were singing　　C. was singing　　D. is singing

4. —How to say 6:35 in English?

  —It's _____.　　(上海,中考)

  A. twenty five to six　　　　　B. twenty five to seven

  C. thirty past six　　　　　　　D. thirty five to six

5. —How do you go back to your hometown every winter holiday?

  —_____.　　(大连,中考)

  A. By 6 o'clock　　B. By sea　　　C. By them　　D. By traveling

6. But today they _____ at 7:00.

  A. are making bed　　B. make bed　　C. makes bed　　D. to make bed

7. But this morning she _____

  A. is drinking coffee　B. drink coffee　　C. drinks coffee　　D. to drink coffee

8. But this afternoon he _____.

  A. swims　　　　B. swimms　　　C. is swimming　　D. is swiming

9. But this evening I _____.

  A. is reading　　B. are reading　　C. read　　　　D. am reading

10. But tonight, we _____ to the radio.

  A. listening　　B. are listening　　C. listen　　　D. listens

11. But tonight she _____ clothes.

  A. are washing　　B. is washing　　C. washes　　D. wash

12. But this afternoon they _____ in the park.

  A. are playing　　B. is playing　　C. play　　　　D. playing

13. But this morning they _____ to school on foot.

  A. goes　　　　B. /　　　　　C. go　　　　D. are going

14. They _____ their homework tonight.

  A. do　　　　　B. does　　　　C. is doing　　D. are doing

15. He _____ reading newspaper this morning.

  A. is doing not　　B. is not doing　　C. not is doing　　D. not doing is

16. Wu Yin gets up _____ six o'clock every day.　　　　　　　　(北京,中考)

　　A. in　　　　　　B. on　　　　　　C. at　　　　　　D. from

17. The headmaster told us _____ at the Science Museum on time.　(北京,中考)

　　A. arrive　　　　B. arrives　　　　C. to arrive　　　　D. arriving

三、翻译句子

1. 这个小孩总是很早上学。

2. 瓦特太太每天早晨看报。

3. 瓦特一家每天晚上 9:00 睡觉。

4. 他们今天正步行去工作。

5. 孩子们通常去公园玩。

6. What time is it?

7. The children do their homework at night.

8. They often go to bed early.

9. We are going to school by bus this morning.

10. It's five o'clock.

四、用动词适当形式填空

1. There _____ (be) a tall tree in front of the building.

2. Look, the boys _____ (play) football on the ground.

3. _____ it _____ (snow) here in winter?

4. _____ (not come) in. We _____ (have) classes now.

5. What _____ you _____ (read) here ? I _____ (read) a magazine now.

五、将下列句子改成否定句、疑问句,并作简略回答

1. There are some newspapers behind the TV set.

2. The boy can put the box on the shelf.

3. It's often cold in December.

4. She is drinking tea in the garden.

5. He usually washes clothes at night.

6. John always plays basketball with his friends after school.

7. She teaches us English this term.

8. There's some coffee in those cups.

六、书面表达

　　假如你的朋友 Mike 最近顺利考取了北京大学(Peking University),请就此写一封信对他表示祝贺。

提示：

　　1. 获知消息的来源；

　　2. 表达祝贺；

　　3. 期盼相逢于北京。

七、完成句子:以一般现在时或现在进行时的形式将括号中的动词填入空内

1. He usually _____ (drink) coffee but today he _____ (drink) tea.

2. He usually _____ (speak) very quickly, so I _____ (not understand) him.

3. Ann _____ (make) a dress for herself at the moment. She always _____ (make) her own clothes.

4. I _____ (wear) my sunglasses(太阳镜) today because the sun is very strong.

5. We _____ (use) this room today because the window in the other room is broken.

6. I usually _____ (go) to work by car but today I _____ (go) by train.

7. He never _____ (listen) to what you say. He alway _____ (think) about something else.

8. What _____ you _____ (have) for breakfast usually? I usually _____ (eat) a piece of bread and _____ (drink) a glass of milk.

9. Why _____ you _____ (walk) so fast today? You usually _____ (walk) quite slowly. I _____ (hurry) because I'll have to meet my mother at 4 o'clock.

10. Tom never _____ (do) any work in the garden; he often _____ (work) on his car.

Lesson 59～60

一、单词拼写：根据所给中文意思补全下列单词

1. p___d（信笺薄 *n.*）　　　2. s___z___（尺寸 *n.*）　　　3. ch___ge（零钱 *n.*）

4. w___t___g p___p___（信纸 *n.*）　　　5. ___ll（所有 *pron.*）

二、语法和词汇：从 A、B、C、D 中选出正确答案

1. "Are you going to eat here _____ take it away?" asked the waiter.　　　（山东，中考）

　　A. and　　　　　B. so　　　　　C. or　　　　　D. but

2. —Would you like something to drink?

　　—_____.　　　　　　　　　　　　　　　　　　　　　　　（宿迁，中考）

　　A. Certainly　　　B. No，thanks　　　C. Me，too　　　D. I'd love

3. Follow your doctor's advice，_____ your cough will get worse.　　　（辽宁，中考）

　　A. or　　　　　　B. and　　　　　C. then　　　　　D. so

4. Liu Xiang an Yao Ming are world-famous sports stars. _____ of them have set a good example for us.

　　A. All　　　　　B. Neither　　　　C. Both　　　　　D. None

5. It is a long journey, and _____ of us four feel it boring.

　　A. neither　　　B. both　　　　　C. none　　　　　D. all

6. My friend and I _____ going to travel this year.

　　A. am　　　　　B. is　　　　　　C. be　　　　　　D. are

7. What _____ do you want?

　　A. else　　　　B. some others　　C. some one　　　D. some ones

8. I want some _____.

　　A. glues　　　　B. glue　　　　　C. chalks　　　　D. pad

9. I want a _____ of glue.

　　A. box　　　　　B. bottle　　　　C. piece　　　　　D. bar

10. I want _____.

　　A. changes　　　B. a change　　　C. change　　　　D. some changes

11. I only have large _____.

　　A. one　　　　　B. some one　　　C. any　　　　　D. ones

12. _____ size do you want?

　　A. Which　　　　B. Whose　　　　C. What　　　　　D. Where

13. —Do you have _____ tomato?

　　—Yes. I have _____.

　　A. some...some　　B. any...any　　C. some...any　　D. any...some

14. Do you have any _____?

　　A. peach　　　　B. peaches　　　C. peachs　　　　D. peach—es

15. _____ me carefully, boys and girls. Can you _____ me?

　　A. Listen to，hear from　　　　　B. Hear，listen to

　　C. Hear，hear　　　　　　　　　D. Listen to，hear

三、翻译句子

1. 我要一大盒巧克力。
2. 你有信纸吗？
3. 我要一本。
4. 你还要什么？
5. 我要我的零钱。
6. Do you want the large size or the small size?
7. I want a large box of chalk.
8. Is that all?
9. That's all, thank you.
10. I want a bottle of glue.

四、变换句型,将下列肯定句变为一般疑问句

1. Mr White usually reads newspapers.
2. My father is shaving in the bathroom.
3. He never does any homework.
4. I want some bananas.
5. My brother has a blue car.

五、介词填空

1. She's waiting _____ her change.
2. She often washes dishes _____ supper and watch TV _____ night.
3. The Greens are watching television _____ the moment _____ the living room.
4. Wang Hai often goes to school _____ bike.
5. They usually have supper _____ six, but tonight they have supper _____ seven.
6. They play games _____ the garden _____ the afternoon.
7. Tom is _____ hospital _____ a broken leg while Mary works _____ the hospital.

70

六、书面表达:仿照例句完成下列句子

假如你是学生会主席,要用英语对外籍学生班的同学口头通知周末安排。请根据下列内容组织一篇口头通知:
1. 星期六去美术馆参观现代艺术展;
2. 愿意去者请举手;
3. 坐车、骑车自便;
4. 集合时间为早9点,地点在美术馆前;
5. 参观之后请北京艺术家协会韩教授作题为"现代油画"的演讲。
注:美术馆:Arts Gallery　北京艺术家协会:Beijing Artists' Association

七、完成句子:仿照例句完成下列句子

Have you any honey? /jam
I haven't any honey, but I have some jam.

1. Have you and Mary any beans? /peas
2. Have you any potatoes? /tomatoes
3. Have you and Mary any beans? /potatoes
4. Have they any cigarettes? /cigars
5. Have you and Jane any steak? /beef
6. Have you any mince? /steak
7. Have you any butter? /cheese
8. Have Mary and Tom any wine? /beer
9. Have you and Tom any bread? /biscuits
10. Have Tom and Mary any grapes? /bananas
11. Have the children any butter? /eggs
12. Have you any lettuces? /cabbages

Lesson 61～62

一、单词拼写：根据所给中文意思补全下列单词

1. ear _____ （耳痛 *n.*）   2. t___p_____ture（温度 *n.* ）   3. fl___ （流行性感冒 *n.* ）

4. b__d（坏的 *adj.* ）   5. m___th（嘴 *n.* ）

二、语法和词汇：从 A、B、C、D 中选出正确答案

1. "IT"means" _____ Technology".   （北京，中考）

   A. Informations   B. Information   C. Intellience   D. Intelligent

2. Please _____ to you father and mother.   （上海，中考）

   A. forget   B. remember   C. remind   D. recall

3. —Is your stomachache getting _____ ?

   —No，it's worse.   （苏州，中考）

   A. better   B. bad   C. less   D. well

4. Her husband is ill. He has been _____ for 7 years.

   A. in bed   B. in the bed   C. on the bed   D. on bed

5. I can see that you are pretty _____ already. Will you go to school tomorrow?

   A. better   B. bad   C. less   D. well

6. Can you remember _____ number?

   A. the doctors'   B. the doctor'   C. the doctor's   D. the doctor

7. "We must call the doctor.""Yes，we _____. "

   A. can   B. must   C. need   D. should

8. Sam has _____ temperature.

   A. a   B. an   C. the   D. /

9. Susan has _____.

   A. mumps   B. mump   C. a mumps   D. the mumps

10. She must take _____ aspirin.

    A. a   B. an   C. /   D. the

11. She must take _____.

    A. medicine   B. medicines   C. medicinees   D. medicine

12. I must stay at home. He _____ stay at home，too

    A. musts   B. mustes   C. must   D. musting

13. _____ the students in your school work hard at English?

    A. Are   B. Is   C. Does   D. Do

14. It is better to settle the problems together than _____ who should be responsible for them.

    A. to argue   B. arguing   C. to be argued   D. having argued

15. Excuse me. Could you please tell me _____ get to the bus station tomorrow.

    A. when to   B. where to   C. what I can   D. where can I

16. Let Harry play with your toys as well，Clare you must learn to _____.   （北京，中考）

    A. support   B. care   C. spare   D. share

17. The students _____ on a farm for ten days. Then they _____ to a factory. Though they

71

_____ back at school, they still remembered those farmers and workers.　（北京，中考）

    A. have stayed；went；were   B. had stayed；go；are

    C. have stayed；go；have been   D. had stayed；went；were

三、翻译句子

1. 吉米怎么了？
2. 吉米不舒服。
3. 他必须去看医生。
4. 他得了重感冒。
5. 他必须吃药。

6. He must stay in bed for a week.
7. He has a headache.
8. He must take some medicine.
9. She has a temperature.
10. He has flu.

四、介词填空

1. You must stay _____ home.
2. He must stay _____ bed _____ two weeks.
3. What's the matter _____ him?
4. Is it good news _____ you?
5. Is that medicine _____ her?
6. They are watching TV _____ that moment.

五、用 must，mustn't，can 或 can't 填空

1. "_____ I come at 6 o'clock?" "Oh no, you needn't."
2. A blind man _____ judge colours.
3. "May I go there?" "No, You _____."
4. Two eyes _____ see more than one.
5. I _____ be off. Thank you very much for supper.
6. You _____ be careful. You _____ be careless.
7. _____ I stay up till midnight, please?
8. The teacher _____ favour some children more than others.

六、书面表达

    按下面提示内容，写一篇100字左右的日记。

1. 早上骑自行车上学。
2. 一辆卡车向右拐，自行车撞在卡车上。
3. 摔倒在地，自行车被撞坏。
4. 卡车司机下车，扶你起来，幸好你未被伤着。
5. 找人修车，乘车上学。
6. 事后想来可能你骑车太快或在想别的什么事情。
7. 以后骑车要当心。

    日期　10月16日　星期天　晴

七、完成句子：仿照例句完成下列句子

Tim/(a stomachache/a headache/take an aspirin)

What's the matter with Tim? Has he a stomachache?

No，he hasn't a stomachache. He has a headache. So he must take an aspirin.

1. Alice/(flu)/a cold /have a good rest
2. Susan/(an earache)/mumps/we... call the doctor
3. Jim/(measles)/a temperature/stay in bed
4. Tom/(a stomachache)/a toothache/see a dentist
5. Mike/(mumps)/a toothache/go to the dentist

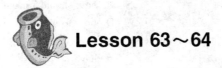

Lesson 63～64

一、单词拼写:根据所给中文意思补全下列单词

1. s ＿（如此 *adv.*）　　2. t ＿＿k（谈论 *v.*）　　3. rem ＿＿n（保持 *v.*）

4. r ＿ch（油腻的 *adj.*）　5. b ＿tt ＿＿＿（更好 *adj.*）

二、语法和词汇:从 A、B、C、D 中选出正确答案

1. You ＿＿＿＿＿ play with fire，Tom. It's dangerous.　　　　　　　（苏州，中考）

　　A. needn't　　　B. may not　　　C. mustn't　　　D. wouldn't

2. Someone is knocking at the door. It ＿＿＿＿＿ my mother. It's time for her to be busy with work.　　　　　　（哈尔滨，中考）

　　A. can be　　　B. may not be　　　C. must be　　　D. can't be

3. —What did the head teacher say at the meeting?

　　—He said，"We ＿＿＿＿＿ be proud of working hard. We mustn't be lazy."　　（福州，中考）

　　A. must　　　B. needn't　　　C. may　　　D. can't

4. Cars，buses and bikes ＿＿＿＿＿ stop when the traffic light is red.

　　A. can　　　B. must　　　C. may　　　D. need

5. Which of the following means "No Photos"? ＿＿＿＿＿　　　　　　　（北京，中考）

　　A.　　　　　　B.　　　　　　C.　　　　　　D.

6. You must keep the room ＿＿＿＿＿.

　　A. warmth　　　B. warms　　　C. warmly　　　D. warm

7. He must ＿＿＿＿＿ in bed.

　　A. remain　　　B. remains　　　C. remaining　　　D. to remain

8. The boy ＿＿＿＿＿ go to school.

　　A. isn't　　　B. aren't　　　C. mustn't　　　D. hasn't

9. He can get up for ＿＿＿＿＿ hour each day.

　　A. a　　　B. an　　　C. one　　　D. the

10. Don't ＿＿＿＿＿ so quickly.

　　A. drive　　　B. drives　　　C. driving　　　D. to drive

11. Don't ＿＿＿＿＿ up.

　　A. to get　　　B. gets　　　C. get　　　D. getting

12. You mustn't ＿＿＿＿＿ rich food.

　　A. to eat　　　B. eats　　　C. eating　　　D. eat

13. You must ＿＿＿＿＿ a doctor.

　　A. call　　　B. calls　　　C. calling　　　D. to call

14. You mustn't ＿＿＿＿＿ in the library.

　　A. talks　　　B. talk　　　C. talking　　　D. to talk

15. You mustn't ＿＿＿＿＿.

　　A. works　　　B. work　　　C. working　　　D. to work

16. I'm sorry, I really don't know _____ the clock.
　　A. to mend　　　　　　　　　　　　B. how should I mend
　　C. what to mend　　　　　　　　　　D. how to mend

17. Please stop _____ a rest if you feel tired.
　　A. to have　　　　B. having　　　　C. have　　　　D. has

18. _____ to take this adventure course will certainly learn a lot of useful skills. （北京,中考）
　　A. Brave enough students　　　　　　B. Enough brave students
　　C. Students brave enough　　　　　　D. Students enough brave

19. He is rich, _____ he isn't happy. 　　　　　　　　　　　　（北京,中考）
　　A. or　　　　　　B. so　　　　　　C. and　　　　　　D. but

20. Most animals have little connection with _____ animals of _____ different kind unless they kill them for food. 　　　　　　　　　　　　　　　　　（北京,中考）
　　A. the ; a　　　　B. 不填 ; a　　　　C. the ; the　　　　D. 不填 ; the

21. —Where is Alice? 　　　　　　　　　　　　　　　　　　　　　　（北京,中考）
　　—She _____ to the library.
　　A. goes　　　　B. will go　　　　C. has gone　　　　D. had gone

22. —Why don't we take a little break?
　　—Didn't we just have _____? 　　　　　　　　　　　　　　（北京,中考）
　　A. it　　　　B. that　　　　C. one　　　　D. this

23. Don't _____ the radio. The baby is sleeping. 　　　　　　　（北京,中考）
　　A. turn off　　　B. turn on　　　C. turn over　　　D. turn down

24. Some boys of Class One enjoy _____ music. 　　　　　　　（北京,中考）
　　A. listen to　　　B. listens to　　　C. listening to　　　D. listened to

三、翻译句子

1. Tom 今天怎么样了？
2. 他好些了,谢谢医生。
3. 他必须再卧床 2 天。
4. 他不能起床。
5. 他不可以上学。
6. You mustn't eat rich food.
7. He has a temperature.
8. Must he stay in bed?
9. You must finish your homework on time.
10. He has a bad cold.

四、用正确的时态填空

1. Jimmy _____ (look) very well.
2. He _____ (be) better.
3. He _____ (have not) a temperature.
4. But he still mustn't _____ (go) to school.
5. He must _____ (remain) in bed for a week.

五、用 each 或 every 填空

1. You've caught a bad cold. Take this pill three times _____ day.
2. She gets up at six _____ morning.
3. Please correct _____ mistake before you hand in your homework.
4. How lovely these children! I know their names. I know _____ one of them.
5. I love my friends. I love _____ one of them.
6. She cuts the cake into pieces and gives one to _____ of the guests.
7. The pencils are £ 1.5 _____.
8. _____ of the boys and girls jumps with joy.

六、书面表达

根据所给的情景,写一便条,至少 50 个单词。要求内容确切,意思连贯。

A Note

假如你叫李磊,去朋友吉米家给他送明晚的电影票,他不在家,于是你留下便条,内容为:

1. 明晚7:30电影票已买到,片名为"泰坦尼克号"(TITANIC);

2. 影片在上海电影院放映,请明晚7:30在影院门口见面;

3. 顺便告诉你父母要晚点回来。只需将事情说明白,不必逐字翻译。开头已给出。

Dear Jim

How are you? I'm leaving this note to tell you that...

七、完成句子:将下列句子变成否定句

1. Pleaes speak fast.

2. You must say it in English.

3. You must talk in the library.

4. Come early tomorrow.

5. I can see someone under the tree.

75

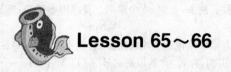

Lesson 65～66

一、单词拼写：根据所给中文意思补全下列单词

1. __nj___（玩快乐 *v.*）　　　　　　2. b__b__（婴儿 *n.*）
3. _____s_l__（她自己 *pron.*）　　　4. _____ms_l____（他们自己 *pron.*）
5. m_s_l__（我自己 *pron.*）

二、语法和词汇：从 A、B、C、D 中选出正确答案

1. Nobody taught _____ ,he learnt it by _____.　　　　（永州,中考）
   A. he/his　　　B. he/himself　　　C. him/his　　　D. him/himself

2. Yesterday I saw _____ enjoy _____ in the park.　　（北京,中考）
   A. her/hers　　B. they/them　　C. she/herself　　D. them/themselves

3. Don't lose _____ in computer games，children.　　（威海,中考）
   A. yourself　　B. yourselves　　C. ourselves　　D. themselves

4. "Help _____ to some meat，Mary. "My aunt says to me.
   A. themselves　　B. ourselves　　C. yourself　　D. himself

5. _____ the twins enjoyed _____ at the party yesterday.
   A. Both/them　　B. Both/themselves　　C. All/them　　D. All/themselves

6. I always enjoy _____.
   A. herself　　B. himself　　C. myself　　D. yourself

7. Mary _____ herself today.
   A. enjoys　　B. enjoies　　C. enjoyes　　D. enjoyies

8. Give _____.
   A. her to key　　B. key to her　　C. key her　　D. she key

9. —How old are you?
   —I am _____.
   A. two years old　　B. two-years-old　　C. two year old　　D. two years olds

10. It is half past eight：_____.
    A. 8：00　　B. 8：30　　C. 7：30　　D. 7：45

11. It is a quarter past eight：_____
    A. 7：45　　B. 8：15　　C. 8：30　　D. 7：30

12. It is ten past eight：_____.
    A. 8：30　　B. 8：10　　C. 7：50　　D. 7：30

13. I always go to work _____ the evening.
    A. on　　B. in　　C. at　　D. of

14. —Enjoy _____.
    —We always enjoy ourselves.
    A. yourself　　B. yourselves　　C. ourselves　　D. themselves

15. It's cold _____ winter.
    A. on　　B. at　　C. with　　D. in

三、翻译句子

1. 今晚打算干什么？
2. 你必须在 10 点半到家。
3. 我能带上门钥匙吗？
4. 你不能超过 11 点 1 刻回家。
5. 好好玩吧。

6. We always enjoy ourselves.
7. I am going to see some friends.
8. It's half past eight.
9. He is five years old.
10. Give her the key.

四、用英语表达下列时间

1. 3：07   2. 5：15   3. 2：30   4. 8：59   5. 12：45

五、用下列单词填空：cup，block，lump，bowl，bag，box，glass，tin，slice，piece，loaf，amount

1. an _____ of money
2. a _____ of soup
3. a _____ of tobacco
4. three _____ of Hami melon
5. five _____ of tea
6. six _____ of rice
7. seven _____ of chalk
8. eight _____ of meat
9. nine _____ of ice
10. ten _____ of bread
11. eleven _____ of wine
12. two _____ of sugar

六、书面表达

假如你是云南穷困地区的一名失学儿童，叫李菊萍。你很幸运得到一位在北京工作的美国人 Smith 先生的赞助，得以重新回到校园继续学习。于是在 2002 年 6 月 1 日你给 Mr. Smith 写一封信表示感谢。

信中内容包括：

1. 收到书和钱能重返校园，非常感谢；
2. 在老师的帮助下学习成绩取得了很大进步；
3. 老师表扬了你，家长也鼓励你；
4. 下决心更加努力学习，取得更大进步；
5. 盼望见到 Smith 先生，但因没有机会去北京，希望 Smith 先生给你寄张照片。

七、完成句子：仿照例句回答问题

When must you come home？/1：0

I must come home at one o'clock.

1. When must you go to bed？/9：30
2. When must they return to the hotel？/7：25
3. When must Tom finish his homework？/8：55
4. When must she go to the library？/1：15
5. When must she wash the dishes？/7：45
6. When must you and Tom see the dentist？/3：45

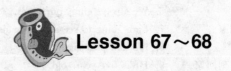

Lesson 67～68

一、单词拼写：根据所给中文意思补全下列单词

1. k___p（保持 v.）　　2. sp_n__（度过 v.）　　3. numb___（数字 n.）

4. st_t___n___（文具商 n.）　　　　5. d___r__（牛奶场 n.）

二、语法和词汇：从 A、B、C、D 中选出正确答案

1. I have _____ uncle. He works at _____ railway station.　　（德州，中考）

　A. an/an　　　　B. a/a　　　　C. an/a　　　　D. a/an

2. —When were you born?

　—I was born _____ Monday, February 2nd, 1989.　　（湖南，中考）

　A. at　　　　B. on　　　　C. in　　　　D. of

3. —When do you usually go to bed at night?

　—At _____ eleven.

　A. half past　　B. a half past　　C. half hour past　　D. a half hour past

4. —Lucy didn't come to school yesterday, did she?

　—_____ , though she was not feeling very well.　　（云南，中考）

　A. No, she didn't　　　　　　B. Yes, she did

　C. Yes, she didn't　　　　　　D. No, she did

5. Our teacher told us the Earth _____ round the Sun all the time.　　（云南，中考）

　A. moved　　　B. travels　　　C. going　　　D. circle

6. —Must I call him now?

　—No, you _____ .

　A. can't　　　B. may not　　　C. needn't　　　D. mustn't

7. Mr. Zhang _____ physics in Beijing since 1990.

　A. teach　　　B. teaches　　　C. taught　　　D. has taught

8. Hurry up, _____ we will miss the train.

　A. but　　　　B. and　　　　C. or　　　　D. so

9. Jack runs as _____ as Tom.

　A. fast　　　　B. faster　　　C. fastest　　　D. much faster

10. —Do you have enough men to carry these chairs?

　—No. I think we need _____ men.

　A. another　　B. two others　　C. more two　　D. two more

11. —You won't follow his example, will you?

　—_____ . I don't think he is right.

　A. No, I won't　　B. Yes, I will　　C. No, I will　　D. Yes. I won't

12. —Where have you _____ these days?

　—I have _____ to Dazhu with my friends.

　A. been, gone　　B. been, been　　C. gone, been　　D. gone, gone

13. The Young Pioneers walked _____ the gates with Uncle Wang.

　A. through　　　B. across　　　C. over　　　D. after

14. It's really not easy to _____ classmates.

    A. go on   B. turn down   C. give back   D. give up

15. When I want to _____ , my teacher always tells me to work harder.

    A. go on   B. turn down   C. give back   D. give up

16. We found _____ useful to use a dictionary when we meet some new words.

    A. it   B. this   C. that   D. what

17. Our teacher did what she could _____ us with English.

    A. help   B. helped   C. helping   D. to help

18. —_____ did you buy the new bag?   （北京，中考）

    —Last Monday.

    A. Where   B. How   C. When   D. Who

19. Frank _____ a film if he's free next Saturday.   （北京，中考）

    A. see   B. saw   C. has seen   D. will see

三、翻译句子：英汉互译

A：你昨天在肉铺店吗？

B：No, I wasn't.

A：在杂货店？

B：Yes, I was.

A：你的男朋友也在杂货店？

B：No，he wasn't.

A：Where was he?

B：他在蔬菜水果店。

四、用动词的适当形式填空

1. The students must _____ in the library.

2. We _____ going to give her the key tomorrow.

3. He _____ in bed the whole day yesterday.

4. Smith and I _____ at the barber's last night.

5. There _____ a tree, a river and many flowers on the picture.

五、就划线部分提问

1. Kate was late for school this afternoon.

2. There was a pencil on the desk during the break.

3. All of our classmates were in the park last Saturday.

4. There were a lot of books in my father's bookshelf last year.

5. I was in the Museum this morning.

6. My father was at the butcher's ten minutes ago.

7. Jim was in his classroom yesterday afternoon.

8. He was a teacher ten years ago.

六、书面表达

    根据下面的简历写一封自我介绍的求职信。（80—120 词）

Name：Li Ming   Sex：Male（男）

Date of Birth ：Oct. 1973   Health：Excellent

Education：1990—1995，Department of Electronic Engineering，Tsinghua University，Beijing

Foreign Languages：English and Japanese

Hobbies：Music and sports

Address：Room 302，Apartment 10＃，Tsinghua University，Beijing 100080

Tel：4214849

79

七、完成句子:用 be 的适当形式填空

1. What _____ you doing here?

2. Jimmy _____ absent from school last Monday.

3. There _____ a lot of people here yesterday.

4. The students must _____ in the library.

5. We _____ going to give her the key tomorrow.

6. He _____ in bed the whole day yesterday.

7. Smith and I _____ at the barber's last night.

8. There _____ a tree,a river and many flowers on the picture.

Lesson 69～70

一、单词拼写:根据所给中文意思补全下列单词

1. cr___d（人群 *n.* ）   2. Ch _n_se（中国人 *n.* ）   3. op___at___（操作员 *n.* ）

4. Jul___（朱丽 *n.* ）   5. st_nd（站 *v.* ）

二、语法和词汇:从 A、B、C、D 中选出正确答案

1. Liu Xiang won the first prize in the men's 110 meters' hurdles _____.   （北京,中考）
   A. race   B. match   C. game   D. competition

2. Dongdong Monitor of Class One, won the top prize in the Speech, _____.   （青岛,中考）
   A. In the way   B. By the way   C. On the way   D. At the way

3. _____, what did you do in the past?   （烟台,中考）
   A. In the way   B. By the way   C. On the way   D. At the way

4. The poor kid was lost _____ to the Zoo.   （广西,中考）
   A. on his way   B. by his way   C. in his way   D. at his way

5. He finished _____ his homework at 10 o'clock last night.   （泸州,中考）
   A. to do   B. did   C. doing   D. do

6. You'd better take the money _____ you.
   A. to   B. for   C. of   D. with

7. Was your father angry _____ you yesterday?
   A. to   B. on   C. for   D. with

8. "Where are you going?" "I'm going to the shop, what _____ you?"
   A. for   B. about   C. in   D. on

9. We usually go to school _____ Monday _____ Friday.
   A. to, from   B. from, on   C. from, to   D. on, to

10. Please turn _____ the radio and listen to the news.
    A. in   B. on   C. into   D. over

11. Please take your dirty shoes away _____ here.
    A. from   B. off   C. of   D. at

12. —May I speak _____ Mary, please?
    —Hold on _____ a moment, please.
    A. to... for   B. for... to   C. to... of   D. to... at

13. _____ bad weather!
    A. How   B. What   C. What a   D. What an

14. It's going to rain. Mary, you'd better _____ the raincoat with you.
    A. take   B. bring   C. get   D. carry

15. We'll give our English teacher a card for _____.
    A. the Teacher's Day   B. teacher's Day
    C. a Teacher's Day   D. Teachers' Day

16. He began to _____ English three years ago.   （北京,中考）
    A. learn   B. learns   C. learned   D. learning

17. Old McDonald gave up smoking for a while, but soon _____ to his old ways.

（北京，中考）

    A. returned   B. returns   C. was returning   D. had returned

三、用 be 的适当形式填空

1. What time _____ (be) it now?

2. What time _____ (be) it when he came back last night?

3. There _____ (be) a football match in our school every week. Last week there _____ (be) an exciting football match.

4. Tom _____ (be) ill last week. He _____ (be) better now.

5. Jimmy and his sister _____ (be) at school. Yesterday they _____ (be) absent from class.

四、翻译句子

1. 你去过美国吗?   6. He was reading a letter then.

2. 去过。   7. Tim was in the office just now.

3. 什么时候去的?   8. There was an old car in front of the building.

4. 去年。   9. They were here last Friday.

5. 你去美国干什么?   10. The young people were in the tall building.

五、用 in, at 或 on 填空

1. They were _____ the dairy _____ Saturday.

2. Were you _____ Australia September last year?

3. When were Tom and Janet _____ the stationer's?

4. There were a crowd of people _____ the street.

5. We were _____ lunch when she called.

6. She's very good _____ Ping-Pong.

7. How many cars were _____ the race?

8. They are standing _____ the right.

9. Were your husband and you _____ the party?

10. Jim got up late _____ the morning and had a meal _____ noon.

六、书面表达

根据中文提示,写一篇有关计算机的短文。

提示:

1. 计算机在当今世界上使用得越来越广泛。

2. 它能控制(control)机器、做家务等等。

3. 科学家正在努力让计算机为人类做更多的事。

七、完成句子:将 on, at 和 in 填入空内

1. I like to spend the summer _____ the country and the winter _____ the town.

2. The train leaves _____ 2∶30 and arrives in Edinburgh(爱丁堡) _____ 6∶15.

3. I will call and see you _____ three o'clock _____ Sunday.

4. Many English people live _____ cities.

5. My uncle lives _____ a large house _____ a village a few miles from Rouen.

6. My wife and my children are _____ the cinema _____ the moment.

7. She will be twenty-five _____ August 11th.

8. Could you meet me _____ 2∶30 _____ Saturday afternoon?

9. He told me that he lived _____ 23 Clarendon Road.

10. When we are _____ London, we always stay _____ this hotel.

11. Mr. Smith teaches Modern Languages _____ the High School.

12. I will call at your office some time _____ the morning.

13. When he retired(退休),he left London and went to live _____ Kent.

14. Christmas Day is _____ December 25th.

15. Would you prefer(更愿意)to work _____ a factory,or _____ a farm?

16. There are a lot of people waiting _____ the bus-stop.

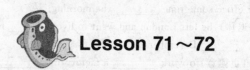

Lesson 71~72

一、单词拼写:根据所给中文意思补全下列单词

1. t__m__ (一次 *n.*) 2. sh_____pen(削尖 *v.*) 3. w_____dr__be(大衣柜 *n.*)

4. tr__s__s(长裤 *n.*) 5. b_____l(沸腾 *v.*)

二、语法和词汇:从 A、B、C、D 中选出正确答案

1. —_____

 —Certainly. One moment, please. （辽宁,中考)

 A. Hello, Ann here.   B. Can you look for Ann, please?

 C. May I speak to Ann, please?   D. OK!

2. There was a strange sound outside. Mary went out and _____ around, but she _____

 nothing. （上海,中考)

 A. looked/saw   B. saw/saw   C. watched/looked   D. looked/find

3. Do you know how to _____ this vegetable is Spanish? （哈尔滨,中考)

 A. say   B. speak   C. tell   D. talk

4. The meeting room was very quiet when she was _____. （北京,中考)

 A. saying   B. speaking   C. telling   D. sleeping

5. —How was your weekend?

 —Great! We _____ a picnic by the lake. （北京,中考)

 A. have   B. are having   C. had   D. will have

6. We live on _____ floor.

 A. fiveth   B. fifth   C. the fiveth   D. the fifth

7. —What _____ is Li Lei in?

  He is in _____.

 A. Row... row five   B. Row... Row Five

 C. row... Row five   D. row... row Five

8. Mrs. Mills _____ in London last week.

 A. loses her way   B. lost her way   C. losed her way   D. losing her way

9. "I can ask the policeman the way," Mr. Mills said _____.

 A. to herself   B. to oneself   C. to himself   D. to him

10. Put your books _____ the schoolbags and take _____ your pencils.

 A. into... out of   B. out... in   C. into... out   D. out... out of

11. He _____ Jane in the street yesterday morning.

 A. meet   B. met   C. meets   D. meeting

12. There are a lot _____ students _____ his class.

  A. in, of   B. of, in   C. in, in   D. of, of

13. Our English teacher _____ us an interesting story this morning.

 A. spoke   B. said   C. told   D. talked

14. The students put down their pens when the teacher _____ them to stop writing.

 A. said   B. spoke   C. told   D. talked

15. This book is useful to me, so I _____ 20 Yuan for it yesterday.

    A. spent   B. cost   C. took   D. paid

三、用所给动词的适当时态填空

1. I _____ (be) busy last night. I _____ (do) my homework and some housework.

2. She often _____ (go) shopping on Monday. But she _____ (stay) at home last Monday.

3. Listen, someone _____ (knock) at the door.

4. It _____ (rain) heavily last night.

5. He _____ (get) up very late this morning.

6. Robert _____ (telephone) you three times this morning.

7. _____ (not drive) so fast. Look, the policeman _____ (wave) to you.

8. I _____ (write) 3 letters this morning.

四、翻译句子

1. He saw the aeroplanes flying over London.

2. They understood the story very well.

3. The children ate too many ices.

4. Hob drank tea for breakfast.

5. He swam in the river an hour ago.

6. 去年秋天,我和玛丽在北京玩得很开心。

7. 他在 1993 年开始在我校学习。

8. 你何时开始学习英语的?

9. 我是 10 年前开始学英语的。

10. 前天他来看你,但你不在。

五、将下列句子改成过去时态,时间状语作相应改变

1. Susan is making her dress by herself.

2. I always get up at seven.

3. They will leave Beijing next Monday.

4. We walk to the cinema.

5. Who's driving that car?

6. Sam sits on that seat.

7. Miss Feng lives in the house.

8. They ask many questions.

9. How much is the meat?

10. Are those students in our class?

六、书面表达

    外国留学生 Tom 和你(王新)是同班同学,他住在友谊宾馆。你到他住处请他参加明天下午李华同学的生日晚会,碰巧他不在。请你用英语给他留个便条,邀请他参加,并告诉他去李华家的路线。

提示:1. 地点:李华家。

       2. 晚会内容:唱歌,跳舞,吃蛋糕。

       3. 字数:100 左右。

七、完成句子:用所给动词的适当时态填空

1. I _____ (be) busy last night. I _____ (do) my homework and some housework.

2. She often _____ (go) shopping on Monday. But she _____ (stay) at home last Monday.

3. Listen, someone _____ (knock) at the door.

4. It _____ (rain) heavily last night.

5. He _____ (get) up very late this morning.

6. Robert _____ (telephone) you three times this morning.

7. _____ (not drive) so fast. Look, the policeman _____ (wave) to you.

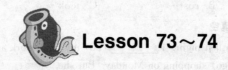

Lesson 73～74

一、单词拼写:根据所给中文意思补全下列单词

1. s __dd___ly（突然地 *adv.*）　　2. h __nd（手 *n.*）　　3. p __ck __t（口袋 *n.*）

4. phr __s __（短语 *n.*）　　5. gr ___t（问候 *v.*）

二、语法和词汇:从 A、B、C、D 中选出正确答案

1. There was _____ no one laughing at that boy. How kind they were!　　（福建,中考）
   A. nearly　　　　B. almost　　　　C. hardly　　　　D. about

2. Everyone says the nurse is very _____. She often helps the _____ people.　　（浙江,中考）
   A. looked for/find　　D. kind/sickly　　C. kindly/sickly　　D. kind/sick

3. The boy _____ his toy everywhere，but he couldn't _____ it.　　（石家庄,中考）
   A. looked for/find　　B. found/look for　　C. looked for/look for　　D. found/find

4. The child _____ his mother carefully but he couldn't _____ anything.　　（广西,中考）
   A. listened/hear　　B. listened to/hear　　C. heard/listen　　D. heard/listen to

5. Susan doesn't look _____. What's the trouble _____ her?　　（甘肃,中考）
   A. happy/with　　B. happily/with　　C. happy/of　　D. happily/of

6. Nothing could make him turn _____ his country.
   A. to　　　　B. against　　　　C. down　　　　D. over

7. _____ animals _____ plants can live without water.
   A. Both...and　　B. Either...or　　C. Not...but　　D. Neither...nor

8. He was pleased. He made _____ mistakes in the maths test.
   A. few　　　　B. a few　　　　C. little　　　　D. a little

9. I _____ the bike for a year.
   A. buy　　　　B. bought　　　　C. have bought　　　　D. have had

10. Stop _____ fire. It's dangerous.
    A. to play　　B. playing and　　C. to play with　　D. playing with

11. Tom enjoys _____ to light music.
    A. listening　　B. listens　　C. to listen　　D. listen

12. Which is brighter，the sun _____ the moon?
    A. and　　　　B. or　　　　C. but　　　　D. so

13. There are _____ books in my home.
    A. three hundreds and twenty-six　　　　B. three hundred and twenty six
    C. three hundred and twenty-six　　　　D. three hundreds and twenty six

14. Mrs. Zhang is too _____ to go on wailing.　　（北京,中考）
    A. strong　　　　B. tall　　　　C. kind　　　　D. tired

三、用 in,at,on,to 填空

1. He is going to telephone _____ five o'clock.

2. My birthday is _____ May 22nd.

3. It is always cold _____ February.

4. My father was there _____ 1942.

5. They always do their homework _____ the evening.

四、翻译句子

1. You came very late last time.
2. My mother is preparing for the meal.
3. He can understand the point.
4. There are some bananas on the wall.

5. 你难道没有告诉他我的电话号码?
6. 不,我告诉他了。
7. 他难道不能在明天早上8点之前来吗?
8. 是的,他不能来得那么早。

五、用 speak，say，talk 或 tell 填空

1. Money _____.
2. It's not good to _____ lies.
3. Actions _____ louder than words.
4. I _____ them my name, address, post code, etc.
5. Can you _____ me what time the play starts?
6. When he first came, he couldn't _____ a word of English.
7. What did she _____ at the meeting?
8. There's an important matter I want to _____ to you about.

六、书面表达

你是一名中学生,设想假期有一段打工的经历。开学初在英语课上,你用英语向同学们讲述你的体会。

试用所给的短语,写一篇100词左右的短文。

1. keep on asking my parents for money
2. learn the value of money
3. get along with others
4. find it's good preparation for/get prepared for
5. get a little bit working and social experience

七、完成句子

1. Mrs. Mills _____ in London last week.
   A. loses her way   B. lost her way   C. losed her way
2. Did you tell _____ to King Street?
   A. him the way   B. his the way   C. himself the way
3. "I can ask the policeman the way," Mr. Mills said _____.
   A. to herself   B. to oneself   C. to himself
4. Be careful. Don't cut _____.
   A. myself   B. yourself   C. himself
5. Put your books _____ the schoolbags and take _____ your pencils.
   A. into...out of   B. our...in   C. into...out

87

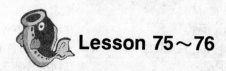

Lesson 75~76

一、单词拼写:根据所给中文意思补全下列单词

1. b__y(买 v.)　　2. f__sh___n(流行 n.)　　3. __n__(一些 pron.)

4. m__n___(月 n.) 5. m__n__t__(分钟 n.)

二、语法和词汇:从 A、B、C、D 中选出正确答案

1. —Can I help you?

　—I want _____ ,please.　　　　　　　　　　　　　　　　　　(浙江,中考)

　A. two socks　　　　　　　　　　　B. two pair of socks

　C. two pairs of socks　　　　　　　D. two pairs of sock

2. Oh,how _____ the cotton sweater feels! I always feel _____ with it.　(上海,中考)

　A. comfortably/comfortably　　　　B. comfortable/comfortably

　C. comfortably/comfortable　　　　D. comfortable/comfortable

3. —There _____ a lot of meat on the plate. Would you like some?

　—Just a little, please.　　　　　　　　　　　　　　　　　　　(北京,中考)

　A. is　　　　　　B. are　　　　　　C. am　　　　　　D. be

4. I don't like this furniture at all. It is already _____.　　　　　(福建,中考)

　A. in fashion　　B. in the fashion　　C. out of fashion　　D. out of the fashion

5. —_____ ?

　—Yes,please,I'd like half a kilo of meat.　　　　　　　　　　　(北京,中考)

　A. Would you like half a kilo of meat　　B. What about something to eat

　C. How do you like this　　　　　　　　D. Can I help you

6. She asked them _____ to late on weekends.

　A. not get up　　B. not to get up　　C. don't get up　　D. to not get up

7. The Yellow River is one of _____ rivers in China.

　A. longer　　　　B. longest　　　　C. long　　　　D. the longest

8. The paper for books and newspapers is made _____ wood.

　A. of　　　　　　B. up　　　　　　C. from　　　　D. in

9. He promised to give the dictionary _____ when he finished using it.

　A. up　　　　　　B. in　　　　　　C. out　　　　D. back

10. How are you getting on _____ your work and study?

　A. for　　　　　　B. about　　　　C. with　　　　D. by

11. If you don't know the word, why don't you _____ in the dictionary?

　A. look at it　　B. look after it　　C. look up it　　D. look it up

12. How did you come _____ that watch?

　A. at　　　　　　B. by　　　　　　C. over　　　　D. for

13. That style of hat first came into _____ last year.

　A. market　　　　B. appearance　　C. fashion　　D. practice

14. Peter didn't go to bed _____ he finished his homework yesterday.

　A. because　　　B. after　　　　　C. until　　　　D. since

15. Thank you for _____ me.

    A. help   B. to help   C. helped   D. helping

三、用所给动词的适当形式填空

    The lady's sister _____ (buy) a pair of shoes in the USA last month. The lady _____ (like) them very much. She _____ (want) to _____ (buy) a pair, too. Yesterday the lady _____ (go) to a shop and _____ (ask) for a pair of shoes like her sister's. There _____ (be) some shoes like those in the shop last month, but now there _____ (be) not any left in the shop. The salesman _____ (tell) the lady that those shoes _____ (be) out of fashion and the shoes in fashion now _____ (be) these uncomfortable ones.

四、翻译句子

1. 我可以在 8 月 4 日 9 点钟去你家吗？

2. 这件衣服去年不是很流行吗？

3. 他能理解那个词语吗？

4. 前天你们在街上遇见谁了？

5. 她怎样？

6. I was born in Shanghai.

7. The train was five minutes late.

8. Did you watch the match last night?

9. He telephoned you a moment ago.

10. He arrived the week before last.

五、改写下列句子

1. Dick drives a car to the office every day. (last Friday)

2. The girl sings an English song well. (at the party)

3. Mary has her birthday party with her family every year. (last year)

4. Lucy helps her mother with the housework every Sunday. (yesterday evening)

5. Bill and Jim talk to each other every day. (this morning)

6. The boys play basketball every Saturday. (last Saturday)

7. The baby cries every night. (last night)

8. She listens to the radio every day. (last night)

六、书面表达

    假定你叫张华，毕业之际，从报上得知广州一家经营有方、在中国享有名气的合资企业东方电脑公司招聘职员(clerk)若干名。2009 年 7 月 3 日，你给该公司经理 Mr. Smith Robert 写了一封自荐信，基本内容如下表：

姓名	张　华	性别	女	出生年月	1984 年 8 月	出生地		湖南
毕业学校	南开大学计算机系		业余爱好		篮球	身体状况		良好
特长	精通微机、英语。可阅读英文科技书籍和用英语写作，懂法语。							
通信地址	湖南省双峰县高中		联系电话		0819－8841679			

    注意：(1)正确使用写信的格式；(2)字数：100 词左右；(3)单词提示：县 county

七、完成句子：以正确的形式将括号内的动词填入空内

1. I _____ (see) that film last week.

2. He _____ (have) his dinner an hour ago.

3. We _____ (have) a very pleasant holiday last summer.

4. The man _____ (repair 修理) my bicycle yesterday.

5. She _____ (sleep) for eight hours last night.

6. It _____ (take) me nearly two hours to get here this morning.

7. I _____ (meet) your friend Peter yesterday afternoon.

8. I _____ (go) to see Mr. Smith yesterday evening, but he _____ (not be) at home.

9. Last Sunday we _____ (visit) some old friends in town.

10. The Second World War _____ (start) in 1939 and _____ (end) in 1945.

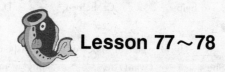

Lesson 77~78

一、单词拼写:根据所给中文意思补全下列单词

1. urg＿nt（急迫的 *adj.*）　　2. wa＿k（走 *v.*）　　3. t＿＿k（谈论 *v.*）

4. ＿sk（问 *v.*）　　5. ＿fr＿＿d（害怕的 *adj.*）

二、语法和词汇:从 A、B、C、D 中选出正确答案

1. —May I go now?

　　—No, you _____ let the teacher know first.　　　　　　（宜昌,中考）

　　A. need　　　　　B. must　　　　　C. can　　　　　D. may

2. —Hi, Jim. I haven't seen you for a long time! You look well!

　　—_____. You look well, too.　　　　　　　　　　（山东,中考）

　　A. Great　　　　　B. Thanks　　　　　C. Oh, no　　　　　D. Not at all

3. —Hi, I'm Tom Smith.

　　—_____.　　　　　　　　　　　　　　　　　　（烟台,中考）

　　A. What a pleasure!　　　　　　　　　B. It's my pleasure.

　　C. I'm very please　　　　　　　　　D. Pleased to meet you.

4. The woman went to see the dentist because she had _____.　（陕西,中考）

　　A. toothache　　　B. a toothache　　　C. teethache　　　D. a teethache

5. —What are you doing _____?

　　—I am reading a magazine.　　　　　　　　　　　（河南,中考）

　　A. at the moment　　B. in the moment　　C. at moment　　D. in moment

6. I want to know _____ in the party yesterday.

　　A. if they had a good time　　　　　B. if did they have a good time

　　C. that they had good times　　　　D. what they had a good time

7. The boy was born _____ January 12th, 1983.

　　A. in　　　　　B. at　　　　　C. on　　　　　D. of

8. Tom's pen was _____ so he needed a new one.

　　A. long　　　　B. cheap　　　　C. broken　　　　D. here

9. Father Christmas lands on top of _____ house and climbs down the chimney into the fireplace.

　　A. each　　　　B. all　　　　C. either　　　　D. both

10. The doctor _____ Mrs. Brown very carefully and then said, "There's nothing much wrong with you."

　　A. watched　　　B. looked after　　　C. operated　　　D. looked over

11. They have been _____ Europe for several times.

　　A. to　　　　B. x　　　　C. gone　　　　D. with

12. There _____ a big increase in our economy since 1999.

　　A. is　　　　B. was　　　　C. has been　　　　D. have been

13. How long _____ it take the workers to build the hospital?

　　A. were　　　　B. does　　　　C. do　　　　D. did

14. If you finish reading my book, please _____ to me.
    A. give it again   B. give again it   C. give back it   D. give it back

15. I _____ my way yesterday.
    A. lose   B. loses   C. lost   D. losing

16. It's going to rain. You'd better _____ an umbrella with you.
    A. take   B. took   C. to take   D. taking

17. It was raining heavily outside. The father made the children _____ in the room.
    A. to stay   B. stay   C. staying   D. stayed

18. We saw him _____ the building and go upstairs.
    A. to enter   B. enter   C. entering   D. entered

19. He drank a glass of beer _____ for he worked hard for a long time on the farm.
    A. slowly   B. hurried   C. happily   D. thirstily

20. —Shall we go shopping now?
    —Sorry, I can't. I _____ my shirts.   (北京，中考)
    A. wash   B. washes   C. washed   D. am washing

21. I don't think I'll need any money but I'll bring some _____.   (北京，中考)
    A. at last   B. in case   C. once again   D. in time

22. —You're drinking too much.
    —Only at home. No one _____ me but you.   (北京，中考)
    A. is seeing   B. had seen   C. sees   D. saw

三、用介词填空

1. He was late _____ Wednesday.
2. There was a sport meet _____ September 20th.
3. My father was here _____ 1990 and 1992.
4. I was there _____ 10：45.
5. Dorothy was with us _____ autumn.

四、翻译句子

1. I want to see the dentist please. Can he see me now?
2. I'm afraid that he can't.
3. Can he see me at 10 a. m. ?
4. No, he can't. He can see you at 2 p. m.
5. You do that work very well.

6. 汤姆在哪？他在教室里上课。
7. 我们常常在晚上7点钟吃晚饭。
8. 在那里你可以玩得很开心。
9. 请稍等，我在吃早餐。
10. 你想要喝杯咖啡吗？

五、用 say 或 tell 填空

1. She _____ good night to each one of her friends.
2. Students shouldn't _____ lies.
3. Then I never _____ her anything again.
4. Does he always _____ the truth?
5. The teacher always _____ good morning to us.
6. The boy could _____ the time when he was very young.
7. They _____ he's a millionaire.

六、完成句子:将下列句子变成否定式的疑问句

1. You came very late last time.
2. My mother is preparing for the meal.
3. He can understand the point.

4. There are some bananas on the wall.
5. The girl speaks Japanese.

91

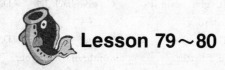

Lesson 79～80

一、单词拼写:根据所给中文意思补全下列单词

1. l__st(单子 n.)　　2. h__p__(希望 v.)　　3. m__n__y(钱 n.)

4. newsp__p___(报纸 n.)　　5. v__g__t__bl__(蔬菜 n.)

二、语法和词汇:从 A、B、C、D 中选出正确答案

1. Many people have donated money to the _____ Project.　　(北京,中考)

　A. Desire　　　B. Wish　　　C. Hope　　　D. Regard

2. I _____ hope you a happy journey!　　(山东,中考)

　A. too much　　B. much too　　C. very much　　D. very many

3. Health is very important to us. We should eat more vegetables and fruit instead of _____ rich food.　　(哈尔滨,中考)

　A. too much　　B. much too　　C. very much　　D. very many

4. There's _____ cooking oil left in the house. Would you go to the corner store and get _____ ?　　(陕西,中考)

　A. little/some　　B. little/any　　C. a little/some　　D. a little/any

5. Don't worry if you can't come to _____ party. I'll save _____ cakes for you.　　(浙江,中考)

　A. the/some　　B. a/much　　C. the/any　　D. a/little

6. We'll listen to a talk _____ British history.

　A. by　　　B. with　　　C. at　　　D. on

7. I have _____ received a letter from my parents.

　A. yet　　　B. are　　　C. just　　　D. just now

8. Where are the students? Are they in _____ ?

　A. the Room 406　　B. Room 406　　C. the 406 Room　　D. 406 Room

9. "I hear your father _____ to Japan once." "Yes. He _____ there last year."

　A. went... has been　　　　　B. has been... went

　C. goes... went　　　　　　D. has been... has been

10. The little baby has two _____ already.

　A. tooth　　　B. tooths　　　C. teeth　　　D. teeths

11. Automative machinery saves manufacturer's space and _____ .

　A. some money　　B. any money　　C. the money　　D. money

12. Don't worry, I'll take good care _____ Polly.

　A. for　　　B. of　　　C. with　　　D. to

13. She always thinks of _____ more than herself.

　A. other　　　B. others　　　C. the other　　　D. the others

14. You may go and ask him. He knows _____ about Japanese.

　A. a few　　　B. few　　　C. a little　　　D. little

15. Please write to me as soon as you _____ Shanghai.

　A. arrive　　　B. reach　　　C. got to　　　D. come

三、用括号内动词的适当形式填空

Mrs. Brown's old grandfather _____ (live) with her and her husband. Every morning he _____ (go) for a walk in the park and _____ (come) home at half past twelve for his lunch.

But one morning a police car _____ (stop) outside Mrs. Brown's house at twelve o'clock, and two policemen _____ (help) Mr. Brown to _____ (get) out of the car. One of them _____ (say) to Mrs. Brown:

"The poor old gentleman _____ (lose) his way in the park and _____ (call) us for help, so we _____ (send) a car to _____ (bring) him home."

四、翻译句子

1. Where did the Sawyers go for the holidays?

2. What did he give you?

3. When did the fire break out?

4. Who told you the way to the post office?

5. 你在做家庭作业吗? 不,我已经做完了。

6. 雨已经下了好几天了。

7. 从92年起他在这个厂工作。

8. 玛丽在哪? 她去买东西了。

五、用 a lot of, many 或 much 填空

1. Do you have _____ money with you?

2. What _____ time you take to dress!

3. Does the singer have _____ fans?

4. On our way to school, he asked me _____ questions.

5. She bought _____ postcards to send her friends.

6. I haven't _____ news to tell you.

7. Do you know _____ people in this company?

8. There aren't _____ things I could do today.

93

六、书面表达

Write a passage with at least 50 words about the topic "The 29th Olympic Games in Beijing". You can use the words or expressions given in the box (以"北京第29届奥运会"为题写一篇不少于 50 个单词的短文。方框内的词语供选用。)

the first Olympic Games	51 gold medals (51 枚金牌),
exciting,	wonderful,
be proud of,	opening and closing ceremonies (开幕式和闭幕式), Champion

The 29th Olympic Games in Beijing

七、完成句子:仿照例句回答下列句子

Have you got any tobacco?   /tobacconist's

I need a lot of tobacco. I haven't got much.

I must go to the tobacconist's to get some tobacco.

Has he got any bananas?   /greengrocer's

He needs a lot of bananas. He hasn't got many.

He must go to the greengrocer's to get some bananas.

1. Have they got any eggs?   /grocer's

2. Has she got any bread?   /baker's

3. Has he got any cheese?   /grocer's

4. Has he got any medicine?   /chemist's

5. Have they got any magazines?   /newsagent's

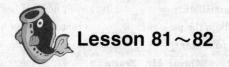

Lesson 81～82

一、单词拼写:根据所给中文意思补全下列单词

1. n＿＿rly (几乎 *adv.*)　　2. d＿nn＿＿ (正餐 *n.*)　　3. r＿＿st (烤的 *adj.*)

4. h＿lid＿y (假期)　　　5. h＿＿rc＿t (理发 *v.*)

二、语法和词汇:从 A、B、C、D 中选出正确答案

1. —Linda had nothing for breakfast this morning, _____?

　—No, She got up too late.　　　　　　　　　　　　　　　　　　(北京,中考)

　A. had she　　　　B. hadn't she　　　C. did she　　　D. didn't she

2. —May I borrow your ruler.

　—Certainly. _____.

　A. Hold on, please　B. It doesn't matter　C. Here you are　D. Not at all

3. —_____ Tom _____ to work hard to help his family?

　—Yes, he _____.　　　　　　　　　　　　　　　　　　　(内蒙古,中考)

　A. Has/不填/does　　　　　　　　　B. Has/不填/does

　C. Does/has/has　　　　　　　　　D. Does/have/does

4. It was hard work carrying the bags. They _____ very heavy.

　A. be　　　　　　B. are　　　　　　C. have been　　　D. were

5. —Jim, it's so nice of you to help me.

　—_____.　　　　　　　　　　　　　　　　　　　　　　　(宿迁,中考)

　A. My pleasure　B. You're right　C. No problem　D. It's my turn

6. There _____ wrong with my radio.

　A. are something　B. are anything　C. is anything　D. is something

7. "_____ do you like the film?" "I like it very much."

　A. How　　　　　B. What　　　　　C. When　　　　D. Where

8. We won't go to the Great Wall if it _____ tomorrow.

　A. snow　　　　　B. snowing　　　　C. snows　　　　D. will snow

9. You look _____ than before, why?

　A. more thin　　　　　　　　　　　B. more thinner

　C. much thinner　　　　　　　　　D. much more thin

10. This morning, I saw a man _____ on the road on my way _____.

　A. lies, there　　　　　　　　　　B. lied, to school

　C. lying, home　　　　　　　　　D. to lie, to the shop

11. Be quiet, please! I will choose _____ for our football team.

　A. anybody strong　　　　　　　　B. someone strong

　C. strong someone　　　　　　　　D. strong anybody

12. I _____ my parents last month.

　　A. heard of　　　B. heard from　　C. heard　　　D. heard about

13. She had _____ apple in one hand and _____ knife in the other.

　　A. an...an　　　B. a...a　　　　C. an...a　　　D. a...an

14. I like playing _____ football and my sister likes playing _____ piano.

    A. ×...×   B. ×...the   C. the...×   D. the...the

15. Li Ming's father is _____ oil worker in Tackhing.

    A. an   B. a   C. the   D. /

16. All the preparations for the task _____ , and we're ready to start.   （北京,中考）

    A. completed   B. complete

    C. had been completed   D. have been completed

17. —Are you coming to Jeff's party?   （北京,中考）

    —I'm not sure. I _____ go to the concert instead.

    A. must   B. would   C. should   D. might

三、用所给动词的现在完成时态填空

1. She _____ (ask) me a question.

2. We _____ (type) that letter.

3. They _____ (turn on) the radio.

4. The children _____ (sharpen) their pencils.

5. The office boy _____ (empty) the basket.

6. Mary _____ (boil) some eggs.

7. Tom _____ (paint) the bookcase.

四、翻译句子

1. They must begin the work now.

2. I need an English-Chinese dictionary.

3. We have got much money.

4. The flower needs some water.

5. We are in need of more time.

6. 他正在洗澡。

7. 喝一杯威斯忌。

8. 我们能在几点吃午饭？

9. 怎么了？

10. 他在楼上。

95

五、书面表达

    Write a passage about the topic "Our Library", use no less than 50 words. You can use the words or expressions given in the box (以"我们的图书馆"为题,写一篇不少于50个单词的短文,要求内容通顺。方框内的词语供使用。)

> after school   reading room   newspapers   magazines   all kinds of   detective stories
> science fictions   borrow   renew

六、完成句子:将括号中的汉语译成英语,用动词 have

1. She usually(吃两个鸡蛋喝一瓶牛奶)for her breakfast.

2. John and Tom(吃午饭) together at a restaurant today.

3. We(度假) last month.

4. My son is going to (理发)this afternoon.

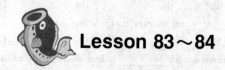

Lesson 83～84

一、单词拼写:根据所给中文意思补全下列单词

1. s＿＿tc＿s＿(小提箱 *n.*)　2. m＿g＿zine(杂志 *n.*)　3. c＿g＿r＿tte(香烟 *n.*)

4. l＿＿＿t(轻的 *adj.*)　5. alr＿＿dy(已经 *adv.*)

二、语法和词汇:从 A、B、C、D 中选出正确答案

1. By the time I ＿＿＿＿ back they ＿＿＿＿ up ten metres.
   A. came/have climbed　　　　B. came/had climbed
   C. come/have climbed　　　　D. had come/climbed

2. The coffee is wonderful! It doesn't taste like anything I ＿＿＿＿ before.
   A. was having　　B. have　　C. have ever had　　D. had ever had

3. The students are sorry to hear that the famous singer ＿＿＿＿ for half an hour.
   (陕西,中考)
   A. has left　　B. has gone　　C. has been away　　D. has gone away

4. It ＿＿＿＿ ten years since we last ＿＿＿＿ in Beijing.　　(河北,中考)
   A. was/met　　B. has been/met　　C. was/meet　　D. is/meet

5. We have worked for three hours. Now let's stop ＿＿＿＿ a rest.　　(河北,中考)
   A. had　　B. have　　C. to have　　D. haing

6. You must work ＿＿＿＿.
   A. hard　　B. hardly　　C. careful　　D. hardy

7. Who does this sweater ＿＿＿＿.
   A. belong to　　B. belong　　C. belong with　　D. belongs to

8. This suitcase is ＿＿＿＿ heavy for him to carry into the car.
   A. so　　B. too　　C. vcry　　D. that

9. He is ＿＿＿＿ that Tom will be here this afternoon.
   A. surely　　B. certainly　　C. x　　D. sure

10. He must be in bed ＿＿＿＿.
    A. each day　　B. each days　　C. every days　　D. each a day

11. "＿＿＿＿ Tom?""He feels ill."
    A. What's matter with　　　　B. What's the matter on
    C. What's matter about　　　　D. What's the matter with

12. He ＿＿＿＿ at home for a week.
    A. has　　B. has stayed　　C. stayed　　D. staying

13. I have a lot of things to buy,so I ＿＿＿＿.
    A. make a shopping list　　　　B. write a shopping list
    C. make shop list　　　　D. write a list

14. Tony often gets up ＿＿＿＿ 9 a.m.
    A. in　　B. on　　C. at　　D. by

15. He ＿＿＿＿ his homework for an hour.
    A. did　　B. does　　C. doing　　D. has done

16. Zhao Lan _____ already _____ in this school for two years.　　　（北京，中考）

　　A. was…studying　　B. will…study　　C. has…studied　　D. are…studying

三、用所给动词的适当时态填空

1. I _____ (get) a letter from Tim last month.

2. The dentist _____ (not be) here. He _____ (go) to Beijing three days ago.

3. I _____ (write) a book at the moment. I _____ (start) last month.

4. My family often _____ (go) to town on Sunday, but next Sunday, we _____ (go to stay) at home.

5. The sun _____ (rise) in the east and _____ (set) in the west.

四、翻译句子

1. We want to catch eight nineteen to London.

2. When's the next train? In five hours' time.

3. He is our new next-door neighbour.

4. Women always have the last word.

5. It's worth every penny of it.

6. 我要两张往返票。

7. 我想这房子要出售吧。

8. 他们正在设法修理它。

9. 我忘了带我的伞。

10. 他打开灯，但是看不见任何人。

五、将下列句子改成否定句、疑问句，并作简单回答

1. The students on duty have closed the windows.

2. I have met him before.

3. They have had a beautiful cake.

4. Mary has received a letter from home.

5. Mother has made a pot of tea.

6. James has washed all the chairs.

7. He has had some bread.

8. I've worked hard all week.

六、书面表达

　　Write at least six sentences about the topic "My Way of Spending Pocket Money"（以"我的花钱方式"为题，写一篇文章，要求内容切题，意思连贯，方框中的词语供选用。）

> my own way of…, get money from, waste money, buy something useful, such as, wise

七、完成句子：以现在完成时的形式将括号内的动词填入空内

1. I _____ (just receive) a letter from my borther.

2. He _____ (read) that novel ten times.

3. The play _____ (already begin).

4. I _____ (never see) that man before.

5. I _____ (not finish) my work yet.

6. _____ she ever _____ (work) in this factory?

7. We _____ (always arrive) at school at eight.

8. _____ you _____ (get) the money back?

9. He _____ (just return) from Britain.

10. I _____ (never have) scarlet fever(猩红热).

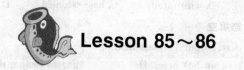

Lesson 85～86

一、单词拼写：根据所给中文意思补全下列单词

1. c_n_m__（电影院 n.）   2. f___m（电影 n.）   3. d____ty（脏的 adj.）

4. cr___d（人群 n.）   5. c_t__（城市 n.）

二、语法和词汇：从 A、B、C、D 中选出正确答案

1. The young girl sitting next to me on the plane is very nervous. She _____ before.

    A. hasn't flown   B. didn't fly   C. hadn't flown   D. wasn't flying

2. —Could you tell me where _____ ?

    —He has gone to the library.   （徐州，中考）

    A. Li Ming is   B. can I find Li Ming   C. has Li Ming gone   C. has Li Ming been

3. I thought she was famous, but none of my friends have _____ heard of her.

    A. even   B. ever   C. just   D. never

4. Linda, do you know what is _____ at the Globe Theater?   （上海，中考）

    A. in   B. on   C. at   D. for

5. —You've never seen dinosaur eggs, have you?

    —_____. How I wish to visit the dinosaur world!

    A. Yes, I have   B. No, I haven't

    C. Certainly, I have   C. Of course, I haven't

6. Tom believed that he could understand _____ the teacher said in the science class.

    A. that   B. how   C. x   D. what

7. He is running _____ enough and he will catch Tom.

    A. quick   B. quickly   C. slowly   D. x

8. This book is _____ better than that one.

    A. very   B. much   C. so   D. enough

9. He _____ to school yesterday.

    A. doesn't go   B. didn't go   C. not went   D. goed

10. Where did you go _____ night.

    A. at   B. tomorrow   C. last   D. ago

11. _____ the way home I met an old friend.

    A. On   B. At   C. In   D. By

12. _____ you absent from school since last term?

    A. Was   B. Have been   C. Are   D. Be

13. We're going to stay home on Saturday and Sunday. So we aren't going to be out _____ the weekend.

    A. at   B. for   C. in   D. on

14. She _____ him before. So she doesn't know him.

    A. hasn't seen   B. didn't see   C. won't see   D. doesn't see

15. Having read this novel, the director decided to _____ it.

    A. develop   B. dim   C. film   D. print

16. I finally got the job I dreamed about. Never in all my life _____ so happy! （北京，中考）

    A. did I feel   B. I felt   C. I had felt   D. had I felt

三、用所给动词的适当形式填空

    Peggy _____（already have）lunch. He _____（have）it at half past twelve. After lunch he _____（have）a cup of coffee. At the moment, he _____（come）to see Tom. Tom and his wife _____（have）lunch now. They _____（leave）tomorrow. They _____（go）to have a holiday. Peggy _____（already have）a holiday this year. He _____（not go）any where. He _____（stay）at home.

四、翻译句子

1. Where are you going for holidays? I am going to New York.

2. My parents will fly to Paris next week.

3. He is only 25 years old, and he has been to many countries.

4. What is Mary doing? She is reading in the library.

5. I have bought a radio to learn English. I bought it last week.

6. 上星期他没上学吧？

7. 你能为我找一双鞋吗？恐怕不行。

8. 我难受极了，牙痛得要命。

9. 我们的茶叶和咖啡不多了。

10. 汤姆正在写购物单。

五、用 have/has been 或 have/has gone 填空

1. My brother _____ in the army for nearly three years.

2. They _____（never）to Yan'an.

3. Miss Green _____ in Beijing since 1997.

4. Lucy _____（always）a good student.

5. A：Where _____ Mary _____?

    B：I think she _____ to the cinema by herself.

6. He _____ to the museum. He was at the museum just now and is now already back.

7. She _____ to the library. She _____ at the library for about two hours.

8. A：_____ you ever _____ to Sydney?

    B：No, I _____（never be）there.

六、书面表达

    Write at least 50 words according to the topic "Don't Waste Any Water"（以"不要浪费水"为题，写一篇至少有 50 个单词的短文，要求内容切题，意思连贯，方框中的词语供选用。）

> important, everyone, drink, wash, use, clean, life convenient, mustn't, all help, save water

七、完成句子：用 have(has)been 或 have(has)gone 填空

1. I have not seen Mr. Smith. He _____ abroad(国外).

2. Ken _____ to the airport many times. He knows where it is.

3. A：_____ you _____ to Paris?

  B：Yes, I _____ there twice.

4. A：Where _____ you _____?

  B：I _____ to the library.

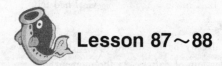

Lesson 87～88

一、单词拼写:根据所给中文意思补全下列单词

1. br__n__(带来 v.)　　2. cl__m__te(气候 n.)　　3. rep_____(修 v.)

4. Br__z__l(巴西 n.)　　5. int_____sting(有趣的 adj.)

二、语法和词汇:从 A、B、C、D 中选出正确答案

1. —Mr. Johnson, we have found our watch.

　　—My watch! Thank you. Where _____ it?　　　　　　　　　　　　(绍兴,中考)

　　A. do you find　　　　　　　　　　B. have you found

　　C. did you find　　　　　　　　　　D. were you finding

2. —Have you mended your shoes, Bob?

　　—Yes, I _____ them twenty minutes ago.

　　　　　　　　　　　　　　　　　　　　　　　　　　　　　　(天津,中考)

　　A. have mended　　B. mend　　C. had mended　　D. mended

3. —Jimmy is leaving for a holiday.

　　—Really? Where _____ he _____?

　　A. has/gone　　B. will/go　　C. did/go　　D. does/go

4. Sarah had her washing machine repaired the day before yesterday, _____ she?

　　A. had　　　　B. did　　　　C. hadn't　　　　D. didn't

5. My friend, who _____ on the International Olympic Committee all his life, is retiring next month.

　　A. served　　　　B. is serving　　C. had served　　D. has served

6. "Whose is that watch? Is it Bill's?" "I'm not sure. It _____ be his. "

　　Λ. may　　　　B. can　　　　C. must　　　　D. should

7. "Happy New Year, Mr. Smith. " "_____. "

　　A. That's OK　　　　　　　　B. That's all right

　　C. The same to you　　　　　　D. Thank you all the same

8. The farmer _____ a special kind of sheep.

　　A. sets up　　　B. brings up　　C. rises　　　D. rears

9. "Where is Jill?" "She forgot his number and went to _____ in the phone book. "

　　A. look for it　　B. pick it up　　C. look it up　　D. pick it out

10. That's a nice watch! Is it _____ in China?

　　A. make　　　B. making　　C. made　　D. makes

11. I'm still hungry. Could I have two _____ pieces of bread, please?

　　A. much　　　B. many　　C. more　　D. most

12. It's very cold today. You'd better put _____ your coat when you go out.

　　A. away　　　B. down　　C. on　　　D. up

13. "Who did better, Bill or Henry?" "I think Bill did just _____ Henry. "

　　A. as well as　　B. as good as　　C. as better as　　D. more badly than

14. I'll try to _____ the damage caused by accident.

A. fix   B. make for   C. repair   D. mend

15. He told _____ that he had finished his homework.

   A. he   B. hers   C. her   D. x

16. She can't _____ mind, can she?

   A. make up its   B. make up her C. make up with her D. do with

17. Tom gave us a good _____ of his school.

   A. decision   B. impress   C. describe   D. description

三、翻译句子

1. I have a brother.   6. 我们还在吃午饭,你吃过了吗?

2. He had dinner at 6 yesterday.   7. 我刚吃过,半小时之前吃的。

3. He is having a bath.   8. 几天前我把一只手提箱忘在开往伦敦的火车上了。

4. Mr. Smith had a haircut.   9. 我想最好请医生来给你看一下。

5. He often has a swim in the afternoon. 10. 我在旅行时留了胡子。

四、用所给动词的适当时态填空

1. It _____ (be) ten o'clock now. I _____ (go) to bed in ten minutes.

2. Winter _____ (be) over. It _____ (get) warm. The days _____ (be) long.

3. She _____ (begin) to learn English three years ago. Now she _____ (speak) good English.

4. The boy _____ (have) a bad cold the day before yesterday.

   Today he _____ (feel) better.

5. The children usually _____ (do) their homework in the evening. But now they _____ (watch) a football match on TV.

五、用动词的适当形式填空

1. I _____ (know) her since she was a little girl.

2. I _____ (not see) him for a long time, but his father often _____ (see) him.

3. My sister _____ (be) not in her room now.

   She _____ (still read) in the reading room.

4. I _____ (not finish) my homework yet. I _____ (still do) it.

5. Don't turn off TV. I _____ (still watch) the programme.

6. The mechanics _____ (still repair) my father's car.

7. It _____ (still rain) heavily.

8. The girl _____ (still sing) loudly.

六、书面表达

   Write a composition according to the situation given below:

   李磊今天病了,他患了重感冒,咳嗽得很厉害,并且还发高烧。所以他要向王老师请三天假

(ask a sick leave for 3 days)。

七、完成句子:将下列句子变成疑问句及否定句

1. My father has already retired.

2. We have waited for you for a long time.

3. Tom and I have finished the work.

4. The rain has already stopped.

5. They came the day before yesterday.

6. He studies very hard every night.

7. I am doing my homework in the study.

8. They are from America.

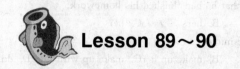

一、单词拼写:根据所给中文意思补全下列单词

1. s＿l＿(卖 *n.*)　　2. ret＿＿n(返回 *v.*)　　3. sti＿＿(还 *adv.*)

4. p＿＿nd(磅 *n.*)　　5. s＿nc＿(自从 *adv.*)

二、语法和词汇:从 A、B、C、D 中选出正确答案

1. Look at the timetable. Hurry up! Flight 4026 _____ off at 18:20.

　　A. takes　　　　B. took　　　　C. will be taken　　　D. has taken

2. —Dear, why not _____ money by yourself for your 8th birthday present?

　　—Good idea. I'll not let a penny(便士) go to waste.　　　　　　　　(广东,中考)

　　A. save　　　　B. spend　　　　C. keep　　　　D. take

3. —_____ you _____ the text yet?

　　—Yes, we _____ it two hours ago.　　　　　　　　　　　　　(上海,中考)

　　A. Did/copy/did　　　　　　　　B. Have/copied/have

　　C. Have/copied/did　　　　　　　D. Did/copy/had

4. —_____ have you been in China?

　　—Since last Wednesday.　　　　　　　　　　　　　　　　　　(上海,中考)

　　A. How soon　　B. How often　　C. How long　　　D. How much

5. —_____ do you help the old man with the housework?

　　—Once a week.　　　　　　　　　　　　　　　　　　　　　　(福州,中考)

　　A. How soon　　B. How long　　C. How often　　　D. How many

6. "Oh, the film is very good." "What's _____?"

　　A. on　　　　　B. at　　　　　C. in　　　　　D. for

7. He drove his car _____ a lamp-post.

　　A. at　　　　　B. into　　　　　C. on　　　　　D. with

8. I have tried _____ you.

　　A. to help　　　B. help　　　　C. helping　　　　D. to helping

9. _____ I use your pen?

　　A. Must　　　　B. May　　　　C. Have　　　　D. Do

10. Please give my _____ to your parents.

　　A. regard　　　B. regards　　　C. questions　　　D. greets

11. I _____ to Beijing for two times.

　　A. have been　　B. go　　　　C. will go　　　　D. went

12. Are these _____ your teachers?

　　A. mans　　　　B. men　　　　C. man　　　　D. manes

13. Jim and Kate _____ at school.

　　A. are　　　　　B. is　　　　　C. am　　　　　D. /

14. This isn't _____ house. _____ is _____ house.

　　A. her, Its, my　　B. her, It, my　　C. she, It, I　　　D. my, Its, her

15. I _____ my homework. So I can go out to play.

A. have finished B. finish　　　C. will finish　　　　D. finished

16. —I believe we've met somewhere before.　　　　　　　（北京，中考）

　　—No, _____.

　　A. it isn't the same　　　　　　B. it can't be true

　　C. I don't think so　　　　　　D. I'd rather not

17. —May I borrow your ruler?　　　　　　　　　　　　　（北京，中考）

　　—Certainly. _____.

　　A. Hold on, please　　　　　　B. It doesn't matter

　　C. Here you are　　　　　　　D. Not at all

18. My parents _____ in Beijing since 1995.　　　　　（北京，中考）

　　A. are living　　　B. have lived　　　C. live　　　　　D. will live

三、用所给动词的适当形式填空

1. A：How long _____ you _____ (study) English?

　　B：I _____ (study) English for ten months.

2. A：Where _____ you _____ (be)?

　　B：I _____ (be) to the dentist.

　　A：_____ he _____ (take) out your bad tooth?

　　B：Yes, he _____.

3. A：I have just heard Peter is in Australia.

　　B：Oh, _____ you _____ (not know)? He _____ (fly) out at the beginning of the month.

4. A：_____ you _____ (hear) from him? Does he like the life there?

　　B：Yes, I _____ (get) his letter last week. He _____ (tell) me about his job. But he _____ (not say) whether he liked the life there or not. Perhaps it's too soon to say. He's only been there for three weeks.

四、翻译句子

1. John will come to see you the day after tomorrow.

2. The mechanics will repair your car the week after next.

3. Linda is going to drive you home.

4. He has studied here for 30 days.

5. Where have you been?

6. 外面下着大雨，孩子们都呆在家里。

7. 你刚拍完一部新电影吗？

8. 今年你们打算去哪里度假？

9. 你打算出售你的房子吗？

10. 我已出售了我的房子。

五、用一般过去时或现在完成时填空

1. A：_____ you _____ (have) enough to eat?

　　B：Yes, I _____ (have) plenty. Thank you.

2. We _____ (live) in London for two years and then _____ (go) to Edinburgh.

3. A：_____ you _____ (plant) your peas?

　　B：Yes, I _____ (plant) them on Tuesday.

4. You can't go out because you _____ (not finish) your homework yet.

5. A：When _____ you _____ (arrive)?

　　B：We _____ (arrive) at 2：00.

六、书面表达

Write at least 50 words about the topic "My Favorite Sport". You can use the words and expressions in the box.(以"我最喜爱的运动"为题,写一篇不少于50个单词的短文,要求内容通顺。方框内的单词和词组供使用。)

like, best, interesting, helpful, often, sometimes, make me strong, take part in

七、完成句子:将 for 和 since 填入下列空内

1. I've studied English _____ almost two years, but haven't learnt anything.

2. I have played football for the school team(校队)_____ last January.

3. I haven't seen Mary _____ a few weeks.

4. He has worked in Paris _____ the summer before last.

5. Mother has been ill in bed _____ five years.

6. Johnny hasn't been to school _____ his illness.

7. Tom hasn't done any homework _____ a week.

Lesson 91~92

一、单词拼写：根据所给中文意思补全下列单词

1. __rr__ve(到达 *v.*)   2. m__v__(移 *v.*)   3. r__m__mb__(记得 *v.*)

4. m__ss(想念 *v.*)   5. lib_____y(图书馆 *n.*)

二、语法和词汇：从 A、B、C、D 中选出正确答案

1. —Look out! The traffic is moving fast!

　—Thanks, I _____ .　　　　　　　　　　　　　　　　　　　　（北京，中考）

　A. do　　　　　B. will　　　　　C. can　　　　　D. don't

2. —Lucy didn't come to school yesterday, did she?

　—_____ , because she was not feeling very well.

　A. No, she didn't　B. Yes, she did　C. Yes, she didn't　D. No, she did

3. _____ Chinese people are _____ hardworking people.　　　　（广州，中考）

　A. 不填/不填　　B. A/不填　　　C. The/the　　　D. The/a

4. —May I speak to John?

　—Sorry, he _____ Japan. But he _____ in two days.　　（焦作，中考）

　A. has been to/will come back　　B. has gone to/will be back

　C. has been in/would come back　　D. has gone to/won't come back

5. —Is Mr. Smith really very ill?

　—_____ . He's in hospital.　　　　　　　　　　　　　　　　（焦作，中考）

　A. I don't think so　　　　　　B. No, he isn't

　C. I hope so　　　　　　　　　D. I'm afraid so

6. If you come to see me, I _____ the money.

　A. pay　　　　　B. will pay　　　C. have paid　　D. pays

7. I don't know _____ you're talking about.

　A. /　　　　　　B. that　　　　　C. what　　　　D. which

8. She _____ Tom to her party next time.

　A. invites　　　　B. will invite　　C. invited　　　D. has invited

9. Please give me two _____ to Washington.

　A. turn tickets　　B. return tickets　C. return ticket　D. come tickets

10. I _____ to him tomorrow.

　A. have written　　B. am writing　　C. wrote　　　D. shall write

11. Tim _____ out next night. Neither will I.

　A. goes　　　　　B. went　　　　　C. will go　　　D. won't go

12. _____ the end, we won the game. We were so happy.

　A. In　　　　　　B. With　　　　　C. By　　　　　D. On

13. What colour is her _____ ?

　A. shoes　　　　　B. coat　　　　　C. trousers　　　D. glasses

14. The black cat is _____ the door.

　A. in　　　　　　B. behind　　　　C. under　　　　D. to

15. This is my shirt. Please _____.

    A. put on it   B. put it on   C. put them on   D. put on them

三、用现在完成时或一般过去时填空

1. A：When _____ you _____(meet) him?

   B：I _____(meet) him yesterday evening.

2. A：_____ you _____(be) to London before?

   B：Yes, I _____(spend) my holiday there last year.

   A：_____ you _____(have) a good time?

   B：No, it never _____(stop) raining.

四、翻译句子

1. 你什么时候出售了你的房子？   6. Mr. West sold his house last week.

2. 上星期。   7. The new people moved into the house yesterday.

3. 你什么时候搬到新房去？   8. I am sweeping the floor now.

4. 明天下午。   9. They have painted the house green.

5. 我会想你的。我们已是多年的好邻居了。 10. I often go swimming in the river.

五、用 do, did, does 或 don't, didn't 填空

1. He always helps others as Lei Feng _____.

2. Jane practises hard, but you _____.

3. Tom didn't like dancing. I _____, either.

4. A：Who won?

   B：Jim _____.

5. My secretary worked later than you _____ at the office.

6. A："Shall I write to him right now?"

   B：Yes, you _____.

7. I studies English harder than you _____.

8. A：Do you like playing football?

   B：Yes, I _____.

六、书面表达

    Write at least six sentences about the topic "On the way to school", use no less than 50 words. You may use the words and expressions in the box (以"在上学的路上"为题，写一篇文章，不少于 50 个单词。方框内的单词和短语供使用。)

> What's wrong with, be lost, see sb. doing sth., son's address, do a good deed (做好事)

七、完成句子：用括号内所给的时间状语改写下列句子

1. He goes to work early in the morning. (tomorrow)

2. My father goes to work by car every day. (tomorrow)

3. We often get up at six in the morning. (tomorrow morning)

4. Mr. West sold his house last week. (the day after tomorrow)

5. The new people moved into the house yesterday. (tomorrow afternoon)

6. I am sweeping the floor now. (tonight)

7. They have painted the house green. (tomorrow)

Lesson 93～94

一、单词拼写:根据所给中文意思补全下列单词

1. p＿l＿t(飞行员 *n.*) 2. rep＿＿＿＿(修理 *v.*) 3. b＿＿＿＿＿tiful(美丽的 *adj.*)

4. T＿ky＿(东京 *n.*) 5. R＿m＿(罗马 *n.*)

二、语法和词汇:从 A、B、C、D 中选出正确答案

1. We'll be away for two weeks because we'll have a _____. （北京,中考）
   A. two-weeks holiday   B. two weeks' holidays
   C. two-week holiday   D. two-weeks' holiday

2. The number of the students in our grade _____ about six _____ — _____ of them are
   girls. （武汉,中考）
   A. are/hundreds/two-thirds   B. is/hundred/two-third
   C. is/hundred/two thirds   D. are/hundreds/two third

3. He wrote a _____ composition in English but there were quite a few spelling mistakes.
   （郑州,中考）
   A. two hundred words   B. two-hundred-words
   C. two-hundred-word   D. two hundreds word

4. Lesson 49 is another way of saying the _____ lesson. （北京,中考）
   A. fourty-nine   B. forty-ninth   C. forty-nine   D. fourth-ninth

5. He spent _____ yuan on the new computer. （上海,中考）
   A. five thousand,three hundred and forty B. five thousand,three hundred and forties
   C. five thousands,three hundred and forty D. five thousands,hundreds and forty

6. Jack broke his leg,_____?
   A. did Jack   B. didn't Jack   C. did he   D. didn't he

7. The model is _____ than that one.
   A. expensive   B. expensiver   C. more expensive D. most expensive

8. Which is _____,the green one,the black one or the red one?
   A. the wellest   B. better   C. more better   D. the best

9. I'll buy the house _____ installments.
   A. on   B. with   C. in   D. for

10. "I can't go to the party with you.""_____!"
    A. What a pity   B. What the pity   C. What pities   D. What pity

11. What colour's it? _____.
    A. It's in red   B. It is blue   C. Its white   D. It does black

12. She _____ TV last night.
    A. watch   B. watching   C. watchs   D. watched

13. I _____ my jobs in two days.
    A. finish   B. finished   C. will finish   D. finishing

14. They _____ a car next month.
    A. buy   B. will buy   C. bought   D. buying

三、翻译句子

1. You must be home at half past ten.
2. We always enjoy ourselves.
3. Aren't you lucky!
4. It was an exciting finish.
5. She doesn't know London very well, and she lost her way.

6. 假期去哪儿? 去纽约。
7. 我父母亲下个星期坐飞机去巴黎。
8. 他只有 25 岁,但他去过许多国家。
9. Mary 在干什么?
10. 她在图书馆里看书。

四、用所给动词的适当时态形式填空

1. _____ your mother _____ (return) from work yet?
   No. She _____ (come) back at 7 this evening.
2. When _____ you _____ (buy) this tape-recorder?
   I _____ (buy) it the year before last.
3. At this moment, he _____ (be) in the library.
   He _____ (read) a magazine there.
4. _____ you always _____ (get) up so late?
   No, I _____ (get) up at five yesterday.

五、介词填空

1. The plane is going to leave _____ a minute.
2. Please give my regards _____ your parents.
3. Who has the last word _____ that matter?
4. Mary can write letters _____ Chinese.
5. Shall I get his hat _____ him _____ the next room?
6. Why can't you decide _____ the moment?
7. We'll be here the week _____ next.
8. He has been _____ nearly every country _____ the world.
9. Nigel was _____ the army when he left school.
10. He is leaving _____ Beijing next week.

六、书面表达

说明:请以《怎样种白菜》为题,写一篇百字短文,简介种植过程。

要求:1.春天是种菜的大好季节。
　　　2.箱种植简要过程。
　　　3.移植到地里。
　　　4.管理,包括浇水、施肥、除草等。

参考词语:Chinese cabbage　　be the best season　　sow...seeds　　find a box　　put soil at
　　　　　put seeds on　　　　cover...with...　　　plenty of water　place...in the shade

七、完成句子:将下列句子译成英语

1.假期去哪儿? 去纽约。
2.我父母亲下个星期坐飞机去巴黎。
3.他只有二十五岁,但他去过许多国家。
4.Mary 在干什么? 她在图书馆里看书。
5.为学英语,我买了一台收音机,上个星期买的。
6.外面下着大雨,孩子们都呆在家里。

Lesson 95~96

一、单词拼写:根据所给中文意思补全下列单词

1. s __ a __ i __ n(车站 *n.*) 2. h ___ dwr __ ting(书写 *n.*) 3. b __ h __ nd(后面 *adv.*)

4. t __ b __ cc __ (烟草 *n.*) 5. pl ___ f ____ m(站台 *n.*)

二、语法和词汇:从 A、B、C、D 中选出正确答案

1. Which of the following sentences is WRONG? _____ （陕西,中考)

   A. Can you stay here a few days more?

   B. Peter knows that I have something interesting to tell you.

   C. Wait a minute. I have interesting something to tell you.

   D. You had better take off your shoes before you enter the room.

2. It's not fine today. You'd better _____ out. Why _____ stay at home watching TV? （上海,中考)

   A. not to go/not   B. not go/not

   C. don't go/不填   D. to not go/不填

3. You'd better _____ football in the street. （苏州,中考）

   A. not play   B. not to play   C. don't play   D. not playing

4. There is _____ money in the bank. （大理,中考）

   A. little   B. many   C. a number of   D. plenty of

5. Hurry up! Or we will not _____ the bus. （内蒙古,中学）

   A. miss   B. catch   C. keep   D. meet

6. What _____ you see in the picture?

   A. are   B. can   C. is   D. /

7. This is an old bike. Do you want a new _____?

   A. one   B. it   C. that   D. /

8. Jack，come _____ ,please.

   A. to here   B. there   C. to there   D. here

9. I have to see the doctor when I _____.

   A. am hungry   B. cross the road

   C. don't feel well   D. do my homework

10. Lesson Ten isn't as _____ as Lesson Nine. It's hard to read.

    A. easy   B. difficult   C. new   D. easier

11. My mother often _____ for a picnic on Sunday.

    A. want   B. wants   C. wanting   D. wanted

12. The old man has two children but _____ of them lives with him.

    A. both   B. none   C. neither   D. all

13. The little boy is very young，_____ he can look after himself well.

    A. so   B. but   C. if   D. or

14. The seats in the middle of the cinema are _____ of all.

    A. better   B. good   C. the best   D. worse

109

15. You had better _____ when you do some shopping.

    A. be polite   B. stand in line

    C. wait for your turn   D. jump the queue

三、翻译句子

1. He must not take the medicine.

2. I must call the doctor at once.

3. Peter had better study hard.

4. We had better go back to the station.

5. Linda had better not tell him the news.

6. 现在是 11 点钟了,你最好去睡觉。

7. 你看上去很苍白(pale),你最好马上去看医生。

8. 两天后我们必须完成工作,我们最好现在就开始工作。

9. 你最好用钢笔写这封信。

四、用所给动词的适当时态填空

1. I _____ (write) a book at the moment. I _____ (finish) it next month.

2. My family often _____ (go) for a picnic on Sunday. But next Sunday we _____ (stay) at home.

3. It _____ (be) ten o'clock now. I _____ (just finish) my homework. I _____ (go) to bed in ten minutes' time.

4. My brother usually _____ (get) up late. But tomorrow he _____ (get) up early, because his friends _____ (come) to see him.

5. _____ you _____ (be) at home tomorrow afternoon? No, I _____ . I _____ (go) to town with my friend.

五、书面表达

110

    根据中文设置的情景和英文提示,写出语法正确,意思连贯,符合逻辑的英文文段。所给的英文提示词语必须都用上,中文提示内容不必逐字翻译。(字数 60~80)

假如你是李玲,现在你给你的英国朋友 Jane 写一封信,告诉他你和同学们上周日去香山公园郊游的活动和感受。信的开头和结尾已给出。

你们早上七点钟在学校门口集合,大约 8:30 到达香山公园……

参考词语:meet, arrive, at the foot of the hill, have a party, play games, climb, on the top of, see, how, beautiful, feel proud(自豪的), live, Beijing, the 2008 Olympic Games, hold

Dear Jane,

    Last Sunday my classmates and I went to Xiangshan Park.

_____

_____

_____

    I hope we will meet in Beijing in 2008.

    Best wishes.

Yours,

Li Ling

六、完成句子:将下列句子译成英语

1.现在是 11 点钟了,你最好去睡觉。

2.你看上去很苍白(pale),你最好马上去看医生。

3.两天后我们必须完成工作,我们最好现在就开始工作。

4.你最好用钢笔写这封信。

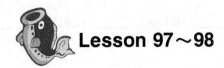

Lesson 97～98

一、单词拼写：根据所给中文意思补全下列单词

1. h __ndl __（提手,柄 *n.*）　2. p ___haps（也许 *adv.*）　3. ___ployee（职员 *n.*）

4. p __nc __（便士 *n.*）　　5. l __ b __l（标签 *n.*）

二、语法和词汇：从 A、B、C、D 中选出正确答案

1. Mr. Huang _____ London for ten years. 　　　　　　　　　　　（浙江,中考）

　　A. has gone　　　B. has been　　　C. has gone to　　　D. has been in

2. Excuse me,does this new car _____ your family? 　　　　　　（福建,中考）

　　A. is belonged to　　　　　　　B. belongs to

　　C. have been belonged to　　　　D. belong to

3. —Can you help me write down my address on this envelope? It is _____.

　　—No problem.

　　A. 87,Island Street　　　　　　B. Island Street,87

　　C. on 87,Island Street　　　　　D. in Island Street,87

4. —_____ meet my old classmate in the street the day before yesterday. 　（江西,中考）

　　A. had　　　B. Happened to　　C. used to　　　D. could

5. He has _____ cold for a couple of days. 　　　　　　　　　　（江西,中考）

　　A. caught　　　B. had　　　C. got　　　D. been

6. He will _____ you on the subject of war and peace.

　　A. address　　　B. say　　　C. speak　　　D. name

7. Let's stand _____ the last(最后的)student.

　　A. next　　　B. in front of　　C. at　　　D. at the back of

8. I can't _____ my ruler. Can you help me?

　　A. find　　　B. see　　　C. look at　　　D. look like

9. "Have you got any milk?""I haven't got _____ milk. I've got very _____."

　　A. much,a little　　B. any,little　　C. some,a little　　D. much,little

10. Can you give me _____ to eat?

　　A. different anything　　　　　B. different something

　　C. anything different　　　　　D. something different

11. We _____ for NewYork next week.

　　A. are leaving　　B. leave　　　C. left　　　D. leaves

12. Do you have any _____ kind of ballpen?

　　A. one　　　B. the other　　　C. other　　　D. another

13. Lucy picked _____ apples.

　　A. only a few　　B. quite a little　　C. a lots of　　　D. much

三、根据括号内的意义,用合适的代词填空

1. _____（他的）brother is a pilot,_____（我的）is a teacher and _____（她的）is an engineer.

2. These shoes are not _____（我的）,_____（它们）are _____（你的）.

3. _____（我）have done _____（我的）homework. Have _____（你）done _____（你的）?

4. These keys are not _____（我们的）. _____（它们）are _____（他们的）.

5. _____（她的）sister is a good friend of _____（我的）.

四、翻译句子

1. Your hat is red, mine is brown.

2. I have my hat, and he has his.

3. That book is hers, not yours.

4. We have done our work.

5. The train is going to leave. We must say good-bye.

6. 我也会想你们的，请代我向你的全家问好。

7. 我明天将飞往上海。

8. 这本书是鲁迅的。

9. 你可以吃饭，但你必须先洗手。

10. 他说他不会用英语写信。

五、用下列词语填空:the other day, describe, leave, miss, be worth, belong to

1. It's an interesting book. It _____ seeing.

2. When _____ you _____ your purse?

3. Would you like to _____ a message for her?

4. China _____ the third world.

5. We _____ him badly since he _____.

6. When _____ he _____? By air or by train?

7. I happened to meet a friend of mine in the park _____.

8. I _____ the accident in detail.

六、书面表达

112

_____
_____
_____
_____
_____
_____
_____
_____

Mr. Larry King
36 Bridge Rood
Richmond
VIC3132
AUSTRALIA

写作:根据中文意思和英文提示词语，写出意思连贯，符合逻辑的英文文段。所给英文提示词语必须都用上，中文提示内容不必逐句翻译，每组英文提示所写出的句数不限。

美国学生 Jim 最近又来到北京,去了王府井,发现这里发生了巨大的变化,请你以 Jim 的身份给父母写一张明信片,介绍……

1. happy, visit, again

2. change, take place

3. go, Wang Fu Jing Street, morning, building, shop market

4. flower, poster（宣传画）, put, for, the Olympics

Lesson 99～100

一、单词拼写：根据所给中文意思补全下列单词

1. f＿ll（跌 *v.*）　2. ＿＿cited（激动的 *adj.*）　3. ex＿m＿n＿tion（考试 *n.*）

4. r＿y（光线 *n.*）5. b＿ck（背部 *n.*）

二、语法和词汇：从 A、B、C、D 中选出正确答案

1. He asked me ＿＿＿＿＿＿＿＿.　　　　　　　　　　　　　　　　　（济南，中考）

 A. if she will come　　　　　　　B. how many books I want to have

 C. they would help us do it　　　　D. what was wrong with me

2. —Could you tell me ＿＿＿＿＿＿＿？

 —Sorry.　I don't know. I was not at the meeting.　　　　　　　（江西，中考）

 A. what does he say at the meeting　　B. what did he say at the meeting

 C. what he says at the meeting　　　　D. what he said at the meeting

3. Which of the following is wrong? ＿＿＿＿＿＿＿＿　　　　　　　　（浙江，中考）

 A. Sue has borrowed the CD disc.

 B. What do you think of the book?

 C. He take 2 hours to do his maths homework.

 D. I found it difficult to understand what he said.

4. Can you tell me ＿＿＿＿＿＿＿ Beijing?　　　　　　　　　　　　（福建，中考）

 A. what time their plane will reach　　B. what time will their plane arrive in

 C. what time their plane will arrive　　D. what time will their plane get to

5. —Do you know ＿＿＿＿＿＿＿？ I'm going to see him.

 —Sorry, I don't know.　　　　　　　　　　　　　　　　　　（北京，中考）

 A. where does Mr. Li live　　　　　B. where did Mr. Li live

 C. where Mr. Li lives　　　　　　　D. where Mr. Li lived

6. There is a watch ＿＿＿＿＿on the ground.　I want to know whose ＿＿＿＿.

 A. lay; it is　　　B. lay; is it　　　C. lying; it is　　　D. lying; is it

7. This is the most beautiful park I have ＿＿＿＿＿visited.

 A. ever　　　　B. never　　　　C. not　　　　D. yet

8. —What about having some drinks first?

 —＿＿＿＿＿？

 A. Well, will you　　　　　　　　B. OK, shall we

 C. Yes, don't we　　　　　　　　D. Sure, why not

9. Lily, please find the city of Beijing ＿＿＿＿＿＿＿.

 A. on the map　　B. on the floor　　C. at home　　　D. in the room

10. Let's go ＿＿＿＿＿＿＿ home together.

 A. to　　　　　　B. at　　　　　　C. in　　　　　　D. /

11. Could you tell me ＿＿＿＿＿？

 A. when will Mary come　　　　　B. when Mary will come

 C. when did Mary come　　　　　　D. when Mary comes

12. This key ＿＿＿＿＿for locking the door.

A. is used   B. used   C. uses   D. are used

13. The teacher told us _____.

    A. don't play on the road   B. not be late again

    C. come to school on foot   D. to cross the road carefully

14. —Where is your father? We haven't seen each other for weeks.

    —_____.

    A. He has been to America   B. He has gone to England

    C. He is going to Australia   D. He would visit my grandparents

15. The Young Pioneers didn't know _____.

    A. where will they go   B. what they would do next

    C. when could they go   D. how did they get there

三、翻译句子

1. That was a long time ago, wasn't it? Not that long ago.

2. I'm not more than twenty.

3. I must water the garden.

4. Did you serve this gentleman half an hour ago?

5. After they had entered the house, they went into the dining room.

6. 老师给了她一本英语词典。

7. 老板马上要和 Linda 小姐谈话。

8. 他告诉我今晚不要外出。

9. 母亲告诉我她明天去北京出差。

10. 她要孩子们别在课堂上交谈。

四、填写句子

1. Ted is afraid that _____(他站不起来).

2. Pat says that _____(Ted 最好去看医生).

3. Pat says that _____(她去给 Carter 医生打电话).

4. The doctor says that _____(他马上就来).

五、用反身代词填空

1. I was thinking to _____ how strange the boys were.

2. Your hair's dirty. Look at _____ in the mirror.

3. The cat enjoyed _____ with the children.

4. The students could only practise with _____ after school.

5. We're teaching _____ English.

6. Did they enjoy _____ at the party?

7. She cut _____ with a knife.

8. He fell off the bike and hurt _____.

六、完成句子:用括号内的动词将句子改成宾语从句

e. g. You had better stay in bed. (I think)

    =I think that you had better stay in bed.

1. He will pass the exam. (I hope)

2. The doors and the windows are all closed. (I believe)

3. She is coming tomorrow. (I'm glad)

4. You missed the train. (I'm sorry)

5. He isn't feeling very well. (He says)

6. I can't help you. (I'm afraid)

7. Tom is right. (She thinks)

8. He will return home next week. (I'm sure)

9. I haven't got any money. (She understands)

10. She has cleaned the classroom. (The teacher knows)

Lesson 101～102

一、单词拼写:根据所给中文意思补全下列单词

1. __ss __c___tion(协会 *n.*)   2. __xc__pt(除外 *adv.*)

3. l__m__n__de(柠檬水 *n.*)   4. kn__ck(敲 *v.*)   5. t___let(厕所 *n.*)

二、语法和词汇:从 A、B、C、D 中选出正确答案

1. Mr. Li would like to _____ us an interesting story?   (北京,中考)

   A. tell   B. talk   C. say   D. speak

2. He has hardly finished his work,_____?   (河北,中考)

   A. hasn't he   B. has he   C. does   D. doesn't he

3. She thinks she can get there on time,_____ she?   (上海,中考)

   A. can   B. doesn't   C. can't   D. does

4. _____ picture books in class,please.   (陕西,中考)

   A. Not read   B. No read   C. Not reading   D. Don't read

5. —You are not going out today,are you?

   —_____. I want to go shopping.   (北京,中考)

   A. Yes,I'm not   B. No,I'm not   C. Yes,I am   D. No,I am

6. Linda often _____ her homework in the evening,but this evening she _____ TV.

   A. does,watches   B. is doing,watches

   C. does,is watching   D. is doing,is watching

7. I often go to work _____ seven _____ the morning.

   A. in,in   B. in,at   C. at,at   D. at,in

8. Kathy isn't _____ school. She is _____ home.

   A. at,at   B. at,in   C. in,at   D. in,in

9. "It's dangerous here. We'd better go out quickly. "

   "But I think we should let _____ go out first. "

   A. woman and children   B. women and child

   C. woman and child   D. women and children

10. Mary says to me that she _____ to Shanghai once.

   A. has been   B. went   C. had been   D. goes

11. The water is too hot. We'd better _____ it right now.

   A. not to drink   B. don't drink   C. not drink   D. drink not

12. —I don't know _____.

   —Let me help you.

   A. which one to choose   B. to choose which one

   C. which one shall choose   D. which to choose one

13. —Thanks very much for your nice present.

   —_____.

   A. I'm glad you like it   B. No,thanks

   C. Oh,it's nothing   D. No,it's very cheap

14. —May I go swimming now?

—No, you _____. You must finish your homework first.

A. mustn't   B. may not   C. couldn't   D. needn't

三、间接引语改为直接引语

1. Mary says that she has finished her homework.

2. The children say that they have never been to London.

3. The mechanics say that I need a new car.

4. Mrs. Blake says that she is waiting for a bus.

5. Tom says that Mary can speak English very well.

6. Mr. West says that he will sell that house.

四、翻译句子

1. I live in a very old town which is surrounded by beautiful woods.

2. Sally was very excited because she never travelled on a train before.

3. After the train left the station, the lady opened her handbag and took out a red powder compact.

4. You're going to have roast beef and potatoes again tonight.

5. I think that I've hurt my back.

6. 你们乘船去,还是乘飞机去?

7. 你刚才一定是以每小时 70 英里的速度开车。

8. 我们的乘客中没人能换开这张钞票?

9. 你好吗?

10. 我们已经做完作业了。

五、用 else 与 something,anything,nothing,nobody,anybody,nowhere,what 或 who 搭配填空

1. _____ is right.

2. _____ is coming?

3. _____ do you want?

4. We went only to the cinema and _____.

5. Are we all here? Is _____ absent?

六、书面表达

假如今天你是值日生,请根据下表的提示,写一篇80词左右的值日生报告。开头语已为你写好。

注意:文中应包括表中所有的内容,可以适当增加细节,使内容连贯。

日　期	4 月 22 日　　星期二
天　气	晴
出勤情况	Jim 缺席(上周回美国度假)
一件事	1. 露西拾到我丢失的一本图书馆的书 2. 送还图书馆 3. 图书馆的王教师告诉我今后应…… 4. 感谢露西

开头语:It's my turn to be on duty today...

七、完成句子:将下列句子变成间接引语

1. The student says:"I always do my homework in the evening."

2. My father says to me:"You must get up at 8."

3. Jimmy says:"I am very hungry."

4. Linda says:"We are going to see a film tonight."

5. The little girl says:"I have lost my way."

117

Lesson 103～104

一、单词拼写:根据所给中文意思补全下列单词

1. p＿ss（通过 v.）　　2. v＿s＿tor（游客 n.）　　3. en＿＿gh（足够的 adj.）

4. emb＿＿＿＿＿＿ed（尴尬的 adj.）　　　　　5. r＿st（其余者 pron.）

二、语法和词汇:从 A、B、C、D 中选出正确答案

1. The math question is so difficult ＿＿＿＿ I cannot work it out.　　（北京,中考）

　　A. what　　　　　B. that　　　　　C. why　　　　　D. when

2. Kate said that she didn't feel very ＿＿＿ today.　　（福建,中考）

　　A. well　　　　　B. good　　　　　C. nice　　　　　D. better

3. The coat I bought last week is too big for me. I'd like to change it for a ＿＿＿ one.

　　（广州,中考）

　　A. small　　　　B. large　　　　C. nicer　　　　D. smaller

4. I was ill yesterday. But now I feel much ＿＿＿. I think I can go to school tomorrow.

　　（海南,中考）

　　A. worse　　　　B. bad　　　　C. better　　　　D. well

5. He eats ＿＿＿ food, so he is ＿＿＿ fat.　　（武汉,中考）

　　A. much too/too much　　　　　　B. much too/too many

　　C. too much/much too　　　　　　D. too much/many too

6. ＿＿＿ in the library.

　　A. Not talk　　B. Talk not　　C. Don't talk　　D. Not to talk

7. The boys are ill. They mustn't eat ＿＿＿ food.

　　A. rich　　　　B. any　　　　C. fresh　　　　D. pure

8. Summer vacation(暑假)usually starts ＿＿＿ July.

　　A. on　　　　B. at　　　　C. in　　　　D. of

9. Before liberation he had no chance ＿＿＿.

　　A. of going to the school　　　　B. to go to school

　　C. to go to the school　　　　　D. going to school

10. You didn't study hard,＿＿＿ you?

　　A. did　　　B. did not　　C. don't　　D. do

11. The students have already left,＿＿＿ they?

　　A. have　　　B. did　　　C. didn't　　D. haven't

12. The radio message ＿＿＿ received yet.

　　A. hasn't been　　B. has been　　C. hasn't being　　D. has being

13. Some people never ＿＿＿ home,others ＿＿＿ all the time.

　　A. live,trip　　B. let,journey　　C. leave,travel　　D. leave,voyage

14. —I'm sorry I ＿＿＿ my homework at home.

　　—That's all right. Don't forget ＿＿＿ it to school this afternoon.

　　A. forget...to take　　　　　B. forget...to bring

　　C. left...to take　　　　　　D. left...to bring

15. Jane will bring her brother here,_____ she?

    A. is   B. do   C. won't   D. will

三、将下列句子改为感叹句

1. He is a clever boy.

2. This is a lovely dress.

3. They are wonderful actors.

4. It is a high building.

5. It is a terrible film.

6. These are beautiful pictures.

四、翻译句子

1. Please show me the pictures which you took on the trip.

2. The story that the teacher told us is very interesting.

3. The students whom I teach are very hard-working.

4. The woman who is typing a letter is his secretary.

5. The man who is sitting there is my English teacher.

6. 这就是他给我的书。

7. 你早上读的书难吗？

8. 他开的那辆小汽车是红色的。

9. 住在楼下的那个男士是个飞行员。

10. 你认识和玛丽一起走的那个人吗？

五、用 too，very 或 enough 填空

1. It was cold _____ to wear a fur coat.

2. The book was _____ easy for her.

3. It's right _____ for reading.

4. We have _____ books for everyone.

5. He's _____ glad that you like his gift.

6. The desk is _____ heavy for me to carry.

7. A：Are you happy?

    B：No, not _____.

8. This is a _____ good apple. May I have another one please?

六、书面表达

    根据下面汉语的提示，以"My Schoolbag"为题，用英语写一篇 50～60 个词的短文。要求内容完整，语言规范。

    1. 书包的形状、颜色、制作材料；

    2. 书包的功能与用途；

    3. 你对书包的感情；

    4. 下列单词供选用：rectangular 长方形的，cloth 布，leather 皮革。

七、完成句子:仿照例句改写下列句子

Example：The car is very cheap. Mr. Smith can buy it.

            The car is cheap enough for Mr. Smith to buy.

1. That house is too expensive. We can not buy it.

2. The pear is very soft. My grandmother can eat it.

3. It was too dark. I could not go out.

4. The wall is very low. You can jump off it.

5. Sue is clever. She can answer the questions.

119

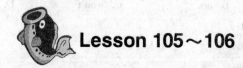

Lesson 105～106

一、单词拼写:根据所给中文意思补全下列单词

1. m＿st＿k＿（错误 *n.*）　　2. sl＿p（滑倒 *v.*）　　3. c＿rre＿＿＿（改正 *v.*）

4. l＿s＿（遗失 *v.*）　　　　5. c＿rry（搬 *v.*）

二、语法和词汇:从 A、B、C、D 中选出正确答案

1. Sorry, I can only remember the pronunciation of the world, but I cannot ＿＿＿＿ it.

（青岛,中考）

    A. say   B. speak   C. spell   D. tell

2. How careless you are! You have ＿＿＿＿ so many mistakes in your writing.　　（烟台,中考）

    A. done   B. made   C. make   D. did

3. Mother told me ＿＿＿＿ take off the winter clothes so quickly. Maybe it would be cold days later.　　（北京,中考）

    A. didn't   B. not   C. not to   D. don't

4. Look! The river is ＿＿＿＿ water and fish.　　（上海,中考）

    A. filled of   B. full of   C. full   D. all

5. I am afraid there might be many mistakes in my paper. Will you help me to ＿＿＿＿ it?

（北京,中考）

    A. make   B. keep   C. correct   D. right

6. Jimmy ＿＿＿＿ Father Christmas.

    A. seemed as   B. looked like   C. looked as   D. seemed

7. The police let him off. They ＿＿＿＿ him.

    A. allowed   B. permitted   C. didn't forbid   D. didn't punish

8. —He doesn't have to go to school tomorrow.

    —That's ＿＿＿＿ good news for him.

    A. a   B. one   C. an   D. /

9. —We're going to the Summer Palace(颐和园)this afternoon.

    —Enjoy ＿＿＿＿!

    A. you   B. yourself   C. ourselves   D. yourselves

10. She reads magazines ＿＿＿＿ one hour each day.

    A. for   B. in   C. after   D. at

11. How many people were ＿＿＿＿ at the meeting?

    A. missing   B. lost   C. appear   D. present

12. On her birthday, the girl is looking forward ＿＿＿＿ a gift.

    A. to be given   B. to being given   C. to give   D. to giving

13. The book ＿＿＿＿ by a famous writer.

    A. believe to write   B. believed to be written

    C. was believed to write   D. was believed to be written

14. Tell him not ＿＿＿＿ so much noise.

    A. make   B. making   C. made   D. to make

15. No permission has ＿＿＿＿ for anybody to enter the building.

A. been given　　B. given　　　　C. to give　　　D. be giving

三、用所给动词的适当形式填空

Mrs. Brown _____ (be) very surprised, but she _____ (thank) the policemen and they _____ (leave).

"But, grandfather." She _____ (ask) the old gentleman. "You _____ (go) to that park every day. How _____ you _____ (lose) your way?"

The old man _____ (smile) and _____ (say):

"I _____ (not lose) my way. I just _____ (feel) tired and _____ (not want) to walk home."

四、翻译句子

1. 家里有人吗?

2. 我肯定 Tom 已经邀请他们过来了。

3. 她又试了一件衣服,但这件衣服还是不适合她。

4. 别打断我的话,我不是在开玩笑。

5. 我不想吃什么,我只是想喝点东西。

6. I found a sign which said, "Anyone who leaves litter in these woods will be prosecuted!"

7. What I saw made me very sad.

8. She began to make up her face.

9. Tell Mary we'll be late for dinner this evening.

10. He said he was busy.

五、请将下面的祈使句改为直接引语

1. Don't play football after school.　　　2. Don't be late for class.

3. Don't drop the vase.　　　　　　　　4. Don't speak here.

5. Please tell them the story in English.　6. Get up early.

7. Sweep the floor please.　　　　　　　8. Go out and see it.

六、书面表达

　　假如你叫李明,因患重感冒今天和明后天不能上学。请你参考右边方框中所给的词语给你的外籍英语教师写一张请假条,说明你这三天不能上学的原因。

not feel well	a bad cold
stay in bed	can't go to school
for two days	get well soon

注意:1. 开头部分已写好,只需接着写。

　　　2. 尽量使用方框中所给的词语,也可适当增加一些词语,使所写的短文正确、连贯。

　　　3. 字数:60 个左右。

Dear Mrs. Green,

　　I'm sorry to tell you that

七、完成句子

1. Is this house large enough for us _____?

　A. living　　　　　B. living in　　　　C. to live　　　　D. to live in

2. He refused _____ the dinner.

　A. to have attended　B. having attended　C. attending　　D. to attend

3. You needn't decide yet _____.

　A. to help him or not　　　　　　B. helping him or not

　C. whether to help him or not　　　D. if to help him.

4. Now the need _____ other people's language is becoming greater and greater.

　A. to learn　　　　B. learning　　　　C. to be learned　　D. being learned

Lesson 107～108

一、单词拼写:根据所给中文意思补全下列单词

1. sh___(给…看 v.)   2. li___en(听 v.)   3. fav___r__te(最喜欢的 adj.)

4. p___nt(油漆 n.)   5. ph__t__grap__(照片 n.)

二、语法和词汇:从 A、B、C、D 中选出正确答案

1. Now air in our town is _____ than it used to be, Something must be done to improve it.

  (北京,中考)

   A. very good   B. much better   C. rather than   D. even worse

2. This book is _____ on the subject.   (河南,中考)

   A. the much best B. much the best   C. very much best D. very the best

3. Usually Xiao Li spends _____ time doing homework than Xiao Chen does.   (山东,中考)

   A. little   B. less   C. few   D. fewer

4. Which is the _____,the train station,the bus station or the airport?   (云南,中考)

   A. far   B. farthest   C. father   D. more far

5. I was feeling tired last night,so I went to bed _____ than usual.   (重庆,中考)

   A. early   B. earlier   C. late   D. later

6. Would you _____ a cup of tea?

   A. as   B. like   C. for   D. of

7. Could you _____ me a favour?

   A. to do   B. do   C. doing   D. does

8. It is the _____ film of all.

   A. interesting   B. interestinger   C. interestingest   D. most interesing

9. Why was he absent from school? He may _____ busy.

   A. be   B. have been   C. is   D. are

10. Mrs. Williams was _____ the butcher's this morning.

   A. in   B. on   C. at   D. be

11. He met an old friend _____ the way home.

   A. to   B. in   C. by   D. on

12. I'm going to stay at my friend's _____ the weekend.

   A. at   B. for   C. in   D. on

13. Mother does most of _____ at home.

   A. clean   B. cleaning   C. to clean   D. the cleaning

14. At the beginning of the class,the teacher asked us to _____ our text-books.

   A. take out   B. take in   C. take off   D. take up

15. Office ladies always _____ their faces before they go to work.

   A. make up   B. make out   C. make   D. make for

三、完成下列反意疑问句

1. It's a fine day,_____?

2. You are studying English,_____?

3. He will write to you,_____?

4. They went to the theatre yesterday evening,_____?

5. She often gets up early,_____?

四、翻译句子

1. He told me that they were joking.

2. He said she looked tired.

3. He told me she had arrived.

4. The reporter said she was making a film.

5. They told me they didn't want their dinner.

6. 他告诉我他已经好久没回家了。

7. 他们告诉我们,他们刚拍完了一部新电影。

8. 我告诉她,我准备买一辆小车。

9. 医生说:"你明天可以出院了。"

10. 她说她那时正在打一封信。

五、用比较级完成下列各句

1. It's _____ in Beijing than in Shanghai. (cold)

2. There are _____ boys than girls in our school. (few)

3. A _____ name is _____ than gold. (good)

4. It's _____ to be healthy than to be _____. (good, rich)

5. The sun is _____ than the earth. (big)

6. It's _____ today than yesterday. (cold)

7. He is _____ than any other boy in the class. (clever)

8. Your jacket is _____ than mine. (short)

六、书面表达

Mr. Li 了解到李香发生车祸的过程后,在班上组织了一次有关交通安全注意事项的讨论。你联系生活实际参与了讨论。请把你的意见整理一下,形成一段 80 词左右的短文。开始语已给出(不计入总词数)。

 1.内容要求:1)行走时的安全事项;

     2)骑车(自行车)时的安全事项;

     3)乘车(公交汽车)时的安全事项。

 2.参考词汇:pavement 人行道;handle bar 自行车把手;watch ahead 向前看;walk;ride;take a bus;should;don't;traffic;while;until;before;line up;play;carry;get on(off)

 When we are walking, we should. . ._____

_____

_____

七、完成句子:用所给形容词的适当级填空

1. This text is _____ (easy) than the last one.

2. Your garden is _____ (large) than mine.

3. Shanghai is _____ (large) city than hers.

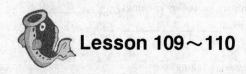

Lesson 109～110

一、单词拼写：根据所给中文意思补全下列单词

1. l __ss（更少 *adj.*）　　2. intro _____（介绍 *n.*）　3. m __ n __（很多 *adj.*）

4. adv __ c __（忠告 *n.*）　5. l ___ st（最少 *adj.*）

二、语法和词汇：从 A、B、C、D 中选出正确答案

1. John came to work _____ of them all yesterday because his bike had broken down.
   （海南，中考）
   A. late　　　　　B. later　　　　　C. latest　　　　　D. latter

2. Now China has joined WTO, so I think English is _____ useful than before.　（兰州，中考）
   A. more　　　　　B. most　　　　　C. much　　　　　D. many

3. If you want a ticket for a round-trip, sir, you'll have to pay ＄80 _____.　（青海，中考）
   A. another　　　　B. other　　　　　C. each　　　　　D. more

4. Jane's brother didn't work so _____ as the others did in his class.　（重庆，中考）
   A. more carefully　　B. carefully　　C. the most carefully D. careful

5. Mike is still _____ with his work as he was when I saw him last.　（天津，中考）
   A. more careful　　　　　　　　B. the most careful
   C. as careful　　　　　　　　　D. as carefully

6. This is one of the best films _____ this year.
   A. which has been shown　　　　B. that have been shown
   C. that have shown　　　　　　　D. have been shown

7. His letters _____ well.
   A. never read　　　　　　　　　B. are never read
   C. read never　　　　　　　　　D. never are read

8. They usually _____ TV in the evening.
   A. watch　　　　B. watched　　　　C. are watching　　　D. watches

9. The sun _____ in the east and _____ in the west.
   A. rose, set　　B. rose, set　　C. rises, sets　　D. rise, set

10. Can't you wait _____ this afternoon?
    A. after　　　　B. till　　　　C. before　　　　D. in

三、完成句子

1. He can't play football well, _____?

2. You haven't been to Beijing, _____?

3. They didn't come here yesterday, _____?

4. They are not watching TV now, _____?

5. You won't be late again, _____?

四、翻译句子

1. 如果你赢了一大笔钱，你将干什么？

2. 我们应该靠自己的双手生活。

3. 她花了一笔钱买了一件大衣。

4. 如果你有假期,你会去哪儿呢?

5. 我肯定她现在一定在学习英语。

6. The garden has already been watered.

7. The floor has already been swept.

8. My car has been repaired.

9. Litter-baskets have been placed under the trees.

10. The thief hasn't been caught.

五、用 few,a few,little 或 a little 填空

1. Will you eat _____ cake?

2. _____ people live to be a hundred.

3. He did quite well. There are _____ mistakes on his test paper this time.

4. There is only very _____ ink left in the bottle.

5. Unfortunately, I had _____ money on me.

6. Luckily, I had _____ bread on me.

7. There are _____ students in the class.

8. Will you please lend me _____ music to listen.

六、书面表达

假如你叫 Li Lei,是个中学生,经常收听音乐节目。请你用英语给节目主持人写一封信。

信的要点如下:

　　1. 你很喜欢这个节目,特别(especially)是英语歌曲;

　　2. 学习很忙,疲劳时,你会打开收音机,听这个节目;

　　3. 从英语歌里你学了很多单词;

　　4. 你最喜欢"My Heart Will Go On"这首歌,希望得到歌词(words of the song)。

注意:1. 信要通顺、连贯;

　　2. 词数 70 左右,信的开头和结层已为你写好,不计入总词数。

No. 28 Middle School

Suzhou

April 8,2001

Dear Madam,

　　I'm a middle school student. _____

_____

_____

_____

Yours sincerely,

Li Lei

七、完成句子:用所给形容词和副词的适当级填空

1. Tom is _____ (lazy) student in our class.

2. There are _____ (few) books in this library than in that one.

3. I have _____ (little) free time than he.

4. Mary is _____ (young) than her husband.

5. My watch runs _____ (fast) than his.

6. The days are _____ (long) in summer than in winter.

7. He knows _____ (many) people than you.

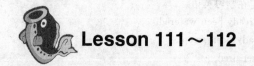

Lesson 111～112

一、单词拼写：根据所给中文意思补全下列单词

1. c＿st（价值 v.）　　　2. th＿＿f（小偷 n.）　　3. p＿rr＿t（鹦鹉 n.）

4. d＿p＿s＿t（保证金 n.）　5. exp＿ns＿v＿（贵的 adj.）

二、语法和词汇：从 A、B、C、D 中选出正确答案

1. Lucy's handwriting is good, but Rose's handwriting is much ＿＿＿＿＿＿.　　　（大同，中考）

　　A. good　　　　　B. best　　　　　C. better　　　　　D. the best

2. As a result, ＿＿＿＿＿＿ people like to travel by air than before.　　（武汉，中考）

　　A. much more　　B. many more　　C. more much　　D. more many

3. ＿＿＿＿＿＿ you eat butter, cream and chocolate, ＿＿＿＿＿＿ you will become.　（陕西，中考）

　　A. The more/the thinner　　　　　B. The less/the fatter

　　C. More/fatter　　　　　　　　　D. The more/the fatter

4. Try to make as ＿＿＿＿＿＿ mistakes as possible.　　　　　　　（广州，中考）

　　A. less　　　　　B. little　　　　　C. few　　　　　D. a few

5. —How will you buy this expensive car, Tom? We don't have enough deposits.

　　—We may buy it ＿＿＿＿＿＿.　　　　　　　　　　　　　　　　（山东，中考）

　　A. on installments　B. at installments　C. by installments　D. in installments

6. ＿＿＿＿＿＿ to have lunch with us today?

　　A. Do you like　　B. Would you like　C. Will you like　　D. Have you like

7. This one is as ＿＿＿＿＿＿ as that one.

　　A. cheaper　　　B. cheapest　　　C. cheap　　　　D. more cheap

8. Mother said that cooking ＿＿＿＿＿＿ much time every day.

　　A. paid　　　　　B. spent　　　　　C. made　　　　　D. took

9. —Hi, Kate.

　　—Hi, Mary. I ＿＿＿＿＿＿ know you are here.

　　A. don't　　　　　B. won't　　　　　C. can't　　　　　D. didn't

10. Will you please ＿＿＿＿＿＿ your shoes on the floor?

　　A. not to drop　　B. not drop　　　C. don't drop　　D. not dropping

11. He doesn't feel like ＿＿＿＿＿＿ anything today.

　　A. to eat　　　　B. eating　　　　C. eat　　　　　D. eats

12. —＿＿＿＿＿＿ has she done ＿＿＿＿＿＿ the tea?

　　—She has just drunk it.

　　A. How, with　　B. How about　　C. What, with　　D. What, about

13. Those Canadians arrived ＿＿＿＿＿＿ Beijing ＿＿＿＿＿＿ a Sunday morning.

　　A. in...in　　　　B. on...at　　　　C. at...in　　　　D. in...on

14. Mary works hard. Her brother works hard, ＿＿＿＿＿＿.

　　A. too　　　　　B. neither　　　　C. either　　　　D. also

15. This car is ＿＿＿＿＿＿ that one. It is ＿＿＿＿＿＿ car in our shop.

　　A. cheaper than...cheapest　　　　　B. cheaper then...the cheapest

　　C. cheaper than...the cheapest　　　D. more cheap than...the most cheap

三、时态填空

1. I _____ (get) up very early yesterday morning.

2. It's raining now. They _____ (stay) at home.

3. It will rain tomorrow. They _____ (hold) the party indoors.

4. I think you _____ (not) wait for him.

5. He _____ (go) to school on foot every day.

6. I _____ (not water) the garden every day last summer.

四、翻译句子

1. I'm sure that he is a middle school teacher.

2. I'm sure that she is not playing the piano.

3. I'm sure that the Yellow River is not longer than the Yangtse River.

4. I'm sure that he is looking for you.

5. 我们英语老师肯定在办公室里。

6. 今天肯定是星期五。看,他们正在开会。

7. 这不可能是他的自行车。

8. 你的书包肯定在房间里某个地方。

9. 他不可能在找东西,他肯定在思考。

五、完成下列句子

1. This book is _____(不如……精彩) that one.

2. Jim is _____(不如……聪明) Simon.

3. He is _____(不和……一样忙碌) you are.

4. The girl on the left is _____(和……一样时髦) the one on the right.

5. That book is _____(和……一样贵) this one.

6. This test paper is _____(和……一样难) that one.

7. Alice can play the piano _____(和……一样好听) her sister.

8. Is this book _____(和……一样好) the first one?

六、书面表达

根据所给的四幅图画,用英语写一篇约 70 个单词的短文,短文的第一句已给出。

要求:短文中必须使用以下词语:

doctor,evening,supper,telephone call,young woman,daughter,ill,bus-stop,home,thanks

Mrs. Smith is a doctor. . .

七、完成句子:仿照例句改写下列句子

Example:Lesson Two is less difficult than Lesson One.

Lesson Two is not as difficult as Lesson One.

1. My watch is less expensive than yours.

2. Tom is less intelligent than Bill.

3. My book is less interesting than yours.

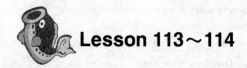

Lesson 113～114

一、单词拼写:根据所给中文意思补全下列单词

1. c__nd__ct____（售票员 *n.*）2. p__ss__nger（乘客 *n.*）3. tr__m____（践踏 *v.*）

4. m__d__m（女士 *n.*）　　5. ____pp____ntment（约会 *n.*）

二、语法和词汇:从 A、B、C、D 中选出正确答案

1. You may _____ stay or go. （太原,中考）

   A. either　　　　B. neither　　　　C. both　　　　D. all

2. Either you or I _____ wrong. （兰州,中考）

   A. am　　　　B. are　　　　C. is　　　　D. be

3. He has _____ brother at all.

   A. not　　　　B. no　　　　C. none　　　　D. no one

4. Mr. Watson won't be here next week, and _____. （上海,中考）

   A. neither his wife will　　　　B. neither his wife won't

   C. his wife won't neither　　　　D. his wife won't either

5. —Are there any pictures on the wall?

   —_____. （广州,中考）

   A. Not　　　　B. No　　　　C. None　　　　D. No one

6. In the UN six languages _____ for business.

   A. have chosen　　B. have spoken　　C. are chosen　　D. are speaking

7. —Which of these two English books will you borrow?

   —I'll borrow _____ of them because they are very interesting.

   A. either　　　　B. all　　　　C. neither　　　　D. both

8. The car broke down and we had to _____ all the way home.

   A. wade　　　　B. go　　　　C. tramp　　　　D. trample

9. We've never seen _____.

   A. everything so beautiful　　　　B. so beautiful anything

   C. anything so beautiful　　　　D. nothing so beautiful

10. —Is it going to rain tomorrow?

    —If it _____, we'll have the match next week.

    A. does　　　　B. is going to rain　　C. will　　　　D. is

11. —Last summer, it wasn't dry, was it?

    —_____. I had to water it every day.

    A. Yes, it was　　B. No, it was　　C. Yes, it wasn't　　D. No, it wasn't

12. May I smoke here? No, you _____.

    A. needn't　　　　B. don't have to　　　　C. mustn't　　　　D. can't

13. What _____ they doing now in the shop?

    A. is　　　　B. are　　　　C. were　　　　D. was

14. He _____ his homework last week. He _____ ill.

    A. doesn't do; is　　B. didn't do; /　　C. didn't do; was　　D. not did; was

15. _____ your mother a bus driver?

A. Are   B. Is   C. Did   D. Does

三、时态填空

1. "Soon he _____(go)to sleep" means "Soon he _____(fall) asleep."

2. His grandpa _____(be)dead for ten years.

3. I think your bike needs _____(repair).

4. He remembered he had _____(put)the football under his bed.

5. I _____(not see)you these days. Where _____ you _____(be)?

四、翻译句子

1. You'll have to come very early tomorrow.

2. We must point out the mistake for him.

3. She had to do all the housework in the past.

4. People have had to work very hard these days.

5. You have to tell me the truth.

6. 明天早上你必须在8点钟之前到火车站。

7. 我得说你看上去好多了。

8. 他们不必来得那么早。

9. 在过去,人们只得用手做很多事情,现在不必了。

10. 我必须用钢笔写这封信吗?

五、用 so 或 neither 完成下列句子

1. He's not happy. _____ his friend.

2. I've got no beer. _____ the boss.

3. The first passenger hasn't any small change. _____ the other passengers.

4. The man wants to go to the Great Wall. _____ the two tramps.

5. Text Three isn't easy. _____ Text Two.

6. Peter has spent little money on books. _____ Billy.

7. They had a good time last night. _____ we.

8. I can't sing this song well. _____ he.

9. He doesn't like the coffee here. _____ Lucy.

10. I like reading. _____ I.

六、书面表达

Make a telephone call.

Allan:(Call up John)_____

John:(Answer the phone)_____

Allan:(Ask John to his birthday party)_____

John:(Say no and give an excuse)_____

七、完成句子:将下列句子译成英语

1. 我有很多英语书。他也有。

2. Tom 在打扫房间。我也是。

3. 我们已经看过这部电影。他们也看过。

4. 他不打算乘火车去。我也不。

5. 我看不见任何人。她也看不见。

129

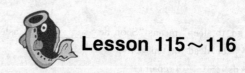

Lesson 115～116

一、单词拼写:根据所给中文意思补全下列单词

1. kn＿ck (敲 *v.*) 2. qu＿＿t (安静的 *adj.*) 3. j＿k＿ (玩笑 *n.*)

4. gl＿ss＿s (眼镜 *n.*) 5. b＿d (床 *n.*)

二、语法和词汇:从 A、B、C、D 中选出正确答案

1. _____ of the three businessmen knew about the document because it was kept as a secret.

   (广州,中考)

   A. None   B. Neither   C. Any   D. Each

2. —Who did you find in the room?

   —_____.

   (上海,中考)

   A. Nobody   B. Not   C. No   D. None

3. Jean is a bright young woman who comes from a rich and famous family. She goes to a good university and has _____ that money can buy.

   (天津,中考)

   A. something   B. everything   C. nothing   D. thing

4. Someone _____ at the door when she was cooking in the kitchen. (广州,中考)

   A. had knocked B. has knocked   C. knocked   D. knock

5. It was Andy's birthday so we booked a _____ -smoking table at Holiday Restaurant for 7:30 p. m. .

   (太原,中考)

   A. keep   B. non   C. not   D. on

6. When I went to bed at ten last night, my mother _____ at her desk.

   A. worked still   B. still worked

   C. still was working   D. was still working

7. _____ is wrong with my watch.

   A. Some thing B. Some things   C. Something   D. Some-thing

8. —Must I come at seven o'clock?

   —Oh no, you _____ come at seven.

   A. must   B. mustn't   C. needn't   D. don't need

9. Mary's mother will _____ in hospital for a few days.

   A. live   B. stay   C. stop   D. keep

10. John likes swimming in summer, _____ he?

    A. does   B. don't   C. didn't   D. doesn't

11. At night the temperature will fall _____ zero.

    A. under   B. below   C. over   D. in

12. —May I borrow your bike?

    —_____, I don't have one.

    A. Thank you   B. Well   C. Sorry   D. Oh

13. —What time _____ I come?

    —Please come at half past seven.

    A. will   B. would   C. shall   D. may

14. Go down the street _____ you come to a cinema.

A. and   B. but   C. until   D. or

15. It'll _____ us two hours to the farm by bus.

A. take   B. use   C. make   D. turn

三、用所给动词的适当形式填空

1. I _____ (receive) your letter by last Friday.

2. Where are the students? They _____ (play) on the playground.

3. When we _____ (get) to the cinema, the film _____ already _____ (begin).

4. We _____ (swim) in the river then.

5. _____ you _____ (read) the novel?

     Yes, I _____ (read) it last year.

四、翻译句子

1. I slipped and fell downstairs.

2. I'm sure I've got a low mark.

3. This letter's full of mistakes. I want you to type it again.

4. It doesn't suit me at all.

5. Eat more and smoke less.

6. 汤姆是个诚实的孩子。

7. 当我们到达电影院时,电影已开始了,我们只好在黑暗中摸索着走。

8. 司机被送到医院后不久就去世了。

9. 我看过这部电影。

10. 你吃过晚饭了吗?

五、改错

1. All is present today.
     A   B   C   D

2. Nothing in the world move faster than light.
       A   B   C   D

3. Not every student do the homework.
     A   B   C   D

4. Everyone should be careful of their behavior.
          A   B   C   D

5. Nobody know his address.
     A   B   C   D

6. Everyone has their duty.
     A   B   C   D

7. Somebody have cleaned the classroom already.
        A   B   C   D

8. Everybody in this class want to go and watch the game.
     A   B   C   D

六、完成句子:将下列句子译成英语

1. 关于中国历史,Tom 一无所知。

2. 今天早上有人打电话来吗?

3. 晚上我总是读点什么。

4. 没有人会相信这个故事。

5. 我到处寻找我的英语书,但哪里也找不到。

131

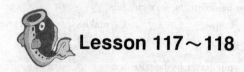

Lesson 117～118

一、单词拼写：根据所给中文意思补全下列单词

1. c___n（硬币 *n.*）　　2. sw___ll___（吞下 *v.*）　　3. t___l_t（厕所 *n.*）

4. l__nch（午饭 *n.*）　　5. n__ce（好的 *adj.*）

二、语法和词汇：从 A、B、C、D 中选出正确答案

1. While I _____ with my friend, she came in.　　　　　　　　　　　　　　（湖北，中考）

　　A. am talking　　　B. was talking　　　C. talked　　　D. am going to talk

2. Someone _____ when she was cooking in the kitchen.　　　　　　　　　（武汉，中考）

　　A. had called　　　B. has called　　　C. called　　　D. calls

3. Nobody _____ how to run this machine.　　　　　　　　　　　　　　　（浙江，中考）

　　A. know　　　　　B. have known　　　C. knows　　　D. is knowing

4. —What is mum doing now?

　　—She _____ some clothes.　　　　　　　　　　　　　　　　　　　　（北京，中考）

　　A. washes　　　　B. is washing　　　C. washed　　　D. has washed

5. We used to be classmates, and 6 years _____ she became my wife.　　　（云南，中考）

　　A. late　　　　　B. later　　　　　C. latest　　　D. the latest

6. _____ the twins sweeping the floor when the teacher came in?

　　A. Are　　　　　B. Were　　　　　C. Is　　　　　D. Was

7. What had Lily _____ by ten o'clock yesterday morning?

　　A. do　　　　　B. does　　　　　C. done　　　　D. doing

8. The noise woke _____ up early in the morning.

　　A. me　　　　　B. I　　　　　　C. my　　　　　D. mine

9. The man was _____ hurt when his bike hit the car.

　　A. bad　　　　　B. badly　　　　C. worse　　　D. worst

10. You'd better _____ late for class next time.

　　A. don't be　　　B. not be　　　　C. no be　　　D. not to be

11. Li Lei was playing football when he _____ his pen on the ground.

　　A. drop　　　　　B. drops　　　　C. dropped　　　D. dropping

12. Don't crowd _____ them. Take them to hospital.

　　A. from　　　　　B. round　　　　C. with　　　　D. to

13. I have had the computer _____ many years.

　　A. since　　　　　B. in　　　　　　C. for　　　　　D. /

14. Don't take off your shoes. _____.

　　A. Put it on　　　B. Put on it　　　C. Put them on　　D. Put on them

15. She has just been to the _____ office.

　　A. teacher　　　　B. teacher's　　　C. teachers　　　D. teachers'

三、用所给动词的适当形式填空

1. We _____（have）a meeting when he came last week.

2. She _____（dust）the windows at that moment.

3. Alice _____（write）a letter at 9 this morning.

4. My wife _____（wash）the clothes while I _____（read）the newspaper.

5. _____ you _____（finish）reading the book?

　Yes，I _____（read）the book the whole morning.

四、翻译句子

1. Susan will leave for Paris next month.

2. We shall fly to Berlin this week.

3. Jane will go to Tokyo next week.

4. She will telephone her mother tomorrow morning.

5. I shall have a shave tomorrow.

6. 他什么时候死的？

7. 你是否也邀请玛丽来吃饭？

8. 她看到了什么？

9. 你为何对他那么粗鲁？

10. 我们什么时候开会？

五、介词填空

from，in，at，out of，into，on，except，through，to

1. We study every day _____ Sunday.

2. There are three boys _____ the classroom. _____ John，they are Peter and Billy.

3. It's impossible to finish the work _____ four hours' time.

4. He looked _____ his exercises before he handed them in.

5. I've got an invitation _____ Jim. He asked me _____ dinner _____ Saturday.

6. Don't look _____ the window. Listen _____ me carefully.

7. When I saw her，she was getting _____ a taxi.

8. He knocked _____ the door when I was having lunch.

133

六、书面表达

请以"MY FIRST JOB"为题写一篇短文

提示：1. 早上睡过了头

　　　2. 没注意听领班(head waiter)的说明(instruction)

　　　3. 自己还穿了双高跟鞋

七、完成句子：用所给动词的适当形式填空

1. We _____（have）a meeting when he came last week.

2. She _____（dust）the windows at that moment.

3. Alice _____（write）a letter at 9 this morning.

4. My wife _____（wash）the clothes while I _____（read）the newspaper.

5. _____ you _____（finish）reading the book?

6. The man _____（repair）your bicycle from 7 to 10 this morning.

　He _____ already _____（repair）it now.

7. Why didn't you come to the party last night?

　I _____（work）in the factory then.

8. What _____ you _____（do）now?

　I _____（play）with snow.

　_____ you _____（do）your homework?

　Yes，I _____（do）it the whole morning.

9. He _____（walk）along the river at ten this morning.

10. I _____（have）a bath at this time yesterday.

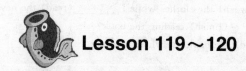

Lesson 119～120

一、单词拼写:根据所给中文意思补全下列单词

1. v__i___(声音 *n.*)   2. st__p__d(愚蠢的 *adj.*)
3. __xp__ns__ve(贵的 *adj.*)   4. c__ll(叫 *v.*)   5. th___f(小偷 *n.*)

二、语法和词汇:从 A、B、C、D 中选出正确答案

1. Though the famous dancer, Tai Lihua, is deaf, she dances _____ most of the people.　　　　　　　　　　　　　　　　　　　　　　　　　　　　　　　　　　　(武汉,中考)

    A. as good as   B. as well as   C. best among   D. better than

2. Don't give up your hope no matter what _____.　　　　　　　(上海,中考)

    A. happens   B. take place   C. occur   D. will be

3. They _____ where to build the new hospital before the work began.　(天津,中考)

    A. have been decide   B. had decided

    C. had been decide   D. will be decided

4. Great changes have _____ in the poor rural area.　　　　　(河南,中考)

    A. been taken place   B. taken place

    C. took place   D. had took place

5. People _____ the annual competition for fun.

    A. enters   B. enter in   C. went into   D. enter for

6. Do you remember _____ your wife when you come to our party?

    A. taking   B. to take   C. bringing   D. to bring

7. Look at the clouds! It _____ rain.

    A. is going to   B. must   C. will   D. is going

8. I'll be back _____ ten minutes.

    A. in   B. at   C. for   D. after

9. She's busy now, but she'll be here _____ five o'clock.

    A. in   B. after   C. for   D. /

10. Before he came to London, he had never heard a single English word _____.

    A. speaking   B. spoken   C. to be spoken   D. speak

11. He asked who was the man _____ on.

    A. to be operating   B. operating

    C. to operate   D. to be operated

12. The pen _____ on the table belongs to me.

    A. which it is   B. lain   C. lay   D. lying

13. I didn't go to bed until he _____ back.

    A. come   B. came   C. had come   D. has come

14. I arrived at the station after the train _____.

    A. left   B. had left   C. leaves   D. has left

三、时态填空

1. My uncle _____ (be) to London twice.

2. He _____ (fall) off his bike when he _____ (ride) to school.

3. I _____ (lose) my bike. So I have to buy a new one.

4. I _____ (not go) much farther before I caught them up.

5. Look! How fast Mary _____ (run)!

四、翻译句子

1. It would be best for us to tell him the truth.

2. If we are going to the theatre this evening，we'll take you.

3. I ought to put on my best suit.

4. It's a long name，I must spell it for you.

5. You ought not to be late.

6. 走完这么长的路我很想喝点冷饮。

7. 他说发生了一些严重的事情。

8. 别做任何蠢事。

9. 你还知道谁想要票吗？

10. 明天见。

五、将下列句子变成复数形式

1. The gentleman is going to speak to us.

2. This lady comes from China.

3. That child is lovely.

4. His life was very interesting.

5. My wife is very beautiful.

6. That knife isn't very sharp.

7. This shelf is clean.

8. This loaf of bread is fresh.

六、书面表达

根据下面的图画,请你用英语写一篇短文。大约包括 8—10 个句子。短文要求达意、正确、连贯。

七、完成句子:用一般过去式或过去完成式将括号内的动词填入空内

1. I _____ (finish) my meal, so I called for the bill, but as (由于) the waiter _____ (go) upstairs, he didn't hear me.

2. As the sun _____ (not rise) yet, we _____ (not see) very far.

3. Our letters _____ (not arrive) when we _____ (leave) home this morning.

4. We _____ (come) home by taxi because we _____ (miss) the last bus.

5. I did not accept their invitation because I _____ (already promise) to come to you.

6. We couldn't answer the policeman's questions as we _____ (not see) anything.

7. We took our little brother to hospital bacause he _____ (swallow) a coin.

8. The plane from Paris _____ (land 着陆) when we _____ (reach) the airport.

9. My brother _____ (never be) abroad before and _____ (feel) a little homesick (想家).

10. The thieves _____ (run) away when the police _____ (arrive).

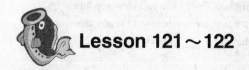

Lesson 121～122

一、单词拼写:根据所给中文意思补全下列单词

1. _____ ['mætə](事情 *n.*)　　2. _____ ['hʌzbənd](丈夫 *n.*)

3. _____ [raɪt](恰好 *adv.*)　　4. c __ st __ m ___（顾客 *n.*）

5. s ___ v __ （服务 *v.*）

二、语法和词汇:从 A、B、C、D 中选出正确答案

1. Do you know the young lady _____ your mother is talking? 　　(上海,中考)

　　A. who　　　　B. whom　　　　C. with whom　　　　D. which

2. —Tom is the _____ one I want to work with. He is always complaining.

　　—Be more patient. He is still a good boy. 　　(山东,中考)

　　A. best　　　　B. last　　　　C. what　　　　D. when

3. I was drawing a horse _____ the teacher came in. 　　(PETS 一级)

　　A. while　　　　B. since　　　　C. when　　　　D. on moment

4. —A latest *China Daily*, please!

　　—Only one copy left. Would you like to have _____, sir? 　　(北京,中考)

　　A. it　　　　B. one　　　　C. this　　　　D. that

5. —Is the girl _____ is interviewing the manager of that company your friend?

　　—Yes, she is a journalist from CCTV. 　　(北京,中考)

　　A. whom　　　　B. which　　　　C. who　　　　D. whose

6. —In England, people eat fish and chips.

　　—Oh, we _____. We eat a lot of chicken.

　　A. don't　　　　B. eat not　　　　C. haven't　　　　D. aren't

7. This is not _____. This is home cooking.

　　A. food take-away　　B. a food take-away　　C. take-away food　　D. a take-away food

8. Which is _____ food in the U. S. A. ?

　　A. the most popular　　　　　　B. more popular

　　C. the popularest　　　　　　　D. popular

9. Let's give him _____ to eat.

　　A. different something　　　　　B. different anything

　　C. something different　　　　　D. anything different

10. —Does Bill like Chinese food?

　　—I've _____.

　　A. no idea　　　　B. not idea　　　　C. on an idea　　　　D. not ideas

11. _____ he is late, I'll go with Mary.

　　A. That　　　　B. Before　　　　C. After　　　　D. If

12. Lily and her mother came _____.

　　A. at the head　　　B. at last　　　C. in line　　　D. at the end

13. If you look carefully _____ you cross the road, you will be safe.

　　A. before　　　　B. after　　　　C. where　　　　D. that

14. It is _____ late to do anything now.

136

A. to   B. too   C. very   D. so

15. It's cold outside. You _____ put on your coat.

    A. will   B. had better   C. have better   D. are going to

16. My father isn't here now. He _____ Shanghai. He _____ there twice.

    A. has gone；has been   B. has gone to；has been to

    C. has been to；has gone   D. has gone to；has been

三、词形转换

1. Which is _____(difficult),English,physics or maths?

2. The third truck is carrying _____(few) of all.

3. The seats in the middle of the cinema are the _____(good).

4. I hope you're well. You look much _____(thin) than before.

5. My brothers is two years _____(old) than I.

四、翻译句子

1. Someone has stolen his bicycle.

2. Her parents will give her a bag as a present.

3. We will discuss the question tomorrow.

4. People in many countries speak English.

5. Mao Dun wrote "Midnight".

6. 他们在吃早饭。

7. 吃完早饭,他们就上班。

8. 那你一个上午在干什么呢?

9. 没干什么。

10. 我在油漆一张餐桌。

五、用关系代词填空

1. The woman _____ invited you to the party is a friend of Jim's.

2. The man _____ is speaking at the meeting is a teacher.

3. He is the man _____ I met last Sunday.

4. Is this the driver _____ they talked about yesterday?

5. The letter _____ I got this morning was from my parents.

6. This is the film _____ I saw the other day.

7. Isn't that coin _____ you found in the garden?

8. The assistant _____ served is standing behind the counter.

六、书面表达

根据图画写句子。每幅图写两句话,表达一个完整的故事。

揭示:时间:母亲节 Mother's Day   人物:Lucy and her mother

图 2 提示:to get up,in the morning   图 3 提示:to buy

七、完成句子:请用关系代词 whom,which,whose,who,that 填空

1. The car _____ he is repairing is very beautiful.

2. The man _____ is reading at the desk is our English teacher.

3. Do you understand the story _____ he is reading?

4. The pen _____ he gave me was made in the U. S. A. .

5. The little girl _____ she is playing with is her daughter.

6. The policeman _____ is helping the old man is my brother.

7. This is the book _____ he is looking for.

8. He is the thief _____ the police caught yesterday.

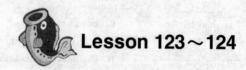

Lesson 123~124

一、单词拼写:根据所给中文意思补全下列单词

1. __ff___(提供 v.)   2. gr___(生长 v.)   3. gr___(成长,过去时 v.)

4. gu__ss(猜 v.)   5. d___ing(在,期间 prep.)

二、语法和词汇:从 A、B、C、D 中选出正确答案

1. The _____ of Marco Polo is one of the most interesting books that I have ever read.

   (武汉,中考)

   A. Travels   B. Trips   C. Journeys   D. Tours

2. She is the woman _____ everybody knows here.   (广州,中考)

   A. what   B. which   C. 不填   D. whose

3. Is this house _____ you are going to buy?   (上海,中考)

   A. what   B. where   C. 不填   D. whose

4. Both my parents like the house _____ windows are all to the south.   (PETS 一级)

   A. what   B. which   C. 不填   D. whose

5. Thank you so much for offering me a _____ in your company.   (郑州,中考)

   A. work   B. career   C. job   D. task

6. Please show me the picture _____ you have.

   A. who   B. whose   C. whom   D. which

7. In summer _____ grows very quickly.

   A. something   B. everything C. anything   D. all things

8. He _____ the letter from my hand and read it quickly.

   A. pulled   B. took   C. brought   D. sent

9. There is _____ in the waiting-room.

   A. anybody   B. everyone   C. somebody   D. all

10. Mike wants _____ tomorrow.

    A. to go swimming   B. to go to swimming
    C. going to swim   D. going swimming

11. The man _____ there is his father.

    A. stands   B. stand   C. standing   D. to stand

12. Don't _____ faces at me, Jack!

    A. make   B. take   C. look   D. put

13. Help _____ to some fruit, please.

    A. you   B. your   C. yours   D. yourself

14. You must _____ of your little sister, and don't let her run on the road.

    A. care   B. careful   C. be careful   D. take care

15. You may go with them, _____ you don't have to.

    A. and   B. so   C. because   D. but

16. It is the ability to do the job _____ matters where you come from or what you are.

    (北京,中考)

    A. one   B. that   C. what   D. it

三、时态填空

1. He _____(learn) some Chinese before he _____(come) to China.
2. What _____ they _____(do) tomorrow?
   They _____(watch) the match on TV.
3. At 5 yesterday morning，we _____ still _____(sleep).
4. My daughter _____(go) to bed before I came home.
5. He _____(wash) the plates after he _____(have) the dinner.

四、翻译句子

1. They have already watered the garden.
2. He has already swept the floor.
3. Someone has repaired my car.
4. We have placed litter-baskets under the trees.
5. The policemen haven't caught the thief.
6. 我有很多英语书。他也有。
7. Tom 在扫房间，我也是。
8. 我们已经看过这部电影。他们也看过。
9. 我不打算乘火车去。他也不。
10. 我看不见任何人。她也看不见。

五、用 a job，work，a trip 或 travel 填空

1. Father always gets home from _____ at 6：00 p. m.
2. All _____ and no play makes Jack a dull boy.
3. She made _____ to Beijing yesterday.
4. We _____ in Europe last spring.
5. Let's do _____ good _____.
6. It's his _____ to teach English here.
7. I got _____ as a bus driver.
8. Light _____ faster than sound.

139

六、书面表达

北京是一座美丽的现代化城市。到处是高楼大厦和干净的街道。我们应该保持周围环境的清洁……，我们不应该……

1. beautiful，modern，city
2. there be，tall building，clean street，everywhere，Beijing
3. environment(环境)，plant，as many flowers and trees as possible，protect(保护) them
4. throw waste(废弃物)，here and there，because，every one of us，hope，live，a wonderful environment

七、完成句子

1. He met an old friend _____ his trip _____ England.
   A. during...to   B. during...of   C. in...to
2. I don't like growing _____.
   A. beard   B. a beard   C. the beard
3. He likes his beard very much，but his wife wants him to _____.
   A. shave off it   B. shave them off   C. shave it off
4. A friend of my father's offered me _____.
   A. job   B. work   C. a job
5. Can you guess _____?
   A. who he is   B. who is he   C. who was he

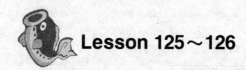

Lesson 125～126

一、单词拼写:根据所给中文意思补全下列单词

1. E_____（英语 *n.*） 　2. b_____（兄弟 *n.*） 　3. p__t（放 *v.*）

4. m___n（意味 *v.*） 　5. w_t_r（水 *n.*）

二、语法和词汇:从 A、B、C、D 中选出正确答案

1. —I don't mind telling you what I know.

　—You _____. I'm not asking you for it.

　A. mustn't 　　　　B. may not 　　　　C. can't 　　　　D. needn't

2. Black holes _____ not be seen directly, so determining the number of the holes is a tough task.

　A. can 　　　　B. should 　　　　C. must 　　　　D. need

3. Yesterday it rained heavily when school was over. We _____ stay in our classroom.

（汕头,中考）

　A. should 　　　　B. must 　　　　C. had to 　　　　D. shouldn't

4. —_____ I leave all the books here?

　—Sorry, you can't. You have to take them back home.

（大连,中考）

　A. Need 　　　　B. Must 　　　　C. May 　　　　D. Should

5. You have already tried your best, so you _____ worry about the matter. （陕西,中考）

　A. can't 　　　　B. needn't 　　　　C. mustn't 　　　　D. couldn't

6. A dog is _____ after a ball now.

　A. run 　　　　B. running 　　　　C. runs 　　　　D. /

7. More and more people _____ something about computers.

　A. learn 　　　　B. learning 　　　　C. are learning 　　　　D. to learn

8. He gets up early every morning. Now he _____ breakfast.

　A. is cooking 　　　　B. cooks 　　　　C. cooking 　　　　D. cook

9. Father likes _____ a plane, but he doesn't like _____ it today.

　A. to make, to make 　B. making, to make 　C. make, making 　D. making, make

10. You are a student, _____?

　A. aren't you 　　　　B. you aren't 　　　　C. are you 　　　　D. you are

11. Let me go and give the coat to _____.

　A. he 　　　　B. his 　　　　C. himself 　　　　D. him

12. They aren't our books. Are they _____?

　A. your 　　　　B. his 　　　　C. her 　　　　D. their

13. What _____ the shop sell?

　A. do 　　　　B. does 　　　　C. are 　　　　D. is

14. Where _____ your friend Linda come from, do you know?

　A. are 　　　　B. do 　　　　C. does 　　　　D. is

15. What time do you leave school _____ weekdays?

　A. in 　　　　B. on 　　　　C. / 　　　　D. at

三、翻译句子

1. This is one of Lu Xun's books.
2. She showed me one of John's pictures.
3. Some of your letters were found on my desk.
4. Some of their friends came to see me.
5. It was one of her ideas.

6. 昨天给我们作报告的妇女是位教授。
7. 大家都忙,他们忙着准备期末考试。
8. 任何人都会回答这个问题,不是吗?
9. 汽车来了。
10. 当心!

四、词形变换

1. He made _____ (many) mistakes than I.
2. Her family is _____ (rich) in the town.
3. Fudan University is _____ (famous) than our college.
4. This road is _____ (wide) than that street.
5. The room is _____ (bright) than mine.
6. Your book is _____ (thick) than Tom's.
7. The water in this river looks _____ (dirty) than in that.

五、用 must,have to,have had to,mustn't,needn't 填空

1. The last bus has left. We will _____ walk home.
2. Everyone _____ talk loudly in the library.
3. She _____ go there every day.
4. I _____ wait for you for one hour.
5. I _____ work hard to make a living.
6. You _____ tell her to come. She has gone to Beijing.
7. You _____ be honest.
8. You _____ try and be more careful.

141

六、书面表达

根据下面五幅图中的内容写一段 5~8 句话的短文。短文首句已经写出。要求:

1. 必须使用提供的关键词;
2. 适当添加相关内容,以使表达连贯。
3. 适当使用过去时态。

关键词语:morning,breakfast,hard,afternoon, playground,supper,homework

首句:John had a busy day yesterday...

七、完成句子

1. Haven't you done your homework? _____. I did it an hour ago.

   A. Yes,I have   B. No,I have   C. Yes,I haven't

2. Last summer,it wan't dry,was it? _____. I had to water it every day.

   A. Yes,it was.   B. No,it was.   C. Yes,it wasn't

3. You _____ take an umbrella. I am sure it won't rain.

   A. mustn't   B. needn't   C. have to

4. May I smoke here? No,you _____.

   A. needn't   B. don't have to   C. mustn't

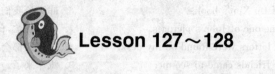

Lesson 127～128

一、单词拼写：根据所给中文意思补全下列单词

1. d _____（画 *v.*）   2. h _____（百 *n.*）   3. Y _____ P _____（少先队员 *n.*）

4. g _____（女孩 *n.*）   5. p _____（双 *n.*）

二、语法和词汇：从 A、B、C、D 中选出正确答案

1. Zhang Yimou is now a famous director, but he was once a wonderful _____ in the movie *Old Well*.　　　　　　　　　　　　　　　　　　　　　　　　　　（西安，中考）

　　A. actor　　　　　　B. actress　　　　　C. player　　　　　D. act

2. I don't have many apples left either. I can only give your two _____.　　（上海，中考）

　　A. at least　　　　　B. at most　　　　　C. at once　　　　　D. at times

3. Can you _____ this letter? Is it "1" or "r"?　　　　　　　　　　　　（焦作，中考）

　　A. recognize　　　　B. see　　　　　　　C. notice　　　　　D. read

4. That was a long time ago, _____?　　　　　　　　　　　　　　　（天津，中考）

　　A. isn't it　　　　　B. isn't that　　　　C. wasn't it　　　　D. wasn't that

5. Girls always like red color, _____?　　　　　　　　　　　　　　（北京，中考）

　　A. do girls　　　　　B. don't girls　　　　C. do they　　　　　D. don't they

6. If you find her, please tell me at once.（选出划线部分的正确译文）

　　A. 一次　　　　　　B. 立刻　　　　　　C. 按时　　　　　　D. 及时

7. New York is _____ its skyscrapers.

　　A. famous　　　　　B. famous for　　　　C. good to　　　　　D. well to

8. A good _____ can play any role.

　　A. actor　　　　　　B. act　　　　　　　C. action　　　　　D. active

9. What have you done _____ the eggs?

　　A. to　　　　　　　B. with　　　　　　　C. at　　　　　　　D. for

10. My grandparents live in Shanghai all by _____.

　　A. himself　　　　　B. themselves　　　　C. themself　　　　D. theirselves

11. Your sister can't drive a car, _____.

　　A. can you　　　　　B. can't you　　　　C. can't she　　　　D. can she

12. I met Jim in the street _____.

　　A. the another day　　B. the other day　　C. other day　　　D. other days

13. Tom's mother usually goes to Shanghai by train, _____?

　　A. isn't she　　　　B. doesn't she　　　　C. doesn't he　　　D. doesn't Tom

三、用所给动词的适当形式填空

1. Who _____ (take) my basket away?

　　_____ you _____ (know)?

2. Somebody wants _____ (see) you, Mr. Smith.

3. I'll go out and _____ (take) a walk in the park.

4. Where _____ they _____ (put) their bikes yesterday?

5. She began _____ (feel) a little afraid.

6. Joan usually _____ (watch) TV before she _____ (go) to bed.

7. What _____ they _____ (do) now?

8. If he _____ (come) tomorrow morning I _____ (give) him the present.

四、翻译句子

1. They must sell the house.

2. You must water the garden now.

3. We mustn't buy the expensive car.

4. He mustn't drive so fast.

5. They mustn't go there on foot.

6. 你好吗？

7. 你怎么了？

8. 我要搬家了。

9. 我已经搬家了。

10. 我正在搬家。

五、完成下列各句

1. Smoking _____（可能）be harmful to health.

2. I _____（必须）finish my work before six.

3. Books _____（决不可）be taken out of the room.

4. I think you're right. You _____（不可能）make any mistakes.

5. It's already eleven o'clock. She _____（一定）be sleeping.

6. The news _____（不可能）be true.

7. A：_____（允许）I go now?

   B：No, you _____（不许）.

8. He _____（不可以）park his car in this street.

六、书面表达

　　假如你是 Hope Middle School 的一名学生,请你用英语写一篇80个词左右的短文,向你的英国朋友介绍一下你们学校的概况(不得使用真实的人名、地名)。短文要包括以下几个方面的内容：

　　1. 校园（school campus）

　　2. 老师和同学

　　3. 学习情况

　　短文的第一句已经给出：

　　I am a student of Hope Middle School...

七、完成句子:将下列句子译成英语

1. 我们英语老师肯定在办公室。

2. 今天肯定是星期五。看,他们正在开会。

3. 这不可能是他的自行车。他的自行车是新的。

4. 你的书包肯定在房间里某个地方。

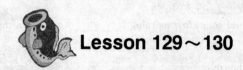

Lesson 129～130

一、单词拼写:根据所给中文意思补全下列单词

1. c _____（能 *v.*）　　　2. f _____（从 *prep.*）　3. A _____（美国 *n.*）

4. w _____（什么时候 *pron.*）　5. l _____（听 *v.*）

二、语法和词汇:从 A、B、C、D 中选出正确答案

1. There's no light on—they _____ be at home.

   A. can't　　　B. mustn't　　　C. needn't　　　D. shouldn't

2. —Could I have a word with you, mum?

   —Oh dear, if you _____.

   A. can　　　B. must　　　C. may　　　D. should

3. It was very kind of you to do the washing-up, but you _____ it.

   A. mustn't have done　　　　B. wouldn't have done

   C. mightn't have done　　　　D. needn't have done

4. You _____ listening to me — your eyes _____ looking outside.

   A. can't be/were　　　　B. can't have been/is

   C. can't have been/were　　D. can't be/was

5. Didn't you see the "No Stamping" _____ on the grassland?

   A. sign　　　B. signal　　　C. gesture　　　D. symbol

6. The station is past the next _____.

   A. turn　　　B. turns　　　C. turning　　　D. to turn

7. The post office is _____ that road.

   A. along　　　B. in　　　C. by　　　D. to

8. He can't _____ for his pen now.

   A. have looking　　　　B. have look

   C. have been looking　　D. be looking

9. Tom _____ to school on foot, and his parents _____ to work by bike.

   A. go, go　　　B. goes, go　　　C. go, goes　　　D. goes, goes

10. I think you'd better not _____ late very often.

    A. are　　　B. were　　　C. be　　　D. bes

11. She is _____ a good player and a _____ good coach（教练）.

    A. quite...very　　　　B. quite...quite

    C. very...quite　　　　D. very...very

12. I like spring _____ than summer.

    A. good　　　B. better　　　C. well　　　D. best

13. He is _____ young to go to school.

    A. so　　　B. very　　　C. too　　　D. much

14. Which is _____ country, Australia or Russia?

    A. larger　　　B. large　　　C. the larger　　　D. larger

15. This basket is _____ heavy for me, I can't carry it. That basket is heavy _____. I can't carry it, either.

A. very...very   B. too...too

C. very...too   D. too...very

三、用所给形容词和副词的正确形式填空

1. This is _____ (useful) book among the four.

2. Which can you speak _____ (fluently 流利), English or French?

3. John's watch was _____ (expensive) than yours.

4. This is _____ (beautiful) film that has ever come out of Hollywood.

5. Hans and Peter are exactly as _____ (old) as each other and exactly as _____ (tall) as each other.

四、翻译句子

1. My watch is less expensive than yours.

2. Tom is less intelligent than Bill.

3. My book is less interesting than yours.

4. Tom is less careful than Bill.

5. Mary is less beautiful than Jane.

6. 我比你上更多的课。

7. 你比我吃更多的苹果。

8. 这是我最漂亮的裙子。

9. 这是我最好的书。

10. 英语老师比数学老师年轻。

五、用下列词语替换句中划线部分:do, phone, at table, take, overtake, famous, neighbour, by yourself

1. The Greens are <u>having lunch.</u>

2. Did you do it <u>alone</u>?

3. Jim <u>caught up with</u> the man.

4. He <u>was driving</u> at sixty miles an hour.

5. We'd better <u>listen to</u> his advice.

六、书面表达

根据画面内容和文字提示,写一篇40～60单词的短文,短文的开头已给出。要求:要点齐全,表达正确,词句通顺,意思连贯。

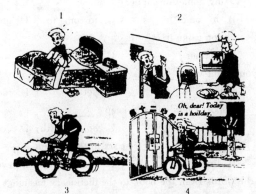

Yang Lei is a student of No. 12 Middle School. Last Saturday ...

七、完成句子:用 can't be,must be,can't have been,must have been 填空

1. The man speaks English very fluently. He _____ from America.

2. The old man looked very pale. He _____ ill.

3. Your sister _____ older than I. I went to school when she was still a bady.

4. She is here now. She _____ in Japan yesterday.

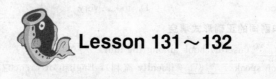

Lesson 131～132

一、单词拼写:根据所给中文意思补全下列单词

1. m _____(分钟 *n.*)　　 2. t _____(树 *n.*)　　 3. w _____(错误的 *adj.*)

4. p _____(图画 *n.*)　　 5. w _____(妇女 *n.*)

二、语法和词汇:从 A、B、C、D 中选出正确答案

1. —Will you please stay here for the party?

　—Sorry,I _____. I'll have to go to an important meeting.　　　　(浙江,中考)

　A. mustn't　　　　B. needn't　　　　　C. can't　　　　D. won't

2. —Where's Mr. Lee? I have something unusual to tell him.

　—You _____ find him. He _____ Japan.　　　　　　　　　　(黑龙江,中考)

　A. may not/has gone to　　　　　　　　B. may not/has been to

　C. can't/has gone to　　　　　　　　　D. can't/has been to

3. The new car _____ us 90,000 RMB. It is too expensive.　　　　(哈尔滨,中考)

　A. takes　　　　　B. costs　　　　　　C. spends　　　　D. uses

4. —Why is Joanna not here yet?

　—She _____ come today,her mother is ill.　　　　　　　　　　(大同,中考)

　A. not may　　　　B. may not　　　　　C. may not be　　D. may not have been

5. What would you like _____,ma'am,lemonade or Sprite?　　　　(北京,中考)

　A. drink　　　　　B. to drink　　　　　C. drinking　　　　D. drunk

6. Would you like _____ my home for supper?

　A. to go　　　　　B. to come　　　　　C. to come to　　　D. go to

7. She doesn't like coffee. I don't like it _____.

　A. too　　　　　　B. neither　　　　　C. either　　　　　D. so

8. Have you finished your homework _____?

　A. already　　　　B. still　　　　　　C. yet　　　　　　D. too

9. Everyone must _____ sport every day and keep _____.

　A. does...healthy　B. do...healthy　　C. do...healthy　D. does...health

10. We have our _____ at about a quarter past six in the evening.

　A. supper　　　　　B. lunch　　　　　C. breakfast　　　D. evening meal

11. You can _____ the words from the book in the dictionary meanings of the words.

　A. look for　　　　B. look up　　　　　C. look out　　　　D. look after

12. They _____ a meeting from 2：00 to 4：00 yesterday afternoon.

　A. were having　　　　　　　　　　　B. were going to have

　C. have　　　　　　　　　　　　　　D. are having

13. Which do you prefer,fish _____ chicken?

　A. and　　　　　　B. to　　　　　　　C. or　　　　　　D. so

14. Please _____ my sister when I'm out.

　A. look after　　　B. take care　　　C. watch　　　　　D. look for

15. _____ country do you like, England or Germany?

　A. What　　　　　B. Why　　　　　　C. Which　　　　D. Where

146

三、用括号中所给单词的适当形式填空

1. People all over the world _____ (like) playing football.

2. Can I _____ (carry) these bags for you?

3. What _____ (be) the weather like today?

4. We _____ (not know) where he is.

5. Would you like something _____ (drink)?

四、翻译句子

1. Tom said that he was not feeling well.

2. The Smiths said that they wouldn't come to dinner tonight.

3. I want to know if you attended the lecture last time.

4. She wants to know if you're going to write him a letter.

5. No one knows why our teacher got so angry.

6. 当他进来时,您在干什么?

7. 我在打字机上打一封信。

8. 当时您的孩子在干什么?

9. 他们正在书房里做作业。

10. 当你在看报时,他们在干什么?

五、将下列句子改成用 it 作形式主语的句子

1. Reading in bed is no good.

2. To walk on such a road is dangerous.

3. Talking like that is no use.

4. That they'll come on time is doubtful.

5. That we have walked to the wrong way is undoubtful.

6. To learn English is useful.

7. To study English every day is necessary.

8. That we have been to Beijing is true.

六、书面表达

就植树节这一天的植树活动写一篇简短的日记。

要求:1.意思表达清楚,文句通顺、连贯;

　　　2.至少写 5 个句子,单词数 50 个左右。

提示:1.穿旧衣服;

　　　2.早餐后乘车到西山;

　　　3.挖坑、种树、浇水,每人种树 3 棵;

　　　4.12 点结束;

　　　5.感想。

七、完成句子:根据下列各句的内容将所给词语译成英语

1. You _____(可以去)there this afternoon.

2. Mr. Way _____(可能不来)today. He doesn't feel well.

3. _____(可以)I smoke here? No,please don't.

4. You _____(可以用)my dictionary.

5. Will Harry come tomorrow? He _____ (可能来)if he is free.

6. What were they doing yesterday morning?

    They _____(可能一直在打信).

147

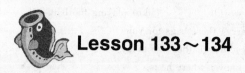

Lesson 133～134

一、单词拼写:根据所给中文意思补全下列单词

1. w _____（谁的 *pron.*)
2. h _____（帮助 *n.*)
3. n _____（附近 *prep.*)
4. w _____（工人 *n.*)

二、语法和词汇:从 A、B、C、D 中选出正确答案

1. A lion escaped from the park and went back to the mountain. This is _____ in our city.　　(辽宁,中考)

    A. sensible　　B. sensitive　　C. sensational　　D. sentimental

2. Obviously the bull is very _____ to the drunk's rude words.　　(北京,中考)

    A. sensible　　B. sensitive　　C. sensational　　D. sentimental

3. Deng Xiaoping is a very _____ leader—he leads China to a correct developing way. (大连,中考)

    A. sensible　　B. sensitive　　C. sensational　　D. sentimental

4. I cannot bear any girl who is like Lin Daiyu—too _____.　　(北京,中考)

    A. sensible　　B. sensitive　　C. sensational　　D. sentimental

5. —Could you lend me your bike, please?

    —Certainly. But don't _____ it too long. I am going out this afternoon.　　(上海,中考)

    A. borrow　　B. stay　　C. lend　　D. keep

6. Did Polly pick _____ apples?

    A. a lot of　　B. many　　C. much　　D. a lot

7. Shall we have a holiday _____ ten days?

    A. to　　B. on　　C. for　　D. at

8. The teacher told me that we _____ an exam very soon.

    A. would have　　B. will have　　C. have

9. Would you please go and _____ me something to eat?

    A. take　　B. bring　　C. carry　　D. get

10. The month after August is _____.

    A. the nineth　　B. ninth　　C. a ninth　　D. the ninth

11. He _____ dancing in public.

    A. like　　B. likes　　C. liking　　D. to like

12. It _____ Jim's birthday yesterday. He _____ good time.

    A. was...had　　B. is...has　　C. was...had a　　D. is...had a

三、用所给形容词或副词的适当形式填空

1. Marile is _____ (young) than Lucille.

2. Fritz is the _____ (small) of the family.

3. Ruth can run _____ (fast) than Frieda.

4. Ruth's hair is _____ (long) than Gretchen's.

5. Li Ming is the _____ (tall) in his class.

6. She works _____ (hard) than her sister.

7. They arrived _____ (early) than you.

四、翻译句子

1. When did he die?

2. You have also invited Mary to dinner.

3. What she had seen?

4. Why you were so rude to him?

5. When we shall have a meeting again?

6. 关于中国历史,Tom 一无所知。

7. 今天早上有人打电话来吗?

8. 晚上我总是读点什么。

9. 没有人会相信这个故事。

10. 我到处找我的英语书,但哪里也找不到。

五、将下列直接引语改为间接引语

1. The monitor said:"We want to help Charles."

2. He said:"My father is watching TV now."

3. Jim told her:"It's an American film and it costs a lot of money."

4. She told me:"I have given you a picture."

5. We said:"We're hungry."

6. The boy said:"This is the best way."

7. A woman said:"The purse is mine."

8. Mr. West told me:"I have sold the car."

六、书面表达

你校与澳大利亚某中学结成姊妹学校,澳方校刊来信了解你校的课外活动情况及你们的有关建议,请你根据下面表格中提供的内容用英语写一篇 80 词左右的短文。文章的开头已给出(不计入总词数)。

活动时间	4∶50～5∶50p. m.
主要内容	1.体育类(篮球、足球等) 2.兴趣小组(绘画、歌舞、电脑等) 3.英语角(周三下午)
建议	1.增加课外活动时间 2.减少作业量

生词:兴趣小组 interest group 英语角 English corner 活动 activity(*n.*)

I'd like to tell you something about the out-of-class activities in our school....

七、完成句子:根据上句完成下句,每空一词,意思不得改变

1. "Please tell me what happened, Helen." her teacher said.

Her teacher asked Helen _____ _____ _____ what _____ happened.

2. "How are you feeling now?" the doctor asked her.

The doctor asked her _____ _____ _____ feeling _____.

3. Mother said, "Don't put it on this table."

Mother told me _____ _____ _____ it on _____ table.

4. He said, "Did you see Tom last night?"

He asked me _____ _____ _____ _____ Tom _____ night _____.

5. She said, "I will come here next week."

She said that _____ _____ _____ _____ _____ next week.

149

Lesson 135～136

一、单词拼写：根据所给中文意思补全下列单词

1. _____ / ˈtrʌbl/(麻烦 *v.*)　　　2. _____ /hɔːs/(马 *n.*)
3. _____ /nɔiz/(噪音 *n.*)　　　4. _____ /sliːp/(睡觉 *v.*)

二、语法和词汇：从 A、B、C、D 中选出正确答案

1. He doesn't know _____ English because he has studied it for only _____ weeks.　　　（哈尔滨，中考）
   A. much/a few　　B. little/few　　C. few/a little　　D. a few/a little

2. _____ of them has an English dictionary.　　　（大连，中考）
   A. Every　　B. All　　C. Both　　D. Each

3. It _____ me about a quarter to go to school on foot every day.　　　（山东，中考）
   A. pays　　B. spends　　C. costs　　D. takes

4. Jim asked Lin Feng _____ forget to change water.
   A. to not　　B. don't　　C. not　　D. not to

5. At last it made them _____.　　　（哈尔滨，中考）
   A. happily　　B. quickly　　C. friendly　　D. slowly

6. —Did she _____ home yesterday?
   —Yes, she did.
   A. walked to　　B. walk to　　C. walks to　　D. walk

7. —Where's Jim?
   —He's _____ the tall tree.
   A. in　　B. on　　C. at　　D. to

8. There are many trees on _____ side of the street.
   A. every　　B. either　　C. all　　D. both

9. What's the date today? _____.
   A. Sunday　　B. July 6th　　C. It's fine　　D. My birthday

10. _____ beautiful garden it is!
    A. What　　B. How　　C. What a　　D. What an

11. _____ nice shoes she is wearing!
    A. What　　B. What a　　C. How　　D. How a

12. Mike is not _____ Jim.
    A. as teller as　　B. so tall as　　C. so taller than　　D. as taller than

三、翻译句子

1. The teacher was asked to tell a story by the students.　　　6. 我被要求站起来。
2. This kind of trees will be seen everywhere.　　　7. 他被要求去关门。
3. I will be sent to study abroad next year.　　　8. 她被要求走出来。
4. Water can be changed into vapour by heating.　　　9. 我们被邀请吃饭。
5. The window has been cleaned by me.　　　10. 我们玩得很高兴。

四、用所给形容词和副词的适当形式填空

1. Tom is _____ (lazy) student in our class.

2. There are _____ (few) books in this library than in that one.

3. I have _____ (little) free time than he.

4. Mary is _____ (young) than her husband.

5. My watch runs _____ (fast) than his.

6. The days are _____ (long) in summer than in winter.

五、用所给句子补充对话

A. Who teaches you English?

B. Does he like China?

C. Can he speak Chinese?

D. Where are you going?

E. How long has he lived in China?

A：__1__ Jack.

B：To Turner's. We are going to have English lessons.

A：__2__

B：Mr. Turner.

A：__3__

六、用现在完成时填空

1. He _____ (just make) the beds.

2. Steve _____ (just return) from America.

3. Jim _____ (just meet) his girl friend at the airport.

4. _____ Sue _____ (eat) all the cream cakes?

5. Billy _____ (just get) a letter from his parents.

6. Sorry, Mum. I _____ (just break) windows.

7. _____ he _____ (already hand) his paper to Mr. White?

8. Jim _____ (just take) the dog for a walk.

七、书面表达

根据所给的八幅图画，以"Li Ming's Happiest Day"为题，按图画顺序写一篇短文，不少于十句话，内容必须符合题意，图外的单词供使用。

1. last Sunday　2. get up　3. breakfast　4. play

5. home　6. supper　7. watch　8. go to bed

八、完成句子：将括号中的汉语译成英语

1. He won't let me _____ (制作一部新电影).

2. _____ (我来自我介绍一下). I'm a student of English.

3. _____ (我们都很高兴), when we heard that we would go to Dalian for our summer holidays.

4. We won't leave her _____ (在最新消息来到之前).

5. She told me _____ (老人前天去世的).

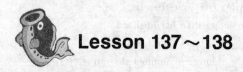

Lesson 137～138

一、单词拼写:根据所给中文意思补全下列单词

1. _____ /weit/(等 *v.*)　　　　　2. _____ /in'dʒɔid/(享受 *v.*)

3. _____ /həul/(整个 *adj.*)　　　4. _____ /'sʌðən/(南方的 *adj.*)

5. _____ /'intrist/(名胜 *n.*)

二、语法和词汇:从 A、B、C、D 中选出正确答案

1. I like exciting trips. I'd love to travel _____ the Amazon jungle next summer,because it's a good place to explore.

   A. across　　　　　B. through　　　　　C. crossing　　　　　D. cross

2. While I _____ with my friend,she came in.

   A. am talking　　　B. was talking　　　C. talked　　　　　D. am going to talk

3. All of us enjoy playing computer games,_____ we can't spend too much time on it.

   A. and　　　　　　B. or　　　　　　　C. but　　　　　　　D. so

4. Would you please tell me _____ ?

   A. what was her name　　　　　　　　B. what her name was

   C. what is her name　　　　　　　　　D. what her name is

5. —We can use QQ to talk with each other on the Internet.

   —Really? Will you please show me _____ it?

   A. what to use　　　B. how to use　　　　C. how can I use　　　D. what can I use

6. We can see there isn't _____ milk in the bottle.

   A. many　　　　　　B. any　　　　　　　C. few　　　　　　　D. some

7. I am _____ . My father is _____ .

   A. at the school. . . at work　　　　　　B. at school. . . at the work

   C. at school. . . at work　　　　　　　D. at school. . . in work

8. _____ the teachers can swim in our school pool.

   A. Only　　　　　　B. There are　　　　C. Some　　　　　　D. Any

9. —What can I do for you?

   —_____ .

   A. Half a kilo bread　　　　　　　　B. Half a kilo of bread

   C. A kilo half bread　　　　　　　　D. A kilo and a half

10. The man _____ many books in the book shop every day.

   A. buys　　　　　　B. wants　　　　　　C. have　　　　　　D. sells

11. I think _____ are wrong.

   A. all of you　　　　B. all you　　　　　C. all of the you　　　D. /

12. _____ forget to bring your homework next time.

   A. Not　　　　　　B. Aren't　　　　　　C. Don't　　　　　　D. Doesn't

13. She often _____ milk and toast for breakfast and doesn't _____ it at home.

   A. have. . . have　　B. eat. . . 'eat　　　　C. have. . . has　　　D. has. . . have

14. I don't like pies _____ apple _____ them.

   A. with. . . in　　　　B. in. . . with　　　　C. full. . . in　　　　D. have. . . with

15. My bike is _____. I think Uncle Wang can mend it.

    A. wrong   B. right   C. broken   D. bad

三、用下列动词的适当形式填空：wait, have, ask, say, knock, stay, walk, watch, lose, keep

1. "I'll come to help you." _____ the teacher.

2. Please _____ at the door before you come in.

3. My friend often _____ at my home when he comes here.

4. "Where did you get this book?" he _____ me.

5. I _____ home yesterday because there was no bus.

6. He _____ a bad cold last week, but he is better today.

四、翻译句子

1. His bicycle has been stolen.

2. She will be given a bag as a present by her parents.

3. The question will be discussed tomorrow.

4. English is spoken in many countries.

5. "Midnight" was written by Mao Dun.

6. 多漂亮的裙子！

7. 你看起来生病了。

8. 他被送进医院。

9. 她被邀请到我家。

10. 他们都出去了。

五、完成下列句子

1. _____ (如果你和我一起去)，your parents won't know where you are.

2. _____ (如果你不给他们留口信)，your parents won't know where you are.

3. _____ (如果你不告诉他们)，your parents won't know where you are.

4. _____ (如果你自己去游乐园)，they won't know where you are.

5. He'll go with you _____ (如果不下雨的话).

6. He'll go with you _____ (如果他不是太忙).

7. He'll go with you _____ (如果他有足够时间).

8. He'll go with you _____ (如果你想去的话).

六、书面表达

    请用英文简要地写出"郑人买履"的故事，以刊登在我国对外发行的某英文刊物上。字数不得少于 70 字，不得多于 140 字。

    故事大意：某人自量脚往市集买鞋，忘带尺度(measurement *n*.)，回家取，再来市集已散。人问："为何不以脚试鞋？"答："宁信尺度，不信自己的脚。"

七、完成句子：以正确的形式将括号内的动词填入空内

1. If it _____ (rain), the match will be called off(取消).

2. If I have time, I _____ (visit) the exhibition(展览).

3. If I see a nice present for her, I _____ (buy) it.

4. If you get a chance to speak to him, _____ (ask) him how his family are getting on.

5. If water _____ (freeze 冰冻), it turns to ice.

6. If you _____ (be) ill, you should see a doctor.

7. If it _____ (be) not too far, we'll go there on foot.

8. If an accident _____ (happen) to you, you should report it at once to the police.

9. If she _____ (have) any free time, she spends it in the garden.

10. If it _____ (be) fine, we always walk to work.

11. If I tell the truth, no one _____ (believe) me.

153

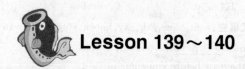

Lesson 139～140

一、单词拼写：根据所给中文意思补全下列单词

1. _____thing.(任何事 *pron.*)   2. ___ rs __lves(我们自己 *pron.*)

3. p ___l(拉 *v.*)   4. f ___(最远的 *adj.*)   5. h ___d(头 *n.*)

二、语法和词汇：从 A、B、C、D 中选出正确答案

1. —Mum，Mary bought a parrot yesterday. Could you please buy _____ for me?
   —Sure. But you must look after it yourself.
   A. one   B. this   C. it   D. that

2. The smile on his face shows that he is _____ his students' work.
   A. worried about   B. pleased with   C. sorry for   D. surprised at

3. —_____ is it from our school to Jingzhu Mall?
   —About half an hour's walk.
   A. How far   B. How often   C. How long   D. How about

4. —Why not swim in the river?
   —Oh，no. Teachers told us _____ here—it's dangerous.
   A. to swim   B. not to swim   C. to not swim   D. to swim not

5. —What a nice MP3 player! Is it yours?
   —Of course. I _____ 300 yuan on it.
   A. cost   B. paid   C. spent   D. afforded

6. He often _____ his car in front of the supermarket（超市）and flies a kite in the _____ near the supermarket.
   A. parks...park   B. park...park   C. parks...parks   D. park...parks

7. I _____ have lunch at school every day.
   A. at not   B. don't   C. haven't   D. /

8. The workers _____ to carry these parts of machines to the truck.
   A. want   B. give   C. like   D. ask

9. Take your dirty socks away. _____ your new _____.
   A. Take off，ones   B. Put on，ones   C. Wear，ones   D. Wearing，ones

10. What about _____ fresh fruits?
    A. have   B. eat   C. to have   D. having

11. You must tell us why _____ late.
    A. are you   B. was you   C. you are   D. you was

12. My bike is broken, so I _____ come here by bus.
    A. must   B. can   C. have to   D. should

13. I _____ to go to school today because it's Saturday.
    A. need   B. needn't   C. don't need   D. not need

14. I _____ do the work myself. No one wants to help me.
    A. can   B. may   C. mustn't   D. have to

三、根据括号内的意义用情态动词填空

1. We _____(必须) finish the work today.

2. You _____(可以) go there this afternoon.

3. _____(能够) you sing any English songs?

4. We _____(一定要) study English hard.

5. _____(一定要) I come tomorrow?

No, you _____(不必要).

四、翻译句子

1. The students asked the teacher to tell a story.

2. You'll see this kind of trees everywhere.

3. They will send me to study abroad next year.

4. You can change water into vapour by heating.

5. I have cleaned the window.

6. 我们玩得很高兴。

7. 他们两人都是老师。

8. 我们都是好学生。

9. 怎么了？

10. 你好吗？

五、将下列副词放入对应句中合适的位置

often   1. Is he late?

never   2. I'll go to that hotel again.

always   3. I do.

already   4. They have gone there.

ever   5. Have you been in an aeroplane?

still   6. Do you live in Beijing?

often   7. I go to the theatre.

never   8. We have been there.

六、书面表达

假定你的名字叫王莉，住在北京东长安街233号。今年六月份，美国青年学生 Jack Cooper 随青年团访问北京，最后一天在青年宫举行告别会(farewell party)，你参加了，坐在 Jack Cooper 旁边。散会时，你和他互相拿错了对方的笔记本，事后你翻开笔记本，发现他的名字地址，才知道拿错了。现在你把笔记本给他寄回去，写一封简单的信说明，同时请他把你的笔记本按你的地址给你寄来。（字数：80～140）

七、完成句子

1. The teacher asked one of the boys _____.

A. if were any mistakes in his homework

B. that there were any mistakes in his homework

C. if there were any mistakes in his homework

D. whether were there any mistakes in his homework

2. Do you know _____ he did not turn off the light?

A. how   B. why   C. what   D. whether

3. Li Ping asked me _____ I would be back.

A. when   B. that   C. what   D. which

4. Can you tell me _____ is going to give us a talk next Monday?

A. who   B. whom   C. whose   D. that

5. Do you know _____ at the bus stop?

A. who they are waiting   B. whom they are waiting

C. who are they waiting for   D. whom they are waiting for

155

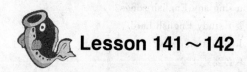

Lesson 141～142

一、单词拼写:根据所给中文意思补全下列单词

1. m__ddl__(中间的 *adj.*)   2. f__nn__(有趣的 *adj.*)   3. f__n(有趣 *n.*)
4. inv__t__(邀请 *v.*)   5. c___(汽车 *n.*)

二、语法和词汇:从 A、B、C、D 中选出正确答案

1. —I'd like to buy that coat.

   —I'm sorry. _____.   (广州,中考)

   A. It sold   B. It's selling   C. It's been sold   D. It had been sold

2. A new house _____ at the corner of the road.   (天津,中考)

   A. is building   B. is being built   C. been built   D. be building

3. The key _____ on the table when I leave.   (武汉,中考)

   A. was left   B. will be left   C. is left   D. has been left

4. _____ many times, the boy still didn't know how to do the exercises. (湖北,中考)

   A. Having taught   B. Having been taught   C. Taught   D. Teaching

5. The blackboard _____ by the girl students after class.

   A. often cleans   B. often cleaned   C. is often cleaning   D. is often cleaned

6. I _____ by them at the door.

   A. saw   B. seen   C. was seen   D. see

7. —Please tell Mary to come.

   —I think she _____ come already.

   A. have   B. has   C. had   D. is having

8. Miss Yang often helps the students. She is very _____.

   A. help   B. helps   C. helpfully   D. helpful

9. They _____ by Tom.

   A. are invited   B. invite   C. invited   D. are inviting

10. Did he catch the train or _____ it yesterday?

    A. get   B. take   C. miss   D. forget

11. What have you done _____ the library book?

    A. in   B. with   C. at   D. by

12. He said _____ the man _____ had bought the radio had long hair.

    A. who; who   B. who; that   C. that; who   D. that; which

13. Do you know the girl _____ a red hat?

    A. in   B. on   C. with   D. at

14. He is the man _____ I served this morning.

    A. which   B. that   C. whom   D. both B and C

15. —Where is Mr. Wang?

    —He _____ the office.

    A. went to   B. is going to   C. has been to   D. has gone to

三、翻译句子

1. Can you tell me what you were doing at 8 last night?

2. I want to know when you will return the book to me.

3. She asks where you spent your last winter holidays.

4. Tom is an honest child.

5. So am I.

6. 我想借这本书。

7. 我想和你在一起。

8. 下课了。

9. 明天见。

10. 你真好。

四、用所给动词的适当形式填空

1. The man _____ (repair) your bicycle from 7 to 10 this morning.

   He _____ already _____ (repair) it now.

2. Why didn't you come to the party last night?

   I _____ (work) in the factory then.

3. What _____ you _____ (do) now?

   I _____ (play) with snow.

五、把下列句子改为被动语态

1. My aunt is making my coat now.

2. I post a letter to my parents every month.

3. They told me to be there before 6.

4. The policemen caught two thieves last Sunday.

5. You can't go into the room. Father is mopping the floor.

6. Jane gave us a lecture last week.

7. I make the bed every day.

8. Before English class, we always sing an English song.

157

六、书面表达

一个国际青年参观团正在访问我国某城市,你负责安排他们的参观活动。请起草一份通知,准备向参观团团员宣读。通知必须用一段话说明以下几点:

   1. 参观日期:7 月 22 日,星期六。

      时　间:早餐后 8 点出发。午餐在参观地点吃。

   2. 参观内容:分四组,每组参观一个地方——工厂、农场、学校或医院。

   3. 欢迎每人参加一组活动。请选择好参观地点,并在今晚 9 点前到服务台(the Service Desk)签名。

注意:1. 通知用英语写,约 70~100 个词。要求意思、语句连贯。

　　　2. 通知只需把要点讲清楚。不要把说明部分逐条译成英语。

　　　3. 通知的开头已写在下面,不计入总词数。

Ladies and gentlemen,

　　May I have your attention, please?

七、完成句子:将下列句子改成被动式,省略动作的执行者

1. They clean the house once a week.

2. Someone broke the window.

3. Someone stole our car.

4. The postman opens the letter-box twice a day.

5. They often wash the car.

6. Someone repaired the clock.

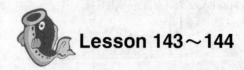

Lesson 143～144

一、单词拼写:根据所给中文意思补全下列单词

1. _____(他们的 *pron.*)   2. b__d(床 *n.*)   3. h____(她的 *pron.*)

4. t____n(城镇 *n.*)   5. __sk(问 *v.*)

二、语法和词汇:从 A、B、C、D 中选出正确答案

1. —Do you like the material?

　—Yes, it _____ very soft.　　　　　　　　　　　　　　　　　(上海,中考)

　A. is feeling　　　　B. felt　　　　C. feels　　　　D. is felt

2. It is difficult for a foreigner _____ Chinese.　　　　　　　　(郑州,中考)

　A. write　　　　B. to write　　　　C. to be written　　D. written

3. I have no more letters _____, thank you.

　A. to type　　　　B. typing　　　　C. to be typed　　D. typed

4. Take care! Don't drop the ink on your shirt, for it _____ easily.

　A. won't wash out　　　　　　　　B. won't be washed out

　C. isn't washed out　　　　　　　D. isn't washing out

5. Nobody noticed the thief slip into the house because the lights happened to _____.

　A. bet put up　　　　B. give in　　　C. be turned off　　D. go away

6. I hope you can come _____ my house _____ my birthday party next Saturday.

　A. in, for　　　　B. for, for　　　C. to, for　　　D. with, for

7. There _____ some milk in the bottle.

　A. are　　　　B. is　　　　C. has　　　　D. have

8. This must be the very _____ where the accident took place.

　A. spring　　　　B. spy　　　　C. spot　　　　D. earth

9. Monkeys are running and jumping _____.

　A. all time　　　　B. all times　　　C. all the time　　D. all the times

10. A bridge _____ over the river.

　A. built　　　　B. was building　　C. was built　　　D. build

11. The plays _____ now.

　A. put on　　　　B. are put on　　　C. are putting on　　D. puts on

12. The patient _____ tomorrow.

　A. will be operated on B. will operate　　C. repairing　　　D. be operated

13. The barber shop is _____ the corner of street.

　A. in　　　　B. on　　　　C. to　　　　D. at

14. —I can't find my key. Have you seen it anywhere?

　—It _____ in your handbag, I think.

　A. may be　　　　B. can be　　　　may　　　　must

15. —Mr. Green isn't a teacher, is he?

　—_____. He's taught in that school for many years.

　A. No, he is　　　　B. Yes, he isn't　C. No, he isn't　　D. Yes, he is.

三、介词填空

1. The Intelligence Test was too difficult _____ Tom. He could answer only half _____ all the questions.

2. I am sure the fellow next _____ Dick did not pass the test. I am sure _____ it.

3. I waited for him _____ the bottom of the hill _____ two hours yesterday.

4. We had our lunch _____ the restaurant next _____ our factory.

四、翻译句子

1. That house is too expensive.

2. We cannot buy it.

3. The pear is very soft.

4. My grandmother can eat it.

5. It was too dark.

6. 我不能出去。

7. 墙太低了。

8. 你能跳下去。

9. 她很聪明。

10. 她能回答这个问题。

五、用下列词语填空：be covered with, among, between, through, excited, exciting

1. He worked _____ the night.

2. On their way they had to pass _____ the busiest street.

3. Divide the chocolates _____ you.

4. The little boy was sitting _____ his parents.

5. His shirt _____ dust.

6. You must decide _____ these two.

7. That was an _____ book. It was worth reading again.

8. We were too _____ to go to sleep.

六、书面表达

请根据下面提示,写一篇以"My Hometown Today"为题的短文。

1. 去年暑假刚开始,你就离开住在城里的父母到你的老家去度假。你的老家离城约 40 公里,乘车要一个小时左右的路程。

2. 你的老家从前是个小山村,四面环山,村前有一条小河。

3. 现在小山村比以前大多了。近年来,由于村民们的辛勤劳动和党的好政策(policy),许多人建起了新房,家家都有了电视机,有人还买了汽车。村民们的生活越来越富裕。

4. 你决心在校更加努力学习,以便将来更好地建设家乡。

(注:不要逐条翻译,字数 80～120 左右)

七、完成句子:以正确的形式将括号中的动词填入空内

1. The joke _____ us all. We _____ by the joke. (amuse)

2. The crowed _____ at the football match. (excite)

3. The snake _____ the dog. (frighten)

4. The little girl _____ by the big dog. (frighten)

5. The news _____ everyone. (surprise)

6. He _____ by the awkward question. (embarrass)

7. They _____ at the news. (surprise)

8. He _____ after his long journey. (tire)

9. I haven't got any money, but this never _____ me. (worry)

10. The good news _____ everybody present. (excite)

参考答案

Lesson 1~2

一、1. pardon   2. skirt   3. dress   4. yes   5. car

二、1. A 2. B 3. B 4. A 5. B 6. D 7. A 8. D 9. D 10. A 11. C 12. A 13. D
14. D 15. C

三、A：Is this your watch?

     B：Sorry，I beg your pardon！

     A：Is this your watch?

     B：Yes，it is.

     A：Thank you very much.

四、1. Excuse me，Pardon，Thank you

     2. Excuse me，Pardon，Thank you

五、1. C F I L N Q T W Z

     2. a d g j m p s v y

六、1. Is everybody

     2. Has she

     3. Does，do any

     4. Did，have，have 在此句中是行为动词，故疑问句不能将其提前。

     5. Has，any；Does，have any

     6. Did，read. 注意原句中的 read 是过去时。

     7. Did，anything. something 用于肯定句，anything 用于疑问句和否定句。

     8. Has，yet

     9. Does，do. 注意 Does 是助动词，do 是实意动词。

     10. Will，meet

     11. Are you. 陈述句的主语是第一人称 I 或 we 变为疑问句时，一般都变为第二人称 you。

     12. Have they；Do they have

     13. Was，built

     14. Has，gone，yet. 陈述句中用 already，疑问句和否定句中用 yet。

     15. Must，finish

     16. Does，go

     17. Do，have，have 在此句中作行为动词。

Lesson 3~4

一、1. number   2. cloakroom   3. daughter   4. teacher   5. here

二、1. C 2. A 3. B 4. B 5. B 6. C 7. B 8. B 9. D 10. A 11. A 12. D 13. A
14. A 15. C 16. B 17. C 18. D

三、A：Please give me my umbrella. This is my ticket.

     B：Thank you，Sir. Number Five.

     B：This is your umbrella.

     A：This is not my umbrella.

     B：Sorry.

四、1. Yes?   2. Thank you.   3. Sorry.   4. Is this your coat?   5. Thank you.

五、1. This is not my bicycle.

Is this your bicycle?

2. This is not my shoe.

   Is this your shoe?

3. This is not my shirt.

   Is this your shirt?

4. This is not my bag.

   Is this your bag?

5. This is not my book.

   Is this your book?

六、1. No. It isn't my skirt. It's your skirt.

2. No. It isn't my house. It's your house.

3. No. It isn't my dress. It's your dress.

4. No. It isn't my watch. It's your watch.

5. No. It isn't my umbrella. It's your umbrella.

6. No. It isn't my pen. It's your pen.

7. No. It isn't my book. It's your book.

8. No. It isn't my shirt. It's your shirt.

9. No. It isn't my car. It's your car.

10. No. It isn't my pencil. It's your pencil.

Lesson 5～6

一、1. Japanese　2. Swedish　3. Italian　4. make　5. morning

二、1. A 2. C 3. C 4. B 5. A 6. C 7. A 8. A 9. C 10. B 11. C 12. D 13. B
14. B 15. D 16. D 17. D 18. B 19. A 20. B 21. C

三、A：Good morning，Mr. Black.

B：Good morning.

A：This is Miss Sophie. She is American and a new student.

B：This is Miss Sophie. She is Japanese and a new student.

A：Nice to meet you.

四、1. D　2. C　3. E　4. B　5. A

五、1. She，She，her，It

2. his，She

3. He，his，It

4. He，his

5. Her，She，her，He

六、1. Where dose Miss Chen teach Chinese?

2. What is Li Lei，"What is (sb.)?"是一个问某人职业的句型,问某人职业还可用 What do（does）
sb. do? 或 What's one's job? 等。

3. How much did the book cost you? 注意原句 cost 是过去时。

4. How often does he write to his friend?

5. How do we write words?

6. How many pens has he? /How many pens does he have?

7. How old is his father?

8. Why can't he ride a bike?

9. Which cat do you like best?

10. How far is it from here to the People's Hospital?

11. What grade are Lucy and Lily in? 如果将 Two 划线,则应用 Which grade 提问。

12. Who often tells the boys about his stories?

Who (Whom) does the old man ofen tell about his stories?

What does the old man often tell the boys?

13. Whose coat is black?

What colour is Han Meimei's coat?

Lesson 7~8

一、1. hairdresser　　2. operator　　3. nationality　　4. milkman　　5. policeman

二、1. A 2. A 3. D 4. C 5. B 6. A 7. B 8. C 9. C 10. C 11. A 12. B 13. C 14. C 15. B 16. B 17. D 18. A 19. D 20. B 21. B

三、1. I am a new student. My name is Robert.

2. What nationality are you? I am Italian.

3. 你是邮递员吗?

4. 不,我不是,我是个工程师。

5. 很高兴见到你。

四、1. an, an　　2. a, a　　3. a, an　　4. a, a

五、1. either　　2. either　　3. too　　4. either　　5. too　　6. either　　7. too

六、1. What's his job? Is he a policeman? Yes, he is.

2. What's her job? Is she a policewoman? Yes, she is.

3. What's his job? Is he a taxi driver? Yes, he is.

4. What's her job? Is she an air hostess? Yes, she is.

5. What's his job? Is he a postman? Yes, he is.

6. What's her job? Is she a nurse? Yes, she is.

7. What's his job? Is he a mechanic? Yes, he is.

8. What's his job? Is he a hairdresser? Yes, he is.

9. What's her job? Is she a housewife? Yes, she is.

10. What's his job? Is he a milkman? Yes, he is.

Lesson 9~10

一、1. thanks　　2. see　　3. today　　4. woman　　5. dirty

二、1. D 2. C 3. D 4. D 5. D 6. D 7. B 8. C 9. D 10. A 11. A 12. C 13. D 14. B 15. A 16. A

三、1. 你好,海伦。你好,史蒂夫。

2. 今天你好吗?

3. 我很好,谢谢你。

4. 很高兴见到你。

5. 我也很高兴见到你。

四、1. is　　2. is　　3. are　　4. Are　　5. am　　6. is

五、Mrs. Helen：Good afternoon, Mr. Steven

Mrs. Helen：I'm very well, thank you

Mr. Steven：thanks

Mr. Steven：How is 或 How about

Mrs. Helen：How is 或 How about

Mrs. Helen：Nice to see you

六、1. How are you, Mr. Brown?

2. How is Mrs. Brown?

3. I'm very well，thank you，And you?

Lesson 11～12

一、1. catch   2. brother   3. her   4. blue   5. whose

二、1. A 2. A 3. C 4. C 5. D 6. C 7. C 8. C 9. A 10. C 11. C 12. B 13. A

  14. B 15. A 16. B 17. B 18. A 19. B 20. B 21. A 22. A 23. A

三、1. Tim，is this your shirt?

2. No，Sir，this is not my shirt. My shirt is blue.

3. Whose shirt is this，then?

4. Perhaps it's Dam's.

5. —Here you are. Catch it.

    —Thank you，Sir.

四、①shirt   ②shirt   ③my shirt   ④Tom's   ⑤Catch it   ⑥Thank you

五、1. Mr. Zhang's office   2. my mother's book   3. Susan's car

  4. my sister's skirt   5. Jim's shirt

六、1. Whose is this tie? It's my brother's. It's his tie.

2. Whose is this shirt? It's Tim's . It's his shirt.

3. Whose is this dress? It's my daughter's. It's her dress.

4. Whose is this skirt? It's my mother's. It's her skirt.

5. Whose is this pen? It's my son's. It's his pen.

6. Whose is this coat? It's Miss Dupont's. It's her coat.

7. Whose is this suit? It's my father's. It's his suit.

8. Whose is this umbrella? It's Mr. Ford's. It's his umbrella.

9. Whose is this blouse? It's my sister's. It's her blouse.

10. Whose is this handbag? It's Stella's. It's her handbag.

Lesson 13～14

一、1. smart   2. same   3. hat   4. dog   5. upstairs

二、1. B 2. C 3. B 4. B 5. C 6. C 7. A 8. C 9. C 10. D 11. A 12. C 13. B

  14. D 15. A 16. C

三、1. What colour is your new suit?

2. It is green.

3. Come upstairs and see it.

4. Thank you.

5. 多么漂亮的帽子！

四、1. the → The   2. are → is，are → is   3. same 前加 the   4. green 前加 are   5. or → and

五、1. yellow bag   2. red car   3. grey shirt

  4. black case   5. green hat   6. white skirt

  7. blue sky   8. brown eye   9. black and grey coat

  10. brown and white cat

六、A：What colour's your car?

B：It isn't black. It's white，but my father's car is black.

A：All right.

A：That is a lovely car.

Lesson 15～16

一、1. Norwegian   2. tourist   3. girl   4. black   5. these

二、1. B 2. B 3. A 4. C 5. C 6. A 7. D 8. A 9. D 10. B 11. C 12. B 13. D 14. B 15. C 16. B 17. D 18. D 19. B 20. C 21. A

三、1. 你们是西班牙人吗?

2. 不,我们是丹麦人。

3. Are your friends Danish, too?

4. No, they are Norwegians.

5. These are our passports.

四、1. He 2. They 3. They 4. her 5. It

五、/s/ books, mechanics, makes, maps

/z/ handbags, teachers, ties, umbrellas

/ts/ suits, coats, tourists, carpets, students

/dz/ beds, friends, Spaniards, Swedes

/iz/ dresses, blouses, boxes, nurses, shoes

六、1. Is, is, is 2. is, is, am 3. are, is 4. are, are 5. is, is, are 6. is, is, are 7. is, are 8. are, Are 9. are, are 10. Are, are, is

Lesson 17～18

一、1. office 2. sales 3. employee 4. lazy 5. very

二、1. D 2. D 3. D 4. C 5. C 6. B 7. C 8. C 9. B 10. B 11. A 12. C 13. A

三、1. Come and meet our employee-Mr. Li.

2. Thank you, Mr. Jack.

3. Those girls are hardworking. What are their jobs?

4. They are keyboard operators.

5. They are hardworking.

6. 这年轻人是谁?

7. 这是吉姆。

8. 他是我们办公室的助手。

9. 你好。

10. 他是非常勤劳的。

四、1. policewomen 2. milkmen 3. books 4. carpets 5. ties

6. students 7. operators 8. housewives 9. boxes 10. nationalities

11. policemen 12. air hostesses 13. houses 14. knives 15. men

16. postmen

五、1. a 2. an 3. an 4. an, a 5. an 6. an 7. a, a 8. a 9. a, a, a, a

10. a, a

六、

Dear friends,

I'm very excited to stand here and express my thanks to you all. I must say I have had a good time in your beautiful city. Your people are very kind and friendly. The beautiful sight of your city will remain in our mind forever.

During my stay here you have done a lot for us. Thank you for your kindness. I am returning home tomorrow. I wish you good luck in everything. If any of you have the chance to visit China, do come to my city.

May the friendship between us remain ever lasting!

七、1. B 2. A 3. A

Lesson 19～20

一、1. Mum　　2. tired　　3. right　　4. big　　5. long

二、1. D　2. D　3. A　4. C　5. D　6. A　7. C　8. C　9. B　10. B　11. A　12. D

三、1. What's the matter,children?
　　2. We are tired and thirsty.
　　3. Sit down here.
　　4. Are you all right now?
　　5. No,we are not.
　　6. 有个卖冰淇淋的。
　　7. 给，孩子们。
　　8. 请给我两个冰淇林。
　　9. 你现在好点吗？
　　10. 谢谢。

四、1. →C　　2. →D　　3. →B　　4. →E　　5. →A

五、1. The small house is theirs.
　　2. My room is untidy.
　　3. My aunt's cat is lovely.
　　4. The clean coats are ours.
　　5. The beautiful dress is your sister's.
　　6. This is Jim's old book.
　　7. My father is a thin man.

六、

Dear friends，

Welcome to China. I'm very glad to tell you what you are going to do during your 3-day stay in Beijing. Our headmaster is to meet you on Monday morning and he'll introduce our school to you. You will be shown around the lab building and the library in the afternoon. On Tuesday morning the students of the two countries are to visit the Great Wall，where Mr. Zhang will tell some interesting stories about it. In the evening we are going to have a party in Room 402. The Chinese and the English students will give nice performances. You'll have a talk with the Chinese students on Wednesday morning. You'll be free in the afternoon. And you will leave for Xi'an by train at 9：45 on Thursday morning.

That's all. Thank you.

七、A：I'm very hot and very thirsty.
　　A：there's a grocery (over there).
　　B：go and buy two bottles of coca-cola.
　　B：What's the matter?
　　A：The shop's shut.
　　A：Look！There's an ice-cream man over there.
　　B：Two ice-creams please.
　　C：Two yuan and four jiao.

Lesson 21～22

一、1. full　　2. sharp　　3. fork　　4. blunt　　5. knife

二、1. A　2. D　3. A　4. A　5. A　6. D　7. C　8. D　9. D　10. B　11. C　12. D　13. A
　　14. B　15. D　16. C　17. C　18. C

三、1. Give me the book,please
　　2. Which one, this one?
　　3. No,the red one.
　　4. This book?
　　5. Yes,thank you.
　　6. 给我一个领带。
　　7. 哪一个？旧的吗？
　　8. 不，新的。
　　9. 给你。
　　10. 谢谢。

四、1. you,it,me　　2. my,They,they,their　　3. They,My　　4. She,Its

五、1. small   2. big   3. little   4. small，large   5. big   6. big

六、

Oct. 28，2002   cloudy

What a day I had today! After school this afternoon，I got on my bike and started going fast. At this moment，an unexpected terrible accident happened. I was riding too fast without any sense of a coming truck from the left. Although the driver was quick to stop the truck，I was knocked down. My bike was broken down. Blood was trickling down my leg. My glasses were broken into pieces. Oh，what a terrible day! I've made up my mind to be more careful on the road next time. Never keep my bike going too fast.

七、1. me，This dirty one? That clean one，Here you are.

2. him，This empty one? That full one.

3. them，Which one? not this one.

Lesson 23～24

一、1. stereo   2. table   3. cupboard   4. plate   5. newspaper

二、1. A 2. D 3. B 4. B 5. D 6. A 7. C 8. D 9. D 10. C 11. B 12. B 13. B

14. D 15. A 16. C 17. B 18. A

三、1. The spoons on the plate are dirty.

2. These cups in the cupboard are empty.

3. The box on the floor is heavy.

4. The books on the shelf are old.

5. Those magazines on the desk are new.

6. 椅子上的领带有点短。

7. 地上的报纸是脏的。

8. 哪些?

9. 给你。

10. 谢谢。

四、1. a→an   2. woman→women   3. works→work   4. American→Americans

5. is→are

五、1. 你桌上的书是有名的。

2. 盘子里的匙很脏。

3. 穿红衣服的女孩是我的同学。

4. 我想买这个书架上的书。

5. 地上的箱子很重。

6. 你手上的书是我的。

7. 很抱歉，餐柜里的杯子是空的。

8. 墙上的画是有价值的。

六、

It is reported that an English party was held at 7：00 p. m. on Dec. 30th(Wednesday) in the No. 2 meeting room of our school. More than two hundred students and teachers came and took part in the evening party. They put on short plays，sang wonderful songs in English. Also they gave some dance performances. Mr. Brown from Australia also joined in the performance. He sang and played his guitar. All those who came to the party had a good time.

七、1. the magazine on the shelf

2. the newspaper on the television

3. the tie on the dressing-table

166

4. the box on the floor

5. the plates on the table

6. the bottles on the sideboard

Lesson 25～26

一、1. middle　　2. electric　　3. where　　4. of　　5. Mrs

二、1. A　2. A　3. C　4. A　5. B　6. A　7. B　8. B　9. B　10. D　11. D　12. C　13. A

14. A　15. D　16. B　17. A　18. C　19. C

三、1. There is a bottle in the refrigerator　　　6. 给我一本书。

2. Is it empty?　　　　　　　　　　　　　　7. 哪本?

3. It is not full.　　　　　　　　　　　　　8. 书架上的那本书。

4. What is in the bottle?　　　　　　　　　9. 有一些书在书架上。

5. There is milk in the bottle.

四、1. in　　　　2. on　　　　3. in　　　　4. on　　　　5. on

五、1. There's　　2. There're　　3. There's　　4. There're　　5. There're　　6. There're

六、　Our school lies in the west of our city. It is not big, but it has a long history. There are about 150 teachers and more than 1,500 students in our school. It has three teaching buildings and a library. To the east of our schoolyard is a large playground.

Our school is beautiful with trees and bushes, grass and flowers everywhere. When spring comes the whole schoolyard is dotted with colorful flowers.

There are the best teachers of the city in our school. The teachers are all kind and ready to help us. We work hard at our lessons and take part in different kinds of activities. Our school life is full of joy.

We all love our school life.

七、A:cooker　　　　　　B:It is on the left

B:a desk/a table　　　A:is the table

A:empty/clean

Lesson 27～28

一、1. door　　2. picture　　3. living　　4. armchair　　5. some

二、1. C　2. B　3. A　4. C　5. A　6. B　7. C　8. C　9. D　10. B　11. C　12. A　13. B

14. C　15. A　16. D　17. C

三、1. Are there tickets on the dressing table?　　　6. 桌子上有一些叉子吗?

2. Yes, there are.　　　　　　　　　　　　　　7. 桌子上一个也没有。

3. Where are they?　　　　　　　　　　　　　8. 食橱上有一些叉子。

4. They are near the box.　　　　　　　　　　9. 这些是谁的叉子?

5. Thank you.　　　　　　　　　　　　　　　10. 是史密斯夫人的。

四、1. Is there a desk near the window?

2. Are there any books on the book-shelf?

3. Is there a picture on the wall?

4. Are there any girls in the shop?

五、1. some, some　　　2. any　　　3. some　　　4. some

5. any　　　6. any, some　　　7. any, some　　　8. some

六、

Dear Carl,

I'm very glad to learn that you are coming next month. I would like to invite you to stay with

167

my family when you visit Beijing. You can have your own room and eat with us. I can also show you around the city. I'm sure you'll enjoy your stay at Beijing.

　　Please let me know when you are arriving so that I can meet you at the airport.

七、1. Is there a desk near the window?

　　There is not a desk near the window.

　　2. Are there any English books on the book-shelf?

　　There are not any English books on the book-shelf.

　　3. Is there a blackboard in the classroom?

　　There is not a blackboard in the classroom.

　　4. Is there a map on the wall?

　　There is not a map on the wall.

　　5. Are there any cars in the street?

　　There are not any cars in the street.

　　6. Are there many people in the shop?

　　There are not many people in the shop.

　　7. Is there any water in the glass?

　　There is not any water in the glass.

Lesson 29～30

一、1. clothes　　2. dust　　3. air　　4. shut　　5. sweep

二、1. B　2. B　3. D　4. D　5. B　6. B　7. D　8. D　9. C　10. B　11. D　12. B　13. C

　　14. C　15. A　16. B　17. C

三、1. Come in，please.　　　　　　　　6. 把衣服放进大衣柜里。

　　2. Please turn off the lights.　　　　 7. 打开窗子给屋子通风。

　　3. The bedroom is untidy.　　　　　 8. 整理床铺。

　　4. What must I do?　　　　　　　　 9. 掸掉梳妆镜台上的灰。

　　5. Sweep the ground and air the room.　　10. 倒空瓶子。

四、1. →C、D　　 2. →D、C　　 3. →A　　 4. →A　　 5. →B

　　6. →B　　　 7. →E、F、D　 8. →G　　 9. →F　　 10. →H

五、1. near　2. under　3. on　4. in　5. of　6. at　7. on　8. in

六、

　　One day，I was doing shopping in the market when I suddenly saw a big fire in the distance. Many people ran to see it and I also went with them. We could see the fire burning on the 11th floor of the Capital Building. Many people escaped from the building. But many others were trapped. Helicopters were sent to rescue them. Because of the heavy smoke，it took the helicopters a long time to land on the roof of the building. About 70 people were saved.

七、1. C　祈使句一般情况下不使用主语，A 可以排除。needn't 用在此句中在语气上和意思上均不妥。won't 更不切意。

　　2. A　根据上下文分析，只有选 A 才符合一般性的逻辑。can't 是"不可能"，而 may not 是"可能不"，but 一词后的那句中必须填 can't 才是正确的。

　　3. D　按照第二句的意思是，用 must 不当，should 和 ought to 虽也可表示猜测，但它们常用于表示经过推断后的结论，它们实际上是 must 的弱化，但其可能性是相当大的，故用在此不当。

　　4. A　最后一句话说，"我已经告诉他了"，因此，用"不必"needn't 才切意，故选 A。

Lesson 31～32

一、1. tooth　　2. basket　　3. type　　4. climb　　5. under

二、1. A 2. B 3. A 4. B 5. B 6. B 7. A 8. A 9. D 10. B 11. B 12. B 13. B
 14. C 15. B 16. A 17. C 18. B 19. A 20. A

三、1. There is a girl in the park.　　　6. 猫正在喝牛奶。

 2. What's she doing?　　　　　　　7. 你正在打开收音机。

 3. She is reading a magazine.　　　　8. 他正在开窗。

 4. What's that dog doing?　　　　　9. 她正在关门。

 5. It is eating the bone.　　　　　　10. 你正在做什么？

四、1. doing，talking　　　2. doing，sweeping　　　3. doing，playing　　　4. having

五、1. Are the children playing on the playground?

 The children are not playing on the playground.

 2. Are the students planting trees?

 The students are not planting trees.

 3. Is Jenny reading a picture book?

 Jenny is not reading a picture book.

 4. Is he drawing on the wall?

 He is not drawing on the wall.

 5. Are they having a good time?

 They are not having a good time.

 6. Are they drinking coffee?

 They are not drinking coffee.

 7. Is his son studying hard?

 His son is not studying hard.

 8. Are they watching TV at the moment?

 They are not watching TV at the moment.

六、

 Ring! Ring! The telephone in the fire station was ringing. A fireman on duty picked it up. "Fire! Fire!" a man's voice came from the other end. "My house is on fire. Please come and put it out!" The fireman asked, "Where is it?" The voice answered, "In my kitchen!" The fireman got angry. He shouted to the receiver. "Yes, I know your kitchen is on fire. But how can we get there?" "Don't you come here in fire-engines?" The man became angry, also.

七、1. is running 2. am reading 3. is going 4. is writing 5. is sharpening

Lesson 33～34

一、1. shave 2. wash 3. jump 4. shine 5. boat

二、1. C 2. A 3. C 4. B 5. C 6. D 7. B 8. A 9. D 10. D 11. A 12. C 13. A
 14. D 15. B 16. B 17. A 18. B 19. D 20. A

三、1. Sholly is sitting under the tree.

 2. There is a cat under the chair.

 3. There is a light over the table.

 4. I live with my parents.

 5. Please give me some glasses.

 6. 现在正下雨。

 7. 天空中有云。

 8. 他们正过桥。

 9. 河中有几条船。

 10. 她正看着船呢。

四、1. on, near   2. over, on   3. with, on, in   4. over, at

五、1. He is eating her breakfast now.

2. She is typing letters now.

3. I am doing my homework now.

4. My father is shaving now.

5. My grandfather is cooking for us now.

6. Bessie is dusting the dressing table now.

7. I am making the bed now.

8. My brother is sharpening his pencils now.

六、

Class 3, Senior Grade 1

No. 1 Middle School

Guangzhou, China

5th, July, 2002

Dear Fred,

I am very pleased to receive your letter of July 2nd. Thank you. In my school, English is an important subject. I like to study it, but I find it difficult to master it. I often make some mistakes in my exercises. For example, the new words and expressions I have learned are easy to forget, some idioms and grammatical rules are hard to grasp. How can I learn English better? Will you give me some advice on it? I'll be grateful to you. If you have time, please write to me more often. With my best regards.

Yours,

Li Ying

170

七、1. What are the men doing? ——They're shaving.

2. What are the children doing? ——They're crying.

3. What are the men doing? ——They're cooking a meal.

4. What are the dogs doing? ——They're eating bones.

5. What are the women doing? ——They're washing dishes.

6. What are the women doing? ——They're typing letters.

7. What are they doing? ——They're walking over the bridge.

8. What are the birds doing? ——They're flying over the river.

9. What are the children doing? ——They're doing their homework.

10. What are the children doing? ——They're looking at the boats on the river.

Lesson 35～36

一、1. off   2. park   3. photograph   4. along   5. into

二、1. B 2. C 3. A 4. D 5. C 6. C 7. D 8. C 9. C 10. D 11. C 12. C 13. B
14. B 15. A 16. B 17. C 18. A

三、1. Tom and I are cleaning the room.   6. 她正在走进一家商店。

2. Mary is teaching Li Ping and me English.   7. 杰克正坐在树下。

3. They and I are sitting under the tree.   8. 飞机在我头上飞。

4. Our daughter is walking between my wife and me. 9. 船在桥下行进。

5. I am going across the road.   10. 我们正沿街道走。

四、1. along   2. on   3. in   4. between   5. with

五、1. Mother is mopping the kitchen floor now.

2. I am sitting on the grass now.

3. They are planning to visit London this summer now.

4. How are you getting along with your classroom now?

5. He is digging a hole in the garden to plant the tree now.

六、

Information and Life

As you know, information plays an important role in our modern society. It affects nearly every aspect of my life. Then how to obtain and deal with information seems to be of utmost importance.

As for me, the first way to obtain information is to go to library. Various kinds of information can be got in it. Of course, library isn't the only source of information. I can learn much information by other means. Even when talking with my friends I can get a lot of useful information.

Information should be made full use in my life. Right now, I try to use information mostly on my studies. When I get into society several years later, information will probably become more and more important.

七、1. along 2. on 3. along 4. in 5. across 6. on 7. between 8. with

Lesson 37～38

一、1. hammer   2. pink   3. make   4. hard   5. homework

二、1. B 2. B 3. B 4. D 5. B 6. C 7. D 8. B 9. B 10. C 11. C 12. A 13. B 14. B 15. A 16. D 17. B

三、1. What are you doing?

2. I'm waiting for the bus.

3. Which bus are you waiting for?

4. Number 401.

5. I am not going to wait for the bus.

6. 你在做你的家庭作业吗?

7. 不,不是的。

8. 你在做什么?

9. 我在看电视。

10. 我看完后将做作业。

四、1. is making, works, is not, is   2. am doing, am going, finish   3. is going, is

五、1. He is going to see Martin the day after tomorrow.

2. I am going to make a phone call to my brother.

3. She is going to give the little girl a present.

4. Laura is going to eat ice cream.

5. Louise is going to write to her mother.

六、

April 14th, 2002

Dear students,

Thank you for your inviting me to the concert at the weekend. But I'm sorry to say I'm not able to attend it, because I have something else to do that evening. I'm sure we can enjoy ourselves some other day. I wish you a good time at the concert. Thank you.

Yours,

Mike

七、1. is going to be 2. is going to sell 3. are going to miss 4. is...going to cut 5. are...going to do; am going to paint 6. is going to rain 7. is going to have 8. is going to fall 9. is going to make 10. am not going to sleep

Lesson 39～40

一、1. careful   2. flower   3. show   4. send   5. go

二、1. C 2. A 3. D 4. C 5. D 6. B 7. A 8. C 9. D 10. D 11. A 12. D 13. D 14. A 15. A 16. C 17. A 18. A 19. A

三、1. What are you going to do with that vase?   6. 不要掉了。

2. I am going to put it on this table.　　　　7. 把它放书架这儿。

3. Don't put it there.　　　　8. 我们到了。

4. Give it to me.　　　　9. 它是一个可爱的花瓶。

5. Be careful!　　　　10. 把它给我。

四、1. Don't make, are having　　2. take　　3. Be careful, is coming

4. Is listening　　5. wait

五、1. on　　2. with, in　　3. out, after　　4. with　　5. at, in　　6. between

7. beside　　8. to, with

六、

My dear classmates,

　　We each are thinking about the future. What is mine? I've made up my mind to become a middle school teacher. Does it sound surprising? I began to have this dream when I was only a child. I love children. I don't think that it is a waste of time to deal with them all the year round. On the contrary, to me it would mean happiness. As we all can see, teachers are badly needed in our country, but not many of us want to become teachers. The main reason for this is that teachers' work is too hard and they get too little. In spite of that, I'm determined to give all my life to the cause of education.

七、1. Don't read in bad light.

2. Don't worry.

3. Be patient.

4. Be kind to the child.

5. Don't leave the office.

6. Don't miss your train.

7. Don't go alone.

8. Don't believe him.

9. Don't put the wine near the fire.

10. Be careful with that knife.

11. Don't be foolish.

12. Don't argue with me.

Lesson 41～42

一、1. bird　　2. cheese　　3. chocolate　　4. coffee　　5. bread

二、1. D　2. B　3. B　4. B　5. A　6. C　7. A　8. D　9. D　10. A　11. C　12. A　13. C

14. D　15. C　16. B　17. C　18. D　19. C

三、1. Is there any tea on the table?　　　　6. 冰箱里有啤酒吗?

2. No, there isn't.　　　　7. 有的,有两瓶啤酒。

3. Is there any coffee on the table?　　　　8. 请给我一瓶。

4. Yes, here you are.　　　　9. 给你。

5. Thank you.　　　　10. 谢谢。

四、1. a loaf of bread　　2. a tin of tobacco　　3. a bottle of milk

4. a bar of soap　　5. a piece of cheese

五、1. There's not any tea in the tin.

Is there any tea in the tin?

2. There's not any cheese on the plate.

Is there any cheese on the plate?

3. There's not any bread on the table.

Is there any bread on the table?

4. There's not any milk in the bottle.

Is there any milk in the bottle?

5. There's not any coffee in the cup.

Is there any coffee in the cup?

6. There's not any soap on the dressing table?

Is there any soap on the dressing table?

7. There's not any fruit in the fruit bowl.

Is there any fruit in the fruit bowl?

8. There's not any meat in the fridge.

Is there any meat in the fridge?

六、

Dear Robin,

    I'm very glad to learn from your letter that you'll come to Beijing. But I am sorry that I can not meet you at the Beijing Railway Station. Now let me tell you the way to my home.

    Get out of the station and take Bus No. 4 to Blue Bridge. Walk across the bridge, until you see a food shop on your right. There is a bookstore next to it. Turn left and cross the street, you'll find a hospital and a bank on your right. Go straight to the south. When you find a white building on your left, find Room 6. My father will be waiting for you at home.

    I will be back in a day or two and I'll show you around Beijing.

    Hoping to see you soon.

Yours truly,

Li Hua

173

七、1. Is there a passport here?

Yes, there is. There's one on the table.

2. Is there any tobacco here?

Yes, there is. There's some in the tin.

3. Is there any bread here?

Yes, there is. There's some on the table.

4. Is there a vase here?

Yes, there's one on the radio.

5. Is there any tea here?

Yes, there is. There is some on the table.

6. Is there a hammer here?

Yes, there is. There's one on the book-case.

7. Is there a suit here?

Yes, there is. There's one in the wardrobe.

8. Is there a tie here?

Yes, there is. There's one on the chair.

9. Is there any chocolate here?

Yes, there is. There's some on the desk.

10. Is there any cheese here?

Yes, there is. There's some on the plate.

Lesson 43~44

一、1. now   2. boil   3. kettle   4. of   5. make

二、1. B　2. C　3. D　4. B　5. C　6. A　7. C　8. A　9. C　10. D　11. D　12. D　13. C
14. D　15. C　16. B　17. B　18. A　19. D　20. C

三、1. Can you make the tea? 　　　　　　6. 快点。

2. Is there any water in this teapot? 　7. 他们在这儿。

3. There is tea behind the teapots. 　　8. 它在这里。

4. I can see them now. 　　　　　　　9. 它在你面前。

5. I can find them. 　　　　　　　　10. 我当然能。

四、boys　foxes　glasses　tomatoes　birds　children　dishes

五、1. pound　　2. cups　　3. pounds　　4. bottles　　5. loaves　　6. bars

7. piece　　8. pound

六、

Give up Smoking

　　Recently more and more smokers are trying to give up smoking, because it is a bad habit and does no good to anyone.

　　First, doctors and scientists have found that smoking is harmful to the smoker's health. It can cause some serious health problems, such as heart trouble or lung cancer. Second, smoking pollutes the air and is also harmful to others' health. Third, fires have been caused by careless smokers. Furthermore, smoking cigarettes is a great waste of money. It is not wise of smokers to spend money on such a bad habit.

　　Smoking does great harm to our health. I advise smokers not to smoke any more. It is time to give up smoking.

174

七、B：I can't　　　　　　　　B：All

A：see the two cars　　　　B：can you see

A：one car/other

Lesson 45～46

一、1. cake　　2. terrible　　3. ask　　4. can　　5. behind

二、1. D　2. C　3. D　4. A　5. A　6. D　7. D　8. C　9. B　10. B　11. D　12. B　13. C
14. B

三、1. Can you type this letter for me? 　　　6. 怎么了?

2. Can you stay here a minute? 　　　　　7. 给你。

3. I can't type this letter. 　　　　　　　8. 这个猫能喝它的牛奶吗?

4. I can't read the letter. 　　　　　　　9. 乔治能带给他这些花吗?

5. The boss's handwriting is terrible! 　　10. 我不能把它放在书架上。

四、1. see　　2. is　　3. open　　4. Are　　5. Sweep　dust

五、1. Can you tell him the truth?

I can't tell him the truth.

2. Can Mr. Zhang speak Japaness? Mr. Zhang can't speak Japaness.

3. Can you see the words on the blackboard clearly?

I can't see the words on the blackboard clearly.

4. Can you help me? I can't help you.

5. Can you go to Hong Kong for a holiday?

We can't go to Hong Kong for a holiday?

6. Can Tom stay up till tomorrow?

Tom can't stay up till tomorrow.

7. Can you do your best for your construction?

We can't do our best for our construction.

8. Can he move the stone? He can't move the stone.

六、

Li Lei, a friend of mine, is much interested in English. Last week when he heard that the English film "The Sound of Music" was in at the Grand Cinema, he went to see it at once. It was a wonderful film. The actress was not only beautiful but also brave; the children, though naughty, were very clever. Li Lei was gripped by the plot and the songs in the film were so nice that he couldn't help liking them. But he couldn't understand the conversations in the film, so after seeing the film, he made up his mind to study English harder.

七、1. can not remember   2. can   3. can not do   4. Can...type   5. can not understand   6. can not come   7. Can...swim   8. can not speak...can understand   9. can climb   10. can not eat

Lesson 47~48

一、1. w<u>a</u>nt   2. <u>o</u>range   3. <u>a</u>pple   4. fr<u>e</u>sh   5. b<u>ee</u>r

二、1. D 2. B 3. C 4. A 5. A 6. B 7. D 8. A 9. B 10. D 11. A 12. A 13. C 14. B 15. C 16. C 17. D 18. A 19. B 20. C 21. D

三、1. It often snows in winter here.

2. He has a big family. There are 10 people in his family.

3. Do you like coffee?

4. Do you want any milk in the coffee?

5. Yes, please.

6. 你想要一杯咖啡吗?

7. 不,谢谢。

8. 你想要糖吗?

9. 我不喜欢在咖啡里放牛奶。

10. 我喜欢黄油,但我不想要。

四、1. opens   2. does   3. studies   4. dresses

五、1. ones   2. ones   3. one   4. one, one, one, one   5. one   6. ones, ones   7. one   8. one

六、1. Yes, I do. I like beer, but I don't want any.

2. Yes, I do. I like whisky, but I don't want any.

3. Yes, I do. I like jam, but I don't want any.

4. Yes, I do. I like biscuits, but I don't want one.

5. Yes, I do. I like butter, but I don't want any.

6. Yes, I do. I like oranges, but I don't want one.

7. Yes, I do. I like eggs, but I don't want one.

8. Yes, I do. I like wine, but I don't want any.

9. Yes, I do. I like honey, but I don't want any.

10. Yes, I do. I like bananas, but I don't want one.

Lesson 49~50

一、1. m<u>i</u>nce   2. tr<u>u</u>th   3. st<u>ea</u>k   4. h<u>u</u>sband   5. b<u>ea</u>n

二、1. C 2. B 3. B 4. C 5. C 6. A 7. B 8. C 9. A 10. D 11. A 12. D 13. D 14. A 15. B

三、1. Do you want any beef?   6. 你喜欢羊肉吗?

2. My son likes bread.   7. 你想吃牛肉吗?

3. I am eating lamb.

4. Do you want patato or tomato?

5. To tell you the truth，I don't like patato.

8. 蒂姆想吃桃吗？

9. 赛姆喜欢卷心菜吗？

10. 她喜欢西红柿，但她不想吃。

四、1. Are cleaning are clean   2. Does watch does is watching

3. Are having   4. answer

五、1. either 2. either 3. too 4. too 5. either 6. too 7. either 8. too

六、

Dear Jack,

Thank you for writing to me.

First of all，join in more sports such as running，swimming and so on. I think you should do running every morning and try to run fast. And I suggest you often play balls with your classmates after class. I believe having more sports will make you stronger and healthier. I'm sure you will get along well with your study if you keep fit and healthy.

Best wishes.

Yours,

Tom

七、1. Are…cleaning，are，clean   2. Does…watch，is watching

3. Are…having   4. answer   5. doesn't live

Lesson 51～52

一、1. Russia   2. Sweden   3. Greece   4. December   5. September

二、1. B 2. A 3. B 4. B 5. B 6. C 7. B 8. D 9. A 10. B 11. A 12. A 13. D 14. B 15. C 16. C 17. B 18. A 19. C 20. D 21. D 22. D

三、1. What's the climate like in your country?   6. 七月和四月总很热。

2. What's the weather like in spring?   7. 秋天总是很暖和。

3. It is hot in summer. The sun shines every day.   8. 冬天很冷。

4. It is cold in winter. It sometimes snows.   9. 十二月下雨。

5. It is windy in autumn. But it is warm.   10. 天气非常宜人。

四、American   English   Norwegian   German   Brazilian   Swedish
French   Russian

五、1. in，in   2. in，in   3. at   4. in   5. from   6. along   7. in   8. in

六、

April 8th,

Dear Mr. Smith,

There will be a lecture on pollution given by Professor Liu from Beijing University in the Science Palace at 9：00 tomorrow morning. If you are interested in the lecture，please get to the Science Palace before 9 o'clock.

The Science Palace is not far from your hotel. You may walk there. Go out of the hotel，turn left and walk down the street until you come to a traffic light. Take a right turn there，and you will see a post office on your right. The Science Palace is next to it. I will wait for you at the entrance.

Li Hua

七、1. What's the climate like in your country?

2. What's the weather like in spring?

3. It's hot in summer. The sun shines every day.

4. It's cold in winter. It snows sometimes.

5. It's windy in spring and autumn，but it's warm. It rains sometimes.

Lesson 53~54

一、1. interesting   2. Korea   3. Nigeria   4. Canada   5. Austria

二、1. A 2. C 3. C 4. D 5. B 6. A 7. C 8. C 9. C 10. D 11. B 12. D 13. B

   14. B 15. A 16. B 17. B

三、1. I like spring and summer best.

   2. My husband doesn't like spring and summer.

   3. The days in summer are long and the nights in summer are short.

   4. The weather is our favourite subject of conversation.

   5. What's the climate like in your hometown?

   6. 你最喜欢哪个季节?

   7. 我最喜欢冬天。

   8. 冬天很冷吗?

   9. 白天长,夜晚短。

   10. 日出早,日落晚。

四、1. Which   2. What   3. Which   4. Which   5. What   6. Whose

五、1. Does Tom come from Nigeria?

   2. Does Mary come from Austria?

   3. Is the climate mild in England?

   4. Does the sun set late in winter?

   5. Does the sun rise early in the morning?

   6. Does he like to go to the south in summer?

   7. Do they both come from Finland?

   8. Does Jim come from Poland?

六、

Saving Our City

   It is very important to deal with the rubbish in cities. Every day people living in our city produce a lot of rubbish. If we don't have a good way to deal with it, or reduce it or reuse it, it will pollute the city, including the air, the water and the land we use. It does harm not only to ourselves but also to animals and trees.

   We have to have the rubbish sorted, have paper and glass reused. The rubbish have to be burried deep. The dirty gas must be made clean before it goes into the air.

   We have made and passed the laws to deal with the rubbish.

   We must do our best to prevent our city from being polluted.

七、1. prep 2. verb 3. prep 4. verb 5. prep

Lesson 55~56

一、1. together   2. arrive   3. afternoon   4. lunch   5. housework

二、1. B 2. B 3. D 4. B 5. C 6. B 7. D 8. C 9. D 10. B 11. A 12. A 13. C

   14. B 15. B 16. B 17. C 18. C 19. B 20. C 21. A

三、1. 他们的父亲每天带他们去上学。   6. He usually drinks milk.

   2. 瓦特先生通常每天晚上看报纸。   7. He goes to school every day.

   3. 她常在中午吃午饭。   8. He goes to bed every night.

   4. 他们经常在晚上听收音机。   9. He comes home very early.

   5. 他们通常做什么?   10. We do our homework every day.

四、1. lives   2. listens   3. does   4. washes   5. do...do   6. stays

五、1. at   2. at,at   3. in   4. in   5. at   6. for   7. at,in   8. on

六、

April 8th，Sunday   Fine

It's Sunday today. Early in the morning my classmates and I went by bus to Xiang Shan to plant trees. As soon as we got there, we began working. Some were digging，some were planting，and there were still some watering. We were going all out（全力以赴）to plant as many trees as we could. Each of us was afraid of falling behind the others. After work, we were wet all over. Looking at the lines of the young trees, we forgot our tiredness. We came back at 12 o'clock.

We all think it's necessary for us to take part in such a physical labour. It not only does us a lot of good，but also benefits the people.

七、1. lives   2. listens   3. are doing，go   4. am going，go

5. washes，is watching   6. shaves   7. stays，is doing，is going   8. do...do

9. does...eat   10. is...doing，Is...reading

Lesson 57～58

一、1. shop   2. usually   3. ten   4. six   5. three

二、1. A   2. C   3. A   4. B   5. B   6. A   7. A   8. C   9. D   10. B   11. B   12. A   13. D

14. D   15. B   16. C   17. C

三、1. The child always goes to school early.   6. 几点了？

2. Mrs. White reads newspapers every morning.   7. 孩子们每天晚上做作业。

3. The Whites go to bed at 9：00 every night.   8. 他们经常早睡。

4. They are going to work on foot today.   9. 今天早上我们乘车去上学。

5. Children usually go to play in the park.   10. 五点了。

四、1. is   2. are playing   3. Does snow

4. Don't come，are having   5. are reading，am reading

五、1. There aren't any newspapers behind the TV set. Are there any newspapers behind the TV set? Yes，there are. No，there aren't.

2. The boy can't put the box on the shelf. Can the boy put the box on the shelf? Yes，he can. No，he can't.

3. It isn't cold in December. Is it cold in December? Yes，it is. No，it isn't.

4. She isn't drinking tea in the garden. Is she drinking tea in the garden? Yes，she is. No，she isn't.

5. He doesn't usually wash clothes at night. Does he usually wash clothes at night? Yes，he does. No，he doesn't.

6. John doesn't always play basketball with his friends after school. Does John always play basketball with his friends after school? Yes，he does. No，he doesn't.

7. She doesn't teach us English this term. Does she teach us（you）English this term? Yes，she does. No，she doesn't.

8. There isn't any coffee in those cups. Is there any coffee in those cups? Yes，there is. No，there isn't.

六、

Dear Mike，

I have just noticed in the newspaper that you passed the entrance examination of Peking University with an excellent record，and I hasten to tender a word of congratulations on your splendid achievement.

Look forward to the day we meet again in Beijing.

Please give my best regards to your parents and your brother.

Yours，

Tom

七、1. drinks...is drinking　2. speaks...don't understand　3. is making...makes　4. am wearing
　　5. are using　6. go...am going　7. listens...thinks　8. do...have;eat...drink　9. are...
　　walking;walk;am hurrying　10. does...works

Lesson 59～60

一、1. pad　　　2. size　　　3. change　　　4. writing paper　　　5. all

二、1. C　2. B　3. A　4. C　5. D　6. D　7. A　8. B　9. B　10. C　11. D　12. C　13. D
　　14. B　15. D

三、1. I want a big box of chocolate.　　　　6. 你想要大尺码还是小尺码的?
　　2. Do you have writing paper?　　　　　7. 我想要一大盒粉笔。
　　3. I want a pad.　　　　　　　　　　　　8. 全部了吗?
　　4. What else do you want?　　　　　　　9. 都在这儿,谢谢。
　　5. I want my change.　　　　　　　　　10. 我想要一瓶胶水。

四、1. Does Mr. White usually read newspapers?
　　2. Is your father shaving in the bathroom?
　　3. Does he never do any homework?
　　4. Do you want any bananas?
　　5. Does your brother have a blue car?

五、1. for　　　　　2. after,at　　　　3. at,in　　　　4. by
　　5. at,at　　　　6. in,in　　　　　7. in,with,at

六、Dear friends,
　　　Your attention, please. I have something interesting to tell you.
　　　Tomorrow is Saturday. We have no class. We've decided to visit the exhibition of modern arts at the Arts Gallery.
　　　Those who want to go please put up your hands. You can go there either by bus or by bike. We'll gather in front of the Gallery at 9∶00 in the morning. Please be there on time.
　　　After that we're going to invite Professor Han from Beijing Artists'Association to give us a speech on modern oil painting. You must be interested in it.
　　　That's all. Thank you.

七、1. We haven't any beans, but we have some peas.
　　2. I haven't any potatoes, but I have some tomatoes.
　　3. We haven't any beans, but we have some potatoes.
　　4. They haven't any cigarettes,but they have some cigars.
　　5. We haven't any steak , but we have some beef.
　　6. I haven't any mince , but I have some steak.
　　7. We haven't any butter,but we have some cheese.
　　8. They haven't any wine,but they have some beer.
　　9. We haven't any bread but we have some biscuits.
　　10. They haven't any grapes,but they have some bananas.
　　11. They haven't any butter,but they have some eggs.
　　12. We haven't any lettuces,but we have some cabbages.

Lesson 61～62

一、1. earache　　2. temperature　　3. flu　　4. bad　　5. mouth

二、1. B　2. B　3. A　4. A　5. D　6. C　7. B　8. A　9. A　10. B　11. A　　12. C　13. D
　　14. A　15. A　16. D　17. D

三、1. What's the matter with Jimmy?

   2. Jimmy feels ill.

   3. He must go to see the doctor.

   4. He has a bad cold.

   5. He must take some medicine.

6. 他必须躺在床上一星期。

7. 他头痛。

8. 他必须吃些药。

9. 她发烧了。

10. 他得了流行性感冒。

四、1. at 2. in ,for 3. with 4. for 5. for 6. at

五、1. Must 2. can't 3. mustn't 4. can

   5. must 6. must，mustn't 7. Can't 8. mustn't

六、

October 16th，Monday   clear

    This morning I went to school by bike. I was riding along the road when a truck turned right in front of me. I couldn't stop my bike before it and hit the truck. I fell off my bike and lay on the ground. The truck stopped and the driver came over to help me up. Luckily I wasn't hurt. But my bike was broken. I had to have it fixed and take a bus to school. Later I wondered how this happened. Maybe I was riding too fast or thinking about something else. I didn't notice the truck turning right. I must be careful while riding a bike.

七、1. What's the matter with Alice? Has she flu?

   No，she hasn't flu. She has a cold. So she must have a good rest.

   2. What's the matter with Susan? Has she an earache?

   No，she hasn't an earache. She has mumps. So we must call the doctor.

   3. What's the matter with Jim? Has he measles?

   No，he hasn't measles. He has a temperature. So he must stay in bed.

   4. What's the matter with Tom? Has he a stomachache?

   No，he hasn't a stomachache. He has a toothache. So he must see a dentist.

   5. What's the matter with Mike ? Has he mumps?

   No，he hasn't mumps. He has a toothache. So he must go to the dentist.

Lesson 63～64

一、1. so 2. talk 3. remain 4. rich 5. better

二、1. C 2. D 3. A 4. B 5. A 6. D 7. A 8. C 9. B 10. A 11. C 12. D 13. A 14. B 15. B 16. D 17. A 18. C 19. D 20. B 21. C 22. C 23. B 24. C

三、1. How is Tom today?

   2. He is better. Thanks，doctor.

   3. He must stay in bed for another two days.

   4. He can't get up.

   5. He mustn't go to school.

6. 你不可以吃油腻食物。

7. 他发烧了。

8. 他必须呆在床上吗?

9. 你必须按时完成作业。

10. 他得了重感冒。

四、1. looks 2. is 3. doesn't have 4. go 5. remain

五、1. each 2. every 3. every 4. each 5. every 6. each 7. each 8. Each

六、

Dear Jim

    How are you? I am leaving this note to tell you that I have got the tickets for tomorrow's film. Its name is "TITANIC". The film will be shown at Shanghai Cinema. It will start at 7：30 p. m. Let's meet at 7：30 p. m. at the gate of the cinema. By the way，the film may end at ten. Don't forget to tell your parents you'll be back late. See you tomorrow.

          Yours，

          Li Lei

七、1. Please don't speak fast.

2. You needn't say it in English.

3. You mustn't talk in the library.

4. Don't come early tomorrow.

5. I can't see anyone under the tree.

Lesson 65～66

一、1. enjoy   2. baby   3. herself   4. themselves   5. myself

二、1. D 2. D 3. B 4. C 5. B 6. C 7. A 8. B 9. A 10. B 11. B 12. B 13. B
14. B 15. D

三、1. What are you going to do this evening?

2. You must come home at half past ten.

3. Can I have the key to the door?

4. You mustn't come home after a quarter past eleven.

5. Enjoy yourself.

6. 我们总是玩得很开心。

7. 我将去看一些朋友。

8. 8：30 了。

9. 他五岁。

10. 给她钥匙。

四、1. seven past three   2. a quarter past five   3. half past two

4. one to nine   5. a quarter to one

五、1. amount   2. bowl   3. tin   4. slices   5. cups   6. bags

7. pieces   8. pieces   9. blocks   10. loaves   11. bottles   12. lumps

六、

Dear Mr. Smith,

　　I'm glad to have received your money and books. Now，I can go to school again. I'm very happy and thank you very much.

　　I have been studying hard since I accepted your gifts. I have made great progress in my study. So our teacher praised me for it，and my parents encouraged me. I have made up my mind to study harder and make even greater progress with the teacher's help.

　　I'm looking forward to seeing you，but I have no chance to go to Beijing. I hope you can post your photo to me.

　　Best wishes!

Yours sincerely，

Li Juping

七、1. I must go to bed at half past nine.

2. They must return to the hotel at twenty-five past seven.

3. Tom must finish his homework at five to nine.

4. She must go to the library at a quarter past one.

5. She must wash the dishes at a quarter to eight.

6. We must see the dentist at a quarter to four.

Lesson 67～68

一、1. keep   2. spend   3. number   4. stationer   5. dairy

二、1. C 2. B 3. A 4. B 5. B 6. C 7. D 8. C 9. A 10. D 11. A 12. A 13. A
14. B 15. D 16. A 17. D 18. C 19. D

三、A：Were you at the butcher's yesterday?

A：Were you at the grocer's?

A：Was your boy friend at the grocer's, too?

A：他在哪儿?

B：不，我不在。

B：是的，我在。

B：不，他不在。

B：He was at the greengrocer's.

四、1. be   2. are   3. was   4. were   5. was

五、1. Who was late for school this afternoon?

2. What was there on the desk during the break?

3. Who was in the park last Saturday?

4. What were there in your father's bookshelf last year?

5. Who was in the Museum this morning?

6. Who was at the butcher's ten minutes ago?

7. Where was Jim yesterday afternoon?

8. What was he ten years ago?

六、

Dear Sir,

I am a 1995 graduate of the Department of Electronic Engineering of Tsinghua University. I know that your company offers a job to young men just out of college. I think this is a wonderful opportunity for me.

I am twenty-five, unmarried and in excellent health. Besides my specialized field，I love music and sports. I can read and write in English and Japanese.

I am hard working and always loyal to any job given to me. I get along very well with people.

I hope to hear from you soon. Here is my address：Room 302, Apartment 10#，Tsinghua U-niversity, Beijing 100080, P. R. China. And my telephone number is 4214849.

Thank you.

Yours Sincerely,

Li Ming

182

七、1. are 2. was 3. were 4. be 5. are 6. was 7. were 8. is

Lesson 69～70

一、1. crowd   2. Chinese   3. operator   4. Julie   5. stand

二、1. A 2. A 3. B 4. A 5. C 6. D 7. D 8. B 9. C 10. B 11. A 12. A 13. C
14. A 15. D 16. A 17. A

三、1. is   2. was   3. is,was   4. was,is   5. are,were

四、1. Have you been to America?   6. 那时他正在读一封信。

2. Yes，I have.   7. 蒂姆刚才在办公室。

3. When did you go to America?   8. 建筑物前有一辆轿车。

4. Last year.   9. 上星期五他们在这儿。

5. What did you do in America?   10. 这个年轻人在高楼里。

五、1. at,on   2. in   3. at   4. in   5. at
6. at   7. in   8. on   9. at   10. in,at

六、

A computer is a wonderful machine. It is used more and more widely in the world today. It can do many things as a man does，faster and better，too. It can control machines, do housework and e-ven play chess. Scientists are working hard to make computers do more things for human beings. Perhaps a computer will take the place of a teacher. But can a computer take the place of a student? I wish it could.

七、1. in...in 2. at...at 3. at...on 4. in 5. in...in 6. at...at 7. on 8. at...on 9. at
10. in...at 11. at 12. in 13. in 14. on 15. in...on 16. at

Lesson 71～72

一、1. time   2. sharpen   3. wardrobe   4. trousers   5. boil

二、1. C 2. A 3. A 4. B 5. C 6. D 7. C 8. B 9. C 10. C 11. B 12. B 13. C
    14. C 15. D

三、1. was,did   2. goes,stayed   3. is knocking   4. rained
    5. got   6. telephoned   7. Don't drive,is waving   8. wrote

四、1. 他看见伦敦上空有一架飞机。

2. 他们非常理解这个故事。

3. 孩子们吃了太多冰淇淋。

4. 哈伯早饭喝茶。

5. 他一小时前在河里游泳。

6. Mary and I enjoyed ourselves in Beijng last autumn.

7. He began to study at my school in 1993.

8. When did you begin to learn English?

9. I began to learn it ten years ago.

10. He came to see you the day before yesterday, but you weren't here.

五、1. Susan made her dress by herself.

2. I always got up at seven when I was at school.

3. They left Beijing last Monday.

4. We walked to the cinema.

5. Who drove that car?

6. Sam sat on that seat.

7. Miss Feng lived in the house.

8. They asked many questions.

9. How much was the meat?

10. Were those students in our class?

六、

Dear Tom,

　　I came to see you but you were out. Tomorrow is Li Hua's birthday. We will have (hold) a birthday party at Li Hua's home tomorrow afternoon. We'll dance, sing songs and we'll also have a big cake. We would be (will be) very happy if you come.

　　Li Hua's home is not very far from your hotel. If you want to come, you may go straight along Blue Road. Turn right at White Road, cross Stone Road, and then you'll find a cinema on your left. Li Hua's home is beside it.

　　Hope to see you at the party.

Yours,

Wang Xin

七、1. was,did   2. goes,stayed   3. is knocking   4. rained
    5. got   6. telephoned   7. Don't drive,is waving

Lesson 73～74

一、1. suddenly   2. hand   3. pocket   3. phrase   4. greet

二、1. A 2. D 3. A 4. B. 5. A 6. B. 7. D. 8. A 9. D 10. D 11. A 12. B 13. C
    14. D

三、1. at   2. on   3. in   4. in   5. in

四、1. 你上次来得很晚。

2. 我母亲正准备饭菜。

3. 他能理解这点。

4. 墙上有一些香蕉。

5. Didn't you tell him my telephone number?

6. Yes，I did.

7. Can't he come here before eight tomorrow morning?

8. No，he can't.

五、1. talks   2. tell   3. speak   4. told   5. tell   6. say   7. say   8. talk

六、

　　Nowadays it is not unusual for many students to find part-time jobs. This past winter holiday, I once worked as a waiter at a McDonald's.

　　I used to keep on asking my parents for money. It's the first time that I've earned money，so I was quite excited. Now I can buy whatever I need without asking others for money. From my working experience，I found it's good preparation for the world outside schools. I understood not only the value of money but also the way of getting along with others. What's more，I've got some (a little bit) working and social experience. It's good for my future work. In a word，I've had a wonderful vacation.

七、1. B 2. A 3. C 4. B 5. C

Lesson 75～76

一、1. buy   2. fashion   3. any   4. month   5. minute

二、1. C 2. D 3. A 4. C 5. D 6. B 7. D 8. C 9. D 10. C 11. C 12. B 13. C 14. C 15. D

三、bought, liked, wanted, buy, went, asked, were, were, told, were, were

四、1. May I go to your home at 9am on August 4th?

2. Wasn't this coat on fashion last year?

3. Can he understand that word?

4. Who did you meet in the street the day before yesterday?

5. How is she?

6. 我是在上海出生的。

7. 火车晚点五分钟。

8. 昨晚你看比赛了吗?

9. 他刚才给你打电话。

10. 他前星期到达了。

五、1. Dick drove a car to the office last Friday.

2. The girl sang an English song well at the party.

3. Mary had her birthday party with her family last year.

4. Lucy helped her mother with the housework yesterday evening.

5. Bill and Jim talked to each other this morning.

6. The boys played basketball last Saturday.

7. The baby cried last night.

8. She listened to the radio last night.

六、

Mr. Smith Robert

Dongfang Computer Company

Guangzhou

Dear Mr. Smith Robert，

Shuangfeng County Senior Middle School

Hunan Province

July 3rd，2009

　　I've learned from a newspaper that some clerks are wanted in your company. I'm eager to be one of them, so I'm writing the letter.

My name is Zhang Hua. I was born in Hunan Province and I'm in good health. I've just graduated from the Computer Department of Nankai University. I've done well in all the subjects and I'm especially good at computer studies and English. I can read science books in English and do some writing in English as well. Besides, I know a little French. And in my spare time, I like to play basketball very much.

Your company is very famous in China and is always well managed. If I have the honour to work for your company, I'll be very glad and work hard for it.

My telephone number is 0819—8841679, I'm looking forward to hearing from you soon.

With best wishes.

Yours,

Zhang Hua

七、1. saw　2. had　3. had　4. repaired　5. slept　6. took　7. met　8. went wasn't　9. visited

　　10. started...ended

Lesson 77～78

一、1. urgent　　2. walk　　3. talk　　4. ask　　5. afraid

二、1. B　2. B　3. D　4. B.　5. A　6. A　7. C　8. C　9. A　10. D　11. A.　12. C　13. D

　　14. D　15. C.　16. A　17. B　18. B　19. D　20. D　21. B　22. C

三、1. on　　2. on　　3. in　　4. at　　5. in

四、1. 我想见牙医。现在他能见我吗？

　　2. 我担心他不能。

　　3. 他能在10点钟见我吗？

　　4. 不，他不能，他能在下午2点钟见你。

　　5. 你的那项工作做得很好。

　　6. Where is Tom? He is having class in classroom.

　　7. We often have supper at 7：00 p. m.

　　8. You can enjoy yourself there.

　　9. Please wait a minute, I am having breakfast.

　　10. Would you want a cup of coffee?

五、1. said　2. tell　3. tell　4. tell　5. says　6. tell　7. say

六、1. Didn't you come very late last time?

　　2. Isn't your mother preparing for the meal?

　　3. Can't he understand the point?

　　4. Aren't there some bananas on the wall?

　　5. Doesn't the girl speak Japanese?

Lesson 79～80

一、1. list　　2. hope　　3. money　　4. newspaper　　5. vegetable

二、1. C　2. B　3. A　4. A　5. A　6. D　7. C　8. B　9. B　10. C　11. D　12. B　13. B

　　14. C　15. B

三、lived, went, came, stopped, helped, get, said, lost, called, sent, bring

四、1. Sawyer 一家去哪里度假了？

　　2. 他给你什么？

　　3. 火是什么时间烧起来的？

　　4. 谁告诉你去邮局的路的？

5. Are you doing your homework? No, I have finished.

6. It has rained for several days.

7. He has worked in this factory since 1992.

8. Where is Mary? She has gone shopping.

五、1. much　　　2. much　　　3. a lot of　　　4. a lot of

5. a lot of　　6. much　　　7. a lot of　　　8. many

六、

The 29th Olympic Games were held in Beijing in August, 2008. It was the first Olympic Games in China. And it was the most exciting games as well as the most wonderful performances in the opening and closing ceremonies since 1896.

In the games we won a great victory with 51 gold medals. The number of medals we got placed first. We are the champion. We are proud of our motherland and the players.

七、1. They need a lot of eggs. They haven't got many. They must go to the grocer's to get some eggs.

2. She needs a lot of bread. She hasn't got much. She must go to the baker's to get some bread.

3. He needs a lot of cheese. He hasn't got much. He must go to the grocer's to get some cheese.

4. He needs a lot of medicine. He hasn't got much. He must go to the chemist's to get some medicine.

5. They need a lot of magazines. They haven't got many. They must go to the newsagent's to get some magazines.

Lesson 81～82

一、1. nearly　　2. dinner　　3. roast　　4. holiday　　5. haircut

二、1. C 2. C 3. D 4. D 5. A 6. D 7. A 8. C 9. C 10. C 11. B 12. B 13. C

14. B 15. A 16. D 17. D

三、1. has asked　　2. have typed　　3. have turned on　　4. have sharpened

5. has emptied　　6. has boiled　　7. has painted

四、1. 他们必须现在开始工作。　　6. He is having a bath.

2. 我需要一本英汉字典。　　7. Have a glass of whisky.

3. 我们有许多钱。　　8. What time can we have lunch?

4. 花需要水。　　9. What's the matter?

5. 我们需要更多的时间。　　10. He's upstairs.

五、

There is a library in our city. I often go there after school. There is a large reading room in the library. We can read magazines, newspapers, and storybooks there. There are all kinds of books there, such as detective stories, novels, science fictions, plays and so on. You can borrow books from the library. But you must return them within five days. If you can't finish reading them then, you must renew them in time. We all like our library.

六、1. has two eggs and a bottle of milk　　2. had lunch

3. had a holiday　　4. have a haircut

Lesson 83～84

一、1. suitcase　　2. magazine　　3. cigarette　　4. light　　5. already

二、1. B 2. C 3. C 4. B 5. C 6. A 7. A 8. B 9. D 10. A 11. D 12. B 13. A

14. C 15. D 16. C

三、1. got 2. is not, went 3. am writing, started 4. go, are going to stay 5. rises, sets

四、1. 我们要乘8点19分的车去伦敦。

2. 下一班火车是什么时候？5小时以后。

3. 他是我们新搬来的隔壁邻居。

4. 女人总是最后说了算的。

5. 它确实值这么多钱。

6. I want two return tickets.

7. I believe that this house is for sale.

8. They're trying to repair it.

9. I forgot to take my umbrella with me.

10. He turned on the light，but he couldn't see anyone.

五、1. The students on duty haven't closed the windows. Have the students on duty closed the windows? Yes，they have. No，they haven't.

2. I haven't met him before. Have you met him before? Yes，I have. No，I haven't.

3. They haven't had a beautiful cake. Have they had a beautiful cake? Yes，they have. No，they haven't.

4. Mary hasn't received a letter from home. Has Mary received a letter from home? Yes，she has. No，she hasn't.

5. Mother hasn't made a pot of tea. Has mother made a pot of tea? Yes，she has. No，she hasn't.

6. James hasn't washed all the chairs. Has James washed all the chairs? Yes，he has. No，he hasn't.

7. He hasn't had any bread. Has he had any bread? Yes，he has. No，he hasn't.

8. I haven't worked hard all week. Have you worked hard all week? Yes，I have. No，I haven't.

六、

　　I have my own way of spending pocket money. Some money is got from my mother every week，and some is earned by myself by delivering newspaper, so I never waste my money. I always stop and think carefully before I buy anything. I always buy something useful，such as pens, books, English tapes and so on. Sometimes I give money to the poor beggars to help them. I think my way of spending money is wise.

七、1. have just received　　2. has read　　3. has already begun　　4. have never seen

5. haven't finished　　6. Has...worked　　7. have always arrived　　8. Have...got

9. has just returned　　10. have never had

Lesson 85~86

一、1. cinema　　2. film　　3. dirty　　4. crowd　　5. city

二、1. A 2. A 3. B 4. B 5. B 6. D 7. B 8. B 9. B 10. C 11. A 12. B 13. B

14. B 15. C 16. D

三、1. has already had　　2. had　　3. had　　4. is coming

5. are having　　6. are leaving　　7. are going　　8. has already had

9. will not go　　10. will stay

四、1. 你将去哪儿度假呀？我去纽约。

2. 我父母下周将飞往巴黎。

3. 他只有25岁，却到过很多国家。

4. 玛丽在干什么？她正在图书馆看书。

5. 我买了台收音机学英语，是上周买的。

6. Was he absent from school last week?

7. Can you get a pair of shoes for me，please?

　　I'm afraid that I can't.

8. I feel awful. I have a terrible toothache.

9. We haven't got much tea and coffee.

10. Tom is making a shopping list.

五、1. has been   2. have never been   3. has been

4. has always been   5. has, gone, has gone   6. has been

7. has gone, has been   8. Have... been, have never been

六、

    Water is very important in our life. Everyone knows that. When we drink, we need water. When we use lights, we need water to make electricity. When we wash things, we need water. Water can make things clean and our life convenient, so we mustn't waste any water.

七、1. has gone   2. has been   3. Have... been, have been   4. have... been, have been

Lesson 87~88

一、1. bring   2. climate   3. repair   4. Brazil   5. interesting

二、1. C 2. D 3. B 4. D 5. D 6. A 7. C 8. B 9. C 10. C 11. C 12. C 13. A 14. C 15. C 16. B 17. D

三、1. 我有一个哥哥。

2. 他是昨天 6 点吃的饭。

3. 他正在洗澡。

4. 史密斯先生理发了。

5. 他经常下午去游泳。

6. We are having lunch. Have you had it?

7. I had it half an hour ago.

8. I left a handbag on the train to London several days ago.

9. I think I had better call the doctor to see you.

10. I didn't shave on my trip.

四、1. is, am going   2. is, is getting, are   3. began, speaks   4. had, feels

5. do, are watching

五、1. have known   2. haven't seen, sees

3. is, is still reading   4. haven't finished, am still doing

5. am still watching   6. are still repairing

7. is still raining   8. is still singing

六、

Miss Wang,

    I am sorry that I can't go to school today, I have caught a bad cold. I cough a lot and have a high fever. I am very weak today. I have gone to see the doctor, he said I would be all right after I took the medicine. So I want to ask a sick leave for 3 days. I will come back to school as soon as I get well. And when I return school, I will catch up with my classmates.

LiLei

七、1. Has your father retired yet?

    My father hasn't retired yet.

2. Have you waited for me for a long time?

    We haven't waited for you for a long time.

3. Have you and Tom finished the work?

    Tom and I haven't finished the work.

4. Has the rain stopped yet?

The rain hasn't stopped yet.

5. Did they come the day before yesterday?

   They didn't come the day before yesterday.

6. Does he study very hard every night?

   He doesn't study very hard every night.

7. Are you doing your homework in the study?

   I'm not doing my homework in the study.

8. Are they from America?

   They are not from America.

Lesson 89～90

一、1. sale   2. return   3. still   4. pound   5. since

二、1. A 2. A 3. C 4. C 5. C 6. A 7. B 8. A 9. B 10. B 11. A 12. B 13. A
   14. B 15. A 16. C 17. C 18. B

三、1. have…studied, have studied   2. have…been, have been, Did…take, did
   3. didn't…know, flew   4. Have…heard, got, told, didn't say

四、1. John 后天将来看你。

   2. 技师们将在下下周修理你的汽车。

   3. 琳达将开车送你回家。

   4. 他已经在这儿学习了 30 天。

   5. 你去哪儿了？

   6. It's raining hard outside. The children are all staying at home.

   7. Have you just made a new film?

   8. Where are you going to spend your holidays this year?

   9. Are you going to sell your house?

   10. I have already sold it.

五、1. Have…had, have had   2. lived, went   3. Have…planted, planted
   4. haven't finished   5. did…arrive, arrived

六、

   I like football best. I began to play football when I was in the primary school. It was so inter-esting that I often played it after school. Now I am much stronger than before. So I became the member of the school football team last year. The teacher of P. E. is our coach. He used to be a good footballer and trained us very well. We often play football with other middle schools. I hope I will be a professional football player sometime later.

七、1. for 2. since 3. for 4. since 5. for 6. since 7. for

Lesson 91～92

一、1. arrive   2. move   3. remember   4. miss   5. library

二、1. B 2. A 3. D 4. B 5. D 6. B 7. C 8. B 9. B 10. D 11. D 12. A 13. B
   14. B 15. B

三、1. did…meet, met   2. Have…been, spent, Did…have, stopped

四、1. When did you sell your house?

   2. Last week.

   3. When will you move to your new house?

   4. Tomorrow afternoon.

   5. I will miss you. We have been good neighbours for several years.

6. 韦斯先生上星期卖了他的房子。

7. 新来的昨天搬进了房子。

8. 我正在拖地板。

9. 他们已经把房子漆成绿色。

10. 我经常在河里游泳。

五、1. does　　2. don't　　3. didn't　　4. did　　5. did　　6. do　　7. do　　8. do

六、

　　One day when Li Lei was on his way to school，he saw an old woman sitting on the roadside. Li Lei went to ask her what was wrong with her. She said she was lost. She forgot her son's address. Li Lei asked her if she remembered her son's phone number. She said her son's phone number was 51680625. It was easy to remember. Li Lei at once made a phone call to her son. Her son came there quickly. They thanked Li Lei. Li Lei did a good deed on his way to school.

七、1. He will go to work early tomorrow.

　　2. My father will go to work by car tomorrow.

　　3. We shall get up at six tomorrow morning.

　　4. Mr. West will sell his house the day after tomorrow.

　　5. The new people will move into the house tomorrow afternoon.

　　6. I shall sweep the floor tonight.

　　7. They will paint the house green tomorrow.

Lesson 93～94

一、1. pilot　　　2. repair　　　3. beautiful　　　4. Tokyo　　　5. Rome

二、1. C　2. C　3. C　4. B　5. A　6. D　7. C　8. D　9. A　10. A　11. B　12. D　13. C
14. B

三、1. 你必须在 10 点半回来。

　　2. 我们过得很好。

　　3. 难道你不幸运吗？

　　4. 那是个令人兴奋的结束。

　　5. 她不熟悉伦敦，她迷路了。

　　6. Where are you going for holiday? To New York.

　　7. My parents will go to Pairs next month by plane.

　　8. He is only 25 years old. But he has been to many countries.

　　9. What is Mary doing?

　　10. She is reading in the library.

四、1. Has...returned，will come　　2. did...buy，bought　　3. is，is reading　　4. Do...get，got

五、1. in　　　2. to　　　3. on　　　4. in　　　5. for，from
　　6. at　　　7. after　　　8. to，in　　　9. in　　　10. for

六、

How to Grow Chinese Cabbages

　　Spring is the best season for growing vegetables. The cabbage is a very common vegetable. When you sow cabbage seeds，first of all，find a box，put some soil at the bottom. Then put the seeds on it and cover them with more soil. Give them plenty of water and place the box in the shade. After a few days，the little cabbage grows up.

七、1. Where are you going for holidays? I am going to New York.

　　2. My parents will fly to Paris next week.

　　3. He is only 25 years old，but he has been to many countries.

4. What is Mary doing? She is reading in the library.

5. I have bought a radio to learn English. I bought it last week.

6. It's raining hard outside. The children are all staying at home.

Lesson 95～96

一、1. station   2. handwriting   3. behind   4. tobacco   5. platform

二、1. C 2. B 3. A 4. D 5. B 6. B 7. A 8. D 9. C 10. A 11. B 12. C 13. B

14. C 15. C

三、1. 他一定不要吃药。   2. 我必须马上叫医生。

3. 彼特最好努力学习。   4. 我们最好返回车站。

5. 琳达最好别告诉他这个消息。

6. It's eleven o'clock now. You had better go to bed.

7. You look pale. You'd better go to see a doctor at once.

8. We must finish the work in two days. We had better start the work now.

9. You'd better write the letters in ink.

四、1. am writing，shall finish   2. go，shall stay   3. is，have just finished，am going

4. gets，will get，will come   5. Will…be，won't，will go

五、

Dear Jane,

     Last Sunday my classmates and I went to Xiangshan Park. At 7：00 in the morning we met at the school gate. We arrived at the park at about 8：30. At the foot of the hill，we had a party and played games. After that，we climbed the hill. On the top of the hill we can see how beautiful Beijing is. We all feel proud that we live in Bejing. We are sure that the 2008 Olympic Games will be held in Beijing.

     I hope we will meet in Beijing in 2008.

     Best wishes.

Yours,
Li Ling

六、1. It's eleven o'clock now. You had better go to bed.

2. You look pale. You'd better go to see a doctor at once.

3. We must finish the work in two days. We had better start the work now.

4. You'd better write the letter in ink.

Lesson 97～98

一、1. handle   2. perhaps   3. employee   4. pence   5. label

二、1. D 2. D 3. A 4. B 5. B 6. A 7. B 8. A 9. D 10. D 11. A 12. C 13. A

三、1. His，mine，hers   2. mine，They，yours   3. I，my，you，yours

4. ours，They，theirs   5. Her，mine

四、1. 你的帽子是红色的，我的是褐色的。

2. 我有我的帽子，他有他的。

3. 这本书是她的，不是你的。

4. 我们已经完成作业了。

5. 火车要开了，我们必须说再见。

6. I will miss you，too. Remember to your parents for me.

7. I will fly to Shanghai tomorrow.

8. The book is written by LuXun.

9. You can have dinner，but you must wash hands before.

10. He says he can't write in English.

五、1. is worth   2. did...miss   3. leave   4. belongs to

    5. have missed，left   6. is...leaving   7. the other day   8. described

六、

Dear Mum and Dad，

    I'm very happy to visit Beijing again. Great changes have taken place in Beijing (here). Today I went to Wang Fu Jing Street early in the morning and I had a good time. Now，there are a lot of new buildings，modern shops and large markets in it (on it/there). Many beautiful posters and flowers are put there (in the street). People in Beijing (here) are working hard (bidding) for the 2008 Olympics. I hope they'll have good luck.

                                                                         Yours，

                                                                               Jim

Lesson 99～100

一、1. fall   2. excited   3. examination   4. ray   5. back

二、1. D 2. D 3. C 4. A 5. C 6. C 7. A 8. D 9. A 10. D 11. B 12. A 13. D

   14. B 15. B

三、1. 那是很长时间以前了，不是吗？

    不，不是很久以前。

2. 我不超过20岁。

3. 我必须给花园浇水。

4. 你在半小时之前给这位绅士服务了吗？

5. 在他们进入房子之后，他们进入餐室。

6. The teacher gave her an English dictionary.

7. The boss wants to talk with Miss Linda at once.

8. He tells me not to go out tonight.

9. Mother tells me that she will go to Beijing on business tomorrow.

10. She tells children not to talk in class.

四、1. he can't stand up

    2. Ted'd better go to see the doctor

    3. she will go to call Doctor Carter

    4. he will come right now

五、1. myself   2. yourself   3. itself   4. themselves

    5. ourselves   6. themselves 7. herself   8. himself

六、1. I hope that he will pass the exam.

2. I believe that the doors and the windows are all closed.

3. I'm glad that she is coming tomorrow.

4. I'm sorry that you missed the train.

5. He says that he isn't feeling very well.

6. I'm afraid that I can't help you.

7. She thinks that Tom is right.

8. I'm sure that he will return home next week.

9. She understands that I haven't got any money.

10. The teacher knows that she has cleaned the classroom.

Lesson 101～102

一、1. association   2. except   3. lemonade   4. knock   5. toilet

二、1. A 2. B 3. B 4. D 5. C 6. C 7. D 8. C 9. D 10. A 11. C 12. A 13. A

14. A

三、1. Mary says："I have finished my homework."

2. The children say："We have never been to London."

3. The mechanics say："You need a new car."

4. Mrs. Blake says："I'm waiting for a bus."

5. Tom says："Mary can speak English very well."

6. Mr. West says："I shall sell this house."

四、1. 我住在一个十分古老的城镇,周围森林茂密。

2. 塞利非常激动,因为她从来没有乘火车旅游过。

3. 火车离站后,这个女士打开手提包,取出一个红色的梳妆镜。

4. 你今晚又要吃烤牛肉和土豆。

5. 我认为,我伤到后背了。

6. Do you go by ship or by plane?

7. You must drive at 70 miles an hour just now.

8. Nobody of our passengers can change this money?

9. How are you?

10. We have done our homework.

五、1. Something else   2. Who else   3. What else   4. nowhere else

5. anybody else

六、

It's my turn to be on duty today. It's Tuesday, April 22nd. It's fine(nice, sunny). Everyone is here except Jim. He went back to America for holiday last week. He won't be back until September.

Yesterday Lucy picked up my lost library book on her way home and returned it to the school library. As soon as I knew this, I hurried to the library and thanked Lucy. Miss Wang told me to be more careful. From now on I should be more careful with everything.

七、1. The student says that he always does his homework in the evening.

2. My father says that I must get up at 8.

3. Jimmy says that he is very hungry.

4. Linda says that they are going to see a film tonight.

5. The little girl says that she has lost her way.

Lesson 103～104

一、1. pass   2. visitor   3. enough   4. embarrassed   5. rest

二、1. B 2. A 3. D 4. C 5. C 6. D 7. D 8. C 9. B 10. A 11. D 12. A 13. C

14. D 15. C

三、1. What a clever boy he is!   4. What a high building it is!

2. What a lovely dress this is!   5. What a terrible film it is!

3. What wonderful actors they are!   6. What beautiful pictures these are!

四、1. 请给我看你在旅行时拍的照片。   6. This is the book that he gave me.

2. 老师告诉我们的故事非常有趣。   7. Is the book that you read in the morning difficult?

3. 我教的学生非常用功。   8. The car that he drives is red.

4. 正在打信的女士是他的秘书。   9. The man who lives downstairs is a pilot.

5. 站在那儿的男人是我的英语老师。　　10. Do you know the man who goes together with Mary?

五、1. enough　　　　2. too/very　　　　3. enough　　　　4. enough

　　5. very　　　　6. too　　　　7. very　　　　8. very

六、

　　I have a schoolbag. It's a rectangular one. It's black and looks very beautiful. It's made of cloth. It is very big and I can put many things in it, like exercise books, the textbooks, dictionaries, the pencil-box and other school things. Every day when I go to school with it on my back, I feel very happy. It's my good friend. I love it very much.

七、1. That house is too expensive for us to buy.

　　2. The pear is soft enough for my grandmother to eat.

　　3. It was too dark for me to go out.

　　4. The wall is low enough for you to jump off.

　　5. Sue is clever enough to answer the questions.

Lesson 105～106

一、1. mistake　　　2. slip　　　　3. correct　　　4. lose　　　5. carry

二、1. C　2. B　3. C　4. B　5. C　6. B　7. D　8. D　9. D　10. A　11. D　12. B　13. D

　　14. D　15. A

三、was, thanked, left, asked, go, did, lose, smiled, said, didn't lose, felt, didn't want

四、1. Is there anyone at home?

　　2. I am sure Tom has invited them over.

　　3. She tried another dress, but it didn't suit her, either.

　　4. Don't interrupt me. I am not joking.

　　5. I don't want to eat anything. I just want to have something to drink.

　　6. 我发现一个标牌上写着:凡在此树林里丢弃垃圾者,将依法处置。

　　7. 我见到的使我很悲伤。

　　8. 她开始打扮起来。

　　9. 告诉玛丽,我们今晚吃饭会迟到。

　　10. 他说他很忙。

五、1. Tell him not to play football after school.

　　2. Tell him not to be late for class.

　　3. Tell her not to drop the vase.

　　4. I don't want you to speak here.

　　5. I want you to tell them the story in English.

　　6. She wants you to get up early.

　　7. I want you to sweep the floor please.

　　8. Tell him to go out and see it.

六、

　　Dear Mrs. Green,

　　　I'm sorry to tell you that I'm not feeling well today. This morning I went to see the doctor and he told me that I had caught a bad cold. And he also asked me to stay in bed for two days. So I can't go to school today tomorrow and the day after tomorrow. I hope I'll get well soon.

　　　　　　　　　　　　　　　　　　　　　　　　　　　　　Yours,

　　　　　　　　　　　　　　　　　　　　　　　　　　　　　Li Ling

七、1. D　　2. D　　3. C　　4. A

Lesson 107～108

一、1. show　　2. listen　　3. favourite　　4. paint　　5. photograph

二、1. D 2. B 3. B 4. B 5. B 6. B 7. B 8. D 9. B 10. C 11. D 12. B 13. D
14. A 15. A

三、1. isn't it　2. aren't you　3. won't he　4. didn't they　5. doesn't she

四、1. 他告诉我他们在开玩笑。　　6. He told me that he had been out for a long time.
2. 他说她看上去很累。　　7. They told us that they had just made a new film.
3. 他告诉我她已经到了。　　8. I told her that I was going to buy a car.
4. 记者说她正在制作一部影片。　9. The doctor said："You may leave the hospital tomorrow."
5. 他们告诉我他们不想吃饭。　10. She said that she was typing a letter then.

五、1. colder　　2. fewer　　3. good，better　　4. better，rich
5. bigger　　6. colder　　7. cleverer　　8. shorter

六、
When we are walking, we should walk on the pavement (sidewalk). At the crossing, we shouldn't cross the road until the traffics stop. Don't read books,play basketball,or listen to music while walking. When we are riding a bike,we should watch ahead and keep both hands on the handle bars. Don't carry anyone on your bike,it is not safe. When we are taking a bus,we should line up and get on (off) one by one. Don't try to get on (off) before the bus stops.

七、1. easier　　2. larger　　3. the largest

Lesson 109～110

一、1. less　　2. introduce　　3. many　　4. advice　　5. least

二、1. C 2. A 3. D 4. B 5. C 6. B 7. B 8. A 9. C 10. B

三、1. can he　　2. have you　　3. did they　　4. are they　　5. will you

四、1. If you win a lot of money,what will you do?　　6. 花园已经被浇过水了。
2. We should depend on our hands to live.　　7. 地板已经被打扫过了。
3. She spent some money on a coat.　　8. 我的汽车已经被修理过了。
4. If you have holiday,where will you go?　　9. 垃圾箱已经被放在树下了。
5. I am sure she must be learning English now.　10. 小偷还没有被抓住。

五、1. a little　　2. Few　　3. few　　4. little
5. little　　6. a little　　7. a few　　8. a little

六、

No. 28 Middle School
Suzhou
April 8,2001

Dear Madam,

I'm a middle school student. I often listen to your music programme. I like the programme very much,especially the English songs.

As a student,I'm busy with my studies. When I feel tired,I will turn on the radio and listen to your programme. I've also learned many English words from these songs.

Of all the English songs, I like "My Heart Will Go On" best. Would you please send me the words of the song?

Yours sincerely,
Li Lei

七、1. the laziest　2. fewer　3. less　4. younger　5. faster　6. longer　7. more

Lesson 111～112

一、1. cost　　2. thief　　3. parrot　　4. deposit　　5. expensive

二、1. C　2. A　3. D　4. C　5. A　6. B　7. C　8. D　9. D　10. B　11. B　12. C　13. D
14. A　15. C

三、1. got　　2. have to stay　　3. will hold　　4. won't　　5. goes　　6. didn't water

四、1. 我敢肯定他是一个中学老师。
2. 我敢肯定她现在不弹钢琴。
3. 我敢肯定黄河不比扬子江长。
4. 我敢肯定他正在找你。
5. Our English teacher must be in the office.
6. Today must be Friday. Look，they are having a meeting.
7. This can't be his bicycle.
8. Your schoolbag must be somewhere in the room.
9. He can't be looking for something，he must be thinking.

五、1. not so exciting as　　2. not so clever as　　3. not so busy as　　4. as fashionable as
5. as expensive as　　6. as difficult as　　7. as beautifully as　　8. as good as

六、

Mrs. Smith is a doctor. One evening，she was having supper when the telephone rang. It was a phone call from a young woman. She asked Mrs. Smith for help because her daughter was ill badly, and having a high fever. Mrs. Smith agreed. Without delay，she hurried to the bus stop and got on the bus to the young woman's home. The young girl felt better after Mrs. Smith examined and treated her carefully. It was already late into the night when Mrs. Smith left the young woman's home. The girl's mother paid Mrs. Smith many thanks.

七、1. My watch is not as expensive as yours.
2. Tom is not as intelligent as Bill.
3. My book is not as interesting as yours.

Lesson 113～114

一、1. conductor　　2. passenger　　3. tramp　　4. madam　　5. appointment

二、1. A　2. A　3. B　4. D　5. B　6. C　7. D　8. C　9. C　10. A　11. A　12. C　13. B
14. C　15. B

三、1. goes，falls　　2. has been　　3. repairing　　4. put　　5. haven't seen，have... been

四、1. 明天你们将不得不早来这儿。
2. 我们必须为他指出错误。
3. 在过去她不得不做所有的家务。
4. 现在人们不得不努力工作。
5. 你得告诉我真相。
6. You must get to the railway station before 8 tomorrow morning.
7. I must say you look much better now.
8. They don't have to come that early.
9. In the past，people had to do many things with hands. Now，they needn't.
10. Must I write the letter in ink?

五、1. Neither is　　2. Neither has　　3. Neither have　　4. So do　　5. Neither is
6. Neither has　　7. So did　　8. Neither can　　9. Neither does　10. So do

六、
Allan：Is that John speaking? /Could/Can I speak to John?

John:Hello,this is John speaking. /Speaking.

Allan:Tomorrow/Next Sunday/This Sunday is my birthday. Could/Can you come to my birthday party? I'd like you to come.

John:I'd love to. But I'll go to see my uncle with my parents. /Sorry,I can't. I'm going to Shanghai tomorrow.

七、1. I have many English books. So has he.

2. Tom is now cleaning the room. So am I.

3. We have already seen this film. So have they.

4. He is not going there by train. Neither am I.

5. I can't see anyone. Neither can she.

Lesson 115～116

一、1. knock   2. quiet   3. joke   4. glasses   5. bed

二、1. A 2. A 3. B 4. C 5. B 6. D 7. C 8. C 9. B 10. D 11. B 12. C 13. C

14. C 15. A

三、1. had received   2. are playing   3. got,had,begun

4. were swimming   5. Have,read,read

四、1. 我滑倒并摔下了楼。

2. 我敢肯定我得了低分。

3. 满封信都是错,我想让你再打一遍。

4. 它一点都不适合我。

5. 多吃点,少抽烟。

6. Tom is an honest boy.

7. When we got to the cinema,the film had begun already. We felt our way in the darkness.

8. The driver died soon after he was sent to hospital.

9. I have seen this film.

10. Have you had your supper?

五、1. B,are   2. B,moves   3. C,does   4. C,his

5. B,knows   6. C,his   7. A,has   8. B,wants

六、1. Tom knows nothing about the Chinese history.

2. Did anyone make a telephone call to me this morning?

3. I always read something at night.

4. Nobody will believe the story.

5. I looked for my English book everywhere but I couldn't find it anywhere.

Lesson 117～118

一、1. coin   2. swallow   3. toilet   4. lunch   5. nice

二、1. B   2. C 3. C 4. B 5. B 6. B 7. C 8. A 9. B 10. B 11. C 12. B 13. C

14. C 15. D

三、1. were having   2. was dusting   3. was writing

4. was washing,was reading   5. Have finished,was reading

四、1. 下个月苏珊将动身去巴黎。   6. When did he die?

2. 本周我们将飞往柏林。   7. Have you invited Mary as well to have dinner?

3. 下周简将去东京。   8. What did she see?

4. 明天早上她将打电话给她母亲。   9. Why are you so rude to him?

5. 我明天将刮胡子。   10. When are we going to have a meeting?

五、1. except　　　　　 2. in, Besides　　　 3. in　　　　 4. through

5. from, to, on　 6. out of, to　　　 7. out of/into　 8. at

六、

　　I took my first job as a waitress in a nice restaurant. At the night before my first day, I was too excited to go to sleep and as a result, I got up late in the morning. I threw on my clothes and rushed over to the restaurant.

　　In a great hurry, I didn't hear clearly the head waiter's instruction that we should go into the kitchen through one door and out from the other. So when I took two plates of eggs and bacon and an orange juice out to the restaurant, I went straight towards the wrong door and collided with another waiter coming in! Worst of all was that I wore a pair of smart shoes but with high heels!

七、1. were having

2. was dusting

3. was writing

4. was washing, was reading

5. Have...finished

6. was repairing, has...repaired

7. was working

8. are...doing, am playing

　Have...done, was doing

9. was walking

10. was having

Lesson 119～120

一、1. voice　　 2. stupid　　　 3. expensive　　 4. call　　 5. thief

二、1. D 2. A 3. B 4. B 5. D 6. D 7. A 8. A 9. B 10. B 11. D 12. D 13. C

14. B

三、1. has been　　 2. fell, rode　　 3. lost　　 4. didn't go　　 5. is running

四、1. 告诉他实情对我们可能是最好的。

2. 如果我们今晚去剧院，我们会带上你。

3. 我应该穿上我最漂亮的衣服。

4. 这是一个很长的名字，我必须给你拼写出来。

5. 你不应该迟到。

6. After the long walk I wanted to drink something cold.

7. He said something serious had happened.

8. Don't do anything stupid.

9. Do you know anyone else who wants a ticket?

10. See you tomorrow.

五、1. The gentlemen are going to speak to us.

2. These ladies come from China.

3. Those children are lovely.

4. Their lives were very interesting.

5. Our wives are very beautiful.

6. Those knives aren't very sharp.

7. These shelves are clean.

8. These loaves of bread are fresh.

六、

It's Saturday today. It's a nice day. Li Lei's family are spending their holiday on a small island. They get there early with some nice food and drink. They are enjoying themselves. Look，Li Lei's playing with the sand. His parents are drinking and talking happily beside him. Behind them we can see two people lying on the sand and enjoying the sunshine. Some children are swimming in the sea. There are two boys playing with a model ship nearby and two girls playing with a model plane over there. The plane is flying high in the sky. Everyone is having a good time.

七、1. (had)finished. . . had gone

2. had not risen. . . did not see

3. hadn't arrived. . . left

4. came. . . had missed

5. had already promised

6. hadn't seen

7. had swallowed

8. had landed. . . reached

9. had never been. . . felt

10. had run. . . arrived

Lesson 121～122

一、1. matter   2. husband   3. right   4. customer   5. serve

二、1. C 2. B 3. C 4. A 5. C 6. A 7. C 8. A 9. C 10. A 11. D 12. B 13. A

14. B 15. B 16.D

三、1. the most difficult   2. least   3. best   4. thinner   5. older

四、1. 有人偷了他的自行车。   6. They are having breakfast.

2. 她父母将给她一个包作为礼物。   7. After breakfast，they will go to work.

3. 我们明天将讨论这个问题。   8. What were you doing this morning?

4. 在很多国家人们说英语。   9. Nothing.

5. 矛盾写了《子夜》。   10. I was painting a dinner table.

五、1. who   2. who   3. whom   4. whom

5. which/that   6. which   7. which/that   8. who

六、

Yesterday was Mother's Day. Lucy got up early in the morning. She wanted to give her mother a surprise. She thought hard and had an idea. Then she went to a flower shop and bought some beautiful flowers. She got home and gave the present to her mother. Her mother was very pleased.

七、1. that/which   2. who

3. that/which   4. that/which

5. whom/that   6. who

7. that/which   8. whom/that

Lesson 123～124

一、1. offer   2. grow   3. grew   4. guess   5. during

二、1. A 2. C 3. C 4. D 5. C 6. D 7. B 8. B 9. C 10. A 11. C 12. A 13. D

14. D 15. D 16.B

三、1. had learned，came   2. will，do，will watch   3. were，sleeping

4. had gone   5. washed，had had

四、1. 他们已经浇过花园了。

199

2. 他已经扫过地了。

3. 有人修理过我的车。

4. 我们已经把垃圾箱放在了树下。

5. 警察还没有抓到小偷。

6. I have many English books. So does he.

7. Tom is cleaning the room. So am I.

8. We have seen this film. So have they.

9. I am not going to go there by train. Neither is he.

10. I can see nobody. Nor can she.

五、1. work　　2. work　　3. a trip　　4. travelled

5. a...job　6. job　　7. a job　　8. travels

六、

Beijing is a beautiful modern city. There are (a lot of/many) tall buildings and clean streets everywhere in Beijing. We should keep our/the environment clean, plant as many flowers and trees as possible and protect them. We shouldn't throw waste here and there because every one of us hopes (that) we can live in a wonderful environment.

七、1. A　2. B　3. C　4. C　5. A

Lesson 125～126

一、1. English　2. brother　3. put　4. mean　5. water

二、1. D　2. A　3. C　4. C　5. B　6. C　7. C　8. A　9. B　10. A　11. D　12. B　13. B

14. C　15. B

三、1. 这是一本鲁迅的书。

2. 她给我看约翰的照片中的一张。

3. 在我的桌上发现了一些你的信。

4. 他们的一些朋友来看过我。

5. 这是她的想法之一。

6. The woman who gave us the talk yesterday is a professor.

7. Everyone is busy. They are preparing for the final exam.

8. Everybody can answer the question, can't they?

9. The bus is coming.

10. Be careful!

四、1. more　　2. the richest　　3. more famous　　4. wider

5. brighter　6. thicker　　7. dirtier

五、1. have to　2. mustn't　3. must　4. have had to

5. have to　6. needn't　7. must　8. have to

六、

John had a busy day yesterday. He got up early in the morning. After breakfast he went to school. He had classes and worked hard all day. After school he played football with his friends on the playground. Then he went home. At home he helped his mother cook supper. He did his homework in the evening and then went to bed.

七、1. A　2. A　3. B　4. C

Lesson 127～128

一、1. draw　2. hundred　3. Young Pioneers　4. girls　5. pairs

二、1. A　2. B　3. A　4. C　5. D　6. B　7. B　8. A　9. B　10. B　11. D　12. B　13. B

三、1. took，Did know   2. to see   3. take   4. did put   5. to feel

   6. watches，goes   7. are，doing   8. comes，will give

四、1. 他们必须卖房子。

   2. 你必须现在浇花园。

   3. 我们不能买贵的汽车。

   4. 他不能开那么快。

   5. 他们不能步行去那儿。

   6. How are you?

   7. What's the matter with you?

   8. I will move to my new house.

   9. I have moved to my new house.

   10. I am moving to my new house.

五、1. can   2. must   3. mustn't   4. can't   5. must

   6. can't   7. May，mustn't   8. mustn't

六、

    I am a student of Hope Middle School. My school campus is big and beautiful. There are many tall trees and beautiful flowers. There is also a playground in our school.

    Our teachers are all very kind and friendly. They work hard and teach us very well. They take good care of us，and they are strict with us.

    There are about 40 students in our class. We get on well with each other. We often study and play together.

    At school，we learn many subjects，such as Chinese，maths and English. We try our best to learn them well.

    I love my school because it's just like my home.

七、1. Our English teacher must be in the office.

   2. Today must be Friday. Look，they are having a meeting.

   3. This can't be his bicycle. His bicycle is new.

   4. Your schoolbag must be somewhere in the room.

Lesson 129～130

一、1. can   2. from   3. America   4. when   5. listen

二、1. A 2. B 3. D 4. C 5. A 6. C 7. C 8. D 9. B 10. C 11. A 12. B 13. C 14. C 15. B

三、1. the most useful   2. more fluently   3. more expensive

   4. the most beautiful   5. old，tall

四、1. 我的手表没有你的贵。

   2. 汤姆没有比尔聪明。

   3. 我的书没有你的有趣。

   4. 汤姆没有比尔仔细。

   5. 玛丽没有简漂亮。

   6. I have more lessons than you.

   7. You eat more apples than I.

   8. This is the most beautiful one of all my skirts.

   9. This is my best book.

   10. The English teacher is younger than the maths teacher.

五、1. are at table   2. by yourself   3. overtook   4. was doing   5. take

六、

Yang Lei is a student of No. 12 Middle School. Last Saturday, he got up at 8：15 and thought he was late for school. So he left home in a hurry without breakfast. He rode his bike as fast as he could on his way to school. When he arrived there, the gate was still closed. Then he remembered that it was a holiday.

七、1. must be　　　2. must be　　3. can't be　　　4. can't have been

Lesson 131～132

一、1. minute　　　2. tree　　　3. wrong　　　4. picture　　　5. woman

二、1. C 2. C 3. B 4. B 5. B 6. C 7. C 8. C 9. B 10. A 11. B 12. A 13. C 14. A 15. C

三、1. like　　　2. carry　　　3. is　　　4. don't know　　　5. to drink

四、1. 汤姆说他感觉不舒服。

2. 史密斯一家说他们今晚不来吃饭了。

3. 我想知道你上次是否出席了讲座。

4. 她想知道你是否要写一封信给他。

5. 没有人知道为什么我们老师生气。

6. When he came in, what were you doing?

7. I was typing a letter.

8. What were your children doing?

9. They were doing homework in the study.

10. What were they doing when you were reading newspaper?

五、1. It's no good reading in bed.

2. It's dangerous to walk on such a road.

3. It's no use talking like that.

4. It's doubtful that they'll come on time.

5. It's undoubtful that we have walked to the wrong way.

6. It's useful to learn English.

7. It's necessary to study English every day.

8. It's true that we have been to Beijing.

六、

Monday March 12th　　　　　　　　　　　　　　　　　　　　fine

Today is Tree Planting Day. After breakfast we went to the West Hill by bus to plant trees. We were all in old clothes and worked very hard. Some dug holes, some put trees in them and others soiled and watered them. Each of us planted three young trees. When we finished our work, it was already twelve o'clock. We felt a little tired, but we were very happy.

七、1. may go

2. may not come

3. May

4. may use

5. may come

6. may have been typing letters

Lesson 133～134

一、1. whose　　　2. help　　　3. near　　　4. worker

二、1. C 2. B 3. A 4. D 5. D 6. B 7. C 8. A 9. B 10. D 11. B 12. C

三、1. younger   2. smallest   3. faster   4. longer   5. tallest

    6. harder   7. earlier

四、1. 他什么时候死的?

    2. 你也请了玛丽来吃饭。

    3. 她看见了什么?

    4. 你为什么对他那么粗鲁?

    5. 我们什么时候再开一次会?

    6. Tom knew nothing about Chinese history.

    7. Did anyone telephone this morning?

    8. I often read something in the evening.

    9. Nobody believes this story.

    10. I have looked for my English book everywhere. But I could find nothing.

五、1. The monitor said they wanted to help Charles.

    2. He said his father was watching TV now.

    3. Jim told her it was an American film and it costs a lot of money.

    4. She told me she had given me a picture.

    5. We said that we were hungry.

    6. The boy said that it was the best way.

    7. A woman said that the purse was hers.

    8. Mr. West told me he had sold the car.

六、

    I'd like to tell you something about the out-of-class activities in our school. We usually have our activities from 4：50～5：50 in the afternoon. We have different kinds of activities. Some students are interested in sports. They play basketball and football. We also have some interest groups，such as drawing，singing and dancing. And now，computer is the most popular. On Wednesday afternoon we go to the English corner. We like talking with each other in English there. We hope we can spend more time on such activities and have a happy middle school time.

七、1. to tell him，had

    2. how she was，then

    3. not to put，that

    4. whether I had seen，the，before

    5. she would go there the

Lesson 135～136

一、1. trouble   2. horse   3. noise   4. sleep

二、1. A 2. D 3. D 4. D 5. C 6. D 7. A 8. B 9. B 10. C 11. A 12. B

三、1. 学生要求老师讲个故事。   6. I was asked to stand up.

    2. 这种树到处能见。   7. He was told to close the door.

    3. 明年我将被派往国外学习。   8. She was told to come out.

    4. 水能被加热成蒸汽。   9. We were invited to dinner.

    5. 窗户被我擦过了。   10. We enjoyed ourselves.

四、1. the laziest   2. fewer   3. less   4. younger   5. faster   6. longer

五、1. D   2. A   3. C

六、1. has just made   2. has just returned

    3. has just met   4. Has ... eaten

    5. has just got   6. have just broken

7. Has ... already handed　　　8. has just taken

七、

Li Ming's Happiest Day

　　Last Sunday was June 2nd. Li Ming got up at 7：50. He had his breakfast at 8：00. Then he played football with his friends/classmates. He likes playing football very much. He had a good time/enjoyed himself. He got home at 5：10 in the afternoon. He had supper with his sister at 6：30. After supper/In the evening they watched TV. He went to bed at 10：00. It was his happiest day.

八、1. make a new film

　　2. Let me introduce myself

　　3. We were all very excited

　　4. before the latest news comes

　　5. the old man had died two days before

Lesson 137～138

一、1. wait　　2. enjoy　　3. whole　　4. southern　　5. interest

二、1. B　2. B　3. C　4. D　5. B　6. B　7. C　8. A　9. B　10. D　11. A　12. C　13. A　14. A　15. C

三、1. said　　2. knock　　3. stays　　4. asked　　5. walked　　6. had

四、1. 他的自行车被偷了。　　　　　　6. What a nice dress!

　　2. 她父母将送她一个书包作为礼物。　7. You looks ill.

　　3. 这个问题明天讨论。　　　　　　8. He is taken to hospital.

　　4. 很多国家说英语。　　　　　　　9. She is invited to my home.

　　5. 《子夜》是矛盾写的。　　　　　　10. They are all out.

五、1. If you go with me　　　　　　　2. If you don't leave them a message

　　3. If you don't tell them　　　　　4. If you go to the Fair by yourself

　　5. if it doesn't rain　　　　　　　6. if he is not too busy

　　7. if he has enough time　　　　　8. if you want

六、

　　Once in the nation of Zheng there was a man who wanted to buy himself a pair of shoes. He took the measurement of his own feet with a piece of string. Then he went to the market. He was looking at some shoes at the shoe-maker's when he realized he had left the measurement at home. He put down the shoes and rushed home to fetch it. By the time he returned with the measurement the market was already closed. So he failed to get his shoes. Somebody asked him,"Why didn't you just try the shoes on your own feet?" He answered,"I trust the measurement I took rather than my feet."

七、1. rains　　2. shall visit　　3. shall buy　　4. ask　　5. freezes　　6. are

　　7. is　　8. happens　　9. has　　10. is　　11. will believe

Lesson 139～140

一、1. anything　　2. ourselves　　3. pull　　4. farthest　　5. head

二、1. A　2. B　3. A　4. B　5. C　6. A　7. D　8. A　9. B　10. D　11. C　12. C　13. C　14. D

三、1. must　　2. may　　3. Can　　4. must　　5. Must，needn't

四、1. 学生们请老师讲个故事。

　　2. 这种树随处可见。

3. 明年他们将送我去国外学习。

4. 你能够通过加热把水变成水蒸气。

5. 我已经擦过窗户了。

6. We enjoy ourselves.

7. They are both teachers.

8. All of us are good students.

9. What's the matter?

10. How are you?

五、1. Is he often late?

2. I'll never go to that hotel again.

3. I always do.

4. They have already gone there.

5. Have you ever been in an aeroplane?

6. Do you still live in Beijing?

7. I often go to the theatre.

8. We have never been there.

六、

233 Dong Changan Street

Beijing，China

July 17，1987

Dear Jack，

In June when you were visiting Beijng, on the last day of your trip a farewell party was given at the Youth Palace. At the party I sat next to you. Then in the end when we went away we took each other's notebook by mistake. I discovered this only when I looked into the notebook and found your name and address inside. I am now sending your notebook by post. Would you please send my notebook to me at the address which is given above? Thank you very much.

I hope you will visit Beijing again soon.

Your Chinese friend，

Wang Li

七、1. C 2. B 3. A 4. A 5. D

Lesson 141～142

一、1. middle 2. funny 3. fun 4. invite 5. car

二、1. C 2. B 3. B 4. B 5. D 6. C 7. B 8. D 9. A 10. C 11. B 12. C 13. A

14. D 15. D

三、1. 你能告诉我你昨晚8：00在做什么吗？

2. 我想知道你什么时候还书给我。

3. 她问你去年冬天在哪儿度的假。

4. 汤姆是个诚实的孩子。

5. 我也是。

6. I want to borrow this book.

7. I want to stay with you.

8. Class is over.

9. See you tomorrow.

10. It's kind of you.

四、1. was repairing，has，repaired 2. was working 3. are，doing，am playing

五、1. My coat is being made by my aunt now.

2. A letter is posted to my parents by me every month.

3. I was told to be there before 6.

4. Two thieves were caught by the policemen last Sunday.

5. You can't go into the room. The floor is being mopped by Father.

6. We were given a lecture by Jane last week.

7. The bed is made by me every day.

8. An English song is sung by us before English class.

六、

Ladies and gentlemen,

May I have your attention, please?

On Saturday 22 July there will be visits to different places. Everybody is welcome. Each person can choose to go to one of the places — a factory, a farm, a school or a hospital. Please sign your name at the Service Desk before 9∶00 p. m. today and tell which place you wish to visit.

We will set out after breakfast at 8∶00 on that day and come back in the afternoon. We will have lunch at the place of visit. (or∶Lunch will be served at the place of visit.)

七、1. The house is cleaned once a week.　　　2. The window was broken.

3. Our car was stolen.　　　4. The letter-box is opened twice a day.

5. The car is often washed.　　　6. The clock was repaired.

Lesson 143～144

一、1. their, there　　2. bed　　3. her　　4. town　　5. ask

二、1. C　2. B　3. C　4. B　5. C　6. C　7. B　8. C　9. C　10. C　11. B　12. A　13. D
14. A　15. D

三、1. to, of　　　2. to, of　　　3. at, for　　　4. at, to

四、1. 那栋房子太贵了。　　2. 我们不能买它。　　3. 梨很软。

4. 我祖母能吃它。　　5. 天太晚了。　　6. I couldn't go out.

7. The wall is very low.　　8. You can jump off it.　　9. She is clever.

10. She can answer the question.

五、1. through　　2. through　　3. among　　4. between　　5. was covered with

6. between　　7. exciting　　8. excited

六、

My Hometown Today

At the beginning of last summer holiday, I left my parents in town for my hometown. It's about 40 kilometres away. It takes around one hour to get there by bus.

There are green hills around my hometown. In front of it is a small river. The town used to be a small mountainous village. Now the village has become bigger. In recent years, the villagers have become richer and richer because of their hard work and the good policy of the Party. Many new houses have been built. Almost every family has a TV set. What's more, a few villagers have trucks of their own.

I must study harder at school in order to make my hometown more beautiful in the future.

七、1. amused. . . were amused　　　2. were excited

3. frightened　　　4. was frightened

5. surprised　　　6. was embarrassed

7. were surprised　　　8. was tired

9. worries　　　10. excited